THEY CAME

THEIR TRAGEDIES AND TRIUMPHS RAN
THROUGH THE FABRIC
OF AMERICAN HISTORY.

THOMAS GAIRDEN—A smokey-eyed Scots-Irish weaver, he left his home for a better life in the New World —and forged a dynasty that would span generations.

SARAH ROBERTS—A headstrong, russet-haired lass, she'd wanted Thomas since they crossed the ocean together —but will she find him on the frontier?

JAMIE LOWE—An Ulsterman and Thomas' rival for Sarah, he has a fiery temper, an eye for straight shooting, and a way with the ladies . . . and the whiskey.

ELIZABETH "CRICKIE" RAWLINS—Her burning black eyes belie her proper English schooling. Even though she longs for love, her absent father's indigo and rice plantation must come first.

MICHEL BORQUE—A crafty Frenchman from the island of Barbados, he likes his horses fast and his women rich.

ALEXANDER GRAY—If there's an easier path to fortune than the sweat of his brow, Thomas' partner will find it —or die trying.

The Founders

Coleen L. Johnston

ST. MARTIN'S PAPERBACKS

THE FOUNDERS

Copyright © 1993 by Colleen L. Johnston.

Cover illustration by Bob Larkin.

All rights reserved. No part of this book may be used or reproduced in any manner whatsoever without written permission except in the case of brief quotations embodied in critical articles or reviews. For information address St. Martin's Press, 175 Fifth Avenue, New York, N.Y. 10010.

ISBN: 0-312-95060-8

Printed in the United States of America

St. Martin's Paperbacks edition/August 1993

10 9 8 7 6 5 4 3 2 1

For my mother, who saved the coverlet,
and my late father,
who taught me that the trip was worth something.

Author's Note

The American coverlets woven by the Gairdens were born of colonial necessity coupled with European know-how. They remain today the only distinctively American textile: linsey-woolsey—handspun woolen yarns woven onto a handspun linen warp—which could be made in the colonies even when the King would not allow the importation of cotton warp yarns. The wool was most often dyed with indigo, an American-produced dyestuff. The coverlet, therefore, was a self-sufficient American unit that defied the Crown at the same time it drew on centuries of English textile experience. Weavers, by the nature of their profession, became active participants in the shaping of a nation.

King's Flower pattern motif

Coverlet names generally reflect the times or places in which they were first woven. The King's Flower coverlet that lends its pattern to *The Founders* dates from the late colonial period, although the pattern continued to be popular well into the mid-1800s. The term "coverlet" comes to us from the French "*couvre-lit*" meaning "to cover the bed." In America, however, the term coverlet took on a more specific meaning, that of a bed covering woven on a large loom, with the pattern determined by the loom's threading. The American coverlet so sought after by today's antique collectors was most often made of two handwoven strips sewn together to form one large piece. Coverlets are not quilts, nor are they constructed of knit or crochet patterns. They are, instead, unique pieces of Americana highly regarded for their enduring beauty and for the legacy of challenge and change woven into them.

THE GAIRDEN LEGACY:
1706–1766

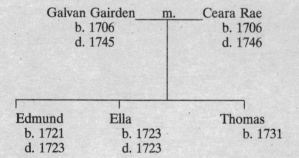

Galvan Gairden ____ m. ____ Ceara Rae
b. 1706   b. 1706
d. 1745   d. 1746

Edmund   Ella   Thomas
b. 1721   b. 1723   b. 1731
d. 1723   d. 1723

❧ Part One ❧

1750

1

Bartram, Pennsylvania
1750

Thomas Gairden edged down the bank, picked up a stone and skipped it easily across the creek, causing ripples that seemed to wink at him in the moonlight. Skip. Skip. Skip. Skim . . . skim . . . skim . . . skim. Gone. He kicked aside the ridge of pebbles at his feet and dropped onto the closest boulder. Crossing his long legs at the ankles, he folded his hands loosely on his lap and hung his head slightly forward. He knew Sarah was watching him, waiting for him to say something.

She sat above him on a slab of granite that cropped out from the bank, her knees drawn up to her small, pointed chin, and arms clasped tightly about her legs. The skirt of her everyday blue homespun sacque was bunched up above her ankles. Any other time he would have sneaked over and tickled the bare feet that peeked out beneath it. But not tonight. Her body—all one hundred pounds of the russet-haired Sarah Roberts—was coiled like a clock spring waiting to strike midnight.

"Thought I'd find you here, lass," he said at last, knowing she wouldn't speak first. His growing-up years in Ireland and his Scottish blood combined to give his words an endearing lilt as they rolled across the cool night air. He stretched his arms leisurely upward in a half yawn, then straightened the tie on his black hair, hoping to look more relaxed than he felt.

"Did you now?" Sarah asked, her accent Scots-Irish like his own. "And why was that?"

Sarah's questions were spoken softly, without ever raising her chin from her knees, and her eyes remained fixed on the silver sparkle of the little rapids before her. Thomas looked at the water, too.

" 'Tis been your habit, has it not, to come here when you've something on your mind . . . when you've wanted to get out of your father's sight for a time and such. I just thought—"

"That I had something on me mind? I'm surprised you noticed, Thomas Duncan Gairden." Sarah's chin came away from her knees at last and the softness went out of her words.

Thomas felt her eyes on him once again, and once again he looked down at his hands. His chest felt tight as he breathed in the damp, dewy air of the April evening. His hands were cold and he rubbed them back and forth, searching for the right thing to say.

"I've noticed, Sarah. Aye, I've noticed it all week. Ever since you told us you'd marry Jamie by midsummer. But I didn't know what to say—I don't now either." He chanced a look at her and found her eyes on him, querying, wondering, waiting. Meeting them, an ache surged through him like a shot of her father's whiskey. "I only want to know if . . . if . . . if you love him?" Thomas looked away as he blurted out the last words, drew in a shallow breath and held it, waiting for her answer.

"Is that any concern of yours, Thomas Gairden? If 'tis, you might've done your asking sooner."

She didn't say yes, Thomas thought, still fixing his eyes on the water. She didn't say yes. He took a breath.

"But you didn't answer me question, lass. Do you—"

"And you didn't answer mine! What concern is it of yours, Thomas Gairden? You've had four years of livin' right here in my father's house to do your asking. Is it jealous you are that Jamie's asked and you haven't?"

Thomas saw an auburn curl slip out from under her cap as she gave her head a defiant bob. She was a gentle lass, but there was that quick temper about her that never failed to catch him off guard.

"Aye, I'm jealous. I admit it . . . I . . . thought you'd be waitin' for me."

"I did." Sarah's eyes met his frankly. "I did wait, Thomas. But I'm eighteen now and me time for waiting's done. Besides, Jamie said you're not the marryin' sort."

"Jamie said? You know me better than Jamie ever has. If Jamie was a man half good enough for you, lass, he'd have spoken to me first before he asked you."

"He spoke to Papa, Thomas. 'Tis the way 'tis done and well you know it."

"Aye, but why is it that your father had ever so much time to speak with Jamie, and every time I tried to speak to him he could only think to interrupt and give me more tasks to do?" Thomas picked up two smooth stones and ground them between his hands. Squeezed them hard but could not break them. Sarah looked off up the creek and did not answer.

"Some lads are ready to marry at nineteen, Sarah, but I'm not. Not that I don't want to. I'd love the touch of your kiss when I wake in the morning and your smile through the day. I'd warm to the nights in your arms. But I've naught to offer a wife, and I'll not ask you to starve and struggle just for the joy of being me wife when I know that with a year or two on my own I can build a weaving business that'll serve us well."

"You've been weavin', Thomas. For the neighbors, for to take to market fair. Has it served you so well?"

"You know who's been served by it, lass. Your father. He's kept what should be mine, first as pay for takin' me in, and now as pay for the new gelding. He takes more than he's owed, you know."

"Aye. I know Father." Sarah's words were quiet now. They'd discussed her father often over these four years in Pennsylvania Colony, most times right here on the smooth granite slab where she sat shivering.

"And I know *you* know I've always wanted you for me own wife."

"But you've never said it."

"I didn't think I had to," he said. The truth sounded weak.

"Did you think I'd say it for you?" Sarah asked, softening the edge on her voice. Brushing away a gnat that flew about her head, she took off her cap, and shook out her unruly auburn curls.

"Nay. I thought 'twould be mutual, I suppose. When we were ready we'd just marry. Simple as that." Thomas's voice was soft. Pained, but not angry. Rising, he drank in a chestful of the evening air that smelled of humus and cold water, then walked to the big rock. He felt the familiar bond suffuse the space between them as he stood leaning against the shelf of granite.

"Jamie thought different," Sarah said plainly.

"The blatherskite—he never told me he was planning to ask you," Thomas said at last. "He bragged of other lasses chasin' after him—but never a word of you. And even if he had told me," Thomas said, "I expected you would tell him no." He shook his head slowly. "When you said yes, I couldn't reason why except that I'd been wrong about us all these years. I decided you must think me more brother than . . . than anything else. And when you lay bundled with Jamie down by the fire last winter, I thought—"

"Thomas, you know bundlin' doesn't mean you've given your body to another. 'Tis a way of spending some private time alone with him when nights are too cold to be out. Father made us use the bundlin' board between us—I knew not the touch of his body then, I swear it."

"You needn't swear it to me, Sarah. 'Tis your own life your leadin'. I'm only saying I thought if you . . . if you . . . loved me, you'd not have given Jamie your word. You knew I saw no other."

"And are you saying Jamie did?" Sarah drew her lips tight, but in her question Thomas heard both choler and concern.

"You know many lasses've caught Jamie's eye," Thomas said quietly. Behind him an owl sang its *who-who-whooo* against the stillness of the forest sky.

"And he picked me," Sarah said, with a trace of pride. "Of all of 'em, he picked me."

"Well . . . I picked you, too, Sarah, the day we left Ballymena I think 'twas, and now I'm asking you." He reached for her hand, taking it in both of his, tender as if he held a day-old chick. "We could marry within the year, I promise."

"Oh . . . Thomas . . ."

He looked into her eyes and saw her want. Her doubt. Then her pride again. "You know I can't," she said once more. "Everyone's been told. The dowry's been offered. And Jamie would—"

"Jamie would what? Rage? Aye, that's just what Jamie would do, lass. Is that what you want? A man who'll rage if you so much as change his plans?"

" 'Tis a rather big plan to change, Thomas, and you know it. You'd rage a bit yourself if your bride left you for another."

"Far better to chance a single rage than live a lifetime of it, Sarah. Jamie's given to temper you know."

"Father calls it 'spirit.' "

"Your father likes Jamie spirited and me meek. . . . Jamie's been a friend to me . . . but not the friend you've been. I'm not afraid of his rage, or your father's. Let me tell 'em you've changed your mind. I can be strong enough for both of us, Sarah, for you know I love you."

His face was close to her now. His words soft. Urgent. Sarah closed her eyes. His lips brushed her cheeks, then her eyelids, and he pulled her close and kissed her lips.

"Sarah," he murmured as the kiss deepened and he felt her response just as he'd known he would. "I love you, Sarah," he whispered, "I—"

He stopped as her hand pressed against his shoulder.

"I can't," she said, "no mind how much I want to." Drawing back, she stood up. Though she shed no tears that Thomas could see in the shadowy moonlight, he heard the tremor in her voice as she spoke. " 'Tis too late. I belong to Jamie now." She turned, giving him one last look he couldn't quite read, then pulled herself up over the top of the bank and ran off up the trail to the house.

2

The morning of her wedding, Sarah Roberts bathed naked
in the kitchen, sponging the hips and arms and breasts of
her small body and remembering how they'd felt under
Jamie's touch. Wondering how they would have felt under
Thomas's . . . She combed impatiently through her waist-
long hair, tugging at tangles and loosening snarls where curl
meshed with curl.

"Sheely, please hurry," she called to her sister. Sheela,
who was one year younger than Sarah, had promised to
fashion her hair into a fetching style for the ceremony.

"Don't want to keep Jamie waiting now, do you?" her
sister teased, following Sarah up the narrow stairs to their
chamber, which was nothing more than attic space divided
in half by a curtain. Though only sixteen, Sheela was taller
than her sister, with lively brown eyes, a dimple in her
cheek and mischief in her ways.

"Nay, I wouldn't. Now hurry or when you marry I'll make
you late by fiddling with your hair all mornin'."

Sheela pulled Sarah's hair back with a playful jerk, then
swept it up the front to form a long roll from ear to ear over
her forehead. The hair in the back of her head was twisted
into a high, flat bun.

In her mother's small looking glass, Sarah checked
Sheela's progress. Never one to fuss with her hair, Sarah
could hardly believe the difference having it piled on top of
her head made. Was the face in the mirror really hers? Her
freckles were still there, of course. They would never leave
her. Still, she was pleased with what she saw. She felt older.

"Ouch!" Sarah cried, as Sheela stuck a comb in her hair.
"Watch what you're doing."

"See there what you get for your threats," Sheela

crowed. "When I marry, which could be any time now, you'll fetch and carry for me as I've done for you this day—and keep a smile on your face while you're doin' it."

"I'll be married and gone, Sheely. Remember that."

"You'll not be gone far—a few miles. You can come and help Mama."

As Sheela chattered on about the kind of wedding she would have when she married John Partridge . . . or James Hunt . . . or whomever it would be, Sarah's eyes fell on the gown that had been Thomas's present—a dress more dear than she should have accepted her mother had said. It was made of a linen he'd woven, then grassed for days and soured in buttermilk to make purely white. He had asked her mother to sew it into a dress, and had woven Iseabal Roberts a warm new wool coverlid for her trouble.

"I'll not be wearing his dress," Sarah said all at once, looking back into her own green-gold eyes in the glass. For a few seconds complete silence filled the room.

"Not wearing the dress? Have you another then?" her sister asked.

"Me other best," Sarah said, laying down the glass and rising to pick an olive wool shift with marigold stomacher and bodice from a hook on the wall.

"That? When you could be wearin' this?" Sheela said, touching the ruffled hem of the wedding gown with longing. "Why? To spite Thomas, is that what it is? You'll hurt him, is all, him who loves you like a sister. Is that what you want?"

Sarah's eyes lost focus as she looked to the delicate white garment her sister held up.

"I didn't want him to love me as a sister," Sarah said at last, still far away with her thoughts. "I decided four years back, aboard the *Endeavor* coming over from Ulster, that someday I'd marry Thomas Duncan Gairden. He was hurting then, havin' just lost his folks to the coughing, and then him so sick on the ship—"

"As we all were but you—which you'll never let any of us forget," her sister put in.

"Aye, as you all were. But Thomas looked to me for help

—had no one but me in the world—and from that day on I wanted no one but him. I thought him coming to live with us the perfect thing. He'd be all mine—"

"Well, maybe just a wee bit mine," Sheela couldn't help but add. "You know I'm the one he always picks the water lilies for, and I'm the one he helps when Papa gives me too many chores."

"A wee bit, maybe. Maybe more than I knew. Now I feel like I don't know anything." Sarah placed the shapeless olive dress on the bed. Thomas had woven it, too. "But mostly he's his own, the way it turned out. Deep inside him there's some piece I've never understood. Until just now."

Sheela pushed a final comb into the back of her sister's hair. "And what's that?" she asked.

"He wants more than what he's got here. He wants to be more than we are. He's restless to be on his own, to get back to his weaving. Father's been wrong to keep him here trying to make a farmer of him when it's weaving he's trained for. He spent seven years as an apprentice with old Kinloch in New Buildings, and he's not willing to give it up."

"No one forced him to stay, did they?" Sheela asked, holding the hand mirror up to pin back her own hair.

"Not so's a person could see, but still I think so." Sarah put a hand at the back of her head where the hair swept up into the bun. Little curls of deep auburn still fringed the neckline, too short to be caught up with the rest. Sarah touched here, there. "He asked me to marry him," she said at last, not looking at her sister.

"He what?" Sheela went around to face Sarah, plunking down on the bed beside her, directly on top of the olive green dress. She looked her sister hard in the eye. "You love Jamie, though, don't you, Sarah? I mean, 'tis Jamie you've spent day and night with these past three months— not Thomas."

"Jamie loves me," Sarah said, not answering her sister. "He'll be a good husband."

"Then Thomas'll be left for me," her sister teased. She rose and went to peer out the small bottle glass window, the only light in the room. Formed from a row of six bottles standing side by side and framed in with rough boards, the window was intended more to let in light than to see out of. Yet, when Sheela put her eye almost directly on the glass, she could see down to the yard below. "Thomas is down there now, getting ready for the race . . . he's looking up here . . . We should be getting down there to see him off."

"Go ahead, Sheely. I'll be down in a minute," Sarah said, still eyeing the white dress as her sister turned back to her.

"Nay, we'll go together or you're like as not to stay here and miss the whole thing. Come along now."

Sheela pulled at her sister's hand but Sarah would not budge. "I can't be seeing Thomas just yet," Sarah said. "Let him ride his race without me. Maybe that's the way he wants it . . ."

"Well, if you change your mind and take Thomas," Sheela said, bending slightly as she stood in the doorway, "then Jamie's left for me—so I cannot seem to lose. . . ." Sheela laughed. "You think about things too much, Sarah. You shouldn't miss the race, I tell you," she said, holding out her hand once again.

"I suppose not," Sarah replied, but made no move to leave. Outside she could hear the sound of hooves and wagon wheels, signalling the arrival of more wedding guests. "But I think I'll wait," she added, and motioned her sister on her way.

Thomas Gairden leaned slightly forward in the saddle, listening for the sound of the gun. Every muscle of his slender body taut, his dark eyes gleamed, narrowing in the morning sun. Lips pursed, jaw tightly set, only his dress marked him as an Ulster Scot immigrant rather than an English lord. Back straight, head erect, even in the saddle he had a graceful bearing that set him apart from most of the ruddy-faced Ulstermen who were settling Bartram and much of the Susquehanna Valley lands west of Philadelphia.

Thomas took a quick glance at the house. Still no sign of Sarah. His breath ran shallow and fast. Again he focused on the trail. With each group of arriving guests shooting their muskets to announce their arrival, an acrid, sulphur odor tainted the warm morning air. Shuttle, Thomas's horse, whinnied and tossed his head, eager to be off and away from it.

The whiskey race was a Scots-Irish wedding day tradition. Thomas would ride for the bride's family, and a neighbor, George Braid, for the groom's. They sat atop their mounts, not speaking, waiting for the signal.

"Away, lad!" Thomas shouted when the signal shot rang out. His knees jabbed Shuttle's trim sides as the horse jumped off to a good lead. The big gelding's hooves swept across the dewy grass, and his nostrils sucked in the perfume of early June clover beneath him. His rider sensed the ripple of Shuttle's smooth chestnut hide and felt the warm air turn cool as the horse flew faster and faster against it.

Beside Thomas, leather-faced George Braid clenched his teeth, crouching over the mane of his dappled mare as he evened the contest. Braid was a fighter, a short man who didn't like to lose, and from the corner of his eye, Thomas saw him lashing the mare with a willow switch. Again and again willow snapped flesh, the crack audible even over the pummeling of hooves on sod. Thomas kept his eyes on the trail and Shuttle stayed a nose ahead.

"Run, Molly, you bitch!" Braid shouted, lashing the switch on his mare's rump. Braid broke ahead by a neck, cursing Molly as the two riders neared the end of the clearing and headed into the patch of woods where the bridle path narrowed. Though the trail through the woods was blazed on both sides, Thomas knew that running Molly and Shuttle side by side was going to mean a lot of branches snapping in his face, and in Shuttle's. He eased back, letting Braid take the lead by a length. Letting Shuttle catch his breath. Letting Braid think he couldn't catch up.

The second clearing wasn't far ahead when Thomas gave Shuttle his chance. Kneeing Shuttle quickly but gently, Thomas felt the gelding read his command and lengthen his stride. A swell of pride in the horse's spirit filled Thomas as he began his cut to the left.

Braid glanced back, still snapping the willow switch and sucking air in through his mouth, his chest heaving, his shirt soaked through with perspiration. Then he swung around and crouched forward. Lashed the mare's left flank. Kicked at her with the sharp toes of his boots.

"Faster, bitch! Faster!" he shouted, licking away saliva from the corner of his mouth. As Braid turned sharply, hearing Shuttle close behind, Thomas saw his eyes narrow with intent. Suddenly, Braid slashed savagely downward with his whip, catching Shuttle across the face.

Instinctively Thomas tightened his grip on the reins. The great gelding reared in agony, thrashing, pawing, throwing his head left, then right, then left again. Down he came, with Thomas holding tight.

"There lad, there." Thomas coaxed the frightened horse, and he tried to regain control. "There, now, let's go," he said, leaning toward Shuttle's ear to speak to him. As he did so, he saw blood streaming from around the horse's eye and felt the quiver of the great neck as Shuttle again threw his head from side to side, his feet dancing in all directions at once.

Braid looked back once more, still racing as if Thomas were at his heels, but he slowed slightly as he crossed the finish line where bridegroom Jamie Lowe and all his family waited with the prize—a bottle of their best whiskey, brought from Derry. Easing his horse to a gallop then, Braid rode back to where Thomas still tried to quiet Shuttle.

With a finely woven linen handkerchief he'd pulled off his own neck, Thomas dabbed gingerly at the horse's cut, hoping to slow the bleeding, but Shuttle flinched at the slightest touch. Thomas slid down from his saddle and drew Shuttle's head close to him, speaking softly as he cradled it, comforting the horse, while blood dripped on his clean shirt.

"Catch a branch, did he?" Braid asked as he rode up, followed by Jamie and his father.

"You bastard," Thomas growled, " 'twas your whip got him and you know it."

"Nay, Thomas, I wouldn't think . . . why I—"

When Thomas took a step toward Braid, who still sat astride his mare, Jamie Lowe intervened.

"I couldn't see what happened, Thomas, but you know 'twas an accident. Now let it go as one. 'Tis only a race—and you're not much of a drinker anyway as I remember it," Jamie said with a wink, "so you won't mind that George here's won the bottle."

The dark of Thomas's eyes flashed over Jamie's face. The groom was ruddy-cheeked and smiling as he sat with his arms crossed loosely on his horse's neck. The full sleeves of his wedding shirt billowed out below the elbow though the shirt was snug across his broad shoulders.

" 'Tis not the bottle I'm angered about and you know it," Thomas said.

Jamie's smile widened. "Aye," he said meaningfully, "I *do* know it." He gave his father and Braid a cocky shrug. They chuckled. It wasn't just the bottle and it wasn't just the horse.

Breathing deeply, to slow the hammering of his heart, Thomas held his tongue. " 'Tis your weddin' day, Jamie, or I'd have you on the ground for that."

"Would you now?" Jamie said, unconcerned, running a hand along the slack reins of his horse. "Maybe another day—"

"Sorry for your horse, lad," Braid said at the same time. The small, squarely built man smiled down at Thomas from the saddle. "Looks like the bleedin's stopped already, though. Naught but a scratch. He'll be fine," he said, then kneed his horse to a lively canter and rode off with Jamie's father, Gavin, to greet the groom's procession still waiting at the finish line.

"He'll be fine if you like a scar by the eye," Thomas said through his teeth. "I'm taking him to the stream for some wet moss to cool it, Jamie. You get back to your family. I'll be along."

"Thomas, I—"

"Be off with you now or you'll miss your own weddin',"

Thomas said through a wry half smile. "I'll catch up with you."

"Hugging that bottle mighty tight aren't you now, Braid? You won it did you?" the father of the bride called out as he crossed the yard to greet the groom's procession. Andrew Roberts was a wiry little red-faced Ulsterman Scot, freckled like his daughter Sarah. "Worried you won't get any?" he teased, waving a welcome to the others on horses and in wagons behind Braid.

"I'll get my share—that you know," said Braid, laughing and patting the bottle of Durnon's Whiskey tucked snuggly beneath his arm. As he spoke to Andrew, his eyes were fixed on the fiery red tresses of Ena Shaw, being helped from a wagon by her cousin, Jamie Lowe. She had been in the colony staying with the Lowes only two months, but in that time she had caught the eye of many a young lad looking for a wife. Older men, too, looked at Ena and harbored such dreams. Andrew watched her along with Braid.

The crossing hadn't hurt Ena any, Andrew thought. She had none of the gaunt, hungry look so many had when they first came. A sheen lit the top of her creamy pink cheeks, and golden brown eyes sparkled lightly above them. He saw the color rise in her cheeks at Jamie's teasing, and heard her laughter jingle on the morning breeze.

"Welcome then, Braid. And congratulations," Andrew said, turning his attention back to his guests. "Where's your rival?"

"Thomas? At the creek." Braid began to dismount. "Horse took a branch in the eye. He's nursin' it."

"Hmmph," Andrew said with a shake of his head. "Too bad. The lad's more often too cautious and would lose before he'd see Shuttle take a branch. Jamie now . . ." he said as his almost son-in-law came sauntering toward them, "Jamie snaps a branch and worries about it later," he boasted.

"Aye, you're an Ulsterman to the bone aren't you, Jamie?" Braid observed, slapping the bridegroom on the back. "Maybe Thomas'll learn a trick or two from you yet."

"Aye," Jamie agreed, laughing at Braid's suggestion. "I'm sure he'll learn a thing or two today." Andrew joined in the joking for a moment before he moved on to greet Jamie's parents, Gavin and Ruth Lowe, and the rest of his family, including the lovely Ena Shaw.

"Whiskey's on the table by the door for those of you thirsty from your trip," Andrew announced. "Come, everyone, help yourselves."

Men drank from the jug and women from cups, and the children, too, had whiskey or metheglin or ale as they stood around the area between Andrew and Iseabal Roberts's house and thatch-roofed barn. The grass had been clipped low by the family's ten sheep who had been allowed to graze there for a few days. Chunks of wood ringed a small area for seating, and plank tables held the food.

Guests were still arriving as Thomas came walking in, leading Shuttle and holding a damp moss pack over the swelling beneath the gelding's eye. His shirt was smeared with blood, and his breeches were wet above the knees. Strands of his lustrous black hair hung loose about his face, and the twinkle was gone from his eye. He skirted the circle of guests and led Shuttle to the shade of a huge chestnut tree near the barn. Conversations ceased as people looked his way, then picked up again as they went back to their friends, no one knowing quite what to say.

As he knotted the reins about the post under the tree, Thomas looked about for Sarah, but instead caught the eye of Ena Shaw for a brief moment. She raised one eyebrow, then lowered her long eyelashes and lifted them once again, never taking her eyes from him. She let her lips almost smile, then stopped. Jamie's cousin for sure, Thomas thought, catching the invitation and ignoring it. He didn't feel like smiling back.

Still stroking Shuttle on the mane and quieting him, Thomas felt the slap of a hand on his back. "You're a good lad, Thomas," Andrew Roberts said, surprising Thomas with his warmth, "and I'm sorry you didn't win."

Thomas looked over his shoulder at Andrew, who was normally tight of lip as well as of purse, and sparing of compliments. His daughter's wedding, and no doubt an early start at the day's whiskey, were bringing out a side of him Thomas had not often seen.

"Thank you, Andrew. I would've but for Braid and his willow switch." Thomas lifted the compress slightly to show Andrew the wound and saw the trace of a question cross the older man's face. Andrew said no more though, anxious to hurry him on to the festivities. He clasped a hand on Thomas's shoulder and kept his arm around him, stretching the seams of his too-tight burgundy waistcoat, which he had worn for his own wedding.

As they covered the short distance across the yard to where men were gathered and waiting to toast the groom, Andrew's voice was low.

"Sarah has you to thank, too, for the dowry she's taking to Jamie. 'Tis a trunkful of linens and finery we couldn't have given her otherwise." Andrew paused, stopped, turned and looked Thomas in the eye. "Might've been yours. You know that, Thomas."

Thomas looked away, then back. Too many feelings tangled inside him to speak frankly just now. Instead he made an easy excuse. "I can make more," he said plainly.

Andrew Roberts again threw an arm around the shoulders of the taller, younger man. Thomas caught the sweet whiskey smell of his breath, unusual for Andrew so early in the morning, and felt himself draw away, but Andrew's grip on him was firm.

"There's still Sheela, if you're inclined to wait a year or two," he said, hopeful, as the two made their way toward the house. "Or is it somewhere else you've got your eye?" Andrew glanced toward Ena Shaw standing a few feet away, laughing with three young men.

Any man who had an eye had had it on Ena as much as possible during the sixty days she had been in the colonies. Married or single, it made no difference, no eye of any age was likely to miss her tiny waist, rounded bosom, or even

the tempting way she held her head. A practiced eye like
Andrew's certainly had taken it all in.

But Andrew never heard Thomas's answer. His words
were lost in the laughter of the several men who stood
waiting for a sip of the fine whiskey Braid had won. Thomas
saw Jamie's pleased and proud look as the older men gave
him both congratulations and advice before beginning their
round of toasts. To leave and miss the toasting would be to
risk a reputation as a poor loser, as less than a man.
Thomas took a place near Jamie and made his toast, a
simple "good luck and good cheer," before he slipped out
to clean up his shirt.

Once out behind the house, where a bucket of cold
springwater rested on a small bench, Thomas felt the ef-
fects of even that small amount of whiskey. He felt oddly
out of balance with his own body—a feeling he hadn't had
since his seasick days on the *Endeavor*. He splashed two
handsful of the icy water on his face, but the wooziness
persisted.

Tugging his shirt off over his head and dunking the fabric
deep into the water, Thomas watched as the bloodstain
began to run. Rubbing the linen shirt back and forth between his knuckles, until they were almost ready to bleed,
he felt an ache for all that should have been—for parents
who lived to old age to know grandchildren and great-
grandchildren, for horses without wounds, for Sarah who
should have been his.

"We're ready over here if you're done at the bottle," he
heard Jamie's mother call from the front of the house,
urging the men to assemble for the ceremony. Thomas gave
the shirt a shake, sending droplets flying in all directions,
then pulled it back on before he noticed that he'd missed
some spots on the sleeve. The damp fabric was clammy
against his skin and he gave a quick shiver as he ran his
hands through his black hair to straighten it. Hardly the way
to dress for a wedding. But then, his other clothes were
upstairs where Sarah and Sheela were dressing. He would
wear the wet shirt. Just now he didn't really care how he
looked.

As Thomas came back around the house, Jamie stepped out the door, taking another long pull from the jug he rested on his shoulder.

"God save the King!" someone shouted inside the open door and several men raised the jugs of local whiskey Andrew Roberts had provided for the celebration.

"God save the King!" came the response from a few.

"What the hell for?" came the question of others, laughing.

"So's he can make sure we have to sell him everything we grow, of course," one neighbor jibed.

"Nay, he's needed to keep the Irish smugglers from starvin'," railed another wit. "If George made no Navigation Acts, the poor bastards'd have no trade." Another chance to twit the Irish. Andrew Roberts laughed loudest of all.

"Nay, God's savin' the King so he can build more of these roads like the fine 'King's Road' to Philly so rutted you can't haul a cart on it," shouted another over a gaggle of voices that now began listing the gripes of everyday life in Bartram.

"No more toasts, Gavin," Ruth Lowe finally said, coming in to take her husband by the arm. " 'Tis time for the weddin'."

Iseabal Roberts made her way up the stairs to Sarah's chamber after the men had left the downstairs.

"You've a handsome lad waiting out there for you," she told her daughter, "but not half as handsome as you are in this dress." She held Sarah at arm's length and looked at her. Petite, but always a lass who loved the outdoors, her daughter could not have looked more ladylike than she did today. "You'll be a bride to remember in this gown of white. Sure 'tisn't a fancy brocade or damask like fine ladies might wear, nor a rich crimson or gold color, but 'tis elegant all the same—shows off your golden skin."

"And freckles," Sarah added.

"It pales your freckles even," her mother assured her, looking her over from top to bottom. Sarah's petticoat of white linen was edged with a ten-inch ruffle, the whole of it hand hemstitched with silk thread. Over it, a stomacher of finest cotton had its whalebone stays stitched in place with overcasting to form satiny stripes on the plain fabric, and it was held in place with emerald ribbons tied in bows. The gown itself, made of fine linen in a delicate open weave, hooked at the waist front and was trimmed with dainty cotton flounces. Around her neck, Sarah wore a loop of emerald ribbon hung with the locket that had once belonged to Jamie's grandmother.

"You must remember to thank Thomas for the dress," her mother reminded her, remembering the countless hours the lad had spent at the loom.

"I will," she said, her words short. She straightened her stays, not looking at her mother.

Iseabal took note. "Don't be harsh, Sarah. You've made your choice—don't blame him for it."

Sarah was not used to talking with her mother about anything more personal than clean sheets or fresh underwear. She kept up her fidgeting with the stays.

"Not everyone's so lucky as to have a choice. My parents forbad me to marry the Irish Catholic lad I loved—"

Sarah looked up. Here was a story she hadn't heard before.

" 'Tis true, lass, and your father knows it though 'tis not spoken of. Life with your papa's not been so bad. You'll do well with Jamie—he's like us. He's much like your papa."

Sarah felt puzzled at this a moment. She had never thought them alike. "Thank you, Mama," she said, trying to ease what seemed difficult for her mother, what was difficult for her.

"Come along now," Iseabal said. "Everyone's ready. You've been up here in your chamber far too long this day. 'Tis time to greet folks."

On the same dewy grass where men had fired their rifles in celebration and where Thomas and George Braid had started their race, there was now an altar made from two cherry planks stretched across an oak trestle, covered with a starched white linen cloth. Behind it stood the Reverend

Darroch, pastor of the local Presbyterians, clothed in his black robe, already perspiring under the early June sun.

James Edward Lowe, looking smart in gray woolen breeches and a crisp white shirt, stood before the minister. Around his neck, Jamie wore the same emerald silk scarf his father had worn twenty-two years earlier. A long black vest reached from his broad shoulders halfway to his knees, but he wore no jacket. Had none. Only a little dulled from the whiskey toasts, Jamie cut a handsome figure with his head of shoulder-length curly brown hair. In his eyes there lurked a perpetual twinkle even the solemnity of a marriage ceremony could not dim, as though some mischief brewed that only he knew. He faced the hundred or so friends and relatives gathered before him with a calm, pleased smile, and with his head held high.

As Sarah stepped out the door of her parents' house and took the arm of her father, the first thing she saw was her mother's proud smile. The second was Thomas standing next to her, wet, disheveled, angry, hurt. It was so unlike him that Sarah quickly looked away. At her father. Then at Jamie, trim, almost elegant, happy, as her father led her toward him.

"Blessings of God the Father, God the Son and God the Holy Spirit be with you all this day," the reverend began, and as the words were said, Sarah looked only at him.

"Let us pray . . ." The reverend was saying, and Sarah felt herself sway, warm under the late morning sun. In a second, Jamie's arm was around her, steadying her. He studied her with concern, not hearing anything the reverend said and Sarah looked into his eyes, then back to the preacher.

"Do you, James Edward Lowe, take . . ." At last the vows began after an eternity of prayer and homily and more prayer. The sun was nearly straight overhead by the time Sarah said "I do" and Jamie pulled her into his arms, holding her close, pressing his lips on and over and around hers as people cheered and clapped.

Tears flowing freely down her cheeks despite her smile, Iseabal Roberts squeezed the new Mrs. Lowe and kissed

her new son roundly on the lips before she opened her arms
to Andrew, then Sheela, and finally to Thomas. Even in a
wrinkled shirt, Thomas carried his slender body with such
noble grace that she wondered for a moment if he'd been
born on the wrong side of the sheets. But there had been no
gossip that way. His parents had been weavers, too, with no
hint of scandal in their lives. Still, behind his brown eyes
there was some mystery she had never been able to unravel.

He returned her embrace, holding her just a moment
longer than she'd expected. Iseabal looked up with a smile
and a sniffle, but already Thomas's eyes were on the bride.

3

Thomas looked about him at those who had stuffed themselves with the roasted hog and pone bread, venison and
smoked fish and sweet maple cakes of the wedding feast.
Some men still stood talking near the table, and others sat,
leaning back on outstretched arms, faces drenched in summer sun. A few women, having found spots in the shade of
the house, sipped cool milk stirred with sugar and whiskey.
No thoughts of hay to get in or ground to be cleared or
fences to be made today. Jamie and Sarah's wedding was
the first excuse for a whole day's celebration, aside from
working bees, in almost a year. Guests came from as far as
twenty-five miles away to feast and frolic, toast and dance.

"Too bad there's not a tree to give some shade nearby,"
Ena Shaw said. Fanning herself with her hand, she came up
behind Thomas who sat on a chunk of wood watching the
children play, waiting for the next contest to begin.

"Trees must be cut if they're too near the house here in
the colonies," Thomas said, taking the hand of the pretty
newcomer as she stepped over the log and sat down beside
him. "Shade brings on malarial fever you see." Ena nodded
and kept on fanning herself.

Thomas saw little Mary Daggins point furtively at them
as she sat waiting her turn at the stone toss, covering a
smirk with her other hand. He gave her a wink and his
special smile. Ena took no notice.

"Ah, 'tis a lovely day for a weddin'—and a wonderful
place," Ena said, shielding her eyes with her hand as she
looked up at the clear blue sky. "At home, of course,
there'd be the kirk and more sisters and cousins . . ."

"Wishin' you hadn't come to the colonies?"

"Nay, not that. Never that. It doesn't take a laird of the

land to see there's more chance here. When me mother died," she continued, "me father wanted only one thing—to die, too. At first I thought he would. He wouldn't go to the fields, wouldn't eat—only took a swallow from the jug and sat starin' at the fire. If it wasn't for my brothers we'd not have got a crop at all that first year. 'Twas William who first put him on the idea of coming here, and me with him. Scared at first I was . . ." Ena dropped her eyes.

"Me, too," Thomas said, remembering how the feelings of wanting to stay in Ulster and yet, wanting to leave, had jostled inside him. It was Sarah who had convinced him to come along with her family. She was always so sure of herself. . . . "Once I saw Philadelphia, though, I knew I was right to come," he added. He omitted the part about the seasickness and telling Sarah he would never cross that ocean again. "I'll never go back," he said instead, and as he spoke he glanced across the yard to where Sarah stood chatting with a few of the neighbors. She looked his way, too, then quickly away again, pretending he hadn't caught her eye. They hadn't spoken more than "pass the mush, please" since that night at the creek.

"Save me the first dance tonight?" he asked Ena suddenly.

"Already saved it for Lewis. And the second one, too." Her heavy lashes shadowed what Thomas thought was a sparkle in the gold of her eyes, half-apologetic, half-pleased with herself. He caught the faint scent of the wildflowers she wore in the pointed cleavage of her dress as his eyes took in all of her though they never really left hers. "Number three for you though, I promise."

"Three 'tis. I'll be honored." Thomas smiled. The acceptance flattered but did not fill. He felt himself a lamp with naught but a bit of oil left in it. Enough for no more than a flicker.

"You can ask for another, you know." Ena's momentary homesickness had obviously subsided.

"Maybe I will," he said, short of a glib phrase. Even so, the words brought a happy curve to Ena's lips.

Thomas's eyes caught the glint of the late afternoon sun

as he got up to join the wood-chopping contest just starting behind the house, glad he had a reason not to have to say any more. Ena's manner was most inviting, and it crossed his mind that spending the evening with her might not be as bad as spending it alone among the guests, but he gave the matter little thought as he went from one contest to the next. From chopping to shooting to footraces, Thomas's mind was occupied more with not appearing a poor loser— of races or of lasses—than with the company of anyone but Sarah.

As the last of the afternoon's heat began to hint at the cool of evening, young and old looked about for partners to join in the dancing they'd all been waiting for. Filled once again from feasting on the bear, pork, quail, pheasant, and rabbit set before them for the evening meal, guests of every age were ready to jump into lively jigs and reels.

Darren Smith played the first notes on his flute and Adam Lypslie joined in on his fiddle. Ignoring the occasional musket blast from those still proving their marksmanship, Jamie and Sarah started the dance. They made a few short turns in the reel before Jamie gave up any pretense of being able to dance and simply took Sarah in his arms for a long, slow kiss. He reeked of whiskey and perspiration, and Sarah held her breath, but all about them people cheered and clapped and called for more. And Jamie loved an audience.

Finally, though, he paused and his new wife led him to the edge of the yard, propping him up against a tree trunk, where he sat in a happy-looking stupor. Sarah's father was already waiting for the next dance, and before she knew it she was circling and stepping along with him just as if she were still Sarah Roberts, his daughter. Only now she wasn't. Not really.

Other couples joined them in the reel. Sarah's mother with Jamie's father. Jamie's mother with her other son, John. Neighbors. Friends. And Thomas, teaching eight-year-old Mary Daggins as they went. Sarah could see his delight in the little girl's determined steps. He did love children, Thomas did.

As the music stopped, Thomas sent Mary scurrying back to her friends and heard Andrew calling him.

"Thomas, lad," he said, his red-veined face moist from the tempo of the reel, "Thomas, 'tis a father's happiest day when he sees his daughter married and knows that grandsons will soon be on the way. Have you kissed the bride yet, lad?"

"No, I—"

"Well then, do it now, lad," Andrew boomed. " 'Tis time the two of you mended fences. And you should never, never pass up a chance to kiss a pretty girl, anyway. She's more than pretty, you know, in the fine dress you and Iseabal made for her." Sarah's father gave a hearty laugh as he pushed young Thomas toward his daughter but made no move to leave.

Thomas leaned forward slightly and touched Sarah's cheek. "You know I hope you'll be happy, you and Jamie," he began, when Andrew pushed him once again.

"Be Jesus, lad," the bride's father insisted, his tongue thick with whiskey, "you can do better than that—remember 'tis your last chance." With his short, muscled arms he thrust the two of them together once again as if they were no more than a pair of young calves.

Sarah felt Thomas's kiss on her lips, charged with the power of all that was denied, forbidden, sought after. Her cheeks burned, and the second her father eased his hold on them, she stepped back. The off-key sound of bow on strings jarred the warm night air as the fiddler did a quick retuning of his instrument between songs.

"Thank you, Thomas," Sarah murmured, looking off over her shoulder, anywhere but into his eyes.

"That's better, lad," Andrew Roberts said, slapping him on the back. He brought his other hand to his mouth as if to whisper something, then asked loud enough for Sarah to hear, "Takin' Ena for a dance, are you?" He looked over his shoulder to where Ena stood with Lewis Harding.

"I am. At least I've asked."

"Well, good luck to you. She's quite an armful, that one." Andrew winked, and the puffiness beneath his eyes fell into saggy wrinkles. "Of course an old man the likes of me wouldn't know," he said, stifling a burp as he chuckled. He slapped Thomas on the back again, leaving his hand there a few moments until Sarah noticed him begin to wobble.

"Papa, can I help you find a seat?"

"Nay, I feel a thirst," Andrew said, his head moving loosely on his shoulders. "Thomas, dance this next one with Sarah for me, will you?" he asked, and headed off listing slightly to the left as the first notes of the next tune came creaking out of Lypslie's fiddle.

"I'll miss you, Sarah," Thomas said as he took her hand to start the reel. The half smile faded from his face as he spoke. "I'm sorry—"

"I'll still be here," she said, as their elbows linked and they circled left. Then right. She felt weightless as her yards of skirts whirled about her.

"So you will," he nodded. "So you will."

Sarah heard the sadness in his voice, but her satisfaction in it was long past. Instead, she felt a sadness of her own. She took his arm, just as she had many other times at many other dances. As they circled and dipped, their eyes looked everywhere but at each other, and their hands barely touched as they kept a careful distance between them.

"Bride ready for another dance?" old man Chalmers wanted to know, tapping Sarah on the shoulder and reaching for her hand before she could answer. Thomas stepped back as the elfin, bent old man whisked her away, but Sarah knew that Thomas watched as she danced away into another life.

The third dance had already begun when Thomas made his way among the dancers to the refreshment table where Ena stood by Lewis.

"My turn, Lewis," he said with a smile. "Lost the whiskey race but I won't lose out on me dances." Ena's hand felt warm and small in his, but she gave his hand two quick squeezes, though she didn't so much as look at him.

"Hmm," was all Lewis had to say for himself as he turned and shuffled toward the house to join his father and several other men. Thomas heard Ena smother a little giggle and felt an unexpected euphoria as they took their places for the jig.

Throughout the evening, Thomas danced with many partners, and danced again with Ena, but it wasn't until the musicians took a break long after dark that Thomas and Ena spoke more than a few offhand words to each other.

"You've not told me where it was you grew up in Ulster, Thomas," Ena said, as they stood alone while other dancers sought out food and drink. Perspiration gave a gleam to her face in the moonlight and Thomas caught the musky scent of her. He wondered how to begin. No secret at all, where he came from, but still talking of what lay back across the ocean came hard to him.

"From New Buildings in the north," he said, finally. "Papa had a little land, spent most of his time at the loom. Mama, too. Sent me to Old Kinloch to learn the trade so I could make me own way, not be at the mercy of the laird."

"You ran away, then?"

"Nay, finished me training. Learned the weavin' trade. But Mama and Papa died of the coughing. I had the choice of taking what little they had to pay the rent on the land, or take passage. Sarah convinced me to come with them."

"A weaver must do well here, I'm sure," Ena ventured. "There's more people settling every day. Soon 'twill be just as crowded here as at home, and all those people will be needin' clothes—and linens—fine things, too."

"Aye. I haven't had much time, though. Been helping Andrew with the farm, weavin' only what we need and a few things for the neighbors."

"Your own land's the way to make a pound. Look how well Uncle Gavin and the others are doin'. Soon you'll be doin' the same." Ena's bright eyes were sure and clear in the moonlight. They made Thomas smile, the first time he'd really felt like smiling all day.

"Been here a month and you know it all—is that it?" he asked her with a mock frown. "How can you be so sure?"

"Two months," she said, correcting him, "and I know you could do it if I helped you."

Thomas blinked, then widened his eyes. Though the night was dark, they were still standing in the midst of a great number of people. Andrew, standing just behind Ena, raised an eyebrow as Thomas looked over toward him, as if he might have heard what Ena had said. Thomas fished for a reply. He looked away, then back down, into her eyes and knew he had heard her right.

"Let's sit a bit before Lypslie and Smith start again," he suggested, offering his arm.

"Nay, let's walk. 'Tis a lovely night for a walk."

Thomas saw Lewis watching them, his massive arms still folded across his chest as he leaned against the house, one foot braced against the wall. He made no move to speak as they walked past, but Thomas sensed his eyes following them. Thomas slipped his arm free of Ena's, distancing himself a bit, but extended his hand at the small of her back to guide her down the path.

In the cover of the edge of the woods, Thomas stopped, and Ena slid into his arms as easily as if they had kissed a thousand times before. He sensed the eagerness of her body and knew the shortness of her breath between the kisses that spilled from them.

She nuzzled close and pressed her lips hard on his, teased him with her tongue. Thomas responded, as she led the way with a passion far removed from the likes of kissing the local lasses at kissing frolics, or even of kissing Sarah that night at the creek. Ena's back felt small in his large hands, and she twisted about against him, the roundness of her bosom soft and inviting.

"Lewis wants me to marry him," Ena whispered as her lips left his to brush the tip of his chin and then his throat, stopping to lick at the curl of hair that wriggled out above the collar. "But I put him off. Told him you'd already spoken to Gavin."

"But I haven't . . ." he started to say, then stopped. She already knows that, he realized. She's made up a lie to put off Lewis. . . . That explained Lewis's sour face. Thomas felt an odd flutter in his eye. He stepped back, the tic in his eye quickening. His eyes narrowed against the tic but already tears had begun to flow, and he felt on the verge of a sneeze.

"I guess I hadn't thought of it—marryin' that is—much until today," Thomas muttered. "I . . . um . . ." Thomas struggled for a word. "I'm pleased you're thinkin' of me, but 'tis Lewis you want. He's a strong lad, that's for sure. Hard worker. You'll—" Ena moved her body restlessly against his as she lay her cheek against his chest and looked up at him.

"But I don't love the fat pug, Thomas. 'Tis you I want. We're both alone in this world, far from home. Let's make a new home, here. Fill it with wee Gairdens, watch 'em grow and give 'em all we didn't have."

He was alone. Ena was right about that. He'd never thought of himself that way before, but today when Sarah stood with Jamie in front of the preacher he had felt it.

Ena lifted her slender arms and took his face between her hands, stretching on tiptoe to press her lips against his once more. Tilting her head slightly back and forth as they kissed, the round contours of her body squeezed softly back and forth against him. Thomas was suddenly aware of his inexperience and the June night with its music of frogs and birds and fiddle and flute began to seem unseasonably warm. Breathing became a gasp and he pulled back, turning sharply away from Ena. Raising a hand to smooth back his hair, he stopped and pressed two fingers to his temple to still the quiver of his eye.

"You're a lovely lass, Ena," he said, still pressing at his temple. "And every man at the wedding and probably every lad between here and Ireland wishes he could be where I am right now. And most of 'em would be more than happy to leave Lewis to chop wood for their weddin's rather than choppin' at his weddin' to you. Some of 'em you'd even be happy with. You might even be happy with me . . . but . . ."

"But what, Thomas Gairden?" Her voice was soft now,

mingled with the song of the frogs that seemed to come from everywhere at once.

"I've come this far, Ena. I've crossed an ocean lookin' for a better life, and I've found one . . . but I don't think it's enough. I'm not goin' to stay put, Ena. I want to try my luck at weavin' in Philadelphia—maybe open a manufactory— and if it's not good there I want to try it somewhere else. I want to keep tryin' 'til it feels right. I've told no one else, but I'm plannin' to leave within the week."

"And you don't need any help, I suppose? I could go to Philadelphia with you—"

"I'll need help. But I'll ask no one, not Sarah, not you, to share in half of nothing should I fail. Sarah has someone to take care of her now. You'll have Lewis or another to take care of you." He spoke with all the care and concern he could muster, hearing in her offer to go to Philadelphia a note of desperation. When she spoke again, that note was gone.

"Half of nothin' is more than you'll ever have, Thomas Gairden, unless you learn to take what God offers you and be thankful for it. I'll find one of those men you mentioned between here and the sea and he'll know what it means to have half of everything. And, you . . . you . . . simperin' double-jugg, I can take care of myself!"

With that, Ena Shaw swept around in the direction of the fiddle music, slicing the quiet air of the forest with the snap of her skirts and Thomas was alone in the darkness of the night.

Thomas headed in the opposite direction. The moonlight threw eerie shadows before him and night birds murmured. About to head in the direction of the creek he thought better of it—too many couples knew it as a spot of peace and privacy. Wandering far off into the woods wasn't wise either, without a musket.

Walking only a few steps farther, Thomas slid down at the base of a towering white pine where many decades' accumulation of needles formed a soft cushion amid the monstrous, tentaclelike roots that reached out above the soil to serve as convenient arms for a natural chair. The tree's pungent scent and the soft cushion of its discarded needles soothed him as he sat thinking back on Ena. The tremor of the tic lessened, then stopped. His thinking switched from Ena to Sarah. Then to the idea that had been haunting him.

He had a little money saved toward starting a place of his own. He had the reeds and shuttles he'd brought from New Buildings, all he had left from his family. He had a few pieces already woven to offer for sale. He would find spinners, take on commissions. He could build up a business, then hire help.

The idea grew in his mind. Staring off into the face of the full moon he imagined his manufactory: many looms, four or five apprentices and journeymen working under him, scallet frames and raiths standing against the wall, yarns piled in the corners, knots of yarn hanging from the beams, himself selling the finest wares to the well-dressed men and ladies of the city who came to order. He knew he could do it. When he'd worked for Kinloch the fancy patterns had been his specialty. He had missed the work since he'd been here clearing land and farming and weaving only a little. He was nineteen. Any debt owed to Andrew and Iseabal was long since paid by four years of work. And now there was no Sarah to hold him here.

Thomas thought of Philadelphia and how it had looked the last time he was there. How he would love to see the ships and harbor once more. To taste the goods of a baker at the fair. To read books from the library society he'd heard about. To talk to other weavers and learn from them. To see fine stores and paved streets. To get copies of Franklin's *Pennsylvania Gazette* when it was fresh, instead of weeks old the way they got them in Bartram.

Thomas went over his plans for a while before the weight of the day's activities caught up with him and he dozed, dreaming an occasional dream of Sarah calling for him. When he woke, dampness chilled the air and he felt a shiver wave through him. There was no music now, he noticed. The woods, too, were silent. Thomas fought the urge to lie down at the foot of the giant pine and spend the rest of the night. But Andrew and Iseabal would worry if he didn't get home at all.

Walking back, he imagined their delight when he told them his news, and their pride when they would come to visit him in the city. The story, though, would have to wait until morning—until Andrew sobered up, probably, Thomas thought. All was quiet around the Roberts' place. The guests had either gone home or gone to bed in their big-wheeled carts. The bride and groom were gone, and no trace of the wedding remained except the wood chunk chairs that ringed the yard. And no candle gleamed in the window for Thomas Gairden.

4

"And next I suppose we'll be gettin' the Reverend Darroch back here for you."

Light scalded Thomas's eyes. Hay scratched beneath him.

"What?" he said through a yawn. Where am I? Thomas wondered, then remembered dropping onto the green hay of the barn loft when he'd come home last night instead of waking the whole house by going in to his bed.

Sitting up, he rubbed his eyes and shook his head, brushing the chaff out of the back of his hair and off his shirt. Looking down, he saw Andrew Roberts looking up at him from his milk stool below.

"The Reverend Darroch," Andrew repeated, louder. "I suppose you'll be wantin' his services one day soon, too, eh?" Andrew wrinkled his eye into a wink, though he pulled down the corners of his little mouth and made a pout of his chin.

"For what?" Thomas stretched his arms wide, yawning as he spoke.

"Out all night with Ena Shaw and not needin' the preacher? Tell me, lad, do you think I ought to believe that?"

"But I wasn't with Ena. I mean—"

"Come now, lad, I saw you lookin' at her. I saw you walkin' to the woods with her. You missed helpin' to steal the bride, and you missed seein' Jamie and Sarah leave because you still weren't back. And now you're sleepin' in the straw like a beggar. Tell me again you weren't out enjoyin' the charms of Ena Shaw."

Thomas swung his legs onto the ladder and lowered himself down from the loft, more awake now. "I went for a walk with Ena . . . to . . . talk. But she came back after just a few minutes. I sat down somewhere along the trail . . . sat down and fell asleep. I wasn't with her more than a short while."

"Then where is she? Gavin couldn't find her when it was time to go. But Lewis Harding said he'd seen the two of you goin' off together, so when Gavin got tired of waitin' he left, thinkin' she was safe with you."

"And what else did Lewis say?" Thomas asked. "He's the one wanted to spend the time with Ena."

Andrew answered with a slow, appraising look. "Said she was pledged to marry you." Andrew raised his bushy eyebrows as he spoke, the whites of his eyes red all over.

"That's what she told him, Andrew, but 'twas a bit of a double-tongue. She told me Lewis had asked her but she didn't want to marry him. She told him I'd already spoken to Gavin about a match . . . she proposed we marry instead."

"And you said nay, lad? Are you crazy? A good-lookin' lass like Ena doesn't come along every day. Are you sayin' Ena lied?" Andrew set his jaw and pulled up his chin in a scowl.

"Not lied, exactly . . ." Thomas groped for words to put it as delicately as he could. "She just tried to work things out on her own so's not to hurt Lewis, him havin' been sufferin' so since Tully died."

"But you said nay, is that right?"

"I don't love her, Andrew, and I'm not ready to marry— or I'd have married Sarah." Thomas, awake now, looked Andrew squarely in the eye. "I'm thinkin' of settlin', Andrew, but not here with Ena." Thomas saw Andrew's eyes widen. Nervous, he bent his head and smoothed his hair back with the palms of both hands, his long fingers touching lightly as they met on the crown of his head. "I'm goin' back to Philadelphia, back into the weavin' business. Settin' up me own shop if I can." He caught Andrew's crestfallen look. "I'm no farmer, Andrew."

Andrew was silent for a moment, then turned from

Thomas to begin milking Hulda. "And how long has this been in the plannin', lad?" he wanted to know.

"A couple of days is all," Thomas admitted, sensing a simmering choler in Andrew and feeling a need to justify his decision. "As I was talkin' to Ena, tryin' to think of reasons why I couldn't marry her, the idea came to me again—and I knew it was right."

"But what about the land here, Thomas? We've treated you like a son. Taken you into our house. Who'll help me now? Who'll clear the fields, plant the wheat?" The tremor in his voice was like a quiet roar, ready to explode. Thomas heard not so much disappointment as anger in Andrew's voice and felt his throat go dry.

"I don't know, Andrew. I don't know. I only know I am goin' to Philly. I'm goin' to do what I was trained to do and I'm goin' to do it better than any other weaver in Pennsylvania. There are more and more people comin' all the time, all needin' things—things I can make. I'm not goin' to die like my father did, with barely enough to pay the next year's rent. I'll be at the mercy of no man." Thomas paused for a moment. "Not even you, Andrew."

Milk shot into the wooden bucket in steady, powerful streams. Even from Thomas's height far above it, the heavy, warm odor filled the air. Hulda flicked her tail to the top of her back, chasing away the flies that were beginning to gather as the day warmed. Frieda mooed nearby, anxious to be milked.

Andrew kept pumping, not looking up, as Thomas tried to explain further.

"I thought you'd be happy for me, Andrew. I thought you'd want me to get out from underfoot here and make me own way. You've still got Sheely. Jamie and Sarah not far away. You've got things nice here, good neighbors, too. You'll find another young lad just off the ship to work for you as I did. But I'm a man now. I must make me own way."

"You'll stay through the harvest," Andrew said, as though it were tomorrow, but still he did not look up.

"Nay, Andrew. I'm leavin' today. I told Ena I was leavin' today. I'm goin' before I change my mind—or you change it for me. The crop is sown, first of the hay is done. If you need me to help with the harvest I'll come home for a while then, but—"

A sharp turn of the head brought Andrew's face full front to Thomas's. "If you're leavin' today, you're not comin' back, lad. Not for the harvest, not at all." Wrath raged in his rigid jaw, and looking at Thomas, he did not blink.

Thomas felt his chest empty of air. "So thanks a lot, Thomas, for workin' your arse off clearin' land and buildin' houses and barns and fences and . . . and . . . I've been no son here, Andrew, have I? Have I? Just a servant you dropped some crumbs to. You're no better than the lairds at home. I'll be takin' me loom and me things today, Andrew."

"You're takin' no loom, lad. Not from this place. You can—"

The reds of Andrew's and Thomas's faces were bleached white by the scream they heard from the far side of the house. Before Andrew could get up and limber his legs, Thomas was halfway across the yard. Thomas rounded the house, crossed the ground where the wood-chopping contest had been held less than twenty-four hours earlier, and followed the screams of terror that pierced the quiet of the June morning. Andrew stopped at the house to get his musket, then ran to catch Thomas. If there were Shawnees out there, they would be running right into them, Thomas thought, but still he ran toward the creek, closing in on the screams with each step.

"Thomas . . ." he heard now, half sobbed, half screamed. Ahead of him he saw Iseabal Roberts kneeling on the ground, her skirts around her like a tent, and as he came closer, he saw, too, the ravaged body of Ena Shaw flung half-naked on the bloodstained ground in front of her. Quickly Thomas stripped off his shirt and lay it over the body, covering the face and torso, but not before Andrew had seen enough to tell him all he needed to know.

"*You* killed her," Andrew roared, his eyes flaming. "You killed her after you'd had your fun with her, didn't you, lad? And thought you could ride out of here before anyone

found her, didn't you?" Andrew raised the gun like a club
and swung hard for Thomas. Iseabal shrieked, not far from
the weapon's path.

"Out of the way, woman," Andrew shouted. "This lad of
our house isn't the lad we brought from Ulster with us. He's
a cheat and a liar . . . and now a killer, too."

"Andrew!" Iseabal screamed. "My God, man, what is
this? What are you talkin' about? This is Shawnee work
here and you know it. Get hold of yourself. Stop, I tell you.
Stop." She clambered to her feet and tugged frantically at
his shoulder as she spoke.

Andrew drew a deep breath and put down the gun. His
wife looked to Thomas for an explanation. The taut skin of
his firm young chest heaved in and out, and every muscle in
his face tensed to hold back the quiver in his eyelid that
wouldn't go away.

"This lad," Andrew said through sobs of his own, "this
lad we raised under our own roof right among our own
daughters has no care for anyone but himself. Had his way
with Ena here, killed her and was plannin' to run off to
Philadelphia—or somewhere—today before anyone found
out about it—isn't that right, Thomas? There were no
Shawnees here. She's got her scalp now, don't she?"

"I did nothin' with her but tell her I wouldn't marry her, I
swear it," said Thomas, his chest rising slower now, but
barely containing the beating of his heart. He remembered
kissing her. How he'd liked it and yet not wanted it. His
face burned.

"Then why were you seen with her and why were you
gone all night and why were you sleepin' in the barn like a
common thief and plannin' to steal away today before anyone found poor Ena? Tell me that, lad?"

Thomas looked to Iseabal, who stood between him and
Andrew, her eyes wide with the shock of death and fear of
her husband's rage. He could not comfort her though, for if
he reached for her hand Andrew would reach for his gun.

"Would I still be around this mornin' if I'd killed her and
wanted to cover it up?" he asked. "Wouldn't I have dragged
her somewhere far away and then kept on goin' myself?"

"Not if you planned to take all your belongin's with you!" Andrew's mouth turned down at the corners and he pulled his upper lip away from his teeth in disgust.

"I had no cause to want to kill Ena," Thomas said softly and slowly, his eyes on the ground. "I just didn't want to marry her."

"And why not?" Andrew thundered. "Look at me, dammit! Why not? Is there somethin' wrong with you?"

Thomas looked up to see Andrew's eyes wild with accusation. Is there somethin' wrong with you? The words echoed and reechoed in Thomas's ears. Somethin' wrong with you? Somethin' wrong?

"You were hungry for her—admit it! Just like you were for Sarah, no matter what you say about her wantin' Jamie. I could see it in you. But you wouldn't want anyone to think you were a man just like the rest of us—you always have to put yourself above the rest. Well, this time you've sunk below all the rest. You're even cryin'." Andrew wrinkled his nose and his narrow lips.

"But look at his clothes, Andrew," Iseabal managed to say. "There's no blood. He hasn't—"

"He probably didn't have 'em on!" Andrew's temper was out of control. "Laid 'em out nice and neat before you took 'er, didn't you? You always was one for neatness. Always lookin' to be a laird yourself."

"Andrew!" Iseabal shrieked, shocked. "Andrew! Get hold of yourself. Why are you accusin' Thomas so? Just because he was sleepin' in the barn? There was many a lad had too much o' the jug last night and slept wherever he fell. Sleepin' in the barn's no crime."

"But runnin' off the morning after a killin' is!" Andrew answered his wife's statement without stopping to think about it. "The lad means to take the loom and anything else he can carry and run to Philly, leavin' us here with not a young body to help us."

Iseabal looked to Thomas for denial.

"I'll leave the loom. Forget it!" Thomas spit the words through lips that barely parted and stepped past Iseabal to leave.

"You'll leave everything," said Andrew, grabbing Thomas by the arm as he passed. "You're not goin' anywhere, lad. You'll stay right here and take your punishment. No lad of my house gets away with murder while I'm here to stop him."

With one swoop of his free arm Thomas could have freed himself from Andrew, but he didn't. Instead he looked into his eyes.

"I swear to you, Andrew. I had nothin' to do with it."

"We'll see about that, lad. We'll see about that," Andrew said, ramming his gun beneath Thomas's nose. "For now you can pick her up one last time and carry her back to the house, though by rights your filthy hands shouldn't touch her."

Thomas bent slowly to gather the tiny body in his arms and Andrew held the musket tight against his back as he stooped. Thomas heard the thudding of his heart as the barrel rammed tighter against him. Andrew was mad enough to kill him, Thomas knew, and he couldn't risk turning his head to look at him, but cornered his eye as he crouched to see if Andrew's face showed any signs of mellowing. Even that small movement was enough to send the barrel bruising against his ribs and Thomas got his answer without even seeing Andrew's face.

The forest grass beneath Ena was matted and damp with the trapped dew of evening, and Ena's body was cold and very stiff. He'd seen his mama and papa, too, and knew the coldness took a while. He also knew Andrew was right about one thing: This was not the work of Shawnees. Still Thomas's eyes scanned the trees before him as he lifted Ena, her full skirts seeming to weigh almost more than the rest of her, their pale green now blood-streaked and dirty.

Thomas felt the quiver of his eye and lips. He smothered a sniffle and held back the tears that started to run from fear and sadness and disgust. But he felt the chill of Andrew's musket and kept about his task, trying to get a firm grip on the body that flopped and slid and seemed impossible to hang onto.

"Get movin' there, Thomas, and get her back to the

house. Then you can go to the barn where you slept off your dirty deeds." Andrew pushed him along with jabs of the rifle barrel. "You can call that home until we talk to a few more good folks who know it couldn't've been anyone but you," he said almost as an afterthought.

5

Large double doors opened on the east side of Andrew Roberts's barn, flanked by a small opening on either side, each with a leather-hinged shutter which could be closed against the cold weather of winter. The barn's hayloft, covering only half of the upper level, was filled by pitching the hay up with a fork, a job Thomas had recently completed. The barn walls had not been rechinked yet this year, and little shafts of light shot in here and there all around Thomas as he sat in the late afternoon heat, wriggling his hands at the wrist to ward off the stiffness and prickliness beginning to set in.

How had it all changed so fast? he wondered. Hadn't he, just hours ago, been sure that Andrew and Iseabal would be pleased for him, striking off on his own? Hadn't he imagined their pride in the success he would make of his weaving business? Now, tied in the barn like a dumb animal, all those dreams seemed far away. Reality was a pile of hay itching against his bare back, sweat running down his brow and chest as the afternoon sun heated the barn with no breeze creeping in to stir the odors of the dung and the straw and the leather of harnesses hung on the wall.

Sheela came to milk Hulda late that afternoon, and Iseabal came to bring him water and some food, but neither so much as loosened a knot on the ropes Andrew had tied so tightly. Thomas sensed both their fear and their uncertainty.

"I need to get to the privy," Thomas said, breaking the silence as Iseabal spooned some corn bread soaked in cream into his mouth. "I'm sorry to bother you, but I need it bad."

She stopped with the spoon halfway to his mouth. The

shocked glaze was gone from her eyes now, replaced by a cautious kind of sadness. Unlike Andrew, she had very little gray hair, her color instead a deep auburn like Sarah's. Dark circles under her eyes and the puffiness of fatigue and tears gave her an aged look far beyond her thirty-five years.

"She had your handkerchief stuck in her sleeve," Iseabal blurted out, looking away.

"What?" Thomas took a moment to process the statement, then knew in one instant all that Iseabal had said in what she hadn't said. "So that proves I'm guilty—is that it? I gave it to her to mop her brow, she was so warm from all the dancin'. It doesn't mean I killed her."

"I know that," Iseabal said softly, "but Andrew doesn't. Won't hear of anything else. I'm sorry, Thomas. So sorry."

Thomas rolled his head back with a loose bob and closed his eyes. "God help me. Please. Help me," he said, straightening once again.

"We'll do what we can, you know that," Iseabal said with a wary reassurance. "I can't let you loose . . . but I can get you a bucket," she said, remembering Thomas's request.

He knew she didn't dare step outside the bounds of Andrew's instructions, but in her offer to help as best she could he felt a bit of hope.

"Let me talk to him alone, Jamie," Sarah said as they stood by their horse in front of the Roberts' house while Iseabal and Sheela were still in the barn.

"Not for a minute! Do you think I'm goin' to let me bride alone with a man who may not be right for this world? Nay, lass!"

"Jamie, you've listened too much to my father. Listen to your heart a minute. You've known Thomas four years now. Have you ever known him to be cruel? To be anything but a friend to you? You owe it to him to stand by him."

"You're my wife. You owe it to me to do as I say." Jamie Lowe's words lit with a sizzle on the humid evening air. Sarah saw the heave of his chest as he waited for her answer.

"I will," Sarah said, "but I also owe it to you to be truthful. Papa has a terrible temper, and he's had the shock of seein' a murder on his own land durin' his own daughter's weddin'. And the shock of hearin' that Thomas plans to leave us. I'm bein' truthful with you when I tell you, Jamie, Papa stretches the truth when it suits him—I've seen it. Think about it. Why just today when he was tellin' your folks about how he's treated Thomas like a son. You know how he's made Thomas work, and for what? He's no son. He'll not inherit this place or anything else of my father's. I ask, who'll speak for Thomas if not me? If you were in trouble, I'd do the same for you."

"You're a Lowe now, lass, and your house has seen one of its daughters beaten and murdered. Should I just forget that? Should I just walk up to Thomas and say I don't mind? He can go free? Tell me, Sarah, who will speak for Ena if we, the livin', don't? Get in the house and comfort your mother. Leave Thomas to me." With a rough shove, Jamie announced the conversation over, and Sarah swallowed back a retort, watching as he stomped to the barn.

"Sarah's in the house," Jamie said with a smile that dismissed Iseabal and Sheela. Once they were out the door, the smile faded. "Fine way to treat Ena." Along with the statement he delivered a kick across Thomas's knuckles to express all the things he couldn't put into words.

"I didn't hear you ask me if I did it," Thomas said, cringing at the pain in his fingers. "I think you owe me that much."

"Owe you? I owe you nothin' as Andrew tells it, and he has no reason to double-tongue. I owe you nothin' but a wagon ride to Philly where they'll hang you—or worse. You make me sick—sicker than I felt when I saw Ena's body all bloody and spent." Closing his eyes in disgust, Jamie shook his head. "How could you?" he asked, almost to himself.

"I couldn't!" Thomas shouted now, for the first time in the ordeal. "And you ought to know it!" He quieted then. "She was puttin' me in a bad spot, that I admit. She'd double-tongued Lewis and wanted me to help her cover it up. Honestly, Jamie . . ." Thomas's voice keened with pain. ". . . she was mad enough to kill *me*, but I had no quarrel with her. Sent her on her way back to Lewis. That's all I did. And you know what? Her last words were 'I can take care of myself.' Guess she wasn't as strong as she thought she was."

Thomas's voice trailed off as he thought back to the conversation and how angry Ena had been. What if she'd told Lewis nay again and he'd struck her for it? One blow from those bulging arms of his could . . .

"Jamie. Has Andrew talked to Lewis yet?" Thomas asked urgently, forgetting his pains.

"What if he has? What would he know about it?"

Thomas told him the story, though he sensed that Jamie listened only in hopes of poking holes in the theory that Lewis might have done the murder. Thomas didn't dare mention he suspected Andrew, himself, for he'd seen the way Andrew's eyes, too, lusted after Ena, and how he was overly quick to point his finger elsewhere.

"Lewis wouldn't," Jamie said flatly. "Not on a chance. Nor was it his handkerchief she'd stuck in her sleeve. You did it. You could at least own up to it."

"Yesterday I toasted you at your weddin' and today you're callin' me a killer, Jamie. Why? Doesn't four years count for anything?"

"You slept in the barn like a thief after bein' in the woods with Ena. Last person to see her alive. The handkerchief . . . Might've been gone already if you hadn't been sleepin' off all the celebratin' you did."

"I'm no drinker, Jamie. You know that. You've known that since the time we took the jug to the river and took a swig for every fish we caught. You were still catchin' fish and lickin' your lips while I was lyin' on the grass wishin' I could die. You *know* that. And Andrew knows it, too, if he'd only stop and think. He's bent on destroyin' me because he didn't like the idea of me leavin'."

"Leavin'?"

Thomas nodded. "Told Andrew this morning I wanted to go back to Philadelphia. Start a weavin' manufactory. I'm no farmer. I can't abide it. I'm trained to weave. Me father was a farmer first and a weaver second, but not me. 'Tis the work I love, and I'm goin' back to it, if not in Philly then on the road."

Jamie quit his glare and raised his eyes to the roof, taking in and letting out a deep breath before he spoke. So Thomas would be gone either way, guilty or innocent. Sarah would never forgive him if he didn't help Thomas. And maybe Andrew did have his own axe to grind.

"I'll talk to Lewis," Jamie said with a sigh. "I'll see what he's got to say for himself. I do owe you that."

"Thank you, Jamie. But 'tis not a matter of debt. 'Tis a matter of justice. You can't let a killer go free—you've a wife to protect now." Thomas saw Jamie's eyes take in the merit of his words, but he did not answer as he hurried away.

✤

6

Lewis Harding lifted his head to see who was coming, but didn't acknowledge the approach of Jamie Lowe before dropping his eyes again. With a rapid, sure stroke he pulled his drawknife over the red oak log he sat straddling.

"Makin' a start are you, Lewis?" Jamie asked in the way of hello, standing only inches away from Harding in the stump-knobbed clearing where Harding planned to build his house.

"May as well get on with it. Expect I'll be livin' here alone anyway."

"You heard about Ena?"

"I did." Jamie heard grief and fury in the low rumble of Harding's voice, and saw them in his sharp pulls against the rough grain of the log.

" 'Twas a shame," Jamie said, shaking his head. "Such a lively lass. Such a head of hair on her. Thomas tells me you'd wanted to marry her. Would've made us cousins."

Harding slid backward down the log far enough to begin shaving down another area. "Suppose," was all he said.

"Will you be wantin' to say a few words at the funeral tomorrow then?" Jamie shifted uncomfortably from right foot to left, then swung the right foot to rest on top of Lewis's log. Bending low, he rested his forearms across his knee and tilted his head to face Harding at his own level. " 'Twould be nice to hear from a friend. I don't know who else would."

The scrape, scrape, scrape of the drawknife set Jamie's teeth on edge as he watched Lewis's powerful hands bear down on the handles and saw the muscles in his forearms bulge at each pull. Staring, his eyes blurred the arm movements, while in his mind he imagined Ena's struggle.

"Will you?" Jamie demanded, angered by the image in his mind.

"Why not ask your friend Thomas?" Lewis said, finally stopping the motion of the knife and looking up, eye to eye with Jamie. "I got nothin' to say. I lost Tully. Now Ena—not that I ever really had her. She didn't want me, you know. Had her eye out for Thomas and every other man at your weddin'. But not me."

"What are you sayin', Lewis?" Jamie asked, straightening and looking down to where Lewis sat, slightly slumped, the drawknife hanging slack from his left hand. "Are you sayin' Ena was of easy virtue?" Lewis was silent. "Well, are you?" Jamie demanded. "She lived in my house, man. I think I'd know somethin' about that. We're talkin' about a murder here, Lewis, and it's soundin' more and more like maybe you had more reason than Thomas!"

Harding stood up, still straddling the log. His yellow hair, damp with perspiration, curled loosely across the top of his head and over his ears, and it hung on his forehead, touching here and there the eyebrows that bushed like awnings over his pale blue eyes. Puffy cheeks and the square lines of his jaw gave him the look of a boxer dog hungry for meat.

"Callin' me a murderer are you, Jamie? You'd better ask a few of the people who were there. I wasn't gone from the weddin' until I went home. I wasn't gone off down the trail with Ena—but Thomas was. I saw 'em leave myself. I heard 'em laughin' and I didn't see 'em come back. What I make of it's plain enough to figure out. But I followed me folks home on me own horse, was with 'em every minute."

Harding stood facing Jamie across two short feet of shaving covered ground. He was powerful. He was angry. Jamie wasn't sure just how angry. He took a step back.

"Sorry, Lewis. I had to ask. Promised Thomas."

Lewis sat down and began to pull the keen-edged drawknife toward him with the same quick rhythm as before. "You won't be so quick to help him when it's your wife he's squirin' off down the lane." Harding didn't look up nor did he pause in his work when he spoke.

Stung, Jamie felt the urge to knock Harding's curly, red-

faced head down among the wood shavings but thought
better of it. "A pail of slops for your supper, Lewis," he
said. "You deserve no better. I'll be goin' now. I've a wife to
get back to."

Jamie turned and started down the road. His head ached
from yesterday's celebrating and today's mourning, but as
he walked he thought about what Lewis had said. Ena had
her eye out for every man she saw . . . Jamie considered
that for a moment, then brushed it off. Ena had made the
most of her good looks—so did lots of others, it was no
crime. But it was Lewis's words about Thomas that bothered him most. When it's your wife he's squirin' down the
lane . . . Won't be so quick to help him . . . So Harding
saw it, too. How many others did? he wondered. There was
something between Thomas and Sarah. They weren't lovers
—nay, Jamie knew for sure Sarah had been a virgin that
first time a few months back—God knew he'd sampled
enough lasses who weren't to know the difference. Jamie
smiled for a moment, then lost it. When Thomas and Sarah
were together they were a clan of two. He thought of how
they'd danced together last night. There was something
about the way they weren't talking to each other he didn't
like. Drunk as he'd been, he'd seen it.

"Damn you, Thomas," Jamie said aloud to the blue sky
that was filled with mountains of clouds. He stopped at a
stream near the road and dismounted while his horse
waded into the cool water. Jamie kicked at a stick. "You're
not the gentleman you think you are if 'tis another's bride
you seek . . ." His horse was still lapping at the ripples of
the stream when Jamie jerked the reins and mounted him
once again, then raced him back to the Roberts' place.

Thomas's horse, Shuttle, stood grazing near the barn and
Jamie heard him whinny softly. He left his own horse by the
house and in a few short steps was in, expecting to see
Sarah's face. He found only Sheela at her needlework.

"Sarah's in the barn," Sheela said before he could ask
where she was, and Jamie was halfway to the barn before
Sheela had finished the sentence.

"I told you to stay in the house!" he shouted as he burst

through the open door to find Sarah sitting on the milk stool at Thomas's feet.

Sarah started to answer, but before she could Thomas spoke.

"I asked for her to come, Jamie. I'm sorry. I didn't think you'd mind, me tied up like I am."

Sarah's eyes never left Jamie's, despite her surprise at Thomas's quick fib. She'd come on her own, but it was like Thomas to take the blame.

"Lewis had no part of it, Thomas," Jamie said, glaring at him as he motioned Sarah to move away. "I'm certain of it."

"You believe him? But you don't believe me? Jamie . . ." Thomas pleaded.

Sarah stood up, planted herself between the two of them. "What makes you so all in heaven sure Lewis tells the truth? Why not Thomas? And what about the Shawnees? You said yourself they've been prowlin' about. And even Papa said they don't always scalp when they kill. Why is it Thomas? I'm waitin' for an answer, Jamie—what makes you so sure 'twas Thomas?"

"Get to the house," Jamie thundered. Sarah twitched, coloring at the command, her freckles stars on a red field. Thomas could not help her now. Eyes on her bare feet, she sped toward the door, careful to keep out of Jamie's reach.

"What did he say?" Sheela asked, wide-eyed, the minute Sarah came through the door.

"That Lewis Harding didn't kill Ena," Sarah answered, her breathing rushed and uneven.

"Nay, I mean to *you,*" her sister prodded. "He looked ready to kill when he ran out of here."

"He's a jealous one this husband of mine, more than I knew. I'm to be his property now, it seems. I'd best like it."

Sheela could find no words for her sister. "I'm sorry," she offered.

"Be not sorry for me, but for Thomas," Sarah said. " 'Tis him that's in danger. 'Tis him Papa'll see hang before the week is out if he has his way. And Thomas with no more guilt in him than a young lamb."

"We must help him get away then," Sheela urged.

Sarah paused a moment, leaning back against the door. " 'Twould do no good. Thomas would never run. You know that."

"Nay, he wouldn't think it right. But that's not the reason, is it? You fear Jamie. 'Tis the reason you say no to helpin' Thomas."

Never, in leaving Ulster or in watching people die and be buried at sea on the *Endeavor,* nor in her first days in the wilderness that was now her father's farm, had Sarah felt as she did now. Powerless. Alone. Filled with a sick dread.

"I fear for Thomas," Sarah said, ignoring her sister's comment. "Papa's not one to say he's wrong, even when he knows it. Remember Colin O'Flynn?" Sheela drew a blank. Shook her head.

"You were too little, maybe," Sarah explained. "But one of Papa's best wee pigs came up missin', and Papa said the Irish boy had stolen it. Papa hadn't seen him do it, just had a feeling—knew it had to be some low Irish and not an Ulster Scot like himself."

The sisters exchanged a knowing glance at this last. No matter that Scots like their grandfathers had taken away the Irish land with the help of good King James I—Irishmen would always be "low Irish" to the transplanted Scots who fumed if anyone called them "Scotch-Irish." Both girls had had their share of warning about not mixing with Irish scum —"Catholic bastards," as their father was fond of calling them.

"Anyway, Papa found the pig one day, half buried in the muck below the stone wall of the barn where it had gotten stuck, but he spent no time in telling of Colin's innocence. Nay, he just buried the pig a little deeper. I saw it all from where I played on the other side of the stone fence—you know where I mean."

"Aye, Sarah, I do." Sheela put down her work. "So what are we goin' to do for Thomas?"

Sarah took a deep breath. Closed her eyes. "Pray?" she said. "I don't know."

" 'Tis for certain Jamie'll be of no help."

"Jamie's just upset. Confused. I can change his mind," Sarah said, hoping to cover the darker feelings she'd allowed to show through when she first came in. "I don't know if he can admit a mistake, though," she added, unable to hold back all of her fears the way she knew a good wife should.

"Can you?" Sheela asked, raising her eyebrows as she framed the question.

Silence hung between them in the still air of the small house. "I don't know," Sarah said finally, truthful as she could be. "I don't know," she repeated, dropping her head back and fixing her eyes on the ceiling.

"Well, you should, but you can't, it seems to me," Sheela said, Sarah's feelings distilled to a thimbleful. "So you'll have to make the best of it," she said, giving her sister a hug. "I'll help if I can."

" 'Tis Thomas you must help. For the first time in my life I'm forbidden to help him—even Papa's never done that before. Right now, I wish I could take back a day . . . be Sarah Roberts again."

"Mama says all brides feel like that at times," Sheela reminded her. "You'll get over it."

"I wonder when?" was all her sister could say before she left Sheela to her stitching and went out the door to head for the big black rock at the creek, her place to think, just as it had been when she *was* Sarah Roberts.

7

Ena Shaw's casket lay in the front room of Gavin Lowe's house, resting on two sawbucks draped with white linen cloth. Sweet clover, daisies and pink rosebuds were strewn across the top of the rough wooden box that held the body of Jamie's cousin. As he stood with his head bowed, his prayer for Ena was a short one. His mind was on the night before.

"I do believe in you, Thomas," he'd half whispered to Thomas after Sarah left. The lie had slipped from his lips easier than he'd expected. "But no one else does. Lewis has a mind to hang you, and the other neighbors think maybe that's too good for you. Thomas, you're goin' to have to get out of here or they'll kill you without so much as a ride to gaol."

Jamie had seen the way fear gripped Thomas. In all of his nineteen years, Thomas probably had never so much as taken a butterfly of yarn from his master's shop, much less taken anyone's life. He'd never faced death—at least not his own. He'd been afraid to die, and Jamie was certain that he was also afraid to run. But Jamie had put the idea to him last night there in the broken twilight of the barn. And he'd put the means at hand, a small knife he'd buried in the straw. The rest was up to Thomas.

Jamie opened his eyes and edged away from the circle of mourners who ringed the casket, then headed for the far end of the room where his mother had set a table with cold pork and pigeon, corn bread and doughnuts. Her big pitcher was filled with metheglin, a drink fermented from honey and water, rather than the whiskey Jamie had hoped to find.

"I'll be outside a bit," he told Sarah, who was busy behind the table. She and Mother Lowe kept the table supplied for the hungry mourners, hearing and participating in a half-dozen conversations as they worked.

"Get your hay in?"

"Looks like a storm comin'."

"Nice weddin' there, Sarah."

Comments all around the table, but few of them about Ena, or her death. Murder was the Devil's work. Unspeakable.

"He's comin' as soon as he's done with his hay," the ample Marva Braid said, stuffing another bit of doughnut into her mouth, when Mother Lowe asked after George. "Insisted on gettin' it in before the rain," she said. Then in a low voice, "And me heart is with you in your loss."

Sarah heard Mother Lowe thank her, and some others who added their condolences once the ice had been broken. She, in turn, apologized that there'd been no wake for Ena, explaining that no one had wanted to take Ena's corpse from house to house at night while there was still a murderer on the loose.

"This hot weather's been leadin' up to a storm, I've felt it in me knees these last days," old man Chalmers said, filling his cup with metheglin and smacking his lips as he gulped. "And are you likin' this married life, Sarah lass?" he asked, giving her a little wink.

"Aye," she said, not looking at him, but keeping her hands busy with the food. " 'Tis fine."

"You're lucky then," he said. "For most folks it takes a mite of gettin' used to. I remember when . . ."

Sarah let the old man ramble on, smiling occasionally so he'd think she was listening. From the corner of her eye she noticed Lewis Harding leaning against the wall at the far end of the room, arms folded across his chest. His eyes narrowed, he wore a surly look on his face, and Sarah quickly looked back to the ale she was pouring.

". . . as I told Andrew yesterday, if 'twas Shawnees, they'll like as not send us another message," old man Chalmers was saying. "They like credit for their deeds—like the rest of us I thinks. And they like games—like the time they took our shoes, your father's and mine. They had a laugh on that one, I'll wager you." Old man Chalmers laughed at the recollection. "Still, when Indians kill they seem to have a reason for it," he added. "Like us. So killin' Ena makes little sense . . . unless they're comin' back for more—"

Old man Chalmers stopped short, noticing at last the silence around him. The women standing about the table couldn't help but hear and be drawn into the old man's theorizing. He'd had many dealings with the Shawnees during his forty-plus years in the colonies. His was a voice of experience. His questions became their questions. Their fear. Until Andrew Roberts spoke.

"Talk no more of Shawnees, old man," Andrew barked. "We've got our killer." The red of his face and wrath in his voice fired the room, and every eye was on him. But no one disputed what he said. "Let's get started, preacher," he said, quieter, tugging his shirt looser about his sweaty neck.

Thunder rumbled in the far-off hills as the Reverend Darroch donned his black robe to begin the prayers for Ena. The air was thick as water under the gray skies of a gathering storm, and the mourners stepped back to give him room and air, as he took his place at the head of the casket.

"Great God, Father Almighty, we ask your blessings on this child, Ena Shaw . . ."

Jamie stood, hands folded in front of him, repeating the litany, and Sarah stood beside him, doing the same. Jamie slipped his arm around her waist, trying to draw her close as the Reverend Darroch prayed on, but she did not let herself be held. She looked at her husband from the corner of her eye, not daring to turn her head away from the minister. She heard him try to sniffle away some tears and was not surprised. Jamie was a sentimental sort, his sadnesses every bit as deep as his joys were great. Her father always said there was Irish blood in the Lowes that made their tempers hot and their songs sweet. She had thought that charming once. Her father liked Jamie, Irish or not. . . . There was no way to figure out her father sometimes.

As Darroch began the eulogy, Sarah let her eyes stray

about the room, taking note of others whose eyes showed
the trace of a tear. Some sobbed openly. Mother Lowe
wept softly as the reverend spoke of Ena's beauty and determination. Sarah's own mother did not weep, but her eyes
were sunken and she was paler than Sarah could ever remember having seen her. Her father stood staring. Not at
the casket, not at the minister, but at the plain wood planking of the wall before him. His eyes were lowered slightly,
and he held his hands folded in front of him, with one
rubbing nervously back and forth upon the other. Lewis
Harding, too, was dry eyed, his face unreadable. Jamie,
though, seemed to ache, more than Sarah had expected he
would. Maybe his bad temper was caused by the shock of
Ena's murder and not by jealousy of Thomas. The thought
gave her some hope, and she gently squeezed Jamie's hand.
Jamie returned it, eyes straight ahead as hers were.

The benediction came after nearly two hours of standing
in the muggy room. Jamie, his father and two others lifted
the casket and carried it on their shoulders out to the small
hillside that would be the family burial ground. Ena was its
first occupant. Placing the casket on wide leather straps at
the head of the grave for a moment while the mourners
found their places, it was lifted again, then lowered into the
hole Jamie had dug.

As the Reverend Darroch spoke the words of interment,
Sarah stood with head bowed but eyes peeking around the
ring of friends and family left with their own thoughts, their
own prayers.

At the sound of the reverend's final amen, lightning
sliced the sky close enough to send a tingle to the skin of
the mourners. They raced for the shelter of Lowe's house
as rain pelted them in heavy sheets. Except for Jamie, who
stayed in the rain to cover the casket. And Lewis Harding,
who looked on.

In Andrew Roberts's barn, Thomas Gairden sat alone, unable to move, hobbled right and left, doubly secured against
escape now that everyone was gone to Ena's funeral. Andrew had done the tying himself, cursing and grumbling as

he worked. Thomas hadn't spoken at all. His efforts to clear himself with Andrew seemed more futile with each passing hour.

Storm clouds had already begun to gather when Andrew and the rest of the family left, yet the sun had forced its hot yellow rays through the blue between the clouds and lent a shadowy cast to the midafternoon heat.

" 'Tis Ena we bury today, Thomas," Andrew had said, coming out to check the ropes one last time. "Tomorrow we'll deal with you." Thomas wasn't sure whether it was triumph or desperation he'd heard in Andrew's voice. Andrew had doused his head with a pail of water, but given him none to drink. The cool water mixed with the salty perspiration of his face and ran across Thomas's lips.

You've all the answers don't you, Andrew, he'd felt like saying. I bet you'd like it if I told you that your son-in-law brought me a knife so I could get away from here while you're gone. He'd felt like asking Andrew the questions he'd been asking God—what he'd done to deserve such blame, and what he could do to save himself. But he had not spoken to Andrew. And he had not licked the dripping water from his lip but wiped it on his bare shoulder, his eyes never leaving Andrew's.

Shifting what little he could against the matted straw, Thomas felt the blade of the small knife beneath his right buttock. Damn but it was close yet miles away. Andrew had seen to it that his hands weren't good for much, one tied to the wall and the other to the stall, legs the same, splayed in all directions like compass points. And even if he could have reached it, he'd never give Jamie the satisfaction of having Thomas in his debt. What would Sarah think of him if he ran? The only one who believed in him, she'd think him guilty for certain.

A horsefly walked leisurely across the width of Thomas's sweaty chest, almost to the edge of the straw, then took a horse-sized bite out of Thomas's hide before flying off again. Jumping at the pain, Thomas felt the knife under him again, a temptation, he had to admit. He wished he had something to use on the flies that were becoming more and

more sticky with each roll of thunder in the western sky. He
itched everywhere and his head ached with heat and hunger
and the dark imaginings of two days imprisoned in the barn.
He didn't know what trials were like in Philadelphia, but
he'd heard about the gaols, where things worse than hunger
and heat got the prisoners. If no one believed him here in
Bartram, surely no one would believe him in Philadelphia.
If he ever got there.

The sound of hooves thumped rhythmically on the grassy
ground outside the barn, startling Thomas. Hearing the
rider dismount and speak something to his horse, Thomas
could not quite place the sounds or imagine who would be
coming back so early. When he saw George Braid's face
come peering around the door frame, he wondered immediately what was wrong.

"Aye, I'm in here, George. Come on in. Is something
wrong at Lowe's?"

"Nay, not so's a man could see," Braid said, looking
about. "So here's your new lodgin's, Gairden . . ."
Dressed for the funeral in his Sunday black breeches, Braid
loosened the tie at his neck as he walked toward Thomas,
the sleeves of his ivory shirt darkened with perspiration.
"Can't say I envy you."

"Few would. Still I could stand it if I thought they'd find
the real killer, but as the hours go by I'm losin' hope."

Braid ambled closer, finally crouching on his haunches at
Thomas's feet and rocking slightly. From a sheath looped
over his belt he drew a knife and deftly sliced the taut ropes
that held Thomas's feet.

"They have," Braid said as he reached to free one of
Thomas's hands.

"George . . . I thank you . . . but who? I—" Thomas,
excited, shook out the numbness in his free arm and got to
his haunches, supporting himself with his free hand, while
Braid's knife balked at the last rope.

" 'Tis you, sure," Braid said, his cocky smile taking
Thomas back to the day of the wedding. "And no thanks
needed, Thomas. You're goin' to have a little accident's all.

Tryin' to get away I see you and shoot you down. Ena's killer done in. No trial. Saves everyone a lot of bother."

"But I'm *not* Ena's killer. You have to believe that! I . . ." Thomas felt saliva drain down his throat though he hadn't swallowed. Felt his hands cold in the afternoon heat.

"Aye, lad. I believe you. But you're goin' to take the blame for it all the same. You could've married Ena and saved yourself all this you know." Braid leaned nearer Thomas, sawing away at the rope of his left hand. "But you wouldn't. Wouldn't save Ena the disgrace of havin' a child out of holy wedlock—"

"But she wasn't—I didn't—I—"

"But she was—carryin' me child, that is. Nobody knew. Nobody knew Ena had a thirst for a man's body from the day she got here. 'Cept me, that is. Saw it in her in the first time she looked me way. And I satisfied it, too. Figured she'd marry up with one of the other young lads moonin' about. But I didn't figure on you."

Braid stopped his cutting with a quarter inch of rope still holding Thomas to the wall and lay the knife against Thomas's throat. "I didn't figure was a man in the world who'd say no to a pair of bubbies like hers—but you . . . you ruined it all. And then Ena said she'd rather tell the world about me than live one minute with Lewis Hardin' or any of these other cod's heads. She was forcin' me, lad."

Every cell of Thomas's skin cringed at Braid's touch. His heart raced and his temples throbbed as he tried to see his way out of this new prison. He felt the quiver begin in his left eye.

"Well, lad, maybe what you didn't get in this world you can get in the next," Braid said, laughing and gesturing crudely.

Revulsion shook Thomas. "You're the one had the thirst, George. Not Ena. Ena was lookin' for a husband so she wouldn't be alone in the world, she wasn't just lookin' for a man."

The back of Braid's hand stung Thomas's face and the image of Braid whipping the horse snapped through Thomas's mind. "Defendin' the lady fair are you, Gairden?

Defendin' but not humpin'. What are you anyway, one of them that likes the lads a little better?"

Thomas's free hand curled to a tight fist and swung for Braid's chin, but Braid had the advantage and jerked clear, catching Thomas by the wrist. Both men's arms quivered as they forced against each other. Thomas's was first to weaken and Braid took his victory with a sick smile, then drew his knife down across Thomas's face before bringing its point to rest firmly at his crotch.

"You wouldn't miss your balls if you didn't have 'em now would you, fair Thomas?" Braid's eyes flared. "You've got no balls, lad. Never did or you'd have left Andrew to do his own work long ago. You've got no spunk, lad," he said, spitting each word with disgust, pressing the knife just enough to make Thomas shrink gradually farther and farther back into the hay bedding.

"You're married, George," Thomas said, trying to make Braid rational again. "Got a family. Carve me up like a pig and they'll know I didn't do it myself. Think, man."

Braid paused a moment, thinking, then rammed the knife harder, and only the heavy cloth of Thomas's wool breeches kept it from drawing blood. "I'll do as I please here, lad, and you'll do as I please, too," Braid growled. "Now get up."

Giving himself a push upward, Thomas's free hand found Jamie's knife in the straw and grabbed it, then made a swipe for his remaining rope and cut himself free. Lunging for Braid's knees, he knocked him off balance and out of the way, then hurdled over the top of the stall for protection.

Braid, leathery and tough as week-old venison, sprang back, sweat pouring from his forehead. Each breath heaved from his chest and whistled through his nostrils. With a single leap he was into the stall, scant inches away from Thomas.

Behind Thomas, somewhere outside the barn, Shuttle gave an anxious whinny as the sky darkened and thunder boomed. Afraid to unlock his eyes from Braid's, Thomas inched backward, Jamie's knife clenched in his right hand, blade down, while Braid's arm extended straight in front of him like a lance. One stumble and Braid would have him, Thomas thought just as his back touched the wall. Braid's eyes widened and he snarled as he charged.

Thomas arched to the right. "Ahh," he gasped. Braid's knife struck him just above his left hip, stopping Thomas in a moment's shock as though he were nailed to the wall.

But Braid did not stop. Never taking his hand from the knife he began at once to pull it out, twisting and ramming it back in once while he watched the terror in Thomas's eyes and breathed heavy, fetid breaths into Thomas's face. Braid grinned as he fed on the sight of Thomas's pain.

Desperately Thomas lashed upward with Jamie's knife. The angle awkward, he swung his arm in a wide, wild arc as Braid threw up one arm in defense, still trying to pull out his knife with the other.

Thomas's knife sliced across Braid's neck and the underside of his forearm. Blood torrented from the wounds and Braid stepped back, eyes bulging like a dead cow.

"Oh, God!" Thomas cried, raising Jamie's knife, sure that Braid would charge him again.

Braid's wild eyes opened still wider, and he swung for Thomas again with his good arm, blood shooting from him now like water from a pump.

"Stop, George! Stop I say!" Thomas screamed, raising his blade once again. "You'll bleed to death!" he screamed, forgetting his own wound.

"Not 'til I—"

Braid stopped midstep. Gasped. Fell back.

This time his eyes closed, and his mouth gaped open in an unfinished threat.

Braid. Got to stop the bleedin', Thomas thought, and headed to get Iseabal's sheet to use as a bandage. One step, two. The white sheet outside the stall seemed so far away. By the third step, Thomas felt his legs go limp beneath him and folded to the floor, his pulse pounding in his ears. Down on his knees in the pine needle bedding of the stall, he felt Braid's knife invading him. With a shudder and a roll of nausea, Thomas pulled it from his side. Pinching the wound together with his hand, he tried to stop the pain, but in less than the space of two breaths weakness whitewashed him completely and the hand fell useless at his side.

A crack of lightning so close it made his hair stand on end brought Thomas back to a groggy consciousness. Rain pelted the barn and blew in through the open door that banged on its leather hinges. Thomas shivered. Even his teeth chattered. He heard the frightened horses outside. Listening, he lifted his head. The simple movement made him dizzy, nauseous. He sank back into the pine straw but did not close his eyes again. Where was Braid, he wondered? He reached for his knife.

Now a *pop, pop, pop, pop* sound announced the beginning of a hailstorm. A roaring wind bashed hailstones the size of June potatoes against the barn wall and in no time the thatched roof was riddled with holes. The sultriness of the afternoon was gone in a matter of minutes, replaced by a brace of icy wind. Shivers racked the shirtless Thomas, who heard the hail begin to slow down, only to be replaced with a driving rain that poured in through the roof.

Thomas raised up on his elbows, roused by the sound of Shuttle's frantic neighing outside, and this time his eyes focused well enough to see the blood that was drying on him. The struggle with Braid flashed through his mind and he bolted upright. Felt the stabbing pain in his side. Saw Braid dead. Looked away and started for the house, rain soaking him before he'd cleared the doorway. But he had to get Shuttle, and he had to get away. Now he *was* a killer.

The house looked far off and seemed to waver slightly from side to side as he walked half staggering, half stumbling toward it. The thunderstorm had given way to a steady downpour, the kind that in early June can last all day and all night, and the spongy grass of the yard was cold beneath his feet.

Once inside he made his way up the narrow stairs to his bed. The urge to fall into it and wait to die came strongly as sweat beaded up on his brow and chills racked his body. He stuffed his belongings randomly into a bag—at the bottom was the shuttle his father had carved for him when he went to work for Kinloch, and on top of it was a stack of weavings he could use for trading. He pulled the blue coverlid from his bed and flung it around his shoulders, then allowed himself one last glance beyond the curtain that divided the upper chamber into a space for him and one for Sheela and Sarah. The room was bare of every touch of the one he loved, just as he must learn to be.

Thomas ducked his head to enter the top step and saw the trail of scarlet he was leaving behind. A fitting farewell. He clasped his bag under one arm and used his right hand to apply pressure to his wound, then sat down to navigate the tiny, angled stairway toddler fashion, his long legs three steps ahead of his buttocks.

The house, oddly dark and silent, seemed to swim about him as he took his last look from the bottom of the stairs. The warp beam of his loom, wedged tightly against the stairway, made a pull-bar by which he raised himself, and he paused to rest his hand on the castle as he caught his breath. His reeds. His long raith for spreading the warp. He couldn't take them now. The half-finished Queen's Delight coverlid. Someone else would have to weave it. He reached to the harness castle to remove the heavy paper pattern he had lashed to it, then stopped. He could remember the 4/1/ 1/8/8/1/4/1 pattern of the threading and figure out the treadling again, just as he'd done in writing this one from memory. Leave this one, he thought. Maybe Sarah . . .

In the hewn posts and beams of the loom he'd made four years ago when he'd arrived in the colony, Thomas felt the framework of his own life. Salty tears fell on the indigo blue weft and natural linen warp of the coverlid rolled on the cloth beam as Thomas stood clutching it for one last moment, giving it the firmest squeeze he could manage before turning his back on it and making his way back outside. Struggling to mount Shuttle, Thomas took a last look. This wasn't home. Not really.

For a moment, he thought of his mother, almost saw her there in front of him, then she was gone. He drooped facedown against Shuttle's wet mane and closed his eyes, the reins slack in his hands. Shuttle waited no more than a moment for the tug of the reins that didn't come before he cantered off. He knew where to go.

Thomas woke to a sunless sky, a wet and feverish body and an empty stomach. Flat on his back in a puddle, he was within sight of Jamie and Sarah's house. Must have gotten off—maybe fallen off—here during the night. Now he watched as Shuttle pawed roughly in the grass of Sarah and Jamie's doorstep, trying his best to wake them. Thomas remembered nothing for a moment—until the image of a dead George Braid appeared before his eyes. Raising his head, he scanned the clearing for pursuers. Found none. Knew he must go before Jamie and Sarah were awakened. Started to get up. Stopped.

"So you used the knife after all," Jamie said, appearing in the doorway in nothing but his drawers. "I didn't think you had the stomach for it." Thomas saw Sarah behind Jamie, her eyes widening at the sight of him on the ground while Jamie made no move to help. Could it be they didn't know yet? It was a fair distance from the Roberts' house to this one. Perhaps the word hadn't reached them yet, but it would soon. Thomas had to take the chance.

"I could stand to break my long fast," Thomas said, not up to being drawn into any kind of confrontation, even verbal. Shuttle made one complete circle in the clearing in front of Jamie and Sarah's one-room cabin before Thomas sat up and took a deep breath, closing his eyes while he tried to think.

"Nay, Thomas, you'd best be on your way. I can help you no more. Goin' against me father-in-law after three days of holy wedlock does not seem a wise choice where Andrew's concerned."

"He's wantin' food, Jamie, and we can give him that at least," Sarah protested. "There's johnnycake and maple molasses left from yesterday's breakfast to warm."

Thomas mumbled a thank-you, and swabbed on some mud to cover the bloodstains on his shirt, then got up the best he could, holding his mud-smeared coverlid tightly against his wound.

"A wee bit stiff after a night in the rain, are you there, Thomas?" Jamie laughed at his rival's predicament, and Thomas allowed himself no more than a slight limp as he walked toward the house, trusting the folds of the coverlid to conceal the dried blood around his wound.

"Seems like when we used to have our tea parties with Sheely, doesn't it, Thomas," Sarah said when they sat down at the table. Thomas heard nervousness, false gaiety, in her voice as she went on. "It seems like we're pretendin' some-how—like this isn't quite real."

"Ah, but 'tis real," Jamie was quick to remind his wife and their guest, "and soon we'll have bairns of our own to prove it. Did you know that, Thomas? Your lovely Sarah's to be a mother sooner than the parson should know about." Jamie tossed a lusty laugh and a smug look Thomas's direction and took another swallow of rye coffee.

The johnnycake felt dry in Thomas's throat and he, too, drank of the bitter coffee, then soaked the rest of his cake more thoroughly with maple molasses before finishing it. Sarah with Jamie's children . . . The thought of it made swallowing hard.

"I've a favor to ask of you, Jamie," Thomas said, clearing his throat. "Would you trade me that old musket of yours for me shoe buckles? You've another you say shoots straighter anyway. I'll be needin' a gun I'm afraid."

Guns were to Jamie as horses were to Thomas—more than just a necessity. Jamie hesitated.

" 'Tis naught to me if you'd rather not," Thomas said, seeing the pause. "I'll find another."

"Nay, I'll trade it. You've shot it more than I have any-way, since Andrew was loath to let you use his." Jamie raised an eyebrow reminding Thomas of warm autumn af-ternoons of hunting and summer evenings of fishing, drink-ing from the secret stash of Jamie's father's whiskey and racing about on any nags they could beg, borrow or— But that was all behind them now, and there was a distance between them that was Sarah. The easy laughter that had so often passed between them was gone now.

"I'd best be goin'," Thomas said, rising as he clutched the coverlid over his wound and felt a stab of pain.

"Wait, I'll get the musket for you. Ah, me cleanin' rod's out by the shed—I was usin' it to poke between the stones where mice had been workin'—but I did it no harm. I'll even clean her for you before you go as part of the bargain."

"Have another piece of cake then while you're waitin', Thomas," Sarah said, motioning for him to sit down.

The door thunked on its leather hinges as Jamie went out, and Thomas did not sit down, nor did Sarah.

"I thank you for the fine food," Thomas said, trying to crowd so much into so little time.

Sarah handed him a small bag he recognized as one he'd made. Inside was a little food, and a half-dozen fine linen cloths he'd woven for the dowry. "I can't—"

"Take 'em," she insisted. "You can sell 'em if you need the money and make me more when this is all settled."

Thomas saw a defeated look on her face. "I wish—"

"Ah, Thomas, we're beyond wishes aren't we?" Sarah said, stepping near him. "If we weren't, I'd be wishin' that night we had at the creek together happened before I ever knew Jamie. I'd be wishin' I had less temper and more brains. I'd be wishin' 'twas your bairn I carry inside me, not Jamie's . . . I'll be ever sorry I brought this on you, as I know I did."

"Sarah, what I've done, and not done, has been no one's fault but me own," he said. "You're Jamie's now, and to tell you all that's in me heart would be wrong. I—" He started to tell her of his fight with George Braid, then stopped. It would be better if she didn't know, no matter what she might think of him. At least she'd not feel pressed to keep his secret. Nay, this was something he was in alone. Thomas's jaw quivered and he took a hard swallow just as Sarah took another half step that put her in his arms.

He held her close, wanting to kiss her once again as he had that night at the creek, as he should have many times before that, as he knew she wanted him to kiss her, but it was not right. He held her there, hoping she could hear in the beat of his heart all he felt but could not say.

"I think 'tis time you're leavin'," Jamie said, eyes flashing as he opened the door on the embrace. His voice rose to a thundering crescendo as Thomas and Sarah sprang apart, stumbling to explain.

"We were naught but—" Sarah started.

"That 'tis," Thomas said at the same time, "though 'tis not as it looks to you, Jamie."

"You've always been one to act the innocent, haven't you, Thomas? 'Tis no wonder Andrew was in such a fit. Get out of here and forget about takin' any musket of mine—or wife of mine—with you!" he shouted.

"I might've said the same to you for takin' this lass of mine without so much as tellin' me this April past. I once thought we were friends, Jamie, but I see now we never were. Still I ask you one thing before I leave. If you promise it, you never need see me again." Thomas looked Jamie in the eye, daring him to look away, daring him to speak. "Promise me you'll never lay a hand on Sarah in anger, that you'll be a good husband to her."

Jamie stood between him and the door, the musket in his left hand. "I made me promises to God," he said, each word edged like a newly whetted knife. "Now get out before I shoot you," he shouted, raising the musket. "You know I'm within the law!"

Thomas crossed the room in two hurried steps that tore at his wound, and was out the door. He heard movement behind him, and as he mounted Shuttle he chanced a look back. There in the doorway stood Jamie, feet planted like pillars and hands gripping the musket barrel hard enough to bend it. Just behind him stood Sarah. And she was crying.

❖ Part Two ❖

1754–1755

8

Charles Town, South Carolina
October 1754

"Faster, Michel, faster!" Crickie Rawlins heard her younger sisters shout as they bobbed up and down next to her, clapping their gloved hands and cheering. Their broad-brimmed Gipsy hats overlapped each other as they stood wedged in among the rest of the crowd at York Course, six miles north of Charles Town. Crickie managed to raise her arms enough to loosen the ties of her straw hat and let it fall loose on her back. Her black hair, parted in the middle, rolled softly away from her face, and felt ever so much better uncovered.

The autumn sun warmed her face, but it was too weak to harm her olive skin and anyway, she didn't care. She had other worries; her beauty wasn't a preoccupation with her the way it was with Margaret and Deborah. She smiled in comfort now as she watched Michel Borque's long-legged bay gelding round the last turn, a nose behind a chestnut horse she'd not seen before.

"Michel, faster," Deborah Rawlins pleaded, her fourteen-year-old exuberance a bit too noisy to suit her big sister.

"Deborah! Margaret!" Crickie spoke their names half under her breath, and let a flash of her black eyes say the rest.

The first horses crossed the finish line just as Crickie scolded her sisters, and she missed it.

"Must you be so proper, Miss Elizabeth Crichton Rawlins?" her sister Margaret said through a forced smile. "Do you not even care that Michel has just lost his race?" Margaret's violet-blue eyes never left Michel as she spoke, and she held her chin with a practiced tilt that showed the fine lines of her neck and head.

Crickie looked to the track once again and saw the chestnut horse slowing to a canter, with Michel's horse following. "Monsieur Borque will have other races," Crickie said, "but you and Deborah will be forever known as loud and without manners should you not try to quiet yourselves."

"You know I'm only a year younger than you and responsible for my own behavior. Besides, we really must cheer for Michel, for he has no other champions here yet." Margaret's porcelainlike face was a picture of innocence under the shadow of her hat.

"As long as mother is ill, I am in charge," Crickie reminded her. "I am to be responsible for all of us—and for High Garden—where, if I may remind you, we need to return before it is dark." Crickie adjusted the lace-trimmed tippet that wrapped around her shoulders. "Days are shorter now, you know, and I've work to see to at home."

Margaret shrugged and turned her attention to where the winner was about to receive his prize. "You think of nothing but work, Crickie," her sister said, unbuttoning the front of her rich rose velvet cape as her eyes drifted about to see who might be watching her. "While Michel is here, you might try to let some work of ye plantation take care of itself and help show our guest ye pleasures of Charles Town." Margaret tilted her head with determination and flashed her sister another fixed smile.

"Isn't his horse the sleekest animal you have ever seen?" Deborah asked, unbothered by her sisters' disagreement. Her hands were clasped beneath her chin in juvenile ecstasy, and her round cheeks were pink with excitement. But neither sister answered her. Instead, they continued their conversation, eyes all the while fixed on the tall young man about to receive the silver tankard that was the day's prize.

"Monsieur Borque was sent here from Antigua by Papa to help with ye indigo processing, Margaret. So far he has done little other than look off the veranda and smile, then go off on his own to race or play at cards. I'm certain he will find all ye pleasures of Charles Town very well on his own without our help." Crickie never raised her voice, and never let the smile leave her face. She spoke in a low tone so as not to be heard by friends standing nearby. Inside though, she burned. It was so like Margaret to bring up her failings in public. Margaret enjoyed taunting her. She always had.

"Ye winner of today's final race, Mr. Thomas Gairden," president of the Jockey Club, Joseph Stansbury, announced.

Crickie wasn't sure she'd heard him. "Who?" she asked over Deborah's head to her friend Lisette Forcher. The cheering of the crowd was so loud she couldn't hear what Lisette answered. "What?" she asked again.

Dressed in a new pompadour cloak and beaver hat, Lisette leaned close to say the name in her ear.

"Thomas Gairden," she said, each word distinct. As she spoke, Thomas held the intricately engraved silver tankard high for the crowd to see, and reined his horse about in a half circle, greeting the applause that rose in his honor. "Do you know him?" Lisette asked, her blue eyes sparkling with surprise.

"No . . . I . . . well, I think I may have met him," Crickie said, wondering if it could be the same one. But it couldn't. "There was someone by that name when I crossed from London the last time—I was just a little girl. I didn't really know him—just heard his name. I remembered it because 'Gairden' reminded me of 'Garden'—High Garden."

"Father knows him," Lisette said with the pleased look of a daughter used to a father's indulgence. "Something with his business. I think he's a factor, though not a large one. And he has a weaving manufactory. Odd combination."

"Yea. Odd." Crickie watched as he dismounted, gave his horse an affectionate rub on the mane, and then shook hands with Mr. Stansbury and Michel, who had been the second place finisher.

"Handsome, though, isn't he?" Lisette asked. "Perhaps I'll have Father introduce us."

"I very much prefer our Monsieur Borque," Margaret

was quick to answer. "A man of wealth and well travelled," she said, now draping her cape over her arm to show off her matching silk sacque and velvet stomacher. Her fingers fidgeted with a pearl drop that hung on a gold chain against her creamy white skin.

"So do I," mooned Deborah, in her typically refreshing little girl fashion, "and Monsieur Borque has promised us a great party while he is here."

"He looks a fascinating prospect." Lisette arched her eyebrows meaningfully at Crickie and Margaret as she spoke.

"A widower? I doubt Monsieur Borque has any interest in another marriage," Crickie observed, watching the curious little man as he moved among the other racers and horse owners, shaking hands, slapping backs, laughing and always, always, moving his hands as he spoke.

Lisette's face brightened into a sly smile. "Your father must hold great trust in him, or he wouldn't have sent him here. Perhaps—"

"In ye three and one-half years Papa has been with ye army in Antigua, he's put forth a good many marriage prospects for me, Lisette. As you know, I've told him I intend to make any such selection myself. Monsieur Borque is here because his family has grown indigo in the islands for three decades, and theirs brings a higher price than Carolina indigo. Papa simply wants me to learn a bit from him. Nothing more."

Actually, Crickie suspected her father had offered a general sort of invitation and Borque had unexpectedly accepted, but since Borque had hand delivered her father's message, Papa had not been able to make the whole situation clear. Anyway, there was no point in explaining it all to Lisette or her sisters. Crickie understood her father and he understood her—and few others understood that.

"We should go to him now," she said, excusing herself from Lisette, "and be on our way home. Please do come to High Garden one day soon, Lisette," she said, waving as she started toward the track.

"Come visit us," Lisette called back to her, then started off her own way.

Crickie and her sisters hurried across the grounds, the grass a bright green contrast to the blue October sky. Most of the planters among the spectators had already left, anxious to get back to their harvest. It was an odd time of the year for a race—a week of racing was usually planned for February—but Borque had talked a few of his newfound racing friends into the fall date, and it had drawn a moderate following. Still it lacked the festive atmosphere of the February races, when there would be balls and midnight suppers.

Borque was still talking with some fellow horsemen, his hands gesturing, when his hostesses approached. Gairden was gone, Crickie noticed.

"Ah, Creekee," Borque exclaimed, pronouncing her name the French way. He greeted her with his usual half bow and sweep of the hand, and then bowed to her sisters, who responded with well-practiced small curtseys and sighs of delight. "My regrets that I could not bring to you the silver cup this day. The horse of Monsieur Gairden was too fast for mine this time, but next time I shall prevail, have no fears." Another little bow.

"I have no fear that you will have many victories during your visit with us, monsieur," Crickie said, "but for now we must begin our trip back up the river to High Garden while there is still some light. It will be late enough before we get back as it is."

"You are all so lovely in your fashionable hats," Borque said, ignoring Crickie's request. "You were, without question, the loveliest ladies at the race. I wish to show you off— not to just go home after such a delightful day. We are all to be the guests of Madame and Monsieur Forcher and their daughter, Lisette, for a small gathering this evening. I've sent your man Dill home with a message that we shall be detained in Charles Town until tomorrow."

"But I have work to—"

"Your indigo can wait one more day," Borque said, anticipating her protest. "I am expert on such matters, am I not?" he asked.

Crickie could hear in his voice that Borque, ten years her senior, was used to giving orders, not taking them, especially from a woman.

"It's just that I always see to—"

"It is time you see to the entertainment of our guest," Margaret reminded her, her face sweet as an angel's as she smiled at Borque while she spoke. "Ye indigo will wait," she added.

"Indigo does not wait," Crickie said, "as you would know if you had ever helped with it. Steeping is the most critical phase. I cannot—"

"I've already given Dill his instructions, Crickie," Borque said, smiling and completely in control. "In Antigua we always let our overseer . . ." Borque groped for the right word, ". . . oversee . . . such things. Yours should do the same or be replaced."

"But I like to see for myself," Crickie insisted.

"Crickie," Deborah pleaded. "Let us stay. Please." Deborah, with her round cheeks and innocent face, was hard for Crickie to refuse.

"All right," Crickie said at last, annoyed with herself for giving in. "Evan Forcher is our factor and it would not be polite to ignore his offer of hospitality. And it's not that I don't like parties, you understand," she said to Borque, "but that my first responsibility is at High Garden."

"Your father had in you a superb planter," Borque said, smoothing his moustache.

"Had?" Crickie asked. Why did he look at her so . . . so . . . ? She couldn't quite put a finger on just how he looked at her as she spoke.

"Ahem . . . 'has' should it be? My English is not what it should sometimes be."

"I did not mean to correct you, monsieur," Crickie was quick to assure him. "I only worried for a moment that perhaps something had happened to our father that you spoke in the past tense."

"Ah. Non, your father *is* well and *has* a fine daughter to see to his affairs," he told Crickie. *"Mais non,* fine daughters," he said, correcting himself to please Margaret and Deborah.

"Well then," Crickie said, taking charge, "let us proceed to ye Forchers, and then make early for High Garden on ye morrow."

"Have no fears, Crickie," Borque said, emphasizing the long *e* sounds of her name as he always did, "we shall be off in good time, and you shall have the greatest indigo harvest of your years at the High Garden. Have no fears," he repeated with a determined nod of the head and wave of the arms.

"Very well," Crickie agreed. Falling in step behind Borque and her sisters who were already laughing and planning the night's fun, she studied this man her father had sent. Small, fine boned, with hair and eyes as dark as her own, he was a good-looking man. The moustaches she did not care for. They made him look older than he was. More cynical. Though her sisters did not seem to mind. Was he so complacent about his own crop at home? Crickie wondered. Was she over anxious? Perhaps a few extra hours wouldn't make any difference, she told herself, falling back a bit from the other three as she looked about at the red earth of the now empty track, rough where the powerful hooves of the horses had thrown dirt this way and that.

She pictured the racers once again. What was in a person's face that made him look evil or good, happy or sad, proud or arrogant? How, and why, did she sense goodness in the face of this Thomas Gairden whose name had reminded her of "garden" and therefore, "home" when she'd been a little girl at sea? He'd had no fine clothes then, and he was travelling with people of the middling sort, still he and the girl who was always with him on board the ship had made an intriguing pair. Watching them had been Crickie's prime entertainment during the eight weeks at sea. She remembered most of all the way he'd looked at that girl, the love that was in his eyes and his every gesture. Someday I, too, will be loved like that, she had told herself. But she'd never expected to see those same eyes again, or to hear that

name. The coincidence of it fascinated her and she began
to hope Lisette Forcher would introduce them so that she
could learn if the real Thomas Gairden was anything like
the long-imagined Thomas Gairden. Perhaps staying the
night at Forchers was a good idea after all, Crickie decided,
and hurried to catch up with her sisters.

After an evening buffet at the Forchers and a glass of Madeira with them and their friends, Crickie had gone up with
Lisette, slept in one of her fine, silk-trimmed nightgowns,
and forgotten some of her anxiety at being away from the
plantation too long. When she had asked Evan Forcher if
there was any word from her father, he'd had none but told
her a schooner was expected within the week. He reminded
her that her father's new post as attaché to the governor no
doubt kept him very busy and prevented his writing as often
as he might like.

Crickie woke at five in the morning, just as she did every
day, tiptoed out of bed and went to the window. A north-
east wind blew a damp, cool breeze in from the sea, and she
closed the window that was letting in the draft. The air was
different in Charles Town, she thought. Though High Garden was only ten miles away, it didn't catch the ocean
breezes that the city did. Life was so different here, too.
The relentless entertaining and gossiping of the women.
The endless talk of Indians and war with the French by the
men—she'd wondered last night if Borque would be of-
fended at the anti-French sentiments expressed, but he
hadn't seemed to be. He was, after all, an English subject
now, just as she was, despite his French background and
language. Of course, he had turned the conversation to
horses at every opportunity anyway. He cared little for politics.

From Lisette's third floor window, Crickie could see all
the way to the harbor. As dawn began to break, masts and
sails stood golden against the flat black of the water. Soon
one of those same ships would carry yet another cargo of
High Garden indigo and rice to England, and she would
have more income to record in her books. Evan Forcher,

acting as her father's factor, would see to the sale, and handle the credit for her. After three years of supervising harvests, Crickie was now comfortable with the process. In fact, she was eager for it, and eager for the rest of the house to wake up so that she could be on her way.

Crickie left the window and tiptoed past the bed where Lisette would probably sleep for hours yet. There was one errand she hoped to accomplish before she left the city this morning, and it would best be done without the knowledge of her sisters or Borque. Crickie slipped once again into the petticoat and blue camlet sacque she'd worn yesterday which had been spot cleaned and brushed by the Forcher servants during the night. She arranged the lace-edged tippet around her shoulders and put on the Gipsy hat, tying its silk ribbon under her chin, then was out the door and down the stairs.

As she walked past, Crickie found the kitchen, a small brick building a few yards behind the house, already busy with the day's baking. Selene Forcher was explaining the day's menus to the cook. Mrs. Forcher, however, took time out to answer Crickie's questions, and a few minutes later Crickie was in the Forchers' carriage, on her way to a place known as the Sign of the Shuttle.

9

Thomas Gairden sat slightly bent over the cloth beam of the huge loom that filled one whole end of his shop, the loom's castle braced and bolted to the room's exposed joists. His slender fingers touched lightly at the right selvage, checking by feel to see if the yarn was drawn in just right, before he threw the next shot of the shuttle from the left. The morning's light was just beginning to wash in through the high arched windows on his left, so Thomas still worked beneath the two betty lamps he'd hung as close over the loom as he'd dared. It would not do for the lamps to be knocked about each time he pulled the laith to beat the cloth.

This morning he was anxious to finish one more of the Lover's Dream double woven coverlids that were in such demand just now. By working before dawn, his beat and his concentration were uninterrupted by customers at the Sign of the Shuttle.

He had started his business with just the one loom he had built with Henry Jones's help. It was a simple loom with only four wings, much like every barn loom in the colonies. Weaving, at first, the same Queen's Delight pattern he'd left standing on his loom in Andrew Roberts's house a few months earlier, Thomas then moved on to one called "King's Flower," and it was that one that established his reputation. He had told his customers it was named for South Carolina, because King George was so fond of calling the state "the flower of the colonies." Charles Town was more like London than any other place in the colonies, founded by the Lords Proprietors and then settled by scores of British aristocrats who maintained a lavish lifestyle and their British loyalty with equal vigor. It was only later that

Thomas made a few subtle changes in the pattern and re-named it "Carolina Beauty," a title more in keeping with his own political leanings. The new pattern, and the others that followed, were even more popular than the first.

Soon, though, Thomas could see that a larger, more complex loom was needed, for slaves were taught to do the kind of weaving that could be done on a four-wing loom. He had taken time to build a loom of sixteen wings on which he could weave the Lover's Dream pattern he'd adapted from Kinloch's manufactory back in Ulster. A double-woven coverlid, it offered the owner two layers of reversible, fancy blanketing—one light, one indigo blue—interwoven in pattern to form a single piece. Such a coverlid required the skill of a professional to make both halves even so that the pattern would match. Its production insured Thomas a niche in the textile market of the city. Payment, though, most often came in the form of rice or forest products or deerskins, leading him to become a natural part of the import/export business, and that work as a factor now earned him much more profit than his weaving did. But still it was weaving he loved.

Between the rapid *boom, boom* of the laith each time the shuttle was passed through the shed, Thomas watched the pattern develop. Although his feet knew the dance of the treadles well, his eye roved the web at each shot, wary for the mistake that could occasionally creep in. Weaving coverlids was, with each development and redevelopment of the pattern, a delight to the eye, the indigo of the woof upon the creamy white of the warp forming little pictures the imagination could make into what it chose. He never tired of imagining what they might be, or of experimenting to alter and change them into other patterns for future coverlids.

The beauty of it, he thought. 'Twas all that kept me going sometimes with Kinloch. Imagining away the patterns I was weaving, that's all that did it. A weaver's mind has much time to imagine, to dream and plan, once his feet know the dance.

Mackay's still learnin', Thomas noted as he looked to the

loom where his indentured man would soon be sitting. Its torn paper pattern nailed to the laith, up aways from eye level, was one of the three Dugald Mackay had mastered so far. He'll get there, though, Thomas thought. Has the makings of a good solid weaver. Not much at making up a new pattern, maybe, but good enough at following someone else's. And strong shoulders, ones that can work fifteen hours at a stretch and not feel it. He'd be competition one day no doubt, Thomas decided. But not for a while. For now he worked without pay because Thomas had bought his passage on the *New Built* from Ireland. An Ulsterman like himself, Mackay had come to Charles Town the son of a crofter, no more. Finding no planter to buy his indenture that day, slaves being a better investment, he had been purchased by Thomas instead and found himself a weaver's apprentice by nightfall. He said Providence had smiled on him that day, and Thomas agreed.

As the pale light of dawn gave way to the brightness of morning, Thomas snuffed out the lamps and paused for a biscuit and drink of ale before climbing back atop the high seat that was bolted the full width of his loom. He'd woven his one yard before dawn, and with luck he could weave one more before the interruptions of the day became too frequent.

"G'day, Thomas," Dugald Mackay called as he ducked slightly to enter the shop. Mackay was tall, and his walk made him look like a collection of unrelated arms, legs and head—all parts seeming to move in opposing directions. At the loom, though, he was surprisingly well coordinated and conscientious. He'd begun by weaving simple fabrics such as shirtings, diapers, sheeting and blankets, but after a year was now weaving coverlids alongside his master, a source of great pride to him.

"Dugald!" Thomas greeted him, barely looking up from his work. "A wee bit late last night, were you?" Three years older than his apprentice, but still master, Thomas took delight in Dugald's off-hours exploits.

"A wee bit. Mary couldn't stand to quit me charms." Dugald's head with its greasy brown hair shook with a swagger. "Aye, and you should find one like her for yourself," he chided, as he did most days.

"I doubt there are any more left like Mary," Thomas said, as he did most days. Mary, the eager daughter of their landlady, helped Dugald pass many a cozy hour while he served out his four-year indenture, though he could not marry until he was out of his time. "Nay, lad, you've got the one and only Mary in Charles Town," Thomas added.

"You must've spotted some fine skirts at your race yesterday, Thomas. If you didn't hurry back to your work so soon you might've met one or two."

"I'm waitin' for one to spot me, don't you see? That way I don't need to waste time on ones that have no interest in a poor weaver."

"Ha! Poor weaver. You're a damn sight richer for your tradin' and lendin' than a man has a right to be—just because you don't show it off don't mean you don't have it. You've got the true Scots blood in you, Thomas. I know."

"Covetin' what your master has now are you? You'll have it yourself one day if times are right. I came to Charles Town four years back and found every shop overstocked with London goods, and prices droppin' by the day. Calicoes, oznaburgs, India goods—they were all there, dumped on us by the Crown, like it or not. Not much room for a weaver with the like o' that goin' on. I found I had to try a different way, and it turned out the better for me, was all." Thomas stopped his shuttle and looked at Dugald. "The better for you, too, I might add. If I hadn't made a pound or two at the wharf to buy your indenture you'd be back in Ulster now, and never've met the lovely Mary."

"Aye, master," Dugald said, with the mock-respect that amused Thomas. "But timin' wasn't all of it, from what I see. You've a knack for takin' a risk this son of a crofter'll never have. I'll go to plantin' yet, I think."

"There's money in plantin' if you like it," Thomas said, speaking louder now to be heard over the beating of the laiths of the two looms. "I just never did," he added after a moment. If I had, I'd still be in Bartram, married to Sarah,

Thomas thought, but kept it to himself. There was no one he could talk to about Bartram. Or Sarah.

Dugald's beat stopped for a moment as he unwove the inch he'd just woven, the first of the day that was always a bit uneven until he hit his usual rhythm. It was one of the many tricks Thomas had taught him.

"And it may be just as well. If the bloody French keep pushin', we're apt to be in a war again soon, and land can be lost. At least we'll always know weavin', and no one can take that away from us."

"Aye, 'tis good to have a trade, Dugald, even if you do end up a planter, you can always do some weavin', too, the way me father did. He'd have been a comfortable man if he'd lived."

"And *me* folks are near starvin'," Dugald grumbled. "Rent's higher and higher, crops poorer and poorer. I hope they get here one day, but I doubt they'll try it. I had to sneak out to get away from it myself."

"And glad you did, aren't you?"

"Aye," Dugald said, resuming his beating. "For Mary's sake," he said with a laugh, and the day's work was begun.

"Thomas Gairden?" Crickie asked, looking from Mackay to Gairden and back, even though she knew full well the face of Thomas Gairden now that she saw it again. His dark eyes were quick. Expressive. His manner cordial. Even warm. Crickie smiled.

"I'm Gairden. And may I be of help to you?" He swung his legs over the loom bench and walked toward her.

Sunlight flooded the big east windows behind him, back-lighting him, and Crickie noticed the fiber dust that drifted lazily about him on the sun rays. His hair, every bit as black as her own, was tied neatly at his neck but not powdered, and the curled ends of it caught loosely on the shoulder seam of his shirt as he nodded politely.

"I hope so," Crickie answered. "I am in need of Negro cloth—forty yards of fustian and forty yards of broadcloth. Might you have that on hand?"

"We have the broadcloth, in eighteen ell lengths, imported from London," Thomas said. "The fustian we'd have to make up for you," he added. "Dugald, forty yards of fustian? How soon?"

Crickie's eyebrows shot up in surprise. Should not the master tell the servant when the work would be completed, rather than asking him when it might be completed? Gairden's attitude reminded her of the way her father handled servants. Father, she thought fondly, and shook her head.

"We've promised those hundred blankets for the militia in three weeks," Mackay replied, never ceasing the beat of his loom. " 'Twould have to be at least another week after that."

"Say mid-November then," Thomas told his client. "Will that be satisfactory?"

"Not at all," Crickie said, shaking her head firmly, though she had expected such a delay. Craftsmen were always trying to arrange things to suit their own schedules. "I'll need ye fustian next week. Ye Negroes are soon to be done in ye fields and then I'll set them on their winter's work. Ye sewing comes first."

"So 'tis, so 'tis," Thomas said, thinking. "A moment please," he asked of her, "while I check my warehouse."

Waiting for the weaver Gairden to check his stores, Crickie looked around the small manufactory. Near Gairden's large loom, there was another wide loom on which a blanket was in progress. Deep wooden boxes of unfinished white pine were packed with skeins of wool yarn, sorted by color, and piled in one corner. Shelves along the far wall bowed under the weight of fabrics, blankets and coverlids already woven, and the top shelf was neatly arranged with spare shuttles, reeds and other equipment required by the weavers. A slant-topped writing desk stood on tall legs near the door, account books stacked to one side, rolls of patterns on the other. A copy of *Gentleman's Magazine* lay open there, too, along with two volumes of essays, she noticed. The magazine was one she'd just finished reading herself, but the essays were new to her and she had to remind herself it would look too forward should

she pick up one of them and look at it without Mr.
Gairden's authorization.

"Have a seat there, miss, if you like," Mackay said, at
last, seeing her shift her weight from one foot to the other.
He motioned toward the bench of the loom where the blanket was being woven, and Crickie nodded, hoisting herself
up onto the high seat. Her feet dangled loosely as she sat at
Mackay's back, watching each beat of his laith against the
cloth jar the high-beamed room.

Three blocks away, at the shop of J. Loggins, London
Importer, another even rhythm could be heard. It was the
rhythm of Thomas Gairden's long fingers drumming on the
counter as he waited for Loggins to find a bolt of fustian.
Thomas smiled as he thought of the knowing wink Dugald
had flashed as he'd gone out the back door of the manufactory—the one that led into Henry Jones's carpentry shop,
for Thomas had no warehouse of fabric. Not yet, anyway.
Thomas drummed his fingers again, silently begging Loggins to make haste.

"Two pieces—fifty yards in all," Loggins said as he returned from his second floor storeroom, puffing slightly and
adjusting the powdered wig he always wore.

"Fine, sir, fine," Thomas said, taking the rolls of coarse
fabric from him. "I'll replace 'em for you as soon as I get a
shipment myself," Thomas offered.

The older merchant paused. "I would find ready payment
more acceptable," he said. "Thirty pounds."

"All me eye and Betty Martin, man! That's half-again
what 'tis worth," Thomas said.

The older man smiled placidly. "Thirty pounds," he repeated.

"You're enjoyin' this aren't you, Loggins?" Thomas said,
taking up a quill to sign for the purchase.

"You seem a bit desperate, Gairden," he said. "Prices do
rise when demand is great." Powder from his wig fell on the
deep blue of his own fustian coat, and Loggins brushed it
away fastidiously. "One does what one must," he said, still
beaming.

"Doesn't one, though," Thomas said as he hurried to the

door, the heavy fabric rolled beneath his arm as if it were nothing more than a down pillow. He was halfway outside when he stopped and poked his head in for one parting shot. "I'll remember the favor, Loggins," he said with a chuckle.

"No doubt," Loggins replied, unruffled. "I shall anticipate it." He let only the trace of a smile curve his lips as he watched the weaver rush off.

Thomas sprinted back to the Sign of the Shuttle down the back street, the way he'd left, so as not to be seen by the lady's driver, and stopped a moment in Jones's shop to catch his breath before letting himself back into his manufactory.

Inside the door, he stopped a moment to dust himself off as if he had been combing through bins of wares in search of the fustian.

"I did find two pieces of fustian, Miss—"

"Rawlins, of High Garden Plantation on ye Bark River— near High Grove Church," Crickie said.

"Aye, Miss Rawlins, I've heard Evan Forcher speak of your fine plantation—indigo, isn't it?"

"Indigo and rice," she said, accepting the hand he offered to help her down from the loom bench.

He watched her finger the fustian, checking its weight and quality. "These pieces are imports," he said quickly. "I had none of my own on hand." She looked rather young, perhaps because she was so petite, but she had a determined way about her that made her seem mature, and very attractive. Her dark eyes gleamed with intelligence and seemed to take in every detail of him, the manufactory, and the fabrics. She had a bright, genuine smile, which Thomas couldn't help but smile back to. Now he knew what Evan Forcher had meant when he said High Garden was beautiful in every way.

"These will do," she said, "if the price is acceptable. How much?"

"Fifteen pounds," he said, matter-of-fact.

Dugald cleared his throat.

Crickie raised her eyebrows approvingly. "Fine," she said.

Thomas could tell she had expected to pay more, and normally he would have charged more. But this time was different. He showed her to the desk, where he wrote her receipt. Her head barely reached his shoulder, and she watched him closely as the quill scratched across the paper. The letters came quick and sure. Well formed.

"Did I see you at York yesterday, Miss Rawlins?" Thomas asked without stopping the quill or taking his eyes off the account book.

"I was there." Crickie smiled. Tilted her head a bit in question.

Still writing, Thomas looked to her from the corner of his eye. "First time?" he asked.

"First since I was a little girl," Crickie answered, conscious of the other weaver listening. "My father used to take me, but since he's been away we haven't attended—until yesterday. We have a visitor who is devoted to racing and insisted we go. I believe you raced him? Monsieur Borque."

The quill stopped. "Borque? I see," he said, surprised. "He very nearly beat me. A good horseman," he added as an afterthought.

"You must have a fine horse yourself, Mr. Gairden," she said, "to best Michel." She was not good at coquettish talk. This last sounded like something Margaret would say—on a bad day.

"Aye, Spinneray can scorch the turf sure enough, but he hasn't the heart of me horse Shuttle. Few do," Thomas said, lapsing into his brogue as he remembered the miles he and the big gelding had travelled together. He went back to his writing.

"I see you do some reading," she said, her eyes falling on some journals stacked on a bench. "I found the article on silkworm culture in the last *Gentleman's Magazine* very informative," she ventured.

" 'Tis a subject I know little of," Thomas said, glancing up from the desk, "though to planters such as yourself I'm sure it has possibilities. I haven't the time or the coin to experiment with it. I more enjoyed the articles on His Majesty's differences with the French, and the Navigation Laws —they affect me in a bit of a more direct way, as they do all of us here in the colonies."

"The King will no doubt take care of it all for us, since he commands the British Army," Crickie said with pride. "My father is a lieutenant colonel, serving in Antigua," she added. "My mother is ill and unable to leave High Garden, so we stayed behind."

"Aye, then, and Dugald and I are serving with the Carolina militia, so we have something in common there," he said, finally looking up from his work, and catching Dugald's wink. There was some enmity between militiamen and the regulars, but that did not concern Thomas just now.

"Your receipt, Miss Rawlins," he said, taking a chance, at last, on looking directly into a pair of eyes as dark—yet as bright—as any he'd ever seen. Her gaze, in return, was direct and honest. Her smile, genuine, though she quickly looked away.

"Thank you, Mr. Gairden," she said. "I shall remember your manufactory when I am in further need of fabric."

"Have you no slaves to weave for you at High Garden, then?" he asked. Slaves. They were beginning to outnumber whites, even in the city, though Thomas had none.

Crickie started to speak, but stopped. Then she started again. "We do—but there's been far too much field work and . . . our Negroes are behind . . . ye indigo seemed more important this year," she managed.

"Aye, the market is strong," Thomas said, opening the door and carrying the yardage out for her. " 'Tis one I hope my partner and I can get into."

"I wish you luck with it." She took his hand as he helped her into the chaise and flashed a quick smile of thanks, then tapped for the driver to commence.

Thomas stood watching the black enameled chaise roll down the street for a moment. Then, going back in to face Dugald, whose laughter he could already hear, Thomas tapped the door frame the way Miss Rawlins had the chaise. Every day should begin so, he thought, and went back to work smiling his jaunty half smile.

Crickie arrived back at the Forchers well pleased with her morning's business. She had been extravagant in purchasing what her slaves could well have woven at home, she knew, but with this year's good indigo crop a small extravagance would be of little notice.

She had the silver-haired driver leave the rolled fabric in the chaise, since they would soon be leaving for High Garden, anyway, and entered the house humming a little tune as she headed for the dining room where she could hear voices at the breakfast table.

"Your disposition seems improved this morning, Crickie," Borque said, ambling down the stairs to her back. His highly polished boots clicked lightly on the polished oak treads.

Crickie stopped, like a child caught sneaking candy, though of course she was doing nothing of the sort, but she stopped anyway. Her fingers fumbled at the ties on her hat, as she half turned and waited for him to catch up.

"You have been out on business already this morning?" Borque said, bowing gracefully as he joined her. "I should have been most pleased to accompany you had I known."

"I had only to see about some Negro cloth," she said. "There was no need for assistance." Did she sound duplicitous? Did she sound too happy? Too abrupt? She found herself suddenly uncomfortable as Borque guided her into the dining room.

"Nevertheless, how pleased I will be if I may be of service to you with some of your many tasks while I am here," Borque said, his eyes almost caressing her.

Crickie slid into her chair, glad to be among this familiar group just now.

Margaret spoke before Crickie could answer, or make her greetings. "We will not allow all of your time here to be spent working," she said, her mile-wide smile beaming to light up Borque's face as well. "You must see the colony and meet its fine gentlemen."

"What—no more racing?" Borque rejoined with his typical aplomb.

Margaret loved these flirtatious exchanges. Crickie busied herself spooning fruit onto her plate.

"Racing—of course. All the racing you want." Margaret laughed and placed her hand elegantly at the open throat of her gown, her index finger playing with the little pearl necklace she wore again today.

As if she were the silliest girl in the city instead of the coyest, her sister thought. And Deborah didn't help matters.

"And we must go to parties while you are here as well," she put in, "and *have* parties, too!"

Crickie took a forkful of what was probably the last melon of the season. Have parties? There had been no parties at High Garden since her father had been gone— Mother would not want to start now. Crickie rolled her eyes a bit as she looked to Deborah, silencing her. Margaret, though, kept up her conversation with Borque as Lisette Forcher and her mother listened and looked on.

Crickie could tell by the look on Lisette's face she was enjoying this flirting, especially when she got a chance to squeeze in a word of her own. Only Selene Forcher and Crickie ate the fruits and warm breads set before them and drank their tea while it steamed; the rest talked about the minuet steps Borque had learned in Paris last year, and the towering wigs of the ladies there. Selene was accustomed to her daughter's frivolity and was amused by it. But Crickie's mind was still back at the Sign of the Shuttle. She had been right. It was the same Thomas Gairden she remembered from the *Endeavor*. She would know those eyes anywhere. On board ship, the look in his eyes had been saved for the girl Sarah. And as Crickie ate the soft, tangy melon, she wondered if he still looked at her that way. If there was still a Sarah in his life, somewhere?

The melon was sweet on her tongue, and Crickie savored it as the conversation drifted on about her. She would find out—or Lisette would find out for her. And she hoped the answer to both questions was no.

10

Marching two rows behind the drummer boy, Thomas kept his eyes straight ahead, with only an occasional peripheral glance to check the straightness of his rank. Other marchers gave not even that much of a glance, so that some men were a full step behind the rank, some a step ahead. "Straight ranks are fine, but straight shootin's better!" the militiamen liked to boast.

"Hie, company left!" barked the sergeant, a sturdy-built man of thirty whose step seemed to falter at times, but in whom the lust for battle burned like a just-oiled torch. "Step smart, step smart!"

The men, aged eighteen to forty, were intent on their task, perhaps so intent they could not keep in step, and were attired in every manner of common dress since the colony had no funds for issuance of uniforms. Looked on as little better than servants by the British regulars who came through the city periodically, the militia had all the more reason to think of itself as battle ready rather than parade ready.

As the last drumroll signalled the order to stand and fire, Thomas and the others formed a single line. Each man stood, feet shoulder width apart, his musket on the ground, holding the long barrel at arm's length and filling it with powder from a horn, then stuffing it with a cotton patch. Next a lead ball was packed in by hand, then forced low into the smooth bore barrel with the ramrod. Thus prepared, the musket was raised and its powder pan primed with a powder fine as black pepper, then cocked for firing.

On this bright October day, there was no need for the call to "keep your powder dry," as a light breeze rustled the drying leaves of the chestnut trees surrounding the green, and even the late autumn grass had a tinder crackle to it.

"Raise arms. Take aim. Fire!" called the sergeant. A *schhhhhh boom, boom . . . boom* went up as the muskets fired at varying times, owing to the variance in amounts of powder and ignition of spark. Still, firing as they did in a solid line of men, the militia would transform the not-so-accurate Brown Bess muskets into weapons of considerable deadliness should they be called.

"Form ranks!" called the sergeant before the smoke had cleared completely. Men hustled into position and began the march back to the powder magazine at the far end of the green to stow arms before heading back to the remainder of their day's work. Militia drill each day at noon for one hour was part of the daily rhythm of the city for all able-bodied British subjects now that England was at war with the French and Indians. At any time, this company could be called to aid the British regulars who were beginning to arrive weekly to defend the western frontier from the vicious attacks of the French, and their allies the Cherokee tribes.

"One day soon we'll be goin', I know it," Dugald Mackay told Thomas as they walked back toward the Sign of the Shuttle. "I can't wait to take aim at a few of them popish bastards. Or redskins either."

"Mighty sure they're bastards, are you, Dugald? I suspect they bleed like the rest of us."

"Sure they do, and they can go bleed somewhere else. They can get off that Ohio land, too—I want to go up and get some of it for myself when I'm done with you, and want no papists tellin' me where. The farmland's rich up there, I hear, and here's at such a premium. I'll go north, and you should go, too. Of course then you'd have to leave your horse racin' behind, and I suppose you'd miss that."

"Aye, I'd miss it, though there's always a race to be found somewhere if a man looks. But I'm not lookin' to go north again. I've been there and I'll not go back." He couldn't say he didn't miss it. That would be a lie. Not a day passed that he didn't think of Sarah. Didn't wonder about her life now.

Didn't wonder how things might have been. But he knew there was no going back.

As the men walked, Thomas's mind strayed back to Bartram. He spoke again, quickly, to shield his thoughtfulness. "Once you're out of your time, Dugald, you can go where you please, but my work is here and I'd best stay with it."

"A weaver has work wherever he goes, you're always sayin'," the indentured man reminded him.

"Aye, but not the work of weavin' for the army, as we're doin' now. That work that's keepin' you busy from daylight to dark is the kind of work you can get only in the city. Weavin' coverlids for folks—only in the city can you keep a loom set up for it in a grand style. And shippin' and tradin' —only in the city." Thomas was firm in his opinion, trying to encourage realism in the hopelessly optimistic Mackay.

"But land, Thomas, is where the money is. Why, they're givin' land away in the Ohio—givin' it away!"

"And why is good King George doin' that, Dugald? He's doin' it so that good Scots like you will go up there and keep the Indians back a bit. The land is not free, Dugald. Nay, 'tis a heavy price." Thomas shook his head, remembering the fear of Indians that had swept Bartram from time to time, whenever an incident stirred the tribes' anger. It had been a sick feeling, a helpless feeling.

"Are you sayin' then you wouldn't fight for your land, Thomas?"

"Not at all, lad. I'm sayin' that by stayin' here, with what's mine, I'll have no fightin' to do. I'm sayin' that the Crown is usin' Ulstermen like us to do their fightin' for 'em. The Crown is usin' us to settle the wild lands and then comin' in behind us to get rich from 'em. Many's the man who likes that kind of work, but I'm not among 'em, that's all. I've the land here that my partner Gray runs and that's all the land I'll ever want."

"And if the French cross the bar out here one day and squeeze us in between their guns and the Cherokees to the west, then what?"

"Then we've a regiment of British regulars and a few hundred in our militia to fight with us, not to mention the navy. Their job is the defendin' of these waters and I suspect they'll keep right on pokin' their nose about just as they always have. So let's get back to work and leave the war to the men in red."

As Thomas closed the shop door behind him, he effectively closed the subject of war and the Ohio to Dugald, but could not close it to himself. What was it like west of the seaboard? Talk during the autumn market fair, just finishing, had almost always come around to the Indians and the French. A young colonel named Washington had been sent by the governor of Virginia to build a fort at the confluence of the Ohio and Allegheny rivers but found the French had beat him to it. When he built another fort some sixty miles south, he'd been attacked by the French and forced to surrender last July 4. Surprise attacks by French-armed Indians seemed to be increasing. The people of the frontier were demanding protection. Plantation owners didn't know which to fear more, attacks by the Cherokees or a slave uprising. Many of them, in fact, wondered if the warring Cherokees would incite the slaves to revolt. Under the blue-skied autumn canopy, carts rolled into the city laden with rice and indigo and furs and hides. With them came an uneasiness. Thomas felt it.

The afternoon was quiet, with most of the business of the market already transacted. Most country folk were headed for home, hoping to make camp for the evening before blue skies turned gray and emptied cold rains on them and their purchases. Clouds moving in dulled the late afternoon light inside the weaving shop, and Dugald and Thomas both leaned just a little closer to the web to see their work. Still, it would be wasteful to light a lamp so early in the day.

A few raindrops were already starting to fall when Henry Jones, the housewright who owned the building in which Thomas rented his manufactory, stopped in on his way home from the new house he was building on Broad Street. The nails in his leather apron jingled as he walked, his spare body as lithe on ground as it was stepping across second-story rafters. Henry nearly always stopped on his way home, for his family lived upstairs here.

Henry Jones stood across the shop, his brown hair pulled neatly back and tied, his brow lined well from days of outdoor work, and in his eyes and manner an eagerness and brightness. With the same ability he used to draw the plan for a house or design the pleasing curve of a stair, Jones could visualize the way things might one day be in the city, despite the dawdlings of a conservative crew who wanted to keep the colony the same as it had been twenty years earlier. Henry was a man with an eye for beauty and a spirit for fairness, and Thomas was thankful he had happened upon him, building a fine home for the Coopers, that first day in July of 1750 when he had ridden Shuttle into town.

"Ho, landlord, are these few raindrops drivin' you from the roof today?" Thomas said in greeting, not stopping the beat of the loom.

"Nay, 'twas the wind that near blew me from the roof that called for an early end to the day. That and Mother Jones's reminder I must seek out firewood and coal before the cold days come. Today's as good a day for that as any other, it seems."

Jones took his usual seat on the bench of the shop's third loom and spoke over the beat of the other two looms the way he always did when he stopped in on his way home from work at night. Most days the talk was of politics, or now, the war.

"Picked up the *Gazette* on my way home today, Thomas," he said. "The Crown doesn't approve the Plan of Union set forth in Albany last June by that man Franklin of Philadelphia. Nor do most of the colonies. There's to be no binding together. Listen to what this Franklin says: 'Everyone cries a union is absolutely necessary, but when it comes to the manner and form of the union, their weak noddles are perfectly distracted. We may like to rely on the Crown for our defenses and to spend but little of our time in thought of preparedness, but, in fact, we face the first line of threat and must rely on no one but ourselves no matter what the quality of distractions!' I can't help but think Franklin had an idea there," Henry went on. "If this war gets worse, we'd be better defended if we all worked together and could raise an army of our own and the money to run it, instead of waiting for help from London."

"Aye. The few militiamen we have here and there are good men all, but possessed of their own opinions . . . isn't that right, Dugald?" Thomas received the exasperated "hrmmmp!" he knew he would and went on. "Myself, I find militia trainin' a bit of a worry, after watchin' the redcoats. We might shoot straighter, but they follow orders better. If the French are more like the redcoats, it could be bad. We need money and trainin' if we're to be ready for 'em."

"Thought you weren't goin' to fight," Dugald Mackay called out over his shoulder.

"I'm speakin' of possibilities now, lad," his master explained. "Just sayin' what might come to be."

"And I was just sayin' that if it come to be, I wouldn't mind takin' a few shots at the bastards." Dugald paused in the beating of his blanket to look squarely into his master's eyes.

"Nor would I." Thomas, too, ceased the action of his loom and met Dugald's eyes, not goaded, not angered. Jones sat in silence, watching the intensity that passed between the two men. "Still, I say, killin's not what it's made up to be and is to be avoided." Another silence, and this time, Thomas shifted back to his work. "I'm just sidin' with the man Franklin in his thinkin' that by bandin' together, the French might not take us for such easy pickin'. And better if the Cherokees were our friends rather than our enemies."

Boom. Clatter, clatter. Boom. Thomas resumed his work, Dugald his. Henry Jones let his eyes scan the *South Carolina Gazette* for just a few moments, then spoke again.

"It comes as no surprise that London does not approve such a plan," Henry said. "They want us to be quiet, like children, while they're busy with France. 'Twas the idea of a president-general, no doubt, that bothered the Crown. Too much power invested in one man. Still Franklin proposed a Grand Council to balance things. For now, it seems, we'll have to continue to rely on the Assembly to do the best it can with the militia and the Indians," he said.

"Is Franklin to give it up then?" Thomas wanted to know.

"It says he's discussing it now with Governor Shirley in Boston. Who knows what may come of it?" Jones lay the paper across his knee and paused to change the subject. Before he could speak, Dugald spoke up. "Ask Thomas about the fine deal he made on fustian today."

"What's this, Thomas? More good fortune come your way?"

"Indentured men can have their rights taken away from 'em by their masters," Thomas observed, eyeing Dugald from beneath raised eyebrows.

"Just ask him about how he bought fustian from Loggins for thirty pounds, and sold it five minutes later for fifteen pounds, Henry," Dugald insisted. "And then ask him about how he smiled as if he'd just sold it for forty-five."

"Sounds like a lass must've been in the transaction somewheres," Jones ventured.

Thomas allowed himself a pleased smile at the thought of the little deception. "Only tryin' to oblige," he said with a wink to Jones. "A new customer, you know."

"A hundred other new customers've come in since I've been here, and not once has he ducked out the back door, run to Loggins, paid dear and run back to sell cheap," Dugald reasoned. " 'Twas a lass all right, and a rich one, too, I'd wager," Dugald teased.

"So, there's a chance yet, Thomas, you might take your mind off your work long enough to pay mind to a lady. I'll inform Kathleen of it as soon as I top the stairs."

"If Dugald hasn't already," Thomas said. He clicked his tongue, and a corner of his mouth curled upward. "He seems to be takin' it upon himself to tell me secrets to the world."

"Your servant, sir," Dugald called out, unrepentant.

"By the way, Thomas, I met a lad today just in from Pennsylvania. Name of Jones, like mine, was how we got acquainted. Said the Ulster Scots are leavin' the Susquehanna in droves, headed to the west and south on the promise of free land. 'Twas where you came from, wasn't it?"

Thomas kept on with his work, nodding in answer to Henry's question, but the rhythm of the loom was broken. "Free land," he said, neither looking up nor expanding on his answer. Then, sighing, "heh" was all he said, shaking his head. All thoughts of Miss Rawlins and the fustian blew away on the wind of such talk.

Jamie Lowe would no doubt be after that "free land." Where would that redheaded ruffian have dragged Sarah to by now? Women went crazy on the frontier from pure, unrelenting fear—Thomas had seen them as he travelled the Great Philadelphia Wagon Road to the Carolinas. The image of one of them, hollow-eyed and vacant, would never leave him.

The conversation with Henry and Dugald continued for a while, but Thomas only half listened. All this talk of Pennsylvania brought back feelings he thought he'd long since buried. Still his thoughts drifted back to Sarah, as they did nearly every day. I wonder where you are, lass . . . How you are . . . But no answer came, and after a time the rhythm of the loom grew even once more.

11

Little clouds of warm air formed in front of Borque's mouth as he spoke into the crisp air of an early October frost. Sitting easily atop the eager stallion he rode, his hold of the reins was loose, as if the horse were nothing more than a nag.

Crickie maintained the posture her mother expected of her and her kidskinned gloves kept a firm grip on the reins of her mare, though the mare well knew the route to the back fields without guidance. Crickie's breathing made its own clouds, and she puffed out air deliberately through rounded lips to watch the wonder of it over and over as Borque spoke.

"Your father speaks often of this neighbor of yours, Eliza Lucas. She helped him begin the growing of indigo here at High Garden? She must be a highly spirited woman, this Eliza."

"Yea," Crickie answered, still watching her breath rather than looking at her companion. "She is. She has been an example to me throughout my years here. She is not only an expert horticulturist but also a great lover of good books, and has loaned me numerous volumes. We miss her presence since she married Colonel Pinckney. They have sailed to London, and it is not known when they may return."

"Ah, then it was wise that your father allowed me to come and be of assistance to you, although I must say your mentor has taught you well. There is truly very little I can add to what you already know. Have no fears, you are a superb planter of the blue dye."

Crickie colored at the compliment, though she knew it was true. "As I told you, it has been my goal to see to the quality of the product, not just the quantity as so many planters do. I will not see my crop shipped in old rice barrels, nor its weight increased with chunks of coal or mud. High Garden indigo will compete with that of the West Indies in every way, not just in terms of price. We owe it to the Crown to grow a crop worthy of the bounty granted us. And, as British subjects we must keep the supply constant despite the war with the French. That we may benefit from it ourselves is, of course, an added incentive."

Borque smiled his too-familiar smile at this last as they rode on toward the vats where a dozen slaves were processing the last of the indigo. Other crews were bringing in the carrots, squash and pumpkins needed for winter from the acreage close to the house. Some were picking apples and pears to save them from the damage of possible hard frost. It was the best kind of day for such work: cool enough to be invigorating, warm enough to work without a coat.

"Then you must expect a sizable profit from such a fine crop as you have this year?" Borque asked.

"Some," Crickie said, automatically withholding information as her father had instructed her to do. She gave her horse a little kick and pranced on ahead, the ties from her hat flying out behind her. Borque, of course, easily matched her and in seconds was at her side once more. As the two rode up to the number five processing station, the work of drying the indigo was already well in progress.

Three cuttings had been taken from the crop this year, making this last one unusually late in the season. The thick, juicy leaves of Bahama indigo had been cut with reaping hooks and placed in clean, cotton bags three weeks back, then brought here immediately, before their leaves could so much as wilt. The leaves were then steeped in a huge, cement-lined brick vat for approximately twelve hours before a cock was opened to let the indigo liquor into what was called a "beater vat," where it was agitated and oil was added to allow the formation of small particles. Next, limewater was stirred in and allowed to settle, this phase being the most critical of the whole process. Without the right amount of acidity the dye quality would be adversely affected. Once the water was drained from this vat, the remaining paste was placed in oznaburg bags and more liquid squeezed out.

The blue paste was at last taken to the drying house, and it was there that Crickie and Borque stopped.

"I must check on my foreman," Crickie said, "and then I can show you around."

Borque nodded, and helping her down he let his hands linger at her waist well after her feet were planted on the ground. Crickie started for the drying house as though she hadn't noticed.

As they walked, Crickie saw Borque eyeing a stack of leaves drawn from the vats after the steeping. In warmer weather the smell of them would have been overwhelmingly putrid, but so far today the sun was not warm enough to stir the odor. Still, the stack crawled with flies and Crickie noted Borque's frown.

Inside the drying house, Moss, the black man who was foreman of the crew, was spreading indigo paste across a long, narrow cypress table. Borque watched him a moment, then looked out through the netting-covered window openings to where the rest of the crew was working. Five young black men were scrubbing out the bottom of the vat to keep mold and fungus from forming in it over the winter months. They worked without more than a glance at the couple beyond the netting.

"The porous fibers of the cypress will soak up even more of ye moisture," Crickie pointed out as they watched Moss's powerful arms trowel the heavy paste into an even layer reaching almost to the edges of the table. "By evening, the crew will turn it over with wooden paddles, there on ye wall, allowing the other side to dry."

Borque nodded his approval of the process, all the while keeping his hand at Crickie's back as they walked the length of the table, guiding her rather than being guided. Moss kept his eyes on his work, not speaking with the stranger Borque.

"How does it seem to you, Moss?" she asked to see if his judgment matched hers.

"Could be drier, miss," he said honestly, "but we give it time."

"Yea, I wish it were better. But we'll not ship this until spring—it will be nicely dry by then. Correct, Monsieur Borque?" she asked, almost as an afterthought. Her father's guest, after all, was supposed to be the expert, not she.

"Time and warmth—the right conditions—these are the only things that can help you, Crickie," he said, still accenting her name on the second syllable so that the *e* sound rang out long after it should have. Crickie smiled politely. "And please, Crickie, do call me Michel. You are far too formal with such an old friend of your papa's."

"Michel, then," she said, looking quickly back to Moss working the blue paste.

"Ah, yes, you must take care to see that when you cut the dried paste into cubes, you allow each cube to dry evenly."

"I know," Crickie said, hoping to conceal her annoyance. Everyone knew that—though few knew how to do it successfully. "How do you manage such drying in Antigua?" she asked. Here was a place where his knowledge might be helpful. She stopped her slow paces along the table and looked at him, waiting for an answer.

"Our temperature does not vary as much as yours does here in Carolina. We do not have such great difficulty as you. Perhaps you should think of shipping your paste to the Indies to be dried?"

"Never," Crickie snapped, then caught herself. "I would never know if mine were exchanged for an inferior grade— or stolen outright—and the cost would be—"

"But if you gained a better quality product, your indigo would command a higher price, and you would make more money, have no fears," Borque said.

"Is that why you've come?" Crickie asked, "to convince me to ship my crop elsewhere to dry?" She looked straight into his eyes, wondering if she might see his true motives there, but he quickly denied everything.

"But of course not, *ma chère*. It was just a suggestion. I would have no personal interest in such an enterprise."

"Then I misunderstood," Crickie said, excusing herself. "Forgive me," she said, polite but not warm, and inside thought her own thoughts.

"But of course you are forgiven, *ma chère,*" he said, using the endearment once again as if speaking to a child.

"And it is you who must forgive me," he went on, "for I must leave this day and go back to Charles Town to see to a new horse I may purchase. If it would not offend you, I should stay in the Planters' Hotel in the city until the day of next week's race."

"We shall miss you here," she managed to say. "But you are our guest, and we wish you to do all of those things that will make your stay with us most pleasant." Especially staying in Charles Town. For as long as you like, she added silently.

"Your mother has suggested that Margaret and Deborah may accompany me and stay at the Forchers'. I have agreed. So you see you will be most solitary here at the High Garden. Does that suit you?"

"It does," she said, feeling hare to his fox. "And I thank you for helping me to see to my sisters' entertainment. I find it difficult to chaperone them in the city as much as they would like."

"Then it will be my pleasure to entertain them for you," Borque said with a gestured bow.

"I will be quite detained here in seeing to this last indigo and setting the Negroes about their new chores, but perhaps I could try to come into the city next—"

"Not at all, not at all," Borque broke in, waving his hands and shaking his head in objection. "Your work is here and I do not mind in the least watching over your sisters for you. It will be my pleasure," he assured her.

She hesitated, then finally agreed. "All right," she said, giving up. Selene Forcher would no doubt do the biggest share of the chaperoning anyway. Crickie was surprised her mother would allow such an arrangement, but now that Mother was feeling better, she was making a few more decisions, and she did want her daughters to take their place in Charles Town society. Perhaps she thought this a

good way for Margaret and Deborah to learn some inde-
pendence. Crickie said a silent prayer that the girls would
do well.

"Let us begin our ride back to the house, then," he said.
"I believe your sisters are waiting."

"I have work out here yet," Crickie said, having no inten-
tion of going back so soon. She had other crews to direct,
other questions to answer. She could not do that from the
front veranda. "You go on along. I shall ride in when I'm
finished."

"Perhaps I should wait."

"That will not be necessary. Our overseer, Mr. Johnson,
will join me at the next station. If I need any help, I'll take
Moss, here, away from his table. Go on," she said.

"Your father has a most able substitute in you," Borque
said, turning to leave. "And he does appreciate your many
efforts on his behalf," he added.

"Papa is very appreciative, that I know," she said, as if it
were nothing. "And I do miss him."

Borque turned back to her, meeting her eyes with an easy
frankness. "Then he is doubly fortunate," he said, bowing
again, lower this time. "Good day," he called, and was out
the door.

Crickie checked Moss's face for a reaction, but seeing
none, dismissed the whole conversation and pulled her tippet in tighter about her shoulders. A cool breeze filtered in
through the fine netting behind her, and she wondered if it
would be warm enough to dry the indigo. Outside, though,
the sun was beginning to warm the stack of indigo leaves,
and squadrons of black flies swarmed about it, their loud
buzzing a dull harmony to the hoofbeats of Borque's gal-
loping horse as he rode back toward the house.

"I think mebbe that man just learned a little somethin'
about High Garden indigo, miss," Moss ventured, looking
up from his work, but never ceasing the broad, sweeping
motions of the trowel.

"I still cannot understand why Papa sent him," Crickie
said, shaking her head. "Ship my indigo to ye Indies in-

deed," she said, with a laugh. "Even Papa would know better than that."

"Your papa a smart man, miss," Moss said, "but he like the army like Mr. Borque here like his horses. They know you the smartes' planter among 'em."

"Well, I don't know about that," she said, "but I can see how they became friends. I'll be back later this afternoon, Moss," she said. "Set the crew to squeezing ye other bags more when they finish the vat."

Moss nodded. "Yea, Miss Rawlins," he said, and Crickie left, knowing with Moss in charge the work would be done. And done well.

It was late afternoon, almost dark, when Crickie walked up the gravelled path from the stable to the house, tired not from any physical work she'd done, or from riding, but from the sheer weight of the details that had to be seen to at harvest. Lost in thoughts of all that still needed to be done, she was surprised to find her mother sitting on the veranda waiting for her, her lap covered with a heavy wool blanket, her feet resting on a tiny needlepoint stool.

"Mama, how good to see you out," Crickie said. She couldn't remember when she'd last seen her mother out of doors. "But aren't you getting cold? There's a chill in the air."

"I'm used to chills," Judith Rawlins said, her voice conveying a chill of its own. "I've had them off and on for close to seven years. One more won't hurt."

"But we don't want you to be sick again. We want you well for when Papa comes home." Crickie took the chair opposite her mother but did not drop into it as she might have if on the porch alone. Instead, she was careful to lower herself slowly and to sit with her back straight, not touching the back of the chair.

"I spoke to Edward Young today," her mother said, as dour as her daughter was cheerful. "He told me an invasion by France is feared. As long as it is, your father will never come home." Disappointment and anger mixed in her voice as she fixed her eyes on the richly colored sunset visible across the now vacant rice fields.

"Then, perhaps if you continue to feel better you can go to him—you know how he would wish it. And you might find ye climate good for you." Crickie tried to remain positive, but her mother did not make that easy.

Judith Rawlins leaned her head against the lace-draped back of the rocker and closed her eyes. "It was coming to a warm climate that made me ill," she said. "Going to another would be of little use. Going to another in time of war would be nothing short of insane."

"Oh, Mother," Crickie said, "you are tired and unwell from sitting here too long. You must not despair of ill health and Father's regard for you. You must simply try to feel better."

"I will feel better only when your father and I return to London. And when I see my three daughters married well—"

At this, Judith interrupted herself, opening her eyes and leaning forward slightly toward Crickie, imploring her with narrowed gray-brown eyes under sagging lids to listen.

"—To young men of our acquaintance and station, rather than riding about on horses and working like common . . . common . . . people." As she spoke, her eyes flared. "Your papa should never have allowed you to come home from London when he did. You should have finished your schooling as Margaret and Deborah did. Your father is far too lenient with you."

"Ye past is past, Mother," Crickie said, having heard all this many times before. "I might like to speak to you, Mother, about Monsieur Borque," Crickie went on. She checked the parlor window to make certain that her sisters were, in fact, gone. "I fear that both Margaret and Deborah are quite taken with him. Margaret, especially, is too old to be allowed such forward behavior. He may mistake it for encouragement of his attentions. Might you speak to her about it? She does not care for my comments."

Judith settled back in the chair once again. "Why is it that you are so opposed to Margaret's interest in dear Michel?" she asked. "Is it because you have an interest in him yourself?"

For an instant, Crickie thought, Mother sounded just like her old self—fondly teasing, loving, attentive. She brightened at this flicker of progress. "Oh, Mama, of course not. But he is far too old for Margaret. He is twenty-eight to her seventeen. And besides, he seems interested in little other than his horses. I fear she will make herself ye fool and then find he has no interest in her. She will be hurt." She will disgrace us all, Crickie thought.

"Let us not judge what has not yet been done," her mother said, seeming to fade off again into her own world the way she had done for most of the past seven years. The flicker of the old mother pouffed out like a wisp of smoke. "Margaret has her beauty to guide her, as does Deborah."

Crickie felt herself conspicuously absent from her mother's list.

"Yea, she is a beauty," Crickie conceded as she watched her mother lift herself slowly from the rocker, still clutching at the blanket on her lap. With baby steps, the frail woman made her way toward the tall, panelled oak door that led into the hall.

"You'll speak to her, Mother?" Crickie asked once more as her mother stood in the doorway, her small frame silhouetted against the light of the hall lamp.

"If need be, I will," Judith conceded, but her tone gave Crickie little hope that she would and the great door swung shut behind her.

As the flaming reds of sunset gave way to the softer shades of twilight, Crickie looked across the hedged gardens in front of her and down the brick walkway to the landing. Sunset came early these late October days and the live oaks made lofty silhouettes against the pink southwestern horizon. Rippled only by the orange feet of three ducks that landed without sound, the wide river was a platter of deep gold. On the crisp air, the smell of dozens of cook fires floated, familiar.

Crickie's tippet, finally, was not quite enough to warm her against the chill air, and she wished she had her mother's blanket so she could stay, not moving, to watch the gold turn to black, then starlit silver. To see the massive, moss-hung oaks cast their all-consuming shadows. To hear the rustling river night sounds. But darkness dropped with only a single star to light her world, and Crickie went in.

12

As the horses lined up at York Course a few days later, Crickie Rawlins scanned the jockeys for the face of the weaver Thomas Gairden. Borque was there, the corners of his mouth turned down slightly beneath his moustaches, his brow puckered a bit as his horse skittered under him more than he wanted. But across the field of ten riders and back again, the face of Thomas Gairden was not to be seen.

Crickie, seated in the gallery with her friend Lisette and Lisette's brother, Jon, just home from Eton, looked from the horses to the crowd and back again, feigning no particular interest in either. She wondered, though, what kept a horse enthusiast such as Gairden from today's race, where a purse of fifty pounds was to be offered. Surely such a man could use fifty pounds. Borque, on the other hand, did not need the money. He said that he raced out of a love of wagering of all kinds. It would be unkind to speak of it to anyone else, but it seemed to Crickie he had another reason as well—that the short little Borque felt himself tall and powerful when on a fast horse. The thought helped her be more charitable toward the man who was otherwise so shallowpated. The longer she knew him, the less she could understand what he and her father might ever have had in common. No doubt her father, like her sisters, was duped by Borque's easy charm and did not know him long enough to discover his lack of substance. She would inform her father of this lack at the first opportunity.

The gun sounded and before her eyes the field was a blur of legs crisscrossing as the eager horses took off.

"I wish Papa could be here to see this," Deborah said, leaning over Crickie's shoulder from her seat in the second row. "Wouldn't he enjoy watching Michel, and betting on ye horses?"

"He would think it fine." Crickie smiled at the thought of her barrel-chested father watching at the finish line with the other men, smoking his pipe, tipping his hat to the ladies.

The crowd cheered loudly, and Crickie's head moved along with everyone else's, but she was not truly watching. She was thinking of her father. A new track, Newmarket Course, closer to the city, would no doubt be in use by the time her father returned—a change he would favor. In fact, Charles Town was growing in all directions before her very eyes, and Papa would notice some mighty changes when he returned—whenever that was.

"Is your father coming home soon?" Jon Forcher asked. Back from Eton only a week, he knew few of the racers but attempted to show a polite interest. His speech had taken on the broad, oval tones of London English, resulting in a voice too old for the boyish face behind it.

"Nay," Crickie explained, stretching a bit to follow the progress of the horses. "There is no word of his leaving Antigua, especially with France and Spain snooping about ye islands as they are. While you were away he was called to service by ye lieutenant governor. The assistance of the army continues to be much needed, I'm afraid."

"I'm sorry," Jon said, his eyes on the race as he spoke. "You must be so alone."

"We do miss him," Crickie said, turning to Jon, "but Papa's duty is to His Majesty, and we accept that. Of course, we would be there with him were it not for Mama's health."

"Cheer for Michel," Margaret demanded, tapping Crickie on the shoulder and pointing to the far side of the track where Borque's horse trailed a half-dozen others. Crickie tightened her fingers and mouthed a "come on, come on," but let her sisters do the cheering. Jon Forcher kept on with the conversation, leaning his head close to her ear to make himself heard over the crowd.

"Has your mother improved at all while I've been away?"

"She has, and even spoke last week of making ye voyage.

Monsieur Borque assured her Antigua's climate would suit her better than does ye Carolinas."

"You wouldn't leave Charles Town now that I've just returned, would you, Crickie?" Jon asked, half-smiling and completely ignoring the race. "I couldn't bear it."

Crickie had not seen Jon in over four years. He had the same dark, handsome features as his sister. He'd grown up during his years at Eton, but still he seemed . . . young.

"It's not likely," she said, keeping her tone light, but her words were swallowed up in the roar of the crowd as the horses rounded the far side of the track, with Borque's stallion and another big gray horse running neck and neck. Crickie cheered, too, cutting off Jon's further comments, but her eyes left the track time and again to check for the one face she most hoped to see today.

As the horses rounded the last turn, now a pack of four jostling in sharp strides to the inside, their great equine nostrils flaring, great dark eyes wide in eagerness, Crickie saw him. He wore a trim-fitting claret coat that hung half-way to his knees over a pair of fawn camlet breeches caught at the knee by silver garters. Tall riding boots of a soft brown leather and a silver snuffbox dangling at his side as well, Gairden looked more the prosperous businessman than a simple weaver. She knew him by the dark knot of black hair that lay in place against the claret coat, by the way he stood, by some sort of aura she couldn't see but could feel. Her stomach gave a little lurch, her mouth a little sigh of satisfaction.

Having seen him before only in his working or racing garb, she found herself surprised that a workingman should dress so. Surprise froze on her face as he turned and looked back at her, as if he'd felt her eyes at his back. He tipped his grosgrain-trimmed cock hat pleasantly, then restored his attention to the horses, now straining toward the finish.

Crickie looked there, too, and saw the crimson of Michel's scarf clearly in the lead. Her face felt just as crimson. She cheered for him. She clapped her gloved hands for him. But as soon as his new thoroughbred had stepped across the finish line, her eyes darted back once more to Gairden, only to find him gone.

"G'day, Miss Rawlins. 'Tis a pleasure to see you once again." Thomas Gairden's smile was a bit cockeyed as he somehow slid his lower jaw to the side. Pleasant. Appraising. Genuine. "You've been pleased with your yardages from the Sign of the Shuttle?"

"Most pleased," Crickie replied, trying not to sound as eager as she felt. Lisette and Jon had left her side to speak with a circle of friends and Crickie had gone back to check on Deborah's whereabouts after the race. Instead she'd come face-to-face with Thomas Gairden. Ever since she'd gone to his shop that day last month, she'd imagined just such a meeting. Now that it had come, she felt her midsection tense.

"In fact," she went on, "I've told others of your favorable prices, and no doubt you'll see an increase in sales of ye fustian."

"Ah, I thank you," Thomas said, pleasant but not effusive. "Madame Forcher has already made a purchase at your suggestion. . . . Of course I cannot say what the price may be on my next shipment."

"Of course," Crickie said. "We all know how prices change in time of war or piracy—still we need insurance on ye ships, even if it does increase prices." She shifted her eyes right, then left, as she spoke. "I'm looking for my little sister Deborah," Crickie said, explaining.

"Would she be the lass with the lovely yellow curls I saw tuggin' at your arm during the race?" Thomas asked. "I couldn't help but notice . . ."

"Yea, that would be Deborah," Crickie said, her eyes taking in the soft curve of his hat brim and the richness of its deep maroon coloring. "She's quite taken with Monsieur Borque, whom I mentioned to you before. No doubt she and Margaret have gone off to find him."

"Another sister?"

"Yea. Margaret's a year younger than I. She's a great beauty." Why did I say that, Crickie asked herself? But somehow she felt she could say it to Thomas Gairden, though she couldn't tell why.

"Then it runs in the family, Miss Rawlins," he said.

It was the sort of thing Borque might say, but it had none of Borque's artifice. Crickie smiled, lowering her eyes.

"You are very kind, Mr. Gairden," she said, letting her eyes meet his for a moment, then pretending to look away after her sisters.

"How did your indigo crop come in?" he asked, going back once again to their last conversation, their only common ground.

"The last of it is drying slowly, but drying. The earlier cuttings were the best we've ever had."

"Then your factor will be a happy man this year," Thomas said.

"Yea, and my father, too, when he learns of it," Crickie said, "though he pays little attention to the affairs of the plantation." Crickie caught herself—business, again. "I don't see my sister anywhere about," she said. "Perhaps she's already outside the gate."

Thomas fell into step beside Crickie as she ceased her search for Deborah and turned in that direction. Unlike most of the gentlemen she knew, he did not offer her his arm and as he talked he looked far off into the distance, as if thinking about something, rather than always directly at her. Crickie did the same. It gave her a wonderfully mature feeling to be walking so.

"So you are a planter then, Mr. Gairden?" Crickie asked, strolling leisurely as if it were a warm spring day instead of a brisk November one.

"Not really," Gairden said. "The nature of my weaving business involves some trading, some lending. I came into land ownership here when one of my borrowers borrowed more than he could pay. He was an old acquaintance and I bought his plantation as a favor more than anything. He runs the land on shares, and will buy River Plum Plantation back from me one day, I'm sure. For now we have an . . . agreement. Aye . . ." Gairden was thoughtful as he described the relationship. ". . . An agreement . . . that benefits us both. He talked me into buyin' more land in the backcountry than I'd ever planned on, and it's there we plan to plant indigo now that the King's bounty makes it so profitable. . . ."

Gairden's words trailed off as the two neared the group of gentlemen and ladies who clustered near the gate, still chatting and laughing, both men and women using fur muffs to keep off the chill of the darkening November day.

Crickie sensed Gairden's slight turn of body away from her and knew he was about to continue walking while she stopped near her friends.

To prevent that, she said quickly, "We are doing quite well with our indigo at High Garden. If you like, you may tell your friend he is welcome to come and look at our processing stations." Crickie shivered under her cape, and she hunched slightly as she folded her arms tight in front of her.

"He may do that, Miss Rawlins. Thank you," Gairden said, still edging away.

"Or you may," she added uncertainly.

"That's generous of you, Miss Rawlins," Gairden said, bowing slightly. "If time permits, I'm certain I could learn from it. G'day," he said abruptly, then continued on his way to where his horse was tied at one of the wrought-iron hitching posts. She recognized the horse as the one he'd raced last month, and wondered why he'd not raced today. She wondered so many things about him as she watched him ride away. Their conversations were far too short.

Still watching, Crickie felt the touch of a hand at her waist and looked around to see Borque at her side. Elation sparkled in his black eyes as he drew her to him, closer than she cared to be, and kissed her enthusiastically on both cheeks.

"A wonderful race, Michel," Crickie said, happy for him anyway. He was warm and smelled of horse sweat and the oiled leather of a saddle, his breathing quick and puffy in the exhilaration of the moment. "Your horse ran beautifully."

"My thanks, Crickie," he said, accenting, as always, the

last syllable. "Aubergine is a wonderful mount, and I hope for the next ones I buy to be even better."

Borque helped Crickie into the chaise, then took his place beside her, settling in comfortably and placing his palms on his knees as he stretched back against the tufted suede of the seat, exhaling deeply as he relaxed. Crickie did not relax but kept looking about for Deborah and Margaret, moving an inch away as she stretched toward the open door.

"Next ones?" she asked after a moment, still not seeing her sisters.

"I have learned from Monsieur Forcher that a shipment of beautiful animals arrives next week from Ireland, and I am to have the opportunity to purchase from the stock should I choose. Forcher assures me they will be of the highest quality and I am most hopeful that at least one of them will be mine."

"That will make, what, five thoroughbreds in your stable, monsieur?" Crickie asked. "You must plan to do much racing in Charles Town this season." Borque's mood at once was less expansive.

"That I do," he said simply, evading Crickie's unstated question "How long will you be staying?" He leaned side to side with Crickie, helping her look for the sisters, while Crickie pretended not to notice him. At last Deborah came hurrying from around the corner of a boxwood hedge, her smile bright and her golden curls bobbing merrily as she drew nearer.

"Oh, Michel, you did win!" she cried. "I've been looking for you. Did you hear me cheering? I called your name at least one hundred times."

"Then it must have been you I heard as I rounded the far side of the track, although at first I thought it must have been a nightingale, the sound was so sweet."

Deborah's pale cheeks colored in a sweet, girlish blush and she dropped her eyes while Borque basked in her admiration and looked immensely pleased with himself, or so Crickie thought. He enjoyed being the center of attention more than anyone else she had ever known.

"Where is Margaret?" Crickie wanted to know as Deborah settled in across from her in the carriage.

"Off with a friend, I think," Deborah said, and Crickie sensed she knew more than she was saying. "She'll be along soon I'm certain." Deborah looked not to Crickie but to Borque as she spoke, and he nodded, amused.

Crickie kept watch for Margaret while Deborah had Borque go over every switch of Aubergine's tail in the race, exclaiming over each detail as though Borque had been crowned king instead of winning fifty pounds. It was several minutes before Margaret came round the same hedge Deborah had, straightening her hat, her hair, her skirt, her cape, as she walked. Crickie saw the defiance in her sister's eyes. Let it pass. They could not speak of her behavior in front of their guest. Crickie would find out from Deborah later where Margaret had been. And with whom.

Borque was down and out of the chaise to help Margaret in, kissing both cheeks before he lifted her. Crickie and Deborah watched, used to Borque's kissing ways by now, but neither was ready when, just as he took her hand to help her into the carriage she bent toward him and kissed him on the cheek.

"Margaret!" Crickie said, shocked.

"Crickie," her sister returned, derisive, then kissed his other cheek even more slowly and fully before she stepped up to join her sisters. Borque, male pride filling his chest, waved and nodded to some other well-wishers before he reentered the chaise.

"We shall be the guests of honor at Forcher's harvest ball tonight, thanks to you, Michel," Margaret said, letting her tongue glide slowly over her full lips after she spoke. She untied her cape of soft scarlet velvet, and arranged it loosely about her shoulders.

"You beautiful ladies are honored wherever you go," Borque said. "I am only pleased to accompany you."

Crickie saw Margaret cross her legs as she made herself comfortable in the small space of the chaise. Margaret's slipper grazed Borque's leg. Crickie cringed at the way she did it. She must ask Mother again to speak to Margaret.

Looking down, Crickie felt Margaret's laughing eyes on her
while Deborah prattled on about the race, repeating all the
details with which Borque had earlier regaled her.

"Give me the first dance, Michel," Deborah begged.
"Please."

"But of course, *ma chère,*" he said, but Crickie looked up
to find Borque's eyes not on Deborah but on Margaret's
graceful neck and full bosom.

"Michel will be required to dance with many ladies tonight," Crickie said, her face as prim and cordial as she
could force it to be, "and we must not unfairly preoccupy
him." She could not be more direct in front of Borque, and
she knew that saying anything to Margaret in private would
only induce her to flirt more openly.

"You pay me too many compliments, Crickie," Borque
said, his moustaches jiggling as the chaise bounced along
the hard earth of the road back to town. Borque drew back
his shoulders slightly, Crickie noticed. He must be the only
man in the world who could swagger sitting down, she
thought.

For herself, she would rather be home just now. Spending the whole evening worrying over her sisters' behavior
and being pleasant to the few single men who repeatedly
paid her attentions in which she had no interest seemed too
much for her. As the chaise bumped along, Crickie gazed
out on the passing countryside, built up here and there with
a house of red brick or cypress. At home she could plan
how she might next see Thomas Gairden. She might dream
of him without interruption as she lay in the quiet of her
bed. Tomorrow she would go home, and perhaps be lucky
enough to leave Michel behind in Charles Town to see to
his horses. Perhaps lucky enough to leave Margaret and
Deborah behind as well . . . but of course she couldn't—
not with Margaret headstrong as she was. Mother was
wrong to give her so much freedom.

From the corner of her eye she saw Borque smiling, his
mouth moving the slightest bit this way and that as if talking
to himself, and having a nice time of it. Crickie adjusted her
slippers on the chaise's small velvet-covered footrest and

closed her eyes for a few moments, letting her sisters' chatter go on unchecked. Her day had begun at five as it always did, while theirs had begun at ten. No wonder they showed no signs of fatigue.

It had been exceptionally busy at High Garden these last weeks, with both rice and indigo harvests to get in, things to prepare for winter. The pace of life in winter was more even, though still demanding. There had been no word from Papa in months, and like her mother, she was beginning to have some concern for his safety. She would write to him on the morrow and ask once more that he give her some indication as to Monsieur Borque's position here and how long he might be expected to stay. She clenched her teeth and hoped once again that it would not be long.

Crickie breathed deeply as she let her head fall back against the chaise wall. Against the black inside of her eyelid she saw the jaunty smile of Thomas Gairden and in her mind she went back over their few words today. He was a fascinating sort, she thought, and knew her face must have the same sort of pleased look on it that Borque's did. Perhaps he found hers just as irksome, but she didn't know. And she didn't care.

The double parlor on the second floor of Selene and Evan Forcher's home glowed under the light of three crystal-prismed chandeliers which were reflected in the gilt-framed pier mirrors that hung at the ends and sides of the long room. Venetian blinds were drawn at the long windows, demure under the apricot and cream silk swags that draped gracefully at either side. Carrara marble mantels framed fireplaces that burned brightly at either end of the room to take off the early winter chill. Negro house servants in stately black uniform tended the fires, the tables of foods that were set up between the two doors that led into the parlors, and any wants or needs of the Forchers' guests.

Crickie stepped into the room, the silk of her fashionable golden Watteau gown rustling softly as it swished over a creamy white, lace-fronted petticoat. The bodice was cut low across the breasts, pushed up by tight lacing underneath, and it was by far the most elegant and sophisticated dress she had ever owned. Her hair, too, had been done up for evening by Lisette Forcher's maid, and powdered lightly. Her face felt slightly windburned from the afternoon at the track, and looking about her she saw other women heavily made up in attempts to hide the same reddish cheeks of which she was suddenly so conscious. The room would be warm, though, with so many people in it, and soon everyone would be red of face from dancing and wine. Crickie thought no more of her face and was in a moment caught up in conversation with Lisette, then dancing with her brother, Jon.

"We've missed nearly as many parties here as you have," Crickie said as she curtsied, "but now that Monsieur Borque is with us, we must see that he is entertained and spend more time in ye city."

"Thank God for that," Jon said, grinning and looking smart in his deep blue velvet evening jacket. "I should not have wanted to miss seeing you at every opportunity—I've thought of you often while I was away." Jon's eyes were friendly and eager, but Crickie was not drawn to them.

She caught sight of Borque across the room, talking to a small group of people. Mama thought of him as their chaperone. That he would pay little or no attention to them over the course of the evening Mama would never know. Or need to. Crickie was more than capable of watching over her sisters and their guest. Still the convention of male protection was given a nod, and Mama was more or less satisfied.

As Crickie and Jon stepped and swirled, Crickie looked to Borque now and again. He had a way of ingratiating himself into any group he chose. He had made a fast friend of Evan Forcher—of course her father would have fostered that with a letter of some kind. But still, he'd made friends among his racing acquaintances and many other wealthy Carolinians. Perhaps he planned to stay in Charles Town. . . . He was dancing now with Selene Forcher, now with Marthe Huger, now with Ann Jennys . . .

"And may I trade partners with you, Monsieur Forcher,"

Borque asked with great formality as he brought Mrs. Jennys over.

"My pleasure," said Jon, all the good breeding of his family and years at Eton poised in the remark, as he took the hand of the silver-haired grandmother he'd known all of his life. Crickie was impressed at Jon's graciousness and smiled broadly as they danced away.

Borque held her ever so lightly by the hand as they stepped politely in time to the stately rhythm of the minuet. He was graceful and danced well—better than Jon, she had to admit. As she bowed her head to Borque, then lifted it and was about to circle beneath his raised arm, Crickie saw Thomas Gairden at the far end of the room, his left arm resting easily on the mantelpiece, the claret of his jacket a vivid contrast to the white of the marble. Warming himself, observing the dance, sipping from a small stemmed glass, he seemed completely at home. Borque, following Crickie's eyes, looked to Gairden as well, the men nodding a hello. Crickie smiled, not too eagerly she hoped, and then turned and dipped as the dance continued.

Margaret stood waiting for Borque's hand when the minuet was through, and Crickie raised her eyebrows to her sister, admonishing her even as she held her hand out for Borque to kiss. She could not be too harsh—it was Borque's place to dance with each of them, she told herself—and went for a glass of Madeira to sip as she watched the dancing.

"Everything is lovely," she told Selene Forcher, joining her on a settee near the table.

"Thank you, my dear. We are all so pleased you can at last join us. And Jon is especially pleased," she said, with a knowing look.

Crickie gave a little laugh. "I've enjoyed seeing him, too," she said, which was mostly true. "Lisette told me Governor Glen might be coming later on," she added.

"He may," Mrs. Forcher said, "though he is quite consumed by Indian affairs."

"Did you hear of the murders of the Guttrey family and others at Buffalo Creek?" asked Amanda Waddill, the bulge-eyed matron on Crickie's other side, breaking into the conversation. Her satin bodice pulled taut as she straightened her buxom chest indignantly. "Seventeen of them murdered by ye Cherokees just this September," she said, twisting her aging, purpled lips in disgust. "Found by a bridal couple on their way home from their *wedding.*" Mrs. Waddill drew out the irony for maximum effect. Crickie and Mrs. Forcher exchanged looks, hoping the woman would stop.

"Yea, I heard. But no one knows for certain it was Cherokees—" Mrs. Forcher began.

"Who else?" Mrs. Waddill shrieked. "And the Assembly's approved the paying of four and a half pounds for any white man or friendly Indian bringing in the scalps of Cherokees caught in such vileness. I say it should be five."

"We must all—" Mrs. Forcher began again, trying to head off the outraged woman.

"Ye Cherokees have already done murders no more than fifty miles from Charles Town," Mrs. Waddill interrupted. "We need protection—and we don't need the governor spending his time at parties and dancing!"

Selene Forcher stood, her stance indicating the unpleasant conversation was over. "I'm certain Governor Glen and the Assembly will see to our protection just as they always have," she said graciously. "Do not worry yourself, Amanda, but enjoy yourself this lovely evening. Crickie, perhaps you might bring Mrs. Waddill a glass of Madeira," she suggested.

Crickie quickly obliged, joining the line at the table just behind Deborah as the musicians took an intermission.

"It's soon time for you to leave," Crickie reminded her. Fourteen-year-olds were allowed to attend parties, but not to stay until the end.

"I can't wait until next year when I'm old enough to wear a fancy gown and powder my hair like you and Margaret," Deborah said.

"You'll soon be a fair lady, sister, and lovelier than anyone else in Charles Town, I'm certain," Crickie said, loading a china plate with sweets for Mrs. Waddill. "For tonight, though, you must retire." Brushing her sister's cheek with a kiss she sent her on her way, and looked up to see Gairden watching the little farewell from the far end of the room. Acknowledging him with a nod, she returned to Mrs. Waddill before joining a long line of ladies going upstairs to refresh themselves.

In the lavishly wallpapered guest room on the third floor, Crickie could hear a bevy of female voices, talking as they primped. She poked her head in and saw wigs being powdered, hair repinned, gowns adjusted, laces tightened—and loosened—women of all ages in all states of repair before the second half of the evening's dancing began.

Crickie took a quick look about for Margaret, and not seeing her started back down the narrow stairs, holding her petticoat just off the top of her slippers. Halfway down she had a view of the parlor, and there was Margaret, her arm linked with Borque's as they talked to a small group gathered near the fireplace. Among the group was Thomas Gairden.

Margaret's brocaded gown reflected the firelight, and Crickie noticed she'd pulled the puffed sleeves down off her shoulders so that the fine lines of her collarbone and shoulders stood bare and gleaming white, her cleavage alluringly shadowed by the glow of the blazing oak logs. Margaret cast a glance at her sister, but then returned her full attention to Borque and his friends—all men. Hurrying in to join her sister, Crickie met Thomas Gairden on his way out.

"Miss Rawlins," he said, with a controlled smile. "I couldn't leave without thanking you for the invitation to look at your indigo works. Before we begin the reclaimin' of the land above River Plum, I'll have Gray come out for a look."

"As I said," Crickie added quietly, "you are welcome, too."

"Aye, thank you. Your man Borque gave me welcome, too. But I've not the eye for the land Gray has. He's the planter, not I. When I left Pennsylvania I planned to leave farmin' behind for good, but Gray convinced me a weaver would starve here while a planter would prosper. So I took it up once again as a kind of silent partner. Gray sees to the planting," he said with a shrug, "and I handle the business. Makes me a planter in name only, I'm afraid."

"And that's how your 'agreement' works then?" she asked, going back to their discussion of the afternoon.

"Somewhat, aye . . ." he said. "We get along better that way," he added. "You, on the other hand, have a knack for plantin' says Borque. He seems quite proud of that."

"Michel? Oh, Michel is an accomplished flatterer. He is taken with High Garden and with Charles Town and with all that is so new and different from his home. He really knows very little of my work—nor should he. He is our guest, and we are all pleased he has found such a consuming pastime in his racing."

"Aye, that he has. Some men do," Thomas said, remembering another race. "I'll expect to race Shuttle once more in February and then retire him. Will you be coming to Charles Town for Race Week?"

"Perhaps," Crickie said, "although once Monsieur Borque is gone I don't know how often we will come in for race days—unless Mother is well enough to accompany my sisters to the city. I'm afraid ye work at High Garden gets ahead of me at times."

"You should have an Alexander Gray then, to help you, Miss Rawlins," Thomas suggested.

"Please call me Crickie," she told him, laughing at his idea. "Everyone else does."

"Crickie," he said with a small bow, as if meeting her for the first time. "And I am Thomas—though I don't recall you've called me by much of any name the times we've met. But Thomas 'tis, and I hope we may meet again soon and you can teach me of plantin' and I can teach you of weavin' and we may both profit a bit. A Scot seeks to make a profit where he can, as you may have heard," he said, his eyes twinkling in the soft candlelight of the parlor.

"Ye Scots have a reputation, it's true," Crickie said, "but they are not alone in their wish for profit—we all like to earn our bread and then some."

"Well, they say of the Scots that they keep the commandments—and every other good thing they can get their hands on. We are savers, I suppose."

"Yea," Crickie agreed, laughing at his easy self-deprecation. "Well, thrift is a virtue."

"I've even saved time for a dance before I go," he ventured. "Might you do me the honor?" he asked, extending a hand as the musicians readied for the second half of the evening.

Crickie felt her cheeks redden, this time not from windburn. He had not danced once the whole evening, she knew.

"Of course," she said simply, slipping her own hand, which knew well the reins of a horse and the feel of an indigo knife, into the larger hand she'd seen throw the shuttle with such confidence and ease, a hand whose long fingers were warm and alive. He danced with the same lightness and grace with which he walked, and Crickie felt her own feet lighter, her movements more agile, than ever before.

Circling arm-in-arm down the row of dancers, Crickie caught Lisette Forcher's look of interest, her wink. Then Jon Forcher's look. Interest of a different kind. Anyone watching could not help but notice Gairden had danced with no one but her all evening. Did she imagine it or were the matrons over on the settee whispering about her behind their fans? Margaret beamed as they passed in the row of couples. She was dancing with Ann Jennys's handsome son, Patrick, but her eyes gave Thomas a quick appraisal.

Borque was watching, too, smoothing his moustaches, shifting from left foot to right, and the reel was not yet half-done when he stepped into the line, touching the dashing young Patrick Jennys lightly on the arm and murmuring a quiet word.

Crickie saw Margaret take Borque's hand a bit too eagerly. Ah, let Margaret have her moment, she thought. I have mine, after all. She scouted again and again the irresistible challenge of Gairden's dark, knowing eyes. Circling left, circling right, their eyes met at every turn, each meet-

ing a question, each answer an intrigue. These were eyes
Crickie had remembered for eight years—the same ones
that had fascinated her as a little girl on board the *Endeavor*. They expressed so much. Withheld so much. The
dance's last note, drawn out on the strings of a fine German
violin, came far too soon to suit Crickie.

"Thank you, Miss Rawlins," Thomas said, bowing.

She curtsied, nodded. "My pleasure, Mr. Gairden. You
are a fine dancer."

"You seem surprised. But Scots love dancing, and I'm no
different. Only I've not done any for . . . a while. I'm
afraid I could use some practice."

"Not at all. You must—"

"Crickie. Gairden." Borque was at their side, Margaret
on his arm. "Thank you, Monsieur Gairden, for taking this
dance with one of my hostesses. I am unable to dance with
them both at the same time as I would like," he said.

Crickie smiled, speechless, while Margaret clasped his
arm a bit tighter in her own.

" 'Tis time for me to be on my way," Thomas said, scan-
ning the room. The rest of the guests were beginning the
next dance. "Morning's not far away and there's work to be
done."

"*Mais non,*" Borque objected. "Stay. Have a whiskey
with me."

"I thank you, but I can't." He nodded all around. "Ladies. Borque. G'night." Then, bidding the Forchers a good
night, he was gone.

"It is my pleasure to escort two such lovely young ladies
this evening. Surely you are the most beautiful ladies at the
ball," Borque said, patting Margaret's arm as he spoke, but
including Crickie in the compliment.

How often it went this way—Margaret was the reason for
the compliment and Crickie was included, politely. Her
eyes strayed to the doorway while Borque's were on Margaret, and her only concern was that her conversation with
Gairden had been too short. For her, the evening had come
to an end. Now, more than ever, she wondered when she
would see Gairden—Thomas—again.

Later, as Crickie and Margaret ascended the narrow stairs to the third floor, the first word out of Margaret's mouth was "Michel."

"You might have let Monsieur Borque take a few dances with the rest of us, Margaret," Lisette Forcher teased, scampering up the steps behind them. "After all, he should get to know people." Reaching the top of the stairs, she took her place between them, catching them both at the waist in a fond hug.

"You looked busy enough yourself with that friend of Jon's—William . . ."

"Leacock," Lisette finished for her. "Yea," she giggled, "I do hope he will stay with us awhile here in Charles Town before joining his family in Boston again."

"I'm certain you do," Margaret said, an air in her voice neither Lisette nor Crickie could miss. "Michel plans to stay at least," she said, her face placid and perfect as a mask.

"He does?" her sister asked. "How long?"

"Indefinitely," Margaret said. "He quite enjoys our company."

"What gentleman would not, when someone monopolizes his attentions." Crickie knew her words were sharp, but she was disheartened by this news.

"Are you speaking of me, sister?" Margaret asked, innocent.

"Yea, you, Margaret. Who else asked him for dance after dance? At Deborah's age I could tolerate it, but at your age it is not at all comely. Obviously Mother has not spoken to you about such behavior, but I—"

"Michel asked. Not I. Can I help it that he finds me appealing?"

"He asked?" Crickie eyed Margaret, whose face remained smooth as china. "Then I beg your pardon," she said as agreeably as she could. "Tell us all about William, won't you, Lisette?" she said, turning to her friend and changing the subject.

"Yea, won't you, Lisette?" Margaret asked, a smile of victory on her flawless face.

Crickie shrugged. Perhaps she'd been wrong. Perhaps Borque had a genuine interest in Margaret, and if her mother saw nothing wrong with it, why should she? Thomas Gairden was older than she, as well. And she hoped Mama would find nothing wrong in that, either.

13

"You're goin' to look at an indigo plantation?" Henry Jones asked. "There has to be something else—pretty lass, maybe?" he teased.

Thomas's eyes danced a bit, but he said nothing. He had no interest in crops and he'd made it clear enough over the years that his interest in plantations was purely financial. He kept his other interests to himself.

"So 'tis not blue dye but maybe blue eyes you're after," Jones ventured. "Ah, this is a change. I think you've seen about as many women as you have indigo plantations in the time I've known you. This one must be special."

"This *one,* as you call her, invited Gray to look at indigo processing. I'm just having a look at it myself before I send Gray. 'Tis not far from the city."

"Umm. I see," said Jones. "I can find out more talkin' to your loom than I can from you."

"If me looms could talk, they could tell some tales, Henry," Thomas said with a wink and a click of the tongue. He slipped into his jacket and adjusted his hat. "But alas, I've bought their secrecy. Look after 'em for me, will you?"

"You know I will," Jones said, "and Dugald, too."

"I thank you," Thomas said and was out the door.

Thomas hoped the note he'd sent last week with the Rawlinses' house servant, Dill, had arrived, and that he would be expected when he rode in today. After ferrying across the Ashley, he and Shuttle made their way along what was beginning to be a rather well-travelled road along the ridge of high ground that paralleled Wappoo Creek, then turned south and followed the Stono. Live oaks hung with moss, and white pine trees stood stately and quiet in the early morning air. A squirrel skittered in the fallen leaves to the side of the trail, his cheeks rounded with the fruit of a pecan tree nearby. Here and there a sign or a road marked the entrance to a plantation, the center of which was somewhere nearer the river, since all of them had originally been entered by water, and the rice and indigo fields were centered on the marshes and wetlands. All was quiet, and Shuttle's hooves made only muffled clip-clops as Thomas walked him slowly, taking in the faint warmth of the early December sun.

It was a little over an hour before Thomas saw the small sign marked HIGH GARDEN, CARLYLE RAWLINS painted with a single indigo plant at the bottom. Nudging Shuttle left down the sandy drive, Thomas felt a sudden urge to turn around. He knew very little of local crops, and would have a difficult time making it look as though he did. And that left Miss Rawlins, the eldest Miss Rawlins, the one with the strange name, the real reason for his visit. Like no one else except Sarah Roberts—Sarah Lowe, he reminded himself —Crickie Rawlins, despite her proper London schooling and wealth, seemed for some reason to take an interest in him, and though he wondered if her family might not consider him beneath her, he could not help the fact that he took an interest in her, too.

It was time to put Sarah behind him. Completely. He would never see her again. His affairs in Charles Town consumed long hours of each day. And even if he did go back, there was no guarantee she would still be there. Or that he would be welcome. In Crickie Rawlins he had found something lacking in every other lass he'd known since he left Bartram. Spirit, beauty, intellect—she had them, but it was more than that. Something intangible, yet something he felt drawn to no matter how elusive it might be.

Through the pine forest, through the forage acres and finally past the garden plots near the buildings, Thomas rode slowly, looking at the land, watching clouds drift across the pale sky. All seemed quiet. Nearer the barn only a few slaves were about—a cooper at work making barrels, women dipping candles at an outdoor fire. Three toddlers played nearby under the watchful eye of an older girl, but no others were to be seen. Coming closer, Thomas saw the reason why. Miss Rawlins had the older children assembled in a log building at the end of the row of Negro quarters, and through the window he saw that she was teaching them their numbers and letters.

"Bonjour, Monsieur Gairden," Borque called just then, waving broadly from in front of the stable. "Welcome."

"G'day," Thomas answered as Shuttle cantered easily toward him. "I was beginnin' to think no one was about."

"Have no fears, monsieur," Borque said. "Your message arrived and you are expected. Your partner could not come?"

"He hadn't time just now. Wanted me to come anyhow."

"Fine. And fine mount," Borque said, catching Shuttle by the bridle as he came near, then stroking him gently above the nose and down the long, proud neck. "How old is he?"

"Six years—nearly seven," Thomas said. "Bought him in Pennsylvania. Was a fine racer back there, too, but gettin' a bit old to compete with the horses here."

"So you bought some others for that purpose?" Borque asked.

"Two others. English. I've had some excitement with 'em, but Shuttle here will always be the favorite."

"Oui, it was your Spinneray that won the October race was it not?"

"Aye, he's a fine one, Spinneray," Thomas said, dismounting as Borque continued to hold Shuttle. "You have some fine ones yourself," he added.

"Ah, that is true, and in fact, I must go into Charles Town today for Evan Forcher has secured a shipment of the finest animals and I am to choose two for my stable. I regret that I will not be available to talk with you about the indigo growing, but Crickie, of course, knows as much as I, and will be happy to help you."

"I see," said Thomas, surprised that Borque should act so much the host here, rather than the guest. "Will you be takin' these fine horses back to Antigua with you when you go, or might a man have a chance to buy one?"

Borque paused, thinking. "I do not know," he said with

an unconcerned shrug of his narrow shoulders. "I have not thought about it, but I shall remember that you have asked. Should I wish to make a sale, I will contact you, have no fears." He smiled and his black moustaches rose and fell again. "I must be on my way, for Margaret and Deborah wait for me at the river, wishing to go along into Charles Town to buy a present for their mama for Christmas. We will be back by the sunset," he said. "Perhaps you will be here still?"

"Nay, I've only a short time to spend. My weavin' waits for me." Thomas caught Borque's look of distaste at the mention of his trade, and chuckled inside. It was a pleasure, at times, to see the gentry squirm at the idea of an artisan with coin of his own.

"Ah." Borque nodded his understanding of the statement through a fixed smile, then showed Thomas into the house before making his good-byes and hurrying down to the wharf.

Thomas had been seated in the library only a few moments when Dill helped Crickie's mother into the room to join him. Judith Rawlins had a fragile look about her, brittle almost, and her steps were tentative and slow. Thomas stood and bowed his head as he introduced himself.

"Sit down, Mr. Gairden," Mrs. Rawlins said. "I hear Irish in your voice, do I not?" There was no smile of warmth from the drawn face. Her veined hands fingered the polished arms of her chair nervously.

"A bit," Thomas conceded, "I'm a Scot by heritage. My people were transplanted to Ulster so the English could make a Protestant Ireland. It made us neither Scot, nor Irish, nor English while I was there. I think of myself as a Carolinian now. This is my home, as 'tis yours."

"London is my home," Mrs. Rawlins said, abrupt. Then, "You landed at Charles Town, as we did?"

"Nay, landed at Philadelphia over eight years ago, then lived four years in Pennsylvania before coming south."

"And what brought you to South Carolina?"

This was the question Thomas always swallowed hard on before he answered. "I thought I might find some family here," he had learned to say, and he repeated it now, "for I'd been told there were many Ulstermen in Carolina. My parents being gone several years, I hoped to find an uncle or some cousins here, but so far have not. Instead I found country and people to my liking, weavin' to be done . . . and a pleasanter winter than in Pennsylvania," he said, smiling as he added the last, for the mild winters were a source of pride to all Carolinians.

"Um," Mrs. Rawlins offered.

Thomas cleared his throat. The woman was not as genial as her daughter. "Your view of the river is a lovely one," he said.

Mrs. Rawlins nodded. Not easily flattered, Thomas thought, wondering what to say next.

"Elizabeth tells me you are a planter," she said, saving him the bother.

"Elizabeth?" Gairden asked.

"Yea—oh—Crickie," Mrs. Rawlins explained. "Her name is Elizabeth, but I seem to be the only one who calls her by it. Crickie is the nickname for her middle name, 'Crichton'—my maiden name. Her father gave it to her and it seems to have stuck. But since it was once my nickname, too, I am less fond of it."

"Elizabeth is a lovely name, Mrs. Rawlins," Thomas said, and for the first time caught the hint of pleasure on the face across the room. Thomas felt the grit of the freshly swept white sand beneath his shoe as he slowly twisted his foot back and forth, considering how to continue. "Well . . . anyway, aye, I'm a planter of sorts. I've a partner who runs the land. I run my business in the city. It works out well for both of us," he said. "We're about to take on more land, and your daughter has offered to have someone show us about High Garden to see how the indigo operation works. My partner couldn't come today, but I hope to take home some ideas with me. . . . I take it Elizabeth is busy just now?" he asked. Mrs. Rawlins showed pleasure once more in his use of her daughter's given name.

"She is giving ye children their lessons as she does each

day when she is not busy with other matters. I've told Johnson, ye overseer, to take you about. He waits for you on the veranda." Mrs. Rawlins stood, and Thomas stood as well, more than ready for the interview to be over.

"Thank you, Mrs. Rawlins, for the time and the help with this indigo business. That it's a good one, but a tricky one, your daughter's already told me. Still, as a weaver, I know 'tis an important one, too, and I hope to see it put to fields on my own land come spring. G'day."

"Good day, Mr. Gairden," she said, turning him over to Johnson and then calling for her maid to see her back to her room.

Thomas could not help but contrast her with her vital, vibrant daughter, and hoped he'd managed to hide his disappointment that his day should be spent with Johnson rather than with Crickie—who was now Elizabeth.

The full-bodied overseer and Thomas made a tour of the indigo plots. They were on their way to the number one processing station when Crickie came riding up behind them at full gallop, tendrils of her black hair flying free above her ears while her bonnet hung loose at her back. Slowing, she pulled up beside the red-bearded Johnson and leaned forward a bit in the saddle to speak across him to Thomas, who rode on the overseer's other side. She learned what had been covered, what he had yet to see, and apologized for having been detained with the children. No one, it seemed, had let her know Mr. Gairden had arrived.

"Johnson, you ride on ahead and open up the sheds for Mr. Gairden. He'll want to see it all."

The overseer did as he was told, leaving Crickie to walk her horse next to Gairden's as it caught its breath after the long run.

"Mama thought me rather bold to invite you and your partner here," she said in the way of an explanation for what she knew must have been her mother's cool reception of the unsuspecting Gairden. "She and Papa . . ." Crickie stopped. Mama and Papa are determined to pick a marriage partner for me? What was she thinking of? She could say nothing of the kind to Thomas. "She and Papa are a bit traditional in the area of manners."

"And yet they allow you much freedom in the management of High Garden . . . Elizabeth," he said, pronouncing her name slowly and distinctly.

Crickie shot a quick and questioning glance, then caught the inference. "So you've spoken to Mama. I had planned . . ."

"Aye. We had quite a little chat. She asked me my background and my occupation, and I asked her how 'Elizabeth' came to be 'Crickie'—a fair exchange, I thought."

Crickie colored, looking down to where her gloved hands held the reins to her favorite mare, looking at every stitch in the three rows of couching on the back of each glove, at the finely rolled hem that rode up above the wrist leaving only a little sleeve exposed below the fringe of her mantua. So he hadn't been put off by her mother's imperious manner.

"It was Papa's nickname for me, I suppose she told you. He thinks all little girls should have nicknames. Everyone else said it fit me because I jumped from thing to thing like a cricket."

"And do you? Are you prone to changes of heart?"

Crickie laughed. "Papa says I'm even more stubborn than he is—nay, I don't lose heart easily—but I do seem to have more interests, more energy . . . more something . . . than my sisters, and I do tend to go from field to schoolroom to kitchen to pettiauger while they are still busy with their first task of the day. But they are young," she said, quickly excusing them.

"And you are old? I think not," Thomas said approvingly. "Your sisters cannot be much younger than you, and one is not yet old enough to stay up for a ball."

"Margaret is but a year younger than I. Deborah is three years younger. But they've no interests outside ye house—"

"And no nicknames," Thomas concluded for her. "Elizabeth suits you, if I might say it, and I'll call you that if I may."

Thomas's melodic tongue had a way of making the name

sound completely different from the way her mother said it. And she was old enough to be Elizabeth instead of Crickie. "You may," she said, looking to him once again and finding that his smoky charcoal eyes were full on her. Familiar and yet not familiar.

"And what will your mother say about us ridin' along here together with no chaperone, Elizabeth?"

"Mama won't know. I'll tell her Johnson was with us—which he was—and she won't ask him about it, for she does not like speaking with him or ye Negroes. Eight years here, but because she's been confined to her room with a bilious fever so much of the time she is still not at ease with them, especially not the field hands. And Mama is . . . well . . . she has not seen people enough, she's been too ill until just lately and she's just sort of . . ." Crickie could not seem to find the words to describe the change in her mother of late.

"Sickness changes folks," Thomas said. "It changed me own mother. You don't have to say more."

"She talks of getting out more," Crickie went on, wanting him to understand, "but still she seems despondent at times. I worry for her, and yet I am short of temper with her." Crickie had never confided this before. There was release in it, and guilt.

" 'Tis the way with folks sometimes—but at least you have your parents, even though you may be angered at 'em now and again. I lost mine near ten years back."

"I'm sorry," Crickie said, hearing a residue of pain in his voice. "Mama is weak, and so different . . . but at least we've not lost her completely."

"I'd like her permission to . . ." Thomas cleared his throat. "To . . . call on you from time to time. Will she give it?" Thomas kept his eyes straight ahead as he spoke, and Crickie did the same, but as he waited for her answer, he turned toward her.

"There are many ways around Mama," she said, her eyes an invitation. "And the best way is through Papa. A letter to Papa from you, and one from me, will be all that is necessary, and at one word from Papa, Mama will be satisfied."

Crickie saw his skepticism and added with a smile, "Truly she will. It has worked before."

"Elizabeth," Thomas said, "ah, Elizabeth. Are you so used to havin' your own way that a man must be ruled by you?"

"I'm not of ye ruling sort, by nature. I've been ruler here at High Garden only by default and my father's love of ye army. And I've ruled in his heart, it seems, all my life, for my sisters hardly know him, having been away at school and then having him gone. I'm loyal to King George and obey his rule, but I'd rule no man—and have none rule me."

"Then a letter to your father it shall be," Thomas said, reining Shuttle to a stop and pulling him around so that he faced Elizabeth in the protection of a grove of pines between the fields and the higher ground of the processing stations. "And I shall pray each day that his answer's a yea."

Taking her gloved hand in both of his, Thomas held it for a moment as Shuttle stood loose reined but not moving. He looked into her eyes, then brought her hand to his lips, not quite touching it, but holding it there as the very soul of him in his eyes sought hers.

Crickie's hand had been kissed many times in her life, gloved and ungloved, but never before had she so wished that the moment would never end. Never before had the work of the plantation or the wishes of her family or her proper British background seemed so unimportant as they did this minute. Never before had she met anyone quite like this Thomas Gairden.

"I will pray also," she said, and Thomas released her hand in a slow, gentle motion.

"Then we will be surely blessed," he said, turning Shuttle once more, and resuming their slow pace.

"Surely," Crickie said, knowing the moment had to be over. Anything more would be improper. Improperly filled with joy as it was, Crickie broke the spell. "But now for more of your indigo lesson—and this is the hard part!" she said, lifting her proud chin and pressing her mare into a run.

At the sheds, Moss and his crew heard the laughter and

the pounding of hooves long before they saw the riders come up the trail.

"Miss Rawlins' not laughed like that since her Papa left," Moss said to the others. "It sounds good."

14

Thomas knew it was little more than two hours from Murry's Rope Ferry on the Santee to the door at River Plum Plantation. His route took him across the River Road, through a narrows in the pine swamp, then across the ripples at the source of Thorn Tree Brook, over the rapids at Stony Run, and finally on to the south bank of the mighty Black River, lined with swamps as it meandered its way to the Atlantic.

This country was a far cry from the Charles Town Parish, he thought, as he always did when he came up this way. The land was richer, drier. The rivers faster. The people poorer. Still River Plum Plantation, a fancy name for the thousand acres Alexander Gray ran with the labor of a dozen slaves here among the other Ulster Scots in the Williamsburgh District, was producing goodly amounts of rice, corn and wheat, along with fattening a few cattle and sheep.

Quarters for the plantation's few Negroes were in the form of five small, square cabins to the west of the house. The straight slope of the wide barn's roof stood to the east. Thomas felt the chill of an icy raindrop on his cheek and tied Shuttle before taking the steps two at a time and knocking loudly on the house's one elegant feature, a wide carved and panelled door.

He was struck once more by the contrast between River Plum and the Rawlinses' plantation at High Garden. Gray's log house was long, but only one room's width. The first floor contained only a spacious parlor and one bedchamber. The kitchen was housed in a separate structure to the back. Upstairs was one long room, large enough for three bedrooms but divided only by some heavy draping Thomas had woven.

The house was furnished surprisingly well with the English pieces Alexander's first wife had purchased from London—pieces that had helped drive them into a debt they
could not get out of. A large chest-on-chest stood proudly
in the parlor, along with a settee and two rush-seated arm-
chairs. A pair of tall brass candlesticks adorned a trunk
beside the settee, and a chinaware bowl sat next to them.
The dining table was of heavy mahogany, its matching
chairs detailed with carving as befitted a planter's house. In
the bedroom, though, the furnishings were local products,
native pine and oak now well-oiled from daily use.

When the door opened, Thomas found not Gray but a
young Indian girl wearing an ill-fitting English broadcloth
dress and a pair of what must have been Alexander's old
shoes. Probably no more than sixteen, she was thin and fine
boned, with the broad, flat face so favored by the Cherokees. Thomas had seen the way they kept babies' heads
pressed between specially-made flattening boards for the
first eighteen months of their lives to achieve this distinctive
look. He remembered how they liked to call white men
"long heads" and laugh.

"Where is Alexander?" he asked, not sure if she would
understand.

"Here," she said, barely moving her lips. She motioned
to his chamber. As Thomas stepped in, the girl clumped
away in the heavy shoes, her skirts dragging on the floor.

"Alex?" he called, hearing nothing, and wondering if the
girl had understood him after all. But then there was a
grunt from under the covers, and Thomas walked closer to
pull back the curtain around the bed.

Gray lay sunken in the middle of his straw tick mattress,
unshaven, his mouth slung open and his eyes half-shut.
Thoughts of smallpox were just about to seize Thomas
when the smell of whiskey caught his attention, and
Thomas realized his partner was not dying, just drunk.
Shaking and slapping the cheeks of the sotted Gray,
Thomas called his name.

"Alex! Alex!" he said, louder each time. "Alex. Wake up,
man! 'Tis Gairden and I've come one hell of a long way to

see about this land you've written of." Gray's eyeballs rolled languidly, fingers of red covering them all over. Eyelids saggy as a bloodhound's lay in loose folds over the sunken eyes. "Alex! Alex! I can't stay a week, man!" Thomas slapped Gray's blue-veined cheeks again, harder. "Come along, Alex, sit up now."

In one motion Gray shook his head and pushed himself up on his elbows, blinking his eyes purposefully as he groped for focus. "Thomas?" he asked, still blinking. "Where's Echoe?"

"If you mean the Indian girl, she's gone out. Wearin' your shoes, too, I might add."

"Aye, that she does. Found she likes 'em better'n her own now she's gettin' used to 'em." Gray belched once, then again, grumbling as he set about crawling out of the drooping middle of the bed.

"Where'd you get her, Alex?" Thomas wanted to know. He remembered that on their trip down the Wagon Road Gray had had quite an eye for the ladies. The idea of Echoe here did not surprise him. Bothered him, but did not surprise him.

"Tribe woman, upriver. Found her on me travels west for hides. Brought her home," he said, then belched loudly as he tightened the strings on his breeches. He mopped a handful of black and silver hair off his forehead, then held his hand tight at the back of his neck, pressing hard to fight a headache.

Thomas suddenly found himself wondering about the sanity of ever having lent money to such a man, much less of buying more land for him to manage. Still he had no complaints about the way Gray had managed so far. "Do you plan to keep her?" he asked.

" 'Til I can find a wife, I do," Gray replied, belching again as he stepped gingerly across the cold plank floor of the room in search of his socks. "Drinks like no woman you ever saw before. Too much. Gets wild then, like a demon. And, of course, she keeps me in bed half the day," he said with a chuckle. "None of these black wenches can match her there, I'll tell you, Thomas, though you can try one

yourself while you're here if you wants—you can try Echoe
if you wants."

Thomas lifted the corners of his mouth in a smile that
wasn't a smile and declined. " 'Tis business I've come on
and you know it, Alex," he told the sobering Gray. "But if
this is the way you're about to conduct your own business,
I'm not so sure I want it to be mine." Thomas looked him
full in the eye and saw Gray stiffen. "You know I could have
you run off this place for abusin' an Indian, not to mention
the Negroes. What's happened to you in six months' time?
What are you thinkin' of?"

"You sound like that damned Anglican preacher come
ridin' through here last month, tellin' all the Ulstermen
what low scum we are, how we stink of sin. Had the nerve to
ride to the meetin' house and say the same things . . ."
Here Gray paused. His face broke into a grin broadened by
inebriation. " 'Til some o' the boys decided to have a little
fun with him—set a few dogs on him while he was preachin'
and the like—and he rode out of here like he'd just seen the
Pope himself." Gray broke up in laughter. Thomas was less
amused.

"You're too damned serious for your own good,
Thomas," he concluded, his good humor gone to surliness
in the length of a sentence.

In the four years since Thomas had met Gray on the
Great Philadelphia Wagon Road, a crude wagon-wide trail
along the Appalachian Ridge from Pennsylvania into
northern South Carolina, Thomas had changed considerably. In the three months on the trail he'd gone from a
despondent runaway to an experienced colonial traveller,
and for much of that experience, he owed Alexander Gray.
Gray taught him the ways of the trail, the ways of the
Indians they met, and the ways of Indian trading he'd been
using for his ten years in the colonies.

But Gray had ideas of quitting the Indian trade, of settling down and getting rich, and he needed someone like
Thomas to help him. Land was the way to riches, he instructed the young weaver—no craftsman could get rich in
Charles Town. But Gray had a scheme to make one last big

trade with the Catawbas. He was willing to cut Thomas in if he'd help him, and then the two of them—partners, seventy/thirty—would apply for joint land grants in Charles Town, pretend joint ownership of a few slaves, getting fifty additional acres of free land for each one they bought, and would be well on their way to the riches Gray dreamed of.

Thomas had to admit, he'd looked the other way a few times as the wily Gray unrolled his plans a little at a time. Gray had weighted the deerskins they'd traded by leaving on hooves and horns. He'd given the Catawbas only watered whiskey and worthless trinkets. And he'd made up names of slaves they'd never bought and forged their bills of sale in order to get five hundred additional acres of land. In return for Thomas's help, he had given Thomas the profit from the first two years' crop on the five hundred acres in Thomas's name.

In the meantime, Thomas had his thirty percent of the deerskins he'd helped transport over some of the roughest country he'd seen since he'd left Pennsylvania, and with it he'd settled in the city, started his weaving manufactory just as he'd always planned, and he'd found he had a knack for trading, buying and selling, that made each ensuing year a more prosperous one for him.

While Thomas stayed single, Gray married and threw himself into debt to impress his new wife, and when in 1752 a hurricane stormed up the coast and flooded lands that had been dry for decades, Alexander Gray lost his wife and his crop. In debt, hopeless, he had once again prevailed upon Thomas as a partner, and once again Thomas had agreed, only this time it was Thomas who put the lion's share of the money into the operation and it was Thomas who would handle the money. It had worked out well, but Gray remained the same devil-may-care adventurer Thomas had met along the trail. He'd always taken solace in draggle-tail women. Now he'd added whiskey.

Thomas crossed the room to look out across the yard to the fallow rice fields near the river and the water beyond. Perhaps one day Gray would find a good woman and straighten himself out, he thought, though single women were scarce in the districts. In the meantime, Thomas knew he would have to take more responsibility for the plantation.

"I've got some new ideas for River Plum," he told Gray. "We're goin' to try some indigo."

"Indigo?" Gray howled, as if he'd never heard the word before. "Why indigo?"

"Because we can use the same Negroes to work it as we do for rice, just time it different. And because there's money in it, and some say it'll grow better here than in near Charles Town. I've brought seed for the spring crop with me, and we'll see to the fields while I'm here. Plus I've bought the five hundred and fifty acres to the back of this place, and we'll plant fifty acres of that, too. Same arrangements as here." Thomas looked to Gray with the sharp raise of his left eyebrow asking if the arrangements were still agreeable. Gray shrugged.

"We'll need more Negroes then. Clearin' the land is more than an afternoon's work, you know."

"I've done it. I know." Thomas remembered Bartram and the cutting of trees and burning of stumps, the plowing of ancient roots and rocks. The sheer exhaustion.

"Say how'd you get that land, anyway?" Gray asked, rubbing the back of his neck as he regained his faculties. "I thought 'twas owned by another of them Charles Town gentlefolk wantin' to buy land up here they never intend to use. I tried to buy it m'self when I bought River Plum."

" 'Twas part of Gabriel Manigault's holdin's—only a small part. He agreed to sell." Thomas's eyes continued to scan the muted gray-brown of the riverfront under the heavy December sky.

"Rubbin' elbows with some pretty fancy company now aren't you, laddie?" Gray chided.

"Don't trouble yourself about me affairs, Gray," Thomas said, ignoring the mean streak of drunkenness in his partner's voice. "You just keep runnin' things here and I'll manage the money so we'll both make a pound or two."

Finishing the difficult job of getting his sock on, Gray now placed his elbows on the table and rested his head in his hands. "You do that now," he said, "you just go on ahead and do that, though it seems you've got the best of it." He tilted his head just enough to see Thomas from the corner of his eye.

"That may be," Thomas said evenly, "but you'd have none of it if it weren't for me. You'd have been in a hut back up the trail somewhere if I'd not lent you money to keep goin' on. And when you're ready you can buy it back from me—I've no wish to be a planter. But I can't just give away what I've put me own money in either, can I now, Alex?"

Thomas did not exactly fear Gray, but he knew that, despite his tippling, the other man was bigger, stronger and infinitely tougher than he was. The thought that Gray might wish him out of the way crossed his mind and reminded him to be watchful when Gray was drunk. His look to Gray was both affirming and warning.

"I doubt it would harm you, Thomas," Gray said, lifting his head with some effort. "Still, we've cut a bargain. I'll keep my part of it."

"Good," Thomas said, nodding his agreement. "Tomorrow, then, we'll look at the new fields. I'll see you get an overseer and another man or two before spring plantin'."

It took most of the afternoon to go over the indigo plans with Alex, even though he sobered up quickly once he'd had something to eat. And Thomas thought he saw a spark of interest in Gray's eyes at the idea of doubling their investment return every three to four years, which Thomas had learned was the common rate for indigo planters. He knew Gray could handle it if he stayed sober long enough.

After Thomas saw to stabling Shuttle for the night, he brought his blanket to the house. Once more, Echoe was at the door.

"I'll be stayin' a night or two," Thomas said. "Sleep." He pointed to the blanket.

"Me?"

Thomas shook his head. "Nay, nay," he said quickly, trying to make her understand. "I sleep on the floor," he said, pointing. "You, sleep . . ." He shrugged his shoulders and continued to shake his head, as she shuffled to the fireplace, still wearing Gray's shoes, and stirred a pot of strong-smelling stew.

Weary from his journey, Thomas took a chair by the fire, closing his eyes as he slouched down, his long legs crossed at the ankle, the back of his head against the top rung of a sturdy ladder-back. The heat from the fire was like a sedative. Echoe stirred the fire and he heard the pop and crack of the new logs she lay on it before he began to doze. Soon, though, Gray was waking him for the late afternoon meal.

"Tired are you?" Gray asked. "Not used to ridin' so far. Where'd you spend the night?"

"Rice Bird Inn," Thomas said, washing down the hot stew with a swallow of ale.

"Crowded?"

"In a manner o' speakin'," Thomas said. "Five of us on the floor by the fire like a rug, 'twas. I'm scratchin' today, too—must've got the fleas from one of 'em."

" 'Tis better than sleepin' by the road, but not much," Gray observed, his mouth full as he chewed the stringy venison of the stew. "I've stayed in worse, though, up toward the Congarees and the Indian lands. Dirt floor, mangy dogs about, bread dry as a plank—a man has to be desperate for company to stay in such a place," he added with a wink to Thomas.

"Aye, I remember you as bein' rather desperate for company of the female sort, Alex," he said. "No change there, eh?"

"None at all that I can see." Gray laughed and slapped his knee, then poured another mug of whiskey. "And yourself?" he asked, tossing down a hefty gulp of the homemade brew.

"I'm busy with me work, you know that, Alex," he said, pretending complete innocence. "Work's me left-handed wife."

"The hell 'tis," Gray said, rejecting the excuse with a wrenching belch. "Good-lookin' lad like you has lots of ladies, I'll wager. Even this one's taken to you, I can see," Gray said, nodding to Echoe who sat on the hearth, eyes fixed on the fire.

"Not likely," Thomas said, uncomfortable at the girl's presence.

"I stayed a night up there past the Congarees with some folks said they knew you," he went on. "Lowe was the name. James Lowe. Know him?"

Thomas drew back slightly, surprised.

"Down from Pennsylvania like yourself, he said." Gray's tongue smacked inside his mouth as he chewed and talked at the same time.

Thomas's chewing stopped. "You're sure that was the name?"

"I'm sure 'twas James. I talked to him quite some time. I think the wife was Sarah. Had three wee bairns. Just made a claim to some of the free lands up there."

"And how'd you find they knew me?" Thomas wondered.

Gray thought a minute. "Mentioned your name just as I was leavin'. Told him me and my partner, Gairden, might be back to look for some land thereabouts. He asked about the name. I told him what I knew, that we'd met on the Wagon Road a few years back, that you'd made yourself some money in Charles Town and we were partners."

"What kind of place did they have?" Thomas asked.

"House. Half a barn. Cow pen. A few pigs. That's about all," Gray said. "Like everybody else from here to Rock Dell, they're sick of havin' the choice land around 'em picked up by the low-country planters while they're left with the poorer sort, and no votes in the Assembly. They took me for a fine Charles Town gentleman," Gray said with a laugh.

"Did they now," Thomas observed. "Well, you do have a way about you," he said, remembering that once he, too, had thought Gray of the better sort. Perhaps once he had been. Thomas didn't know much about his past.

"Lowe's a feisty one," Gray went on as if Thomas hadn't spoken. "Said none of us'll get decent roads, or protection from the Indians or anythin' else as long as the parishes control the Assembly, and I had to agree with him. Shared a jug, we did," Gray said, as if this gave credence to the idea.

"And he's no doubt right about that," Thomas said, talking of government while he thought about himself. "I've heard it spoken of in Charles Town, too, for there are a few planters willing to let others in. There are many, though, who think they must run it all to suit the King so as to curry his favor, and who care little for the rest of the people. They see to their own interests first."

"Aye, a greedy lot they are."

Thomas nodded absently, looking off toward the horizon where the sun hung low against the almost white of a December snow sky. There was bad weather ahead, he thought, and not just what the sky promised. If enough men like Gray banded together against the rich, low-country planters, the Assembly would have a storm of its own to weather. Thomas would have to stand with Gray, no matter how many friends he had in Charles Town. The backcountry folk, all that stood between the Indians on the frontier and the dignity of Charles Town society, were entitled to be heard, and if the Ulster Scots of Williamsburgh were like the Ulster Scots Thomas had known at Bartram, they would make themselves heard, by whatever means was necessary. They were a scrappy lot, he thought, remembering Gray's tale of the Anglicans with a smile.

"What news did Lowe have of Bartram?" Thomas asked, wondering just how much they'd talked. So far his past had not followed him to Carolina.

Gray thought a moment. The conversation must have been a bit hazy in his mind. "None that I can remember. We spoke mainly of the Cherokees and their troublemakin'. Lowe's done some Indian fightin' in his life, he says."

"So he has, eh?" Thomas said. "Close to home?"

"Some, I fear. Indians prowlin' about day and night, he told me, not likin' it that folks are farmin' their huntin' grounds. 'Tis like it was here when I first came. Give 'em a few years, it'll be a good place . . . if they stay. Sounded to me like they've been on the move a bit—took over a claim in Virginia for a while, now here." Gray shook his head, but Thomas knew that a certain degree of wanderlust tickled Gray's fancy from time to time as it did every other man who wondered what was over the next hill, and the next.

"His wife asked after you," Gray told him. "Looked a might older'n him—got religion bad. Still a pretty one, though," Gray added with the wink of a practiced eye.

Despite its lewd implications, Thomas was relieved at the last comment. If she was still pretty, perhaps life with Jamie hadn't been too hard on her. But he couldn't ask about that.

"Do they have a church yet?" The Williamsburgh Presbyterians had built a church within months after the first settlers had come. The building was also used as a school. Presbyterians were set on the importance of worship and education, and sometimes the building of the church came before their own houses were even finished.

"Not Presbyterian, that I saw. 'Twas Baptists, I believe, the Lowes were. New Light Baptists."

"Baptists? I doubt that," Thomas said, shaking his head. "The ones I knew were raised Presbyterians and would not falter. You've got 'em confused with someone else." Still, Gray said Sarah had asked after him. That would be like her. So like her.

"Why not take a trip up there?" Gray asked. " 'Twas a two-day trip, no more. I'll go with you. We stay a couple of days, see your friends. Maybe steal you a little wench like Echoe here for your fun. See the land—'tis good land, I tell you, Thomas. Some we get free, some you buy . . ." Gray paused, yawning. "Remember how we did it last time?" He looked hard into Thomas's tired eyes, and Thomas saw that Gray's eyes were shrewd and foxlike at the thought of such a project. He was a schemer, no doubt about that. "We can sit on it as well as those Charles Town lads can," Gray added, throwing back his shoulders and straightening at the idea. He waited for Thomas to answer.

"Well . . . I don't know." Thomas shrugged, stumbling about for an excuse. The idea of having Sarah Roberts—Sarah Lowe—within such easy distance unsettled him in a way he could never have predicted. Having tried for nearly five years to put the sight of George Braid's bloody corpse out of his mind and having finally almost succeeded, Thomas now saw it anew. Wondered what Sarah thought of him? Wished he'd explained it all to her. Remembered why he hadn't. The past was again part of the present.

Gray persisted. "They're waitin' on you, Thomas. Acted anxious to see you again," he said. "I told 'em we'd be comin' back that way soon."

"Another time, Alex. 'Tis too far to go . . . in December, especially. And you'll have your work cut out for you in the new fields. . . . I've got work waitin' for me in the city. And as you said, maybe some land hereabouts is more what we need now we know 'tis the indigo business we're headin' for. More land, more expense. And we need to keep our spendin' down if it's money we're to be makin'. Nay, we can't go now."

We can't go at all, he thought. Not unless I want to risk being accused of murder. Hard telling what Jamie might say. He did not need old wounds opened once again. And he certainly had no desire for the Indian wenches Gray kept offering him.

Then there was Elizabeth Rawlins. A year ago no one could have told him anyone would ever replace Sarah in his heart, but as he sat geographically between the two of them, it was toward Elizabeth he wished he could ride yet tonight. She was the confidant he'd not had since he'd left Bartram. Like Sarah she had a spirit that touched something deep inside him. She was a part of this new life he'd made for himself—the life he'd always promised himself. He hoped she'd be a big part. His wife.

He'd written a letter asking her father's permission to court her and sent it on the schooner *New Elder* a fortnight back. One from Elizabeth had gone on the same vessel. He'd sent copies on two other schooners as well, for ships could easily be lost in storms, or to pirates.

He and Elizabeth had managed to see each other the past two Sundays, meeting in the High Garden parlor the first time, by the river, secretly, the next, since they had no permission to court as yet. She'd told her mother she was going out for a Sunday ride as she often did, but this time her ride had delivered her into his arms. They'd been as comfortable together as old friends. Eager for each other's touch as young lovers should be. The memory of her kiss lingered with him. Filled him.

How odd that news of Sarah should come just now, he thought, then brushed it aside. She was a wife, with children and a home of her own. Soon, he hoped, he would be a husband, with a real family at last. He thought of the house he planned to build in Charles Town. Of the new manufactory he was planning. Of the life he and Elizabeth Rawlins would build together. It was the life he had wanted once for Sarah, the life he'd once thought only she could complete.

"You're makin' a mistake, lad," Thomas heard Gray telling him later that evening as they sat by the fire. "You should take time to go back up to the Cherokee country with me. You could be addin' to your riches if you'd let me help you," Gray was saying, his tongue once again thick with whiskey. But Thomas was only half listening. His mind was on Elizabeth. On Sarah. On what was, might have been, would be.

"Another time maybe, Alex. Spring, perhaps," Thomas said, putting him off. "Tomorrow we'll stake out the new ground and figure up what we need for the vats and all." He paused at the door before he went out to relieve himself before bed. "You'd best get some sleep."

Closing the door behind him, Thomas blew out a deep breath. His heart pounded. Jamie and Sarah must not have told Gray about Ena's death. Or George's. Why not? Why by the grace of God not?

In the raw wind of the December evening, Thomas stood for a moment looking west. How I loved you when we were young, Sarah, he thought, before life lost its innocence that stormy afternoon in your father's barn. I was wrong to run. But I wasn't wrong in killing George Braid. I'll never believe I was, no matter how it may have looked. I'm asking for a second chance now with Elizabeth. And I'm asking you to forgive me, Sarah. Somewhere in your heart, please forgive me.

15

With only two days left before Christmas, Crickie was barely able to find enough hours in the day to do all the things she wanted to do. She had set Margaret and Deborah to helping Polly the cook make sweet potato tarts flavored with lemon and orange to be passed out as special treats for all the slaves on Christmas Day. Nuts and fruits for the fruitcakes were chopped as the cooks waited for each ovenload of tarts to finish, and mincemeat pies and plum puddings would eventually take their place in the list of delicacies to be prepared.

Crickie, meanwhile, checked the supply of hair ribbons for the ladies and handkerchiefs for the men and small toys for the children that would be distributed on Christmas morning before the day was spent roasting racks of spareribs and fresh pork chops. Thanks to the fabrics she'd been able to purchase from Thomas, new clothes for all the servants and hands had been sewn these past weeks, and on Christmas morning all eighty-six High Garden Negroes would be dressed for the celebration.

Excitement filled her, especially when it came to cutting greens for the house, her favorite part of the celebration. Taking young Mully, the houseboy, to help her, she cut branches of white pine and pruned her holly trees of shoots dotted with red berries. Drupes of scarlet berries from the yaupon bushes that grew around the house came next, followed by a whole pile of glossy-leafed myrtle. Then Crickie sent Mully scurrying to the top of an oak tree just beyond the house where each year some mistletoe was cut to hang in the front hall.

"Cut a nice big piece," she called up to Mully.

"Yea, Miss Crickie!" the young boy's reply came, eager

and full of anticipation. Crickie heard the smile in his words and smiled back, though he could not see her. "Hurry," she called, shifting from foot to foot as she waited. There was much to do, and yet the day could not come soon enough to suit her.

Her mother watched from the parlor as Mully and Dill toted in huge baskets of greenery, which Crickie directed to various parts of the house she would be decorating.

"We'll be doing no entertaining during ye holidays," her mother said. "I see no reason to make such elaborate preparations. Perhaps next year when I'm able—"

"Yea, then we'll have some parties, but for now, this is just the way I remember Christmas in London, and it's so much fun to bring it here. The smell in the house from ye greens and ye cooking is just too good to miss."

"But we've never done all this in Carolina . . . although I suppose we should see that we observe our customs for Monsieur Borque's sake. I'm certain he'll enjoy seeing the differences in our customs and his own."

"Do you suppose he misses his home?" Crickie asked, wondering if perhaps her mother knew something about Borque's plans.

"He makes no mention of it, if he does. I think he rather likes it here."

"Yea, he seems to," Crickie agreed dryly. Her mother caught the inference.

"We must think of him as your father's guest, nay—as your father's envoy for now. It will make ye Christmas pleasanter to have a man about to help with gifts for ye Negroes."

"I suppose," Crickie said, just stepping down from the ladder as she finished fastening the mistletoe to the center of the pewter chandelier in the hall. Mama was in favor of anything that helped her keep her distance from the slaves. "But I think we've done quite well without him these past years."

"That may be," her mother said emphatically. "But this year we have him, and we must include him."

"He's invited some friends out from Charles Town for

Christmas dinner, you know," Crickie informed her mother, aware that she didn't know. "A young French couple he met at York Course, new here, with no family, and our neighbors ye Youngs. I've asked Mr. Gairden to come as well."

"Mr. Gairden? Elizabeth, dear, surely you've no interest in such a man with no family." Judith rubbed her hands back and forth, half wringing them, half warming them.

"He's written to Papa asking to call," Crickie said as she stood resting one hand on the ladder and the other on her hip. "And I've written to Papa as well. I intend to see Thomas Gairden. He has ambition and a good mind, Mother, more of both than ye other callers you and Papa have selected for me. And as for family, he cannot help it that his parents died and forced him to make his own way in the world. He's done well for himself in Charles Town. And he's just purchased more land in the Williamsburgh District. Why, even now he will have a house built in Charles Town. He's a man of some means, all gotten by his own hand."

"I don't approve," Judith said. "He's smitten with your position, not you. These people of the middling sort hope by marriage to better themselves. They—"

"Do you not think that people of every sort hope to better themselves by marriage? Why is it that every suitor you and Papa send my way seems to be of a better sort than we?" Crickie felt her heart pound inside her.

"We want only the best for you, dear," Judith said. "That is all." The look of her mother's eyes told Crickie she wished the conversation to end.

"What's best for me, Mother, is to let me make my own choices, just as I've had to do in these years while Papa has been gone. I've made good choices these past three years. Papa knows that. Trust that I may take the same care in making the choice of a mate—which Mr. Gairden may never—"

"It is my rest time," her mother said, cutting her off. She rose and excused herself, leaving Crickie to finish decorating the hall, her cheeks nearly as red as the holly berries

that dropped here and there from boughs placed over door-
ways and mirrors. At least she hadn't forbidden him to
come, Crickie thought. But how would she behave toward
him? Perhaps inviting him had been too bold. Perhaps she
should have waited for Papa's letter. Perhaps she should
have lied and told her mother Borque had invited
him. . . .

No, she had done the right thing. She had spoken the
truth to her mother, she had confronted rather than cod-
dled her, and now she would have to see that it all went
well. Thomas would help with that.

The holly tied in place with red ribbons, Crickie finished
by tying several stems of mistletoe in the center, then
stepped down to admire her work. It was all she had hoped
—just like the Christmases she remembered in London.
And waiting for Christmas this year would be almost as
hard as when she was a little girl in London, too.

Cries of "Christmas gift, Christmas gift" woke Crickie this
morning as they had every Christmas she'd been in Carolina. It was the custom for all the slaves to gather under the
master's window to ask for presents. At High Garden, for
the past three years, that window had been Crickie's, and as
was the custom she opened her window and called back
"Christmas gift after breakfast!" at which time the slaves,
except for the house staff, gathered at a huge bonfire lain
the day before to fry the fresh bacon and eggs that were
special treats each year.

The morning flew by. Crickie distributed the new clothes
and small "Christmas gifts," then served a dram of rum to
the men and ale to the women, all the while watching the
road and the river. It was not until almost two o'clock that
she saw a pettiauger slip noiselessly up to the wharf carrying four of the guests. Margaret and Borque hurried down
to greet them. Crickie stayed in the house to call her
mother from her rest, and to oversee the last of the preparations for the feast table she and her sisters and the cooks
had been preparing for days.

Crickie entered the hall from the back of the house just

as Borque and Margaret were ushering the guests in through the front door. Dressed in a new green lutestring gown trimmed with pale Flanders lace, Crickie noticed at once that the deep green of Thomas's knee-length coat and breeches matched her well.

"Be careful where you stand," Margaret said, "or you might find yourself under some mistletoe." Stopping to loosen her cape, she stood directly beneath it. Edward Young, her neighbor, was quick to give her a peck on the cheek. Thomas followed. Georges Ghiselin, Borque's friend from Charles Town, was next. Borque finished the lineup. Crickie watched as Margaret fawned and giggled.

"Welcome, and a blessed Christmas to you all," she heard herself saying, hoping to draw attention away from her sister, who was stepping even nearer to Borque, poising herself for another kiss. "Mama," Crickie called, wishing her mother would hurry and join them. She was never around to witness Margaret's thoughtless behavior.

Borque's lips had barely left her sister's cheek, and his eyes had not left Margaret's eyes, when Judith Rawlins finally arrived but appeared not to notice. Her gait was slow and halting, but her carriage elegant and majestic. At once, Crickie began to make introductions, hoping to divert her mother's attention from Thomas.

Borque's guests, Georges and Marie Ghiselin, were smartly dressed, and their two-year-old daughter, Celeste, wore a pale blue frock fine enough for a princess. Her long, dark sausage curls framed a chubby-cheeked, blue-eyed face. The fine Brussels lace of her collar set off her clear white skin like a tiny Christmas angel, and Crickie felt a rush of pleasure as Thomas scooped her up in his arms, carried her to the mistletoe and gave her a gentle kiss of her own.

"We've made friends on the trip out from Charles Town haven't we now, Celeste?" he asked the little girl who looked at him, bright-eyed, and squirmed to get back down.

"Oui, she *has* found a friend in you, monsieur," Marie Ghiselin agreed, taking the little girl by the hand to keep her from running off through the house on her own.

". . . and I believe you know Monsieur Thomas Gairden," Borque was saying to Judith Rawlins as Thomas and Marie were speaking.

"I do. A blessed Christmas, Mr. Gairden," she managed to say.

"And my warmest Christmas greetings to you and your family, Mrs. Rawlins," he said, reaching above him and picking a small sprig from the mistletoe. Then he took her hand as if to kiss it, but with the other hand held the sprig over her head and kissed her cheek instead. "Merry Christmas," he said, smiling.

"Why . . ." Words were lost to the flattered and surprised Judith Rawlins, but the rest of the small group in the hall joined in laughter and a round of hugs and kisses for her. A nobleman at court could not have handled her more smoothly, Crickie thought, watching him charm her. Inside, of course, she wished she had been under that sprig of mistletoe, but outside she kept a discreet distance from Thomas so as not to jeopardize in any way her chances of her mother's approval of their future courtship. Still their eyes met here, there, and spoke a secret language.

"The Ghiselins," Borque explained as they went in for dinner, "are sugar planters like myself. They have come from Jamaica to Charles Town for business and pleasure."

"And that pleasure is the horses, is it not?" George Ghiselin replied, raising the glass of wine Dill offered him in a toast to Borque.

"Ah, oui. To horses, and to Charles Town," Borque said, raising his glass in an arc about him, including the others in the toast.

"Charles Town," came the response.

"And we hope you will all stay in Charles Town," Deborah put in, her words, of course, meant for Michel Borque, who so captivated her youthful imaginings.

"Thank you, thank you," Marie Ghiselin said. "We do feel so very welcome here."

Deborah smiled politely, then gave Margaret a surreptitious sisterly look.

"Please take your places, everyone," Judith Rawlins announced to Crickie's surprise. Mother was not only joining them at the table, she was hostessing as well. Borque and her mother took the seats at the table's ends, and Margaret scurried to Borque's left, Thomas sat to his right. Crickie sat in her usual place, to her mother's right, which put her as far away as possible from Thomas, but in his full vision. And she felt very close to him just then, felt a touch of what it might be like if someday . . . But the small talk of the meal diffused such thoughts.

The holiday feast of terrapin stew and boned turkey, smoked capon and pheasant, oyster pudding and every manner of creamed vegetable, pastries and cakes was served in the High Garden dining room on the table Crickie had made Mully polish for over two hours yesterday. The sideboard, festooned with boughs and berries, held still more tarts and sweets, along with Judith Rawlins's crystal punch bowl, steaming with warm rum punch.

"We've prepared a traditional London holiday meal for you," Judith explained to the Ghiselins, "though of course it contains some Carolina specialties, too. Elizabeth sent to London for chestnuts and spices, and had the capon specially dressed by a butcher in Charles Town. You realize, of course, that while life in the colonies is very pleasant, we will return to London one day. In the meantime, we try to maintain tradition."

Crickie caught Thomas's glance. Back to London? They'd not discussed this, of course.

"We may not all go back to London," Crickie said before her mother could go on. "I, for one, should very much miss High Garden were I forced to leave it. London holds no special appeal for me."

"I should love to go to London again," Deborah was quick to add in a dreamy tone. "I should love ye endless shopping, ye rows of milliners' shops, ye gowns . . ."

"Ah, but you have such fine things here in Charles Town," Marie Ghiselin said. "Your city is growing before our very eyes. Jamaica is a very sleepy place by comparison."

"I'm sure it is," Judith agreed, her own biases firmly in

place. "My husband is quite content in Antigua, but I fear it not at all to my liking."

"One day these colonies will be a fair match for London, if they aren't now," Thomas said. His words had a way of cutting through generalizations. "Already Philadelphia is the second largest city in the British lands, and our Charles Town third."

"But still, London is the center of it all. Without ye Crown there would be no colonies," Judith said, straightening proudly on her seat.

"Aye, 'tis so," Thomas agreed, "but as we grow here on this side of the Atlantic, 'tis becoming somewhat a case of the tail waggin' the dog now isn't it?"

While the rest of the table laughed heartily at the analogy, Judith Rawlins failed to see its humor.

"The power of ye Crown circles the globe, young man," she said. "Carolina is but a part of it—a small part at that— but England will always be home." Her tone was pleasant, but firm.

"Ulster was my home, as you know, Mrs. Rawlins," Thomas said, without rancor. "Scotland was my family's home before that. But now I've lived in the colonies eight years, and though I sometimes miss the green rollin' hills or the old churches, this is now my home and were I to go back there I would miss the warm Charles Town evenings, the live oaks, the mix of folks who live here. Maybe I'm too much of a traveller, but I find home's where you make it."

"Exactly!" Borque broke in, exuberant. "Life in the islands has its own flavor, but here, too, I find much that is pleasing to me, have no fears."

Agreement rippled around the table, but Judith Rawlins stood her ground. "You are young," she said. "When you are my age, your ideas may well be different. Still it is fitting that no matter where we are or where we plan to go we remember our King. God save the King!" she said, lifting her glass.

"God save the King," the others rejoined, but Crickie did not hear Thomas's voice booming among them. She looked his way, and he raised his glass, just a trifle, to her.

The afternoon passed far too quickly to suit Crickie, before the party once again made its way to the hall, gathering mantuas and cloaks to bundle for the cool river trip back to the city. Borque invited them all to stay, as Crickie found herself wishing they would despite the fact that no rooms were readied for overnight guests. Little Celeste, however, was tired and begging to go home, and Thomas pleaded the need to be back for work the next day, and so the party continued its preparations to leave. Then, bidding their good-byes, they made their way down the brick path to the landing with Crickie, Margaret, Deborah and Michel to see them off. Out of sight of Mother, Crickie was at last able to have a word with Thomas.

" 'Twas a fine table you set in there," he told her as he offered his arm when they set off down the path. "The finest Christmas meal I've ever tasted, in fact."

"I hope you'll come for many more meals at High Garden, Thomas," Crickie said, drawing his arm tighter into her own.

"And I," he agreed. "For now, I must be gettin' back to my work. Mackay and I are backlogged, and I'm bound to hire an overseer to help my partner, Gray. Forcher's found me someone he thinks may take the job and I'm to talk to him tomorrow, too."

"When will I see you?" Crickie whispered, squeezing his arm just a bit closer.

"How soon will your mother let me come back?" he asked, his eyes roving restlessly across hers and over her face and down her slender neck to where lace ruffles were held in place by a jeweled brooch.

"Mama was most pleased with the linen cloth from your shop, as I was with the laces you brought for me—"

"And not so pleased when I suggested the colonies might be a better place than London," Thomas said. "I'm sorry, Elizabeth, I spoke too boldly. 'Tis just my way sometimes. And 'tis hard to hold me tongue about the Crown when I see the ways the Crown is usin' us over here to fatten coffers in London."

"No apology needed. And anyway, most talk of politics

or business is of no interest to Mama. All she cares of is
allegiance to ye Crown, and as long as that's not in question, she carries no ill will."

"She carries a bit more allegiance than I do, Elizabeth,"
Thomas said, looking down into her eyes as they strolled
along, "and you may as well know that. I'm no treasoner—
don't worry—but I'll not sit back and take whatever's
dished to us from London either. We deserve our rights just
as any other Englishmen—maybe even more so, for we're
the ones takin' the risks here across the drink."

Crickie patted his hand. "I am not worried in the least
that you're a spy or a pirate or anything of the kind. . . .
I'm only worried about seeing you again. Soon."

They stopped, lagging behind the rest of the party, and
Thomas turned to her, kissing her slowly, tenderly, on the
lips.

"Mistletoe," he murmured, looking up. Crickie looked
up, too, and saw nothing but a dark sky overhead, lit by a
single evening star.

"Mistletoe?"

" 'Tis up there somewhere," he said, taking her arm once
more and continuing toward the dock where the Ghiselins
were already climbing on board. "With luck, perhaps, a
letter from your father will arrive before the February
races."

"Surely there will be a schooner in from Antigua within
the month. And when it comes we will come to Charles
Town for ye races and balls, and you will come here for
riding and—"

" 'Twill be a long wait," he said, stopping a few feet behind the others and taking her hand in his. "I'll be back as
soon as I can."

"Promise?" Crickie asked, raising one eyebrow. Knowing
the answer.

"Elizabeth Rawlins," he said, turning so that his back was
to Borque, who was speaking in rapid French to his own
departing guests, "I told you once before I don't promise
what I can't deliver. I'll be here." He raised her hand to kiss
it, his eyes never leaving hers until the moment his lips

touched her skin. He closed his eyes then, and for a moment Crickie closed hers, both savoring the moment.

"Gairden, good wishes for the new year," Borque said,
extending his hand as he stepped between them to make his
farewells. Margaret stood by, watching.

"Thank you, Michel," Thomas said, "and to you. We will
see you at York in February no doubt."

"Have no fears," Borque assured him. "It is the finest
racing of the year they tell me."

" 'Tis fine," Thomas concurred, nodding. "Even those
who care little for racing find the February races a time of
special gaiety in the city," he said. "Am I right, Elizabeth?"
he asked, his eyes holding hers.

"You are so very right," Crickie answered, filling her
words with meaning only Thomas could understand.

"I shall be ready then!" Borque announced with his usual
vigor.

"And I, too," Thomas agreed. "Deborah, Margaret, Elizabeth, Michel—my thanks for a fine Christmas," he said,
stepping down into the stern of the pettiauger. Moonlight
on the creek made for little need, but Georges Ghiselin
held up the customary pine knot torch to guide them on
their way.

Crickie heard the gulp of a paddle eddying the water
before the craft rode silently down the waterway, then
watched until the glow of the torch went out of sight around
the Townshend point. Margaret's hoops were already
swinging happily up the path, budged against the white
stockinged leg of Michel Borque, when Deborah and
Crickie left the landing and started toward the candlelit
windows of the house.

"Wasn't little Celeste adorable?" Deborah asked. "Leave
it to Michel to invite the gayest company to our table."

"Umm," Crickie said, only half listening.

"Mr. Gairden was quite fine, too," Deborah went on,
"for a mechanic or whatever he is. Did he kiss you?" she
wanted to know.

Crickie flashed her older-sisterly look of disapproval.

"Did he kiss *you?*" she asked, knowing Thomas had given her a peck on the cheek during the greetings in the hall.

"Yea," Deborah admitted, "but only under the mistletoe."

"Well, that is the only place he kissed me," she said, immensely satisfied to be lying and not lying at the same time, for surely if Thomas said there was mistletoe above them, there was. And while Deborah chattered on, Crickie recalled the touch of his lips, and even more, the touch of a kindred soul. She had, indeed, received a magnificent "Christmas gift" herself.

16

"I was afraid you hadn't gotten my note," Crickie said as Thomas rode into the white pine grove three days later. She'd been waiting for nearly a half hour in this, their secret meeting spot, wondering what could have gone wrong. She made no sound as she ran to meet him, her slippers skimming the brown carpet of needles on the floor of the grove. A cool breeze rustled the wispy needles of the pines, but the afternoon sun was warm and a jay sang overhead.

"Me man Dugald received it from your servant—and held it back on me as a prank. I'm sorry I'm late." Stepping down easily from Shuttle's back, Thomas took her small hands in his and kissed them lightly in turn. "So cold, Elizabeth," he said at her touch, and drew her hands between his, rubbing them slightly. "I'll have to see that Mackay pays dearly for this bit of deviltry."

"He's got to have his fun, too," Crickie said. "I know you give him ample reason in teasing him about his Mary."

Her black eyes shone with delight as she spoke, and Thomas drew her hands to his lips, blowing puffs of warm breath on them, then kissing them once again, before he slipped his hands beneath her cloak and drew her close. Her hands clasped about his neck, she met his lips eagerly. Each day since Christmas she had thought of little other than being close to him once more, of the tender way he touched her, of the soft cocoon that seemed to form around them when they were together.

"The kiss under the mistletoe wasn't enough, was it, lass?" he said when their lips parted long enough for them to catch their breaths. "For me either. 'Twas hard to act the friends when 'tis much more we've become to each other. . . . I love you, Elizabeth," he said, holding her, his lips

tasting of her cool cheek, her ear, a tendril of black hair
that smelled of rose water, the curve of her neck, warm
inside her cloak's high, red velvet collar. She slipped the
button of the velvet cape and felt it drape noiselessly to the
ground behind her. She needed no cloak. And she wanted
nothing between them. Thomas read her message, and the
two of them eased down to the soft bed of needles, gently
loosening buttons and ties as their lips explored each
other's newness. Elizabeth felt the cloak's silky softness on
her skin as Thomas drew it up to cover them. No stiff
petticoat had ever sent such sensation through her.

Against him, her tiny body was alive and her every movement spoke a message to him that he answered wordlessly
in the hour that passed between them there in the privacy
of the pine grove, a half-hour's ride from the big house at
High Garden. This was their own garden, where love grew
between them.

"If only we could stay all day—and night—in a fairyland
such as this, Thomas. I'd wear a silken gown so thin it could
be woven by none but an elf, and you'd be my prince in rich
velvet and ermine collar. We'd do naught but love," she
said, her lips skimming the black hair of his chest as they lay
resting in each other's arms.

"We will, Elizabeth—and soon, but not near soon
enough to suit me. 'Tis enough to want to make me hire an
elf in place of Dugald to weave such a garment—though in
our marriage bed you'll have no need of such a thing—just
as you are will be most satisfactory." Propped on one elbow, Thomas lay content, his hand absently caressing the
gentle slope of torso, waist and hip that was part of the
wonder of this Elizabeth.

She blushed a proper English blush. "I want none, either," she said. "Those who truly love, as we do, have no
need of finery between them—though, of course, we'll want
finery for our wedding."

Thomas smiled at the bright eagerness of her face, at the
honesty of her love for him. "We'll have all the finery the
Sign of the Shuttle can make or buy. Be thinking of what 'tis

you want, and I'll see to it . . . Christmas next, perhaps? A nice time for a weddin'?"

"A lovely time—but must we wait so long?" She snuggled in close, and he put his arm around her, so filled with her that time had no meaning. There was no today or tomorrow, this month or next. Only now.

"We must do only as we please, and as it pleases your parents, once we've the letter from your father. But I do love you in this scarlet cloak, your white skin against the soft shadows of the velvet—I love the winter look of you only because I've not had the glory of the summer look of you."

Another blush. "I love you, Thomas," she said. "I can't say it enough now I've said it once. I love you. I love you. I—"

"I love to hear it," he said, kissing her lips to stop the words, "but there'll be no weddin', no finery, if we're not careful with our meetings. We've been here too long already, I'm afraid, for the sun's now lower—dinnertime, or past. You must get back."

"Yea, though cook is used to my odd hours and won't suspect."

" 'Tis not cook that worries me. 'Tis your mother's suspicions, should she have any." Thomas stood and brushed his breeches, then extended a hand to Elizabeth and helped her straighten her clothes and brush them as well. He fastened the cloak about her shoulders and pressed one last kiss to her lips.

"Sunday?" she asked, smiling broadly while he mounted Shuttle.

"In the parlor. With your mother. I wouldn't miss it," he said smiling back, and blew her a kiss as he cantered off and out of the pine grove where the breeze was now a wind that whistled in the branches, but never lifted a needle from the pine carpet where Elizabeth stood watching him go. Three more days until Sunday. Once again time became real for Thomas.

* * *

In each of the days that followed, through New Year's, and Little Christmas and well on into January, Crickie watched the river. On her way to bind the cut hand of the slave Frederick, wounded when his end of a two-man saw slipped and gashed across his left palm, she looked to the river. On her way to see to the digging of furrows for the spring indigo crop, she looked to the river. Each time she went from house to barn, or house to the street of slave quarters behind it, her eyes roved restlessly to the river beyond the broad stand of rushes where stood the High Garden landing.

And sometimes she saw a pettiauger there. Sometimes a bateau. Some days there were callers. Other days she saw people passing by to or from the other plantations on the river. One day Thomas had come by the river, but most often he came by the road and they met in the pine grove. They talked. They loved. Those were enchanted days. She smiled at the thought. But still she watched the river for one craft yet to arrive.

It was not like Papa to be late with his Christmas presents. Gifts of pearls, or stones set in gold, exotic shells and special sweets, bottles of dark rum and Madeira always arrived neatly crated well before Christmas. Why not this year? And where was her letter?

There is a war on, Crickie reminded herself, going about her work. Still she found herself distracted, even irritable at times. Why did this one thing that was so important to her have to take so long? Papa is busy, she told herself. Papa is in the field. Papa may be on his way home. Papa is so exasperatingly inefficient at times. This last she admitted to no one but herself.

For the sake of her mother, who seemed more and more to see the worst in each situation, she tried to remain positive. In the months that sometimes stretched between letters from Antigua, Mother became increasingly certain that Father was at least wounded, if not dead, despite the fact they'd heard nothing of actual fighting on the island. "By the time news reaches us," she liked to say, "the fighting could well be over."

"That's possible," Crickie would reply. "Still we've heard nothing of aggression there. The French pushing in at our Carolina from the west is a bigger problem—that and their encouraging the Cherokees to fight against us. At least the King has sent General Braddock to fight them in the Ohio Valley. Perhaps the fighting shall stay up there and we shall be spared danger."

"In Antigua there are no Indians," her mother would say, returning to one of her recurring themes, "but the Spaniards incite ye Negroes to revolt at every turn, and no white man or woman is safe from that." Her unspoken message that the same could happen in Carolina did not go unnoticed by her daughter, who nevertheless put such notions aside.

The Rawlinses had come to South Carolina well after the Stono Rebellion of '39 when slaves revolted against their unsuspecting owners, killing them as they slept in their beds, but somehow the retelling of the tale managed to reach Judith Rawlins's ears the first week they were in Charles Town. During her years as an invalid it took root and grew in her mind, making her mistrustful of the High Garden staff whom Crickie trusted implicitly, and especially of the field hands and children.

"The Spanish are no threat to us here, Mama," she said, "nor I'm certain to Papa either. We have merely to be patient and word shall come from Antigua."

Her advice was easier to give than to follow. Her own patience now turned to impatience. For the first time since she'd returned from England, Crickie found herself absorbed in something outside High Garden. The feeling was delightful. For the first time she imagined herself living in Charles Town. Married. Oh, she could make frequent trips to High Garden, too. She would help see to Thomas's land as well if he and his partner agreed. There would be children—she still remembered the way Thomas had enchanted little Celeste. Crickie caught herself daydreaming at her desk, in the fields, at the table. Look only to what is, not what will be, she scolded herself. Watch the river. But again and again her daydreams returned. And she scolded herself less and less.

"Come quick, Miss Crickie. Presents are here!" Mully called one day as he came running far back into the woods where Crickie was checking on the annual drawing of turpentine. The pettiauger had finally arrived. Waving wildly, Mully shouted again, "Come quick, Miss Crickie."

Something inside her somersaulted as the boy ran toward her. It was finally here. Even her mare sensed the excitement and began to step about nervously.

"Thank you, Mully. I'll be done here shortly. Tell Mama I'll be back within the hour."

Mully turned and ran the other way, barely pausing to catch his breath, and Crickie started to watch the turpentine being barreled, then changed her mind.

"Mr. Johnson, see that there's no leakage," she said, and turned her horse around to ride for the house before her overseer could answer. Giving the mare her head, she smiled as she passed Mully.

"Never mind, Mully, I'll tell her myself," she called with a wave to the startled boy as she flew by, skirts billowing, cloak trailing loose at her back.

Crickie swung her light frame down from the mare and tied the horse at the post behind the house, then ran in the back door and down the hall toward the parlor, where her mother and sisters already waited. Borque was there, too. Somehow that surprised Crickie, but it shouldn't have. After all, Papa would certainly include something for his guest. Still, it felt odd to have someone present at what was always such a special family occasion.

On the freshly scrubbed, unfinished pine floor of the parlor, Crickie saw one crate, marked "Rawlins, High Garden Plantation, Bark River, South Carolina."

"Where are ye others?" Crickie asked.

"There is just one. So far," Margaret said. "Perhaps ye others are still in Charles Town or were sent elsewhere by mistake," she reasoned.

Crickie felt the somersault once again. Suppose the letter

was in another box? Oh please, please God, let the letter be here, she prayed inside. "Dill, bring in a pry bar please," she said, wiggling her toes inside her boots. "Perhaps there is just one box," she said, not wanting to encourage false hopes though she was quite certain there were more somewhere. "Great things *do* come in small packages," she added.

"*Oui*," Borque said, smiling, but quiet.

No doubt he was as uncomfortable with them as they were with him, Crickie thought, returning the smile. Papa, I hope you remembered to send something for Monsieur Borque, she said to herself, then sighed. Would Dill never return? Fortunately Deborah's speculation about the box filled the long moments.

"Bar, Miss Crickie," the big-framed black man said, returning at last. "Should I—"

"Allow me, Crickie," Borque said, taking the bar. Dill took a step back, watching as the little islander fumbled with the tightly nailed box. When he finally began to get one end open, Dill faded away in the quiet manner the Rawlinses' servants managed so well.

The packing of finely chopped palm leaves began to spill onto the floor as soon as the lid was off. Margaret and Deborah were first to dig in for their presents.

"Here's a letter," Deborah said, tossing it aside as she continued to dig.

"I'll take that." Judith motioned for one of the girls to hand it to her.

"Let me, Mama. It's to all of us," Crickie said, getting there first. Her eyes began to scan the lines immediately, and as she backtracked to read aloud to the group, her jaw tightened.

December 2, 1754

My dearest Judith and daughters,

I am late in sending to you these few small gifts, and know this will not reach you in time for the holidays. Would that I might explain such lateness by battle or the strain of my duties in the office of the lieutenant governor here, but I cannot. In truth, I could have written this letter last July but did not, wishing instead to give you the opportunity to become known to Monsieur Borque and him to you, for you see, and I can obscure it no longer, Michel Borque has not come to High Garden in order to assist you, my dear Crickie, with the indigo processing, but because he is now the owner of High Garden.

I cannot begin to describe to you my anguish, guilt and shame in my loss of all you have worked so very hard to build up, but alas in the life of the army man there are but few diversions, among them drink and games of chance. When mixed, the two are deadly. My debts, over a period of time, began to exceed my ability to pay, and at last nothing but the land beneath your feet would support me. That it has gone to so wealthy a man as Michel Borque is of some solace to me, for he knows plantations well and will see to it that High Garden continues to grow and prosper. Now it is we who must grow and prosper elsewhere.

All is not lost, for my debts were satisfied before the loss of our London house, and the lieutenant governor assures me that my family is most welcome here in Antigua for as long as I am attached to his service. Thus it is now time to pack clothing and such small articles as you wish, but leave the house furnished for its new owner, and to book passage on the next schooner bound for the south. I know, Judith, that Carolina has never been to your liking, and hope you may find Antigua pleasing both to your temperament and your health.

To my daughters, let no one know of our loss. Monsieur Borque has agreed that no mention of the circumstances of his ownership of High Garden will be made known. Evan Forcher, who as you know, is of the utmost trust, has handled the papers and will see to it our standing in Charles Town is in no way diminished. Similarly, here in Antigua you will be received by the best English families and your lives will go on much as they always have. And perhaps another roll of the dice will one day favor me.

    I await your arrival.

Your loving husband and father,
Carlyle Rawlins

Crickie's hands shook and tears ran slowly down her suddenly pale cheeks as she finished reading, and refolded the letter, then handed it to her mother who sat in shocked silence in her chair.

"I am sorry you had to learn of this in a letter," Borque said, rising and making a slight bow and flourish as he shook his head in a most solemn manner. He took a step toward Crickie. "Your father thought it best this way."

Borque's French accent screamed in Crickie's ear.

"You . . . you . . . could have told us. You've watched us work—let us run things—acted like a . . . a . . . fop! All the while knowing you owned us like slaves." Crickie pulled up her chin in defiance, trying with all that was in her to push back the tears of humiliation trying to flood out. No mention of Thomas. Nothing from her father but disaster. She pulled her shoulders up straight, took a deep breath and saw Deborah comforting her mother, both of them sobbing. Only Margaret remained cool. Even serene.

"All the while laughing at us—weren't you? Weren't you?" Crickie shouted to Borque, her anger at her father and at Margaret all directed toward him.

"Not at all," Borque said, again moving slightly in Crickie's direction. *"Au contraire,* I have admired very much your abilities in managing this plantation, and although it is small compared to my family's holdings in the islands, its rich land and closeness to Charles Town make it most attractive. I could not so much as smile either at it or at the lovely ladies who see to it."

Margaret fairly purred at this last, while her older sister fumed.

"Ha," Crickie scoffed. "Please, no further gallantries. It is obvious we have long overstayed our departure thanks to Papa's lack of enthusiasm for telling the truth. Pray endure us yet one week, until we can pack and find lodgings in the city to await the sailing of a vessel bound to Antigua."

Borque left Crickie's side to move to her mother's before he spoke again.

"There was one more part of our agreement, which your husband does not speak of in his letter," Borque said, looking Judith full in her already red-streaked eyes. "Carlyle offered the hand of his eldest daughter as part of the agreement should I choose."

Crickie actually heard herself gasp. "Absolutely not!" she said. "Father would not! You are a liar!"

The set of Borque's jaw tightened and his eyes left Judith's to narrow on Crickie's. "You have only to ask Monsieur Forcher," he said, his lips pursed beneath his moustaches. "Have no fears, the written agreement between your father and me which Evan Forcher holds describes this well . . ." He paused, slipping his left hand inside the lapel of his waistcoat, resting it on the top button. "I thought you might be pleased at this opportunity to stay on at this place you love so much . . . and in time . . ."

"Never in a thousand times!" Crickie shouted, bringing Judith to her feet.

"Elizabeth Rawlins! Your manners!"

Crickie had often felt her mother's discontent with her through icy words and cutting comments, but never in recent memory could she recall the actual raise of Judith Rawlins's voice. She lowered her own.

"Manners, Mama? Father has lost our home in a game of chance, and you worry about my manners?"

"You will do as your Papa and I say you will do!" she said, clipping each word through clenched brown teeth before sinking like a stone back into her chair.

"Perhaps Monsieur Borque will solve the problem by not choosing to agree to Papa's offer," Margaret said, her bosom heaving rapidly under the tight lacings beneath her bodice. Her eyes fluttered over her mother's head to the sharp black eyes of the little islander.

"Would that my choice might be you, dear Margaret," he said smoothly, noting the quiver of her full lips. "Still

Madamoiselle Crickie was her father's choice . . ." He paused. Crickie's anguish magnified with each second. ". . . And thus she is mine also." He crossed the room to stand by Crickie once more, this time letting his hands fall on her shoulders in a gentle caress and looking her in the eye, for he was no taller than she. "It is an arrangement that will work out quite well for all, have no fears. And you, Madame Rawlins, are most welcome to stay for as long as you wish. Your daughters, also."

"My daughters and I will stay to see you married," Judith said with as much dignity as she could summon, which seemed very little to Crickie, "and then we shall sail for London. Carlyle can—"

"I've not said I agree to this 'arrangement,' Mama. Am I not to be consulted?" Crickie asked, trembling, wishing to tear herself from Borque's increasingly firm hold. Her eyes avoided Borque's, much as they had throughout his stay here these past few months. "You know I've asked Papa's permission to see Thomas Gairden."

"You know your father would not grant permission for such a person to call, nor would I. Such a man of ye middling sort is beneath—"

"You know Papa has never before denied me," Crickie snapped.

Borque made a quiet interjection into the exchange. "Your father made the agreement before he received your request, I believe. Had he not asked that we keep the agreement secret, you would have known and never have asked permission to see Gairden. As it is, I find your mother is right. Gairden is no more than a common—"

"Horseman? Like you?" Crickie snapped. "He's beaten you at York Course and that's all you know of him isn't it? He may not have plantations around the world and generations of money behind him, but I venture he's read more and worked more and done more in his twenty-four years than you have in twenty-eight. He's done more than win property in card games—"

"Loaning money is little more than a game of chance," Borque replied smoothly, allowing that he knew more of

Gairden than Crickie realized. She hung her head. She would not embarrass Papa further by carrying her challenge to Evan Forcher, only to be beaten again. Her father had given her away, as he'd been trying to for over two years to other rich old men. She knew his thinking. She was almost eighteen, getting past marriage age. With her father's fortune slashed, her marriage candidacy would be lessened. Better a life free of financial worry with Borque, who could afford to be generous to the rest of the family as well, than some other, less favorable, match.

Hearing Thomas maligned, though, when it was men like her father and Borque himself who were ineffectual and improvident, was finally too much for Crickie. "Loaning money is what enables this colony to thrive. You'd know that, Mama, if you were forced to handle the accounts as I have had to." Crickie's eyes flashed to her mother, needing to make her see Borque's slander for what it was, but bewilderment was all she could read in her mother's eyes. "I'm thankful factors like Evan Forcher and Thomas Gairden extend credit to those of us who need it. They, at least, use money to improve lives, not destroy them!"

Borque flicked a finger across her chin, then held his hand, palm up, in mock salute. "You honor your father," he said, his pleased smile gone.

"I always have," Crickie said, untouched. She looked out the window to the river once again. "No doubt I always shall."

For each of the next few days, Crickie watched not the river, but the road, hoping to see the big chestnut gelding, Shuttle, gallop in ridden by Thomas Gairden, who would swoop down to tell her he'd received a letter from her father granting the permission he'd asked for. But such a scene never occurred.

"Moss, I want ye back acres dug for planting by the end of the week," she demanded of her foreman one cold morning about a week later.

"But, Miss Crickie, those fields too wet. We can't—"

"I said get them dug," she snapped and rode off before

he could object further. But she took little satisfaction from the command. Moss was right. It was too wet. Yet something inside her said, "Make them suffer, too—make them work."

Back at the house she found Deborah sitting at her mother's bedside writing down names for the wedding guest list.

"I want no wedding, Mama, and you know it," Crickie said, her words cold as the January wind. "Certainly no celebration of the kind you're suggesting. One hundred guests? Never!"

"Elizabeth," her mother said, "you have been given great responsibility here during these years while I have been ill. And you have carried it well. But it was your father's responsibility to see to your marriage, and it is mine to concur with his choice. It is yours to accept what those older and wiser than—"

"Older, yea. But wiser? Papa loses High Garden through wanton gaming and you call him wiser? Papa—"

"Your father is the head of this family, Elizabeth. Please remember that."

Crickie stopped cold. "Papa does not deserve to be the head of this family. When Papa left for Antigua he left us so far in debt to Evan Forcher it has taken me three years to lift us out of it. Had I not managed things for him he'd have had no High Garden to gamble away. And yet my life is to be controlled by his gift of me to Michel Borque, a man with no other thought in life but racing and gambling of his own? Why even now, is he riding about High Garden, taking charge of ye Negroes at their work? Readying for spring planting? Nay! He's in Charles Town. With his horses!" Crickie snapped the riding crop she still held against the soft camlet of her skirt, and a tear rolled from her eye.

"Elizabeth!" Judith Rawlins said, sitting up in her bed. "You would do well to remember that without your Papa's fortune, there would never have been a High Garden for you to enjoy. Your Papa is a wealthy man whose connections are among the finest in the colony or in London. You seem to forget that in your pursuit of a common weaver, this Gairden, who has nothing."

"Better a man with nothing but goodness and ambition, like Thomas, than a man with everything money can buy but a base spirit and aimless ways, Mama."

Crickie did not hear the swish of hoops behind her until Margaret was nearly at her side.

"Mama, if Crickie finds Michel so odious a mate, let me marry him. It is me he finds most fascinating, despite what Papa says." Margaret lifted her nose in the air, posing.

"You are too young, Margaret," her mother said.

"I'm seventeen," Margaret said. "Old enough to know what I want."

"And why would you want Michel Borque?" Crickie asked.

Both Deborah and Margaret giggled.

"He is the most charming, the most—" Margaret began to gush.

"That is why you shall not marry him," her mother said. "There is far more to a marriage than charm. Your father and I will choose for you and Deborah as we have chosen for Elizabeth."

Margaret's pose broke like a china cup on slate. "But it is me Michel wants. I know it!" she huffed.

"Has he told you that?" her mother asked solemnly.

Margaret hesitated. "Nay," she said, closing her eyes deliberately as she answered, giving nothing away. "But I know it and I shall have him!"

"Your ideas are only girlish imagination," her mother said, ignoring her willfulness. "With your beauty, you will find many a young man of good connections wanting you for his wife. Your father will have no trouble making a match for you."

Crickie reddened at the implication. She'd heard it often enough before. "Mama," she said, forcing the shakiness from her voice, "if it's to be done, then let us do it as soon as possible. Arrange ye wedding for next week."

Judith's mouth dropped open in surprise, the sagging skin below her chin hanging loose upon her nightgown.

"That is more the attitude I would expect from you, Elizabeth," she said, "but Monsieur Borque has asked that ye wedding not be held until after the February races."

"His wedding second to a horse race? Does that not tell you something about his character, Mama?" Crickie said, then turned to Margaret. "Would that he might be yours, dear Margaret." Crickie whipped her skirts as she whirled from the room.

"Mama, are you going to let her speak to me in that vile way?" Margaret asked.

"Dear Margaret," her mother said, "if the choice were mine, you might most certainly marry Monsieur Borque. But such choices are made by men among themselves and we must accept them and make the best of them. You must, and Elizabeth must."

"At least I shall be his sister," Deborah said with a sigh, unflapped by the charge in the room.

"Both of you will find the young men in London far more refined and educated than those here in the colonies," their mother told them.

"But it may be years before we go there," Deborah said, agonizing at each and every word.

"Not all that long, I believe," their mother told them with a raise of her finely plucked eyebrows, but would say no more. "I must rest," she said, shooing them out despite their questions.

The next morning at seven, just as the pale light of a lazy sun was rising in the east, Crickie woke her mother.

"Mama," she whispered, "I'll be going in to Charles Town today. I'm going to speak to Evan Forcher."

"What . . . you've nothing to speak to Evan about, my dear," her mother said, loosening the strings of her sleeping bonnet as she propped herself up on an extra pillow. "We own nothing and have no business there any longer. You will not bother Mr. Forcher." Her eyes drifted shut as she spoke.

"Perhaps. But it has occurred to me that since Monsieur Borque told us Evan has the written copy of his agreement with Father, it would be well for me to examine it. Perhaps there is nothing written about my marriage to him at all—perhaps he was bluffing." Crickie whispered, though there was no reason. Borque was already in Charles Town—had been for a week. He would not hear them.

"Bluffing or not," Judith Rawlins said, her eyes open narrowly now, "you'll marry Michel Borque to save this family's good name." Again she closed her eyes.

"But why could we not tell people that High Garden was sold to Monsieur Borque? They would never need to know what really happened."

Judith Rawlins did not move her head from the pillow, did not turn her head, but opened her eyes and looked up at the netting rolled atop her high, poster bed.

"Because people know your father would never sell this land," she said, admitting to Crickie what she had not been able to admit to Margaret and Deborah. "He would be a fool to. People would make the worst of it. This way they will think your father has given you a most generous dowry."

"But then why not give such a dowry to Margaret in my place?"

"Monsieur Borque is, no doubt, a man of his word. If it was you that he and Carlyle agreed on, then it is you he will have."

"We do not know that, though," Crickie said in a hushed tone. "If only I can find a clue in ye document Evan holds, perhaps I can stop this affair."

Judith shifted her eyes to meet her daughter's, her look full of warning. "By discretion we will not risk the disclosure of your father's shortcomings. Nor will we demonstrate your willfulness."

"Still I must see the contract and find out for myself what it is that Papa has signed. We do not know what Borque may be up to. You cannot dispute that." Crickie knew her mother trusted her judgment more even than her father's on matters of paperwork.

"I cannot," she said. "But you must draw Evan Forcher into this no more than absolutely necessary. I feel we can depend on his discretion, but I cannot be sure. Tell him as little as possible."

"That is a certainty, Mama. I intend to satisfy myself on this matter and that is all. I shall be back before dark." She turned to leave the room but stopped before she opened the door. "Should Michel return before I do, tell him I've gone to see about wedding arrangements. It will be the truth, after all."

Judith Rawlins closed her eyes, raising her eyebrows as she did so. Crickie caught the look, but took no time to respond. The pettiauger waited at the landing. She was going to Charles Town. And while she was there, she was going to see Thomas.

❦

17

Wearing a high-collared, dark blue sacque trimmed with satin ruching, Elizabeth Rawlins stepped briskly into Evan Forcher's office at 21 Bay Street as she had many times before on her father's business. Today, though, it was her own business she wished to conduct.

"Crickie, how good it is to see you. It's been nearly two months since you last dined at our table. Lisette misses you." Evan Forcher was warm and gracious, ever the image of a generous benefactor.

"I miss her, too, and look forward to seeing her on race day. Today, though, my business is here." Crickie rose from her black horsehair seat near Evan's desk and closed the door to his office. "I thank you for your discretion in this matter with Papa and Monsieur Borque—" Crickie saw the pity in the older man's eyes and felt the sadness well within her once again. "I understand you've known about this for some time and yet said nothing, nor let anyone else know the situation."

"It is part of my job," Evan said, "and no one is less deserving of such bad fortune than you, my dear Crickie, who have managed so well in your father's absence. His loss is—" Forcher stopped himself. "Let us say, had your father been here for me to advise him, this might have been avoided."

"I have long known that chance runs hot in my father's blood," Crickie said, trying to make it sound as though she were not shocked and destroyed by her father's caprice. "I doubt either of us could have changed anything."

"I might have kept his debts from rising, though, had he been here. He did not lose High Garden on a roll of the dice, you know. He had been gaming heavily and borrowing

from Michel until at last Michel insisted on collateral."
Forcher rose and looked out his window to the bay, where
ships large and small dotted the blue water. "Michel is a
pleasant sort," he said, not looking at her. "You may be
very happy together."

Crickie sat in silence for a moment. So it was true. Michel was not bluffing. The marriage was arranged if he was
so inclined, and he was. "May I see a copy of the agreement, Evan?" she asked, as if there might still be a pinhole
of daylight somewhere in this drape of darkness.

"Most certainly," he replied, taking a key from his pocket
and unlocking the bottom drawer in a cabinet behind his
desk. From a box inside the drawer, he drew a single sheet
of paper covered with what she recognized as her father's
hand and marked at the bottom with Borque's familiar
flourish as well. It was all there, the directions to Forcher to
transfer the deed for High Garden, including all Negroes
and other properties. Then, at the bottom, almost a post-
script, the marriage agreement. "Shall Michel Borque so
agree, he shall take as his wife my daughter, Elizabeth
Crichton Rawlins, at my request, that she may continue her
days there for as long as she shall live."

So Papa had seen to her welfare. Or thought he had.
Papa knew she loved High Garden. He had tried not so
much to make a match for her as to keep her where he
thought she wanted to be. Crickie looked at the words until
they blurred upon the page. "Have you spoken to Michel?"
she asked finally.

"Often," Forcher said. "He regrets the situation of your
family, and is at the same time quite taken with your family." Forcher's tone turned solemn. "You might have done
considerably worse, it seems."

"But then, not all things are as they seem," she said,
pursing her lips to keep them from quivering. "Why would
not Monsieur Borque wish to choose his own wife? He is
not bound to me by this."

"Nay, but you are bound to him. And you are his choice."
Forcher softened once again. "Most matches are made to
some degree by parents, Crickie, you know that. And you

are promised to no one else." Forcher caught her slight cringe. "Are you?" he asked.

"Not promised, nay, but there is someone who had asked Papa's permission to call . . . but not until after all of this was already done—except that I knew nothing of it."

Forcher's eyes asked the next question, and Crickie replied. "Thomas Gairden," she said quietly.

"Gairden? Really? I had no idea. I . . . Nice young man. May be better than me at this game one day if he keeps at it—but he has no family, no money, behind him. No, Crickie, Michel Borque, with his family's holdings in the islands and capital to invest here, will provide for you far better than Gairden ever could—probably far better than your father ever could. You will not be unhappy in this, I hope. I've come to know Borque rather well these past few months. He is a gambler, too, I must admit—but a good one it seems."

Evan Forcher was used to making the best of bad times. A factor had to be, Crickie knew. He was also used to doing favors for clients. She would ask him for one more.

"Evan," she said, "I can only hope you are right, for it seems I am to wed Michel like it or not. I had hoped perhaps he was bluffing about the marriage agreement, but you've proven he wasn't. Still, I owe Thomas an explanation. I wish to speak to him privately. Will you arrange it?"

How bold would Evan Forcher think her? Her cheeks colored. The room blurred about her. But only for a moment. Forcher's answer was surprisingly quick.

"Of course I will. Immediately, if you wish it." Forcher was a businessman once again.

"I wish it," Crickie said. Shoulders erect, head high, her fine, high-bridged nose slightly raised, she met his questioning eyes with her determined ones.

"You may wait here. I will send a messenger for him. In the meantime, I must have some words with Henry Laurens anyway and will seek him out in his offices." Forcher crossed to the door, picking up a thick packet from the desk as he passed. "Take your time, my dear," he said with a warmth Crickie would always remember. "I know that a

delicate matter such as this could not have been discussed
at High Garden, and I am pleased to be of assistance. If I
may help in any other way . . ." His upturned hands offered all that he had to give.

"Thank you, Evan," she said, and sat waiting for what
seemed an endless time, planning how to say good-bye to
the one person she had hoped never to say good-bye to.

Thomas mounted the stairs of the building at 21 Bay Street
and wondered what could be so pressing that Forcher
needed to see him immediately. Some problem with preparations for race day, maybe. They did very little business
with each other. Certainly nothing of an urgent nature. This
call to come running left him with a sour taste in his mouth
—the great one calling to the little one—and he was in no
mood for it.

Knocking and opening the office door at the same time,
Thomas was determined to get the business taken care of as
quickly as possible. He had no time to idle away.

"Elizabeth," Thomas said, looking about to see who else
was in the richly appointed space and finding no one.
"What are you doing here?" A glow came over his face,
erasing concern and all distraction, and without pausing, he
closed the door behind him. Bending to take Crickie's
hand, he pressed it to his lips, holding it there as he looked
into her eyes. "Where's Evan?"

"He's out . . . I . . . asked him to send for you. I had
. . . to see you." Crickie carefully spaced the words. She
had to be truthful, but not tell all. She had to let him know
she cared, yet not show him how much she needed him. She
had to let him go.

As if he sensed something, Thomas drew away but
perched lazily nearby on the corner of the heavy English
walnut desk usually occupied by Evan Forcher.

"Not bad news, I hope. I've had all the bad news I can
manage. Lost me man, Dugald—King's Navy took him
away this week past. 'Tis why I've not been to High Garden
the last few days. First I searched for him, then I learned
what had happened. They found him on the street a bit too

late one night, in his cups, and pressed him into His Majesty's service—impressed him. That leaves me without the man I paid for, and with no one to work for me." Thomas stood and walked to the window, resting his palms on the sill. He hung his head. "I'm sick to death of the English just now," he said. "Forgive me."

"Done," she said, "and I'm sorry about Dugald. The *Gazette* says the press gangs are at work in all the colonies, but the Crown has agreed to make repayment to the masters of the men taken."

"My eye an' Betty Miller," Thomas fumed. "We need as much protection from England as we do from France and the Indians." Thomas turned quickly back to her. "I'm sorry, lass. I don't mean to criticize the service your father's in . . . but I find it hard not to be angry at such goings-on."

Crickie felt his eyes searching her as she looked down at her lap. Silence fell between them, while he tried to fathom what she wanted, and she pondered how to say what she had to say.

"But let's not be talkin' of press gangs, Elizabeth, for I can tell there's somethin' on your mind. What is it, lass?" He returned to the corner of the desk and leaned back against it. "You've heard from your father?"

"We had a letter last week. It . . . was written before he could have received ours."

"And?"

"He and Mama have agreed to a match for me," she said, looking down at the indigo blue of her skirt. "I am to be married before next month's out." She ventured a look up. His eyes smoldered; his heavy eyebrows drew in upon each other, questioning. "Michel Borque," she told him.

Thomas rose and walked again to the window, just the way Forcher had only an hour ago. Studying the ships in the harbor, he spoke. "Borque. Why Borque? I thought your father never refused you. Why Borque?" he asked, tossing his head about to look at her over his shoulder.

"He thought it a financial advantage, I suppose. Michel's family is quite wealthy."

"Financial advantage! Your father would sell you for a financial advantage? I don't believe it. Your father and mother found Thomas Gairden a bit of a weed in their garden, didn't they? Their 'high' garden . . ." Thomas wheeled to face her, his hands gripping the back of Evan Forcher's leather desk chair so hard his knuckles bleached from the force.

"It was not you, Thomas," Crickie pleaded, rushing toward him. "Papa did not even know about you until it was too late. The agreement had already been made and—"

"And what? He sent Borque here to give you the eye, and if you passed he'd take you? I'll be goin'," he said, brushing past her.

"Nay, Thomas . . . don't." Crickie caught him by the arm as he passed, the touch vibrating between them. "I . . . I . . ."

What could she tell him without telling him too much? His eyes burned on her hand where it gripped the soft sleeve of his claret coat, then followed the curve of her arm and swept back up to her face. Nothing but the truth would do for him.

"Papa lost High Garden to Borque at cards," she said, looking him straight in the eye, trying to sound dispassionate but failing.

"Nay, Elizabeth, nay," he said, drawing her into his arms and comforting her, rocking back and forth, side to side.

"He tried to do his best," she went on, fighting back sobs. "He tried to help us save face by a match between me and Borque—he knew I could not bear to lose High Garden completely. He didn't know about us . . ."

"What about Margaret? Does she not have a sweet spot for Borque? It seems I remember her dancin' with him several times at the Forchers' party. And sneaking kisses under the mistletoe. Would she not be the envy of every girl in Charles Town, married at seventeen to a wealthy planter? And you . . ." Thomas leaned his head back a bit, to look down into Elizabeth's face. "Would you not be happy married to an honest—"

"Stop, Thomas. Don't say it. You know I would. But it's

my hand that's been offered and accepted," she said, "and he would not hear of Margaret's. I know not why, for she bears him greater affection than I do. She offered herself. Willingly."

"Let me talk to him, Elizabeth. Please." Thomas's black eyes were persuasive. "Let me help you. There is a way to get through this. Your father's made a mistake is all. Stall on the weddin' until the next schooner comes from the south."

Thomas's eyes pleaded, searched hers, caressed her with a caring warmth. He drew her closer, as if he could will away this awfulness just by holding her tight. His kiss flooded her with its sweetness.

"I saw you kiss a girl named Sarah once on board ye schooner *Endeavor* eight years ago," she said, almost as if talking to herself. "Ever since, I've wanted to be loved the way it looked like you loved her."

"I don't understand." Thomas's eyes narrowed, questioning her.

"I was there, too. Coming home from London to care for Mother. You didn't know me. But every day I watched you two. I saw love between you. Didn't I?"

Thomas's eyes left hers and took once again to the harbor. "Ah, I loved her all right, I'll admit it. But she married another." He was silent for a moment. "Why haven't you told me of this before?"

She smiled a sad smile. "I was saving it. I thought I had a lifetime to talk about the past with you." Again her lips quivered. "How little we know of life, Thomas."

Thomas pressed his lips to hers, feeling the quiver even as they kissed. He kissed her harder, deeper, to stop it. "Cry it out, lass. Cry if you want. I'm here, and I don't intend to lose you, too."

"And you never will, you know—certainly not to Michel." She sniffled, and forced back her tears. "I have remembered you and imagined you from the time I was ten years old, though I never thought to even see you again. But life is as unpredictable as the weather, it seems, and you turned out to be all I remembered and more than I'd imagined. Still I am not to have you any more this time than I did eight years ago. That time Papa took me off the ship at Charles Town while you continued on to Philadelphia. This time Papa takes me out of your arms while you continue on to the arms of another, which surely you will. . . ."

"You're no longer a little girl who must do as her father says," Thomas reasoned. "You've a life of your own to live."

"But I cannot turn my back on my family. I must do everything I can to—"

"And what if Borque turns on you and tells the world how he came to live at High Garden? What then? Your secret's out, and you're still stuck with the blatherskite."

"That is a chance Mother insists we take. Papa has placed great trust in him, as he always has in me. I must take faith in that."

"Your father . . . aghhh." Thomas shook his head. "We should have spoken to your mother. Or I should have asked Evan to act in your father's behalf. I don't know why—"

"We will never know why, Thomas. But I know I am bound by my parents' agreement. This day I've seen that contract signed by Papa and Michel. I'm so sorry, Thomas."

Again her tears began to roll. Her lip began to quiver. "You must do what you must do. And I must," Thomas said. His eyes filled with tears, which he quickly wiped away with his thumb and forefinger. He felt the familiar tic in his left eye and closed it briefly, then drew away from Elizabeth, taking one last, good look at her. "Maybe God in his ultimate wisdom and your father in his bad luck have made the right choice for us—but I don't believe it. I won't believe it. I know me own heart, Elizabeth. And I believe I know yours as well."

With that, Thomas bent and placed one last kiss light upon her lips, so gentle he felt more the aura of her than the real touch. Like the kiss that first day on horseback at High Garden, or the kiss under the mistletoe, this one was chaste, fleeting. Yet he felt the whole of him respond to her even as he drew away. He turned, and in four sharp strides, was out the door.

18

A square of newsprint, folded twice over, carried the names of the entrants in each of the day's four heats at the York Course this first Tuesday of February. Crickie Rawlins, having read it, now twisted it in a tight roll between her gloved hands as she waited for the day's fourth heat to begin. Across the length of the track, near the post, she could see Thomas speaking to Borque, and the anxiousness that had plagued her over the past few weeks once again caused a burning feeling in the pit of her stomach.

"Too bad Michel did not finish in the top three," Lisette Forcher said, carrying on the conversation she'd begun with Crickie before the first heat.

Crickie attempted enthusiasm. "Yea, I know he was hoping for at least one first place. Of course, today there are so many fine horses in the competition. He could not have known what a horse like Shamrock Gold, or the stallion Hero, would be like. Ye Virginians are bringing in some fine stock down here."

"Of course," Lisette said. "Every year the animals are finer. That little Chickasaw mare Thomas Gairden's man rode was a fine runner, too. . . . I suppose Mr. Gairden was surprised to hear of your betrothal."

"I suppose," Crickie said, unable to comment further. She had not seen Lisette since Little Christmas, January 6, and had had no opportunity to share her feelings about Thomas. Or Borque. And this was certainly not the place. Even if it were, she was not certain she could talk about it.

"Well, some may find him of the middling sort, but I find him most handsome." Lisette giggled, then changed the subject. "Every year the parties after the races are finer. We

shall have such fun this evening. Mama has planned a grand
supper for midnight, and we shall dance until dawn."

Crickie managed a smile. A whole evening. At Borque's
side. Accepting congratulations. Dying inside. Another
party tomorrow evening. One next weekend. Then only a
month until her own wedding. "Yea, racing does put people
in a spirit of gaiety. My mama is looking forward to this
evening. It will be her first party in over seven years."

"She has made a wonderful recovery of late, Crickie,"
Lisette said, her eyes, like Crickie's, at the post, where the
winners of the first three heats were lining up for the fourth
race. "It has come so suddenly. To think she will now make
the voyage back to London. And your sisters—how they
must be looking forward to returning home to their school
friends."

"Yea, they are. At least Deborah is. . . . Margaret is
thinking of staying on at High Garden with me."

At this, Lisette took her eyes away from the track. "Staying on? I don't believe it. She loves London so."

"Perhaps this is more home to her than she knows. In any
case, she does not like to leave me here alone." Crickie
fixed her eyes once again at the post.

"Crickie, my dear. You'll hardly be *alone*. A bride . . .
alone?" Lisette laughed. "Surely your mother needs her
more than you do. She will go. I'm certain of it."

"Perhaps you are right, but I'm not certain she knows her
own mind," Crickie said.

"Or perhaps she has her eye on someone here? That
lovely Major Heath perhaps? The one who knew your father in London? There is something about the sight of
those uniforms that sets a girl's heart to pounding—why,
the more of them I see in Charles Town, the more I seem to
fancy them."

"That may well be," Crickie agreed, just as the horses left
the post and neared the inside curve of the long oval track.
The cheering and clapping and shouting were deafening as
the three two-year-olds thundered around the track, their
jockeys hugged low to their necks, silk scarves in their stable's colors flying brightly over their shoulders.

As they rounded the far turn, with Shamrock Gold leading by almost a full length, Borque once more came into Crickie's line of vision, but this time Thomas was nowhere to be seen. She cast a hesitant glance to the rail beyond Borque, and there he was. The gleam of his dark hair, the profile with its almost aristocratic nose and high cheekbones, the small mouth caught in a jaunty smile—it was Thomas, watching the horses, mouthing an aside to a fellow horseman, and apparently giving no thought to what might have been were her father not a gambler.

"Hero! On, Hero, on!" Lisette was shouting, bouncing up and down on tiptoe. "Papa says he may buy a colt out of Hero next spring if he can arrange it," she babbled. "Think of it. We may be winners here one day."

"Yea," said Crickie. "Perhaps by the time the Newmarket Course is ready, Forchers will be taking the prizes instead of these Virginians."

"Of course, Michel's grey did so well today—perhaps Papa should look in his direction instead," Lisette said, afraid she might have hurt Crickie's feelings.

"That I cannot tell you," her friend answered. "You know that my only interest in horses is to ride them slowly and comfortably. Your father must talk to Michel about brood stock."

"Racing will be in your blood, by marriage at least, by next February, and you'll be cheering louder than everyone else put together, I know it."

"Perhaps." Crickie's answer was short, disinterested. Again her eyes strayed to the end of the track, and this time she saw Michel and Thomas leading their horses to the post.

"Papa says Michel made a donation of five-hundred pounds toward the building of Newmarket Course," Lisette said. "You must be so proud."

"Why, yea . . ." Crickie managed, smiling politely. She turned her eyes back to the track where Shipley Dibble, organizer of this year's race, was speaking to the crowd through a small megaphone, trying to get its attention. Crickie strained to hear his words.

"While the three-year-olds ready for the third and final four heats of today's racing, the contenders from our two-year-old gate will run three exhibition races for your racing enjoyment. First to run, each riding his opponent's horse, will be Mr. Michel Borque from Antigua and Mr. Thomas Gairden, Charles Town. In the second race, Mr. John Helmsley of Charles Town and Mr. Edwin Louis of Mulberry Hill. In the third race . . ."

Crickie failed to hear the last names. Whatever was this for? "There will be no purse for these events. Any wagers must be purely private and will not be governed by the rules of the course . . ." she heard Dibble saying. She tried to edge closer to the front of the crowd for a better look at what was happening. Never before had she seen such a competition, although race day always included some sort of exhibition riding. She felt Lisette slip her arm about her waist.

"Good luck to your fiancé," Lisette bubbled. "I'll cheer for Thomas—just to make things fair," she teased. Her cheeks gleamed rose red with anticipation.

"Fine," Crickie said, nodding, her stomach burning once again.

As the gun sounded, the horses broke away from the gate neck and neck, Thomas slung low to the neck of Borque's stallion, Prince, while the smaller Borque rode in the crouch of a jockey, buttocks raised from the saddle, head low. Side by side they sped, neither rider taking so much as a moment to look to the other, their shirts billowing, air-filled, as they rounded first one turn and then the next. Then Borque pulled ahead slightly, kneeing the Chickasaw mare Snowball to run faster and faster.

"He'll save nothing for the end," Crickie said under her breath, embarrassed by his technique.

"He's pulling ahead!" Lisette cheered Thomas on as he edged up on Borque and held him even for a time going into the far turn. "Run, Prince, run, boy!" she shouted.

But even as Lisette clapped her hands to urge Thomas on, Prince dropped a few footfalls short of the lively Snowball, and once more Borque took the lead. This time he held it to the finish line more than a length ahead of Prince. Crickie released the breath she'd been holding. Lisette hugged her.

"Aren't you proud?" Lisette gushed. "Michel riding that little mare and beating the powerful stallion? What skill . . ."

Crickie only half listened as Lisette went on, joined by Deborah and a handful of other friends. She watched as Gairden swung down from the stallion, as easily as if he'd been nowhere but out for an afternoon ride. She saw him look toward where she stood in the ladies' gallery, his eyes searching over the rows of faces and not finding hers. She could not wave, or even smile the way she wanted to. There were appearances to be kept up.

Borque, of course, waved his hands, talking in his emphatic, French-laced style, to Dibble and the other men gathered at the post to congratulate him. And Margaret waited there, too, her hoops swinging smartly as she greeted him and held her hand out to be kissed.

Crickie saw Lisette watching them. "Margaret seems to like your Monsieur Borque," Lisette observed smoothly.

"So do I," Deborah said, sighing her most affected sigh.

"He's quite a favorite," Crickie said, smiling but nonspecific. "You must excuse me, Lisette," she said then, "while I send Dill home for Mama. I will join you all again at home."

"Let me send a servant with the message," Lisette offered.

"Nay, I need to speak to Dill," Crickie said. I need to quit this place for a time, she wanted to say, but couldn't.

Dressed in a jewel-toned gown of garnet silk hung with rounds of matching lace ruffled below the elbow and down the petticoat, her hair combed straight back and plaited over the crown, Crickie entered the familiar double parlor that evening on the arm of her betrothed. She looked elegant, and much older than she had that very afternoon at the races in her blue camlet and bonnet. Heads turned, and thanks to Lisette Forcher, most in the room already knew what Evan Forcher was about to announce. Crickie tried to give her most winning smile, and wondered if it looked real enough.

"If I may have your attention," Evan Forcher said, ringing the silver bell that usually called guests to dinner, "your attention, please." The guests quieted and smiled in anticipation of the news. "In the absence of my dear friend, Carlyle Rawlins, faithful servant of His Majesty George II, attached to the office of the lieutenant governor in Antigua, I am pleased to welcome tonight a face long absent from Charles Town, his lovely wife, Judith."

Crickie's mother sat in an ornate armchair to Forcher's right, and nodded regally to the room at her introduction, not speaking.

Forcher continued: "And furthermore, I am pleased to have the privilege and honor to announce to you tonight the betrothal of Elizabeth Rawlins, known by all of you as our amiable and energetic Crickie, and a fine gentleman from Antigua, recently come to Charles Town and already a member of the Jockey Club, Mr. Michel Borque. Their vows will be said on the sixteenth of next month at High Grove Church."

Applause and cheers went up from the guests and Crickie found herself lowering her eyes and blushing as Evan and others continued with toasts and good wishes. Looking up once again, across the room her eyes met the incredible darkness of the eyes she would know anywhere as Thomas Gairden's. He did not smile, nor did she. There was just the look. The almost imperceptible narrowing of the eyes and the furrowing of brow that just momentarily interrupted the pleasant facade required of the evening. Crickie was first to look away.

"And you are all to be our guests," Borque was saying, gesturing expansively, his accent charming the guests as it always did.

Crickie could not believe it. How many of these people, some of whom she did not even know, would take such an offer seriously? She had planned to make some verbal invitations, and to have some written ones delivered to people like the governor and his staff, for whom a verbal invitation was not suitable—but this? Crickie sent him a smile accompanied by a pair of highly raised eyebrows but received only his usual complacent smile in return. He, of course, would assume the cost of the affair now that her family had next to nothing. He was welcome to invite whomever he chose, though he might have been less vulgar about it.

Margaret was next to him now, offering congratulations Crickie knew were shallow and forced. Borque did not seem to notice.

"Soon enough you will be married, Margaret," Crickie told her, speaking across her fiancé, "and perhaps you'll have both Papa and Mama there. I shall miss Papa's presence next month."

Margaret gave her the briefest of smiles, then barely a nod before she resumed her chatter with Michel. Crickie began to be embarrassed by her behavior, seventeen or not.

"Mama," she said, bending low to her mother's chair. "Will you speak to Margaret? Michel must speak to the other guests, and she must do the same."

"Do I hear jealousy in my little bride?" her mother wanted to know, surprised. "Margaret is just enjoying herself. She will move on to someone else in good time."

They are to be in-laws soon, Crickie told herself. And she is young. Still another look at Margaret's laughter, and the way she stayed at Borque's side, continued to irritate her older sister.

Crickie surveyed the room and did not see, as she'd thought she might, the eye of every matron present fixed upon her sister with scorn. No, people were dancing now. Men stood in groups and went over again the horses and races of the afternoon. And the servants began to bring in the trays of perfectly arranged delicacies, pheasant en croate, sliced hams and bacon curls, sweets and nuts, cakes and fruits that would comprise the midnight meal. Crickie had no appetite.

Staring at the tables until the foods blurred before her, she felt a familiar presence behind her as she stood in front of the serving table which was festooned with silks and silver tack, racing programs and the crest of the Charles Town Jockey Club. She did not dare to turn around, but caught a quick breath.

"I doubt I can take you up on the invitation, Elizabeth," the familiar voice said softly, "and you know I hope Borque has a change of heart before the Ides of March." Thomas stepped beside her, picking up a plate as the buffet line began to form at either end of the long table.

"You know he won't," she said, resigned.

"Aye, I know," Thomas said slowly. "I spoke to him."

Crickie's face showed her surprise. "You did? He never mentioned—"

"He offered to sell me High Garden."

Surprise turned to disbelief and Crickie stopped cold in the middle of bringing a forkful of sliced capon to her plate. "He wouldn't," she said, asking it not to be true.

"Ah, I daresay he would." Thomas's face betrayed no emotion, but his words had a bitter tone. He nudged her along in the line so as not to attract attention.

"Eat more than that, Crickie, or your wedding dress will hang loose on you," Mrs. Forcher chided, touching Crickie warmly on the shoulder as she came to the end of the line. Then she indicated a settee at the other end of the room where Crickie might sit, near where Michel spoke with a group of racing friends. Crickie paused a moment before she headed in that direction.

"Yea, Mr. Gairden, I'll come 'round for that fustian first thing tomorrow if it's ready," she said, turning to him slightly as he was greeted by Mrs. Forcher in turn.

"Indeed 'tis, Miss Rawlins," he said, picking up her meaning instantly.

"Thank you," she said, relieved that Michel had not once turned around and so had not seen her in any proximity to Thomas. Borque would no doubt sleep late in the morning, and she would go to pick up her order. Simple and reasonable. Selene Forcher might guess her reason for going, but was not likely to say anything. Still, Crickie felt the burning in her stomach once more as she picked at the food on her plate. If Borque had offered, why hadn't Thomas purchased High Garden from him and ended this whole business? Why had Borque offered? And what was to become of her and her family after all? For the answers to these questions, Crickie would have to wait until morning, all the while pretending to celebrate. For once, she wished the Forchers' parties were not so gay and well attended. For once, morning could not come too early for her.

The Sign of the Shuttle was quiet in the morning, just as it had been on Crickie's last visit four months ago before so much had happened. Before she had known she would love Thomas Gairden and marry Michel Borque. Thomas was already at the loom this morning, just as he had been on her last visit, except that today he worked at the loom Mackay had used last time.

"You haven't slept, have you?" Thomas asked before a good morning or any other greeting.

Crickie shook her head. "Nay, when ye guests left and all went to bed, I lay awake. Soon day was breaking. . . . I had to come and hear the rest of your story or I might never sleep again."

"I know," he said, taking her cape and hanging it on the same hook where his coat, worn last evening, hung. He had not been to his rooms but had come here to work, and to wait. "I shouldn't have spoken of it at all. 'Twasn't fair," he said, now guiding her across the shop to where a fire burned low in the corner fireplace, only slightly warming the large space. Thomas took two splits of pine from the wood box and threw them on the fire, setting the fire board back in front of the hearth to guard the rest of the room from sparks.

"I had to let you know I'd tried, was all, and found out what you're up against." Thomas's eyes were full of meanings Crickie could only guess.

"What did happen then?" she asked. "Michel offered High Garden at too rich a price, no doubt."

"The price was dear, no question there," Thomas said. " 'Twas the rest o' the bargain I didn't like." He paused, turned away. "He wouldn't agree to let you go, Elizabeth," he said. "Said you've caught his fancy, though as I watched him last night I'd say he takes a mean way of showin' it. He's a gambler, that one. He gambled that if I couldn't have you I'd not want High Garden either, and he was right. Still, he was naught but playin' with me and I knew it. When I called his bluff he laughed. He'll not sell High Garden because he needs the income from it for his habits. And he plans to have you do his own work for him so he has time for his . . . other pursuits."

"Gambling?"

"Aye—at least." Thomas could not even mouth the other vices he suspected Borque had.

Elizabeth warmed her hands above the fire board and despite the heat, she felt cold. Even anger no longer warmed her these days. She hung in a cocoon of cool white oblivion.

She couldn't respond at first. She stood, vision blurring into the golden flames. "You did what you could, Thomas," she said at last. "I knew it was hopeless. I told you so. He has it all his way and he plans to keep it that way. If only I could have talked to Papa . . ."

"I say it to you again, Elizabeth—you're not a little girl anymore."

"Nay, I'm a penniless woman now. Fine distinction," she said.

"Penniless? Is it pennies you're worried about? You know I'm doin' well. You know—"

"Yea, I know, but as long as I'm at High Garden there's the chance we may get it back once again. That Papa—"

"Do you think your Papa cares very damn much about High Garden since he'd gamble it away in a game of cards? Think, lass! If you're marryin' Borque to save High Garden, do it for no one but yourself. Your Papa did as it pleased him. You're entitled to the same license, I'd say. But you must choose. Me. Or it."

She had never seen Thomas show any kind of temper, never seen him be anything but gentle, calm. Until now. Her eyes still on the fire, she sensed his rage and frustration. She closed her eyes a moment.

"I must do as my parents ask, Thomas, though you are ever my choice."

A heavy quiet filled the room, punctuated by the snapping of the pine pitch in the fire. Slowly, Crickie took her eyes from the hands she still held out for warmth and turned to Thomas. "I do not own High Garden, Thomas, but it owns me."

Thomas took one step toward her, then stopped. He walked back to his loom. "I'll be leavin' next week," he said. He threw the shuttle and caught it on the other side, changed sheds and threw again, the massive loom clattering in the empty silence between them.

"For where?"

"For the districts. Militia unit's goin' north on maneuvers for a month. I'll close the shop—no one to keep it for me anyway." *Bang, clatter, bang, bang.* The loom kept its frantic pace. Thomas kept his eyes on the shuttle. "Then I plan to look at some land in the backcountry Gray's scouted for us." Thomas felt a familiar tic in his left eye as he spoke. Laying down the shuttle he held a finger to his eyelid, but the quiver would not cease. Deftly he moved his hand from the eye back along his hair, smoothing it, not wanting her to see.

"I spoke to Charles Simms of the Assembly about your man Mackay," she said. "He says you are not alone in your anger. Many like complaints are coming to ye Assembly. The Crown has agreed to recompense masters for their contracts, but beyond that he was not certain he could get Mackay back for you."

"Aye, they'll pay. They'll pay for the little left on the contract, never admittin' that the last of the contract's the most valuable. Once the man's learned the trade, that's when he's worth somethin'. They—" Thomas caught himself. "I do appreciate your askin', Elizabeth," he said. "It's just that, like you, I feel I'm at the mercy of forces beyond myself. I could weave enough to export, do more business than I do, but the Crown doesn't want anyone over here in competition with her—only wants to unload on us all that she has no need for. Then she takes away what help I do have . . . Then her subjects gamble with what they shouldn't . . ." Thomas looked over his shoulder to find Elizabeth looking back. "I'm ready to quit the weavin' business for good, just as good King George wants me to, and make me money elsewhere."

"Back to Philadelphia?" Crickie asked, suddenly afraid she might never see him again.

"Ah . . . that I don't know," he said, dropping his head back in exhaustion and closing his eyes. "I doubt it, though. . . . New York maybe. Or Boston."

"Then you wouldn't go back to your family in Pennsylvania?" Crickie still remembered the *Endeavor,* and knew Thomas must have family near Philadelphia somewhere.

"I've no family there," he said, not explaining. "You're the closest to family I've had in a long while. Must be I've not the spirit to have a family 'round me. Or the luck for it." Thomas kicked at the corner post of his loom. "That's why I'm no match for a gambler. No luck."

"I'm sorry you didn't beat Michel yesterday," she offered. "I wanted you to. So much."

Thomas narrowed one eye in a confidential sort of way, and shrugged. "Don't be too sorry," he said, one corner of his mouth turned up just a smidgeon. "I didn't run young Prince like I might've."

"You mean to say you let Michel win?" Crickie could not believe this. "Surely not to please me?"

Thomas laughed. "If I'd thought it might please you, I'd have let him win by much more." His smile had tenderness, but no joy in it. Crickie still did not understand.

"There are many ways to beat a man like Borque," he explained. "One is the fair, square way, which is best. Another is to let him think he's won and stroke him a bit, which I did—*he* won the race, but he was ridin' *my* horse," Thomas said. "And after we rode, a half-dozen men asked about a foal from my mare while Borque had nothin' but a ribbon to show for his efforts."

Crickie saw the trick of it. "And did you make a sale?"

"That I did," Thomas said. Then his smile faded. "I sold Snowball—at a fine price. Spinneray, too. I won't be here to see to 'em. I thought it best. My racin' days are done it seems. Shuttle will be me only horse once again, and a finer one there'll never be," he said.

Crickie watched him, wishing she could know all of him that she would now never know.

"I must go," she said, sensing a change in him as she left the fire and walked toward him. "I should have wished not to have to say farewell to you once more, and I shall wish it again. But I thank you for what you tried to do with Michel. . . ." She was so close she could smell the Thomas smell of him, of wool and leather and soap. Drawing in one deep, full breath of remembering, she walked away, crossing to take her cape from the hook and go out, wishing he would stop her.

Her hand upon the latch, she heard his voice one last time. "May God go with you, Elizabeth," he said.

"And also with you," she responded through the lump in her throat. But she did not look back.

It was still early when her carriage pulled in at the rear of the Forcher home on Tradd Street. A mist hung over the garden, its condensing droplets sparkling as sunlight forced through from above. The smell of bacon frying and date bread baking sweetened the garden space, but Crickie barely noticed as she shuffled up the walk, scuffing the toes of her slippers.

Careful to open and close the door quietly behind her, she was about to go up to her room again when she heard the clink of a cup and saucer in the dining room.

"There was no need to leave so quietly this morning," Michel said. He sat alone at Selene Forcher's dining room table, sipping a cup of strong black tea, and his voice lacked its usual ebullient cadence. "I was not yet asleep, and I doubt the rest of the household could have been roused . . . I take it you had urgent business."

Crickie rummaged for a reply. "Not urgent. I couldn't sleep . . . I thought it best to see about—"

"Some weaving from Monsieur Gairden?" He smiled as he watched her squirm. "Ah, I see. And did he tell you of our little talk? He really loves you very much," Borque said as if he were talking about a puppy or a horse. "He wanted to buy High Garden from me—putting himself quite in debt in the doing if I am not wrong." Borque chuckled. "Quite gallant actually."

"And why did you not sell?" Crickie asked, regaining her composure. "Was his silver not shined enough for you? You care nothing for High Garden—and nothing for me. Why, then, not let us both go?"

"You are wrong, Crickie," Borque said. "I care a great deal for High Garden. It is going to make me rich. And you are going to see to it." His smile was imperious. Crickie stepped back.

"But you are rich. Papa said—"

"I will be *more* rich, I meant to say, with your help."

"While you—?"

"While I busy myself here in Charles Town, *ma chère,*" he assured her, chewing slowly on a piece of the fresh date bread from the kitchen.

Crickie took another step back toward the wide, double archway. "You know I bear you no affection. And you know Johnson can handle such work." Her heart thudded inside her as she spoke. "He knows High Garden well now. I wish to marry Thomas Gairden." Her black eyes flashed indignantly at his smug indolence.

"And let the whole city know what has happened to the Rawlins fortune? Ha." Borque took another sip of tea and smoothed his moustaches. "The agreement I made with your father clearly states that I am to have you for my wife," Borque said, laughing softly and shaking his head. "In fact, I believe you've read the contract." His eyes accused her of doubt. Of checking up on him. His eyes assured her he would not tolerate it further. Then his fixed smile returned. "With the plantation came the wife who would manage it expertly—your father's promise. But have no fears, Crickie, as my fiancée, or as my wife, you may see whom you like—as I will."

"But—" Crickie's eyes widened in protest. She heard

herself gasp as she swirled about-face and ran to the staircase.

"Ah, Crickie," Borque called after her, "when you are angry you are nearly as beautiful as your sister Margaret is." The sound of his laughter followed her up the stairs.

❧ Part Three ☙

1756–1757

※

19

Fort Ogchachee, South Carolina
March 1756

The three months spent here at the settlers' fort high on the Saluda River had been long ones for Sarah Roberts Lowe. Discontent among the Cherokees—from too many settlers disturbing their hunting grounds, too many white traders cheating them, too many treaties broken—had resulted in murders and scalpings during the last six months, and Jamie had been only too willing to take off in pursuit. He had little concern that while he was off in Indian territory, she was left at Turkey Creek alone. After a few weeks she'd made her way to the fort, where she'd endured life with sparse provisions, and endless condescension from the four British regulars assigned to protect settlers like herself. Even with three small children to care for, her time inside the palisaded walls passed slowly. While the children napped and after they quieted for the night, she spent time in prayer, alone with her petitions. The five other women confined within the walls did not join her, preferring the company of the British regulars to that of the Holy Spirit.

Just this morning, with a bright, warm sun beaming down inside the walls, the children were begging for a trip to the creek, and Sarah had to admit she longed for one herself. Ordinarily only the regulars left the fort, but today might be different. She took the children by the hand and walked to the gate where the fort commander stood surveying a large group of militiamen camped outside the walls.

"Would it be safe to take the children to the river this mornin', sir?" she asked Major Thornton. The commander was a stocky, purse-lipped Englishman of about thirty, and

he stood by the gate, watching the militiamen with a scow
on his face.

"I'm not certain the likes of these can give you much
protection," he said, lifting his nose, "but you have my
permission."

"Thank you, sir," she said evenly, ignoring the slur and
hurrying the children down the hill toward where the mili
tiamen were camped.

"Which unit are you from?" she asked one of them who
was frying fish at a small fire as her eyes scanned the small
groups of men about their morning routine.

"First Charles Town," the red-bearded man said with a
bit of a Scottish burr. "Lookin' for someone?"

"Aye, me husband, James Lowe," she said, still studying
the men who, with their growth of whiskers and dirty
clothes all seemed to look the same. "But he'd not be with
the Charles Town men," she said, "he's—"

She caught herself midsentence when two men came
striding into view, returning from the river, each carrying
two fish stuck through the gills with a sharp stick. She
looked from one to the other, then back to the first. Black
bearded and taller than the other man, his hair was pulled
back tight at the neck. Above his beard the skin was pale,
set off by the profound darkness of his eyes. He wore the
same leather breeches and heavy shirt as the man next to
her, but beneath it a half inch of ruffled collar snuck out.
His leggings fit snug along the calf and he wore tall boots
stained dark now from wading in the river. This was no
Charles Town militiaman. This was Thomas Gairden. No
one else.

Sarah ran toward him and by the third step he was running toward her, too, hurdling rocks and logs with an easy
step.

"Thomas!" she shrieked, eyes wide with joy, as they
rushed into each other's arms. The skewered bass fell to the
just greening spring grass, forgotten, and for a moment the
whole world lived through the bond of lost years and found
memories.

"Come see the wee ones," she said, recovering herself,

hen stepping back and slipping her arm through his.
"They'll be wonderin' what their mama's doin'." She waved
o them as she fell into step beside Thomas who once again
carried the fish, and saw that many eyes were on them, from
he guard posts of the fort to the camp in front of its gates.

The children, their eyes still caked with sleep sand and
heir bellies rumbling, looked up shyly at the tall stranger
with their mother.

"This is your uncle Thomas," she told them. "He used to
ive with your grandmother and grandfather Roberts all the
way back in Pennsylvania. He came over with us on the big
ship from Ireland and he helped grandfather Roberts start
his farm in Bartram." Sarah raised her eyebrows to prompt
he children into a greeting.

"Hello, Uncle Thomas," they said in unison, with Gavin,
he oldest of the three, leading.

"I didn't know I was an uncle," he said, crouching down
on haunches to speak with them. "You'll have to tell me
your names now, since your mother's not done it."

"I'm Gavin. I'm five," said the red-haired boy whose eyes
were every bit as blue and piercing as his father's, but lacking their mischief.

"Aye, that's as it should be. Named for your grandfather
Lowe," Thomas said, nodding seriously.

"Martha," the little girl next to him was quick to say.
Thomas guessed her to be about four, and was taken immediately with her golden curls and small round mouth.

Looking to the smallest of the three, still a toddler,
Thomas waited for one more name, but this child would
only look at him warily. Thomas held out his hands to her,
but she puckered up to cry and hid her face in her mother's
skirts.

"I didn't mean to frighten you, little one," he said to her
back, leaning near her. "My name is Thomas, and I'll have
to guess yours now won't I? Let me see . . . is it Mary?"
The baby turned her head just enough to peek at Thomas
from the corner of her eye and almost smiled. "Nay? Not
Mary? Well then, Katherine?" The list kept going for a

couple of minutes before Martha could take the suspense no longer.

" 'Tis Anna," she said, at which the baby turned full face to Thomas, though still clinging to her mother's skirts, her round, chubby face a bit suspicious.

"Anna is it? What a lovely name." Thomas looked up to Sarah, her face radiating a mother's pride. "Quite a family you've got here, Sarah. Jamie must be proud."

"That he is, though he's had little time home with 'em these past two years. Off to the Cherokee lands every chance he gets." Sarah spoke without malice. "You know Jamie. Every fight is his fight."

"Aye, a true Ulsterman, Jamie. Never one to walk away from trouble." Thomas stood up. "Not like me. I ran from it."

"You had to, Thomas," Sarah said, taking his hand, "but that's over. They know why you ran—everyone in Bartram does. They know you thought you'd be tried for murderin' George Braid along with Ena—but you won't. George's wife stepped forward with the bloody clothes she'd seen him buryin' in the moonlight the night of the weddin'. She'd gone home early because the baby was ailin', remember? George walked home toward mornin'. Marva kept her suspicions to herself at first, afraid he'd kill her if she accused him. But she knew he'd been sneakin' off with Ena. Once he was dead, she wasn't afraid anymore."

Sarah felt the tension ebb from Thomas in the droop of his shoulders. He was silent for a moment.

"Did anyone ask how I'd freed myself? How I'd managed to fight off a man with a knife when I was bound like a sheep for slaughter?"

Sarah tried to remember. She recalled only that Marva Braid's disclosure hadn't lessened Andrew Roberts's choler any. He'd refused to admit he was completely wrong and sworn out a warrant against Thomas as a horse thief. Accused him of stealing money as well. But she could not tell Thomas that. Not yet.

"Nay," she said. "I suppose they thought you outfought him."

"Ha! What else? I was always known as a fighter, wasn't I now, lass? Aye, and Jamie can keep his lips silent when it serves him, too. It was your husband, lass, who gave me a knife to use to cut myself free. Jamie who wanted me to run so I'd look guilty. I didn't see it right away, but once I calmed down I figured it out—and I've lived these four years certain the whole of Pennsylvania thought me just that. But for Marva Braid, I'd still be a wanted man."

"Why didn't you tell me what had happened, Thomas? That morning . . ."

"I wanted to. But it wouldn't have been fair to you. I thought there'd be less burden on you if you knew nothin'."

"So you bore it all yourself. All this time. You could have gone to the Lord with it."

Sarah saw bitterness in his eyes as he replied, "I did." At least he hadn't forsaken God, she told herself. Not entirely. That was good. She could help him. She could bring him to the New Light where his sins would be forgiven. She would have the joy of saving him—something she was certain she could never do for Jamie—but she would have to go slowly. "What are you doin' here?" she asked, carefully changing the subject.

"Laws, you know. Every man between sixteen and sixty must leave his work and drill with the militia monthly. We've spent at least one month a year practicin' in the field —only now 'tis more than practice. The French keep the Cherokees so damned stirred up that even in Charles Town people fear attack, and though most don't say it, they fear the French and Indians may stir the Negroes as well. We're to try to keep the troubles here in the backcountry, and to try to make the land safe for settlers like you, so you won't have to spend your time in forts like this. We've seen forts with thirty families in 'em, packed tight as rice in a hogshead. . . . Have you been all right, Sarah?" he asked, his voice soft.

"Not pleasant, but all right," she told him. Now that the subjects of the murders, and Jamie, were behind them, Thomas once again became the caring, thoughtful man she'd loved. "And you?" she asked.

"Like you, I expect. I'm headed to Williamsburgh to help me partner plant some new indigo land, see to some business, then I'll be back here again. The redcoats can take care of it 'til we get back."

"You've land and business here? In the Carolinas? We met a man who said he knew a Thomas Gairden, but we never thought it really you. I never knew—"

"I started for Baltimore," he said, standing and looking into her eyes, "all those many years ago. But it seemed a bit too close to your father."

Again Sarah saw a trace of bitterness flash through his dark eyes, then disappear as he went on with his tale. "When I crossed the Wagon Road I met a man named Alexander Gray—the man you saw—who convinced me to come south with him. He did some Indian tradin' . . . so we traded some of my belongin's and some of his for a few dickers of deer hides from the Catawbas. When we got to Charles Town we sold 'em and got some land and a few Negroes for him, a building and a place to stay for me. He went to be a planter, me a weaver once again. He had some troubles, though, and soon I was lending him money. After a couple of years I was a partner at his plantation, River Plum."

"So you've done well for yourself," she surmised. "And you're minglin' with the rich down there in Charles Town I suppose." Sarah raised her eyebrows just a shade and saw Thomas tighten at the barb. After a moment she lifted the baby to her hip, rocking her back and forth slightly as she and Thomas talked while he gutted the fish and put them on a small tin plate to fry for breakfast. Heads and tails extended well over the edges and began to sear immediately.

" 'Tis you and Jamie I want to hear about—how you got here, how long you've been here—all of that," he said, poking at the fish with a green stick as they waited.

Upwind from the smoke of the hot fire, Sarah sat down cross-legged on the ground next to Thomas with Anna on her lap. Gavin and Martha played tag only a few feet away,

nd Sarah saw Thomas watching them, smiling at what he
aw.

"We stayed in Bartram over a year," she said, watching
he tag match, too, " 'til Papa and Jamie could no more be
n the same house together without ragin'. And then Jamie
ust told me one morning to pack up little Gavin, for we
vere leavin'. Jamie's folks left, too. We all started west, for
)etter land . . . Mother and Father Lowe picked the
vrong piece of land for their cabin . . . I found them
.calped and ravaged . . ."

Sarah paused, remembering it all so clearly. She barely
10ticed as Thomas handed her a piece of fish, and called
he children to come have some, too. She chewed, mushing
.he fish about in her mouth to sort out the bones and
;pitting them on the ground, but her thoughts remained on
:he Iroquois attack. She spat another fish bone out in dis-
;ust.

" 'Twas when Jamie got started on his Indian war," she
;aid as though there'd been no pause. "He rode after 'em
for a time, then came back. Before long he had ideas of
movin' again. This time south, for he'd heard the governor
of Virginia was givin' free land to folks on the western side
of the colony. We headed down the Wagon Road ourselves
and found a place—barely got it started when he heard
about the land down here, so we moved again. In each
place 'tis a new fight for him. In each place he lasts only a
while and then moves on."

"And will you move again, Sarah?" Thomas wondered.

"We will. I know it. One day Jamie'll come back from the
Indian territory and he'll be mad, and tired of land that
needs work and more work and sayin' he wants to go
lookin' for land that's ready for the plow, where corn and
squash'll come up without bein' planted, when all he really
wants is a new fight. Aye, we'll move again."

Thomas stopped eating and looked at her. "The Sarah I
knew wouldn't give in to Jamie's every mood," he said.

"He's my husband," she answered, looking at him, not
blinking. "The Lord commands me to follow him."

"No God commands you to hardship and starvation. You or the children," he added.

As she raised another handful of fish to her mouth, picking it from the common bowl she and Thomas shared, the fish became the ravaged bodies of her in-laws, and she spat meat and bones alike to the ground, searching the inside of her mouth wildly with her tongue to cleanse away any last bits of them.

"I've learned," she went on, "to put my faith not in Jamie but in God, for only in the Lord is there safety and goodness."

Thomas nodded. "God's been with me, too, lass, but—"

"He's right here with us now, you know—not in some faraway cathedral in London or some graven image in a church! No 'buts'! God walks with us if we live His commandments, and Satan will lead if we don't. You've not let the dark one into your life have you, Thomas?"

Thomas looked at her, but did not rush to answer. "You've changed, Sarah," he said after a deep breath, "or you'd not ask me such a question."

"I ask such a question for I want you to be saved," she said. "And if you could come before me church and confess your evilness, you would be saved. . . . I'm Baptist now," she said, "so you're right, I've changed. We find no need for fancy buildings or ministers from across the ocean. Ministers preach from their heart, not from some book, and they've brought me a promise of salvation. They can do as much for you if you'll just let 'em."

"And confess my sins?"

"Aye, you must confess 'em," Sarah said, praying he would agree. She could not bear to think of his soul, newly found to her, lost to eternity.

"Confessin' is something left for the Pope." Thomas stood up and brushed off the seat of his breeches. "I'll see to me own sins."

Sarah let a long silence fall between them, remembering well how Thomas took time to think things over before he made decisions. He could not be pushed, that she knew only too well. "Don't shut the Lord out," she said gently, rising and laying her hand on his arm.

He met her eyes, then looked away. "You can walk with God without tellin' the world how you do it, that's all I'm sayin'."

Sarah looked from the face of his determination to the total innocence of Anna's cherubic eyes so near her own. She heard Thomas exhale a deep breath.

"I'm sorry, Thomas," she said, letting Anna wriggle to the ground. "I'm only thinkin' of your soul."

"And I should be glad for that, shouldn't I?" he said, looking down into her eyes once again. "A man can't have too many people prayin' for his soul. Especially a man who's killed another, even if it was in his own defense. I thank you, Sarah."

She saw the familiar smile creep onto his face and returned it. "You've never left my prayers, Thomas," she said, but sensed his discomfort.

"Looks as though these lads are ready to move on now their bellies are full," he said, looking everywhere but at her. "I'll be leavin' with 'em. . . ."

"I'm leavin' as well," she said, and saw his surprise. "There've been no Cherokees about for weeks now, and I can stay no more at such a place as this is. I'm off for Turkey Creek this day." The idea popped into her head so suddenly she surprised even herself, but still it felt right. She breathed deeply of the clear morning air.

" 'Tis not safe, lass," Thomas protested. "You must wait for Jamie."

"The officers here are a bawdy bunch and not fit to be with women nor wee ones I've found. 'Tis just as safe at home."

"The commander will not let you and the wee ones go alone," Thomas said.

"Ah, but he will. He cares naught for the settlers—only for cards and rum." The more she defended the idea to Thomas, the more she wished she'd left weeks ago.

"I'll not let you ride alone, lass. I've only now just found you . . . how far is it?"

"A day's ride's all. I'll be there by dark if I can find a horse. 'Tis not far away."

"Some of these lads are leadin' spare mounts—findin' a horse's no problem. But you shouldn't be goin'."

"I've lived six long years in the wilderness without you, Thomas Gairden—most of 'em without Jamie, too—and I'll live many more. For all I know, Jamie may be dead. He should've been back by now."

"I doubt any Cherokee's a match for him, lass, but you're another matter. What if you had the bad fortune to meet with a Cherokee war party? And what about the vagrants loose in the countryside lootin' every place where settlers have left to take cover from the Cherokees? There are mean, low sorts lurkin' about, Sarah, and no sheriffs or courts to stop 'em. Do you even have a musket?"

"I have God's mighty sword of justice. And I am not afraid." Sarah saw the Evil One before her eyes as she spoke, urging her to tempt this man not her husband. Smiling, beckoning, calling to her, the Evil One was a fluid mass of red and orange and purple swirling about a glowing face. Then He was gone. "I leave this day," she repeated, her hands firm on her hips.

"All right, then, lass. I'll get you a horse," Thomas said with an indulgent smile very different from that of the Evil One. "But I'll be goin' with you."

Sarah's eyes swept over Thomas as he walked off toward the horses. The sheen of his black hair was brilliant as ever, but the untrimmed black beard he wore kept her from seeing the cut of the jaw and shape of the lips she remembered so well. He's not as handsome as he was, she told herself. He has no faith. What was between you is between you no longer. God will keep you free from sin. You did not tempt him. He insisted.

Within the hour they were on their way to Turkey Creek.

Contentedly Sarah cradled Anna against her, the small child a soft, limp bundle as she napped against the rough cloth of her mother's dress. The newly bought horse plodded along, well used to this walking pace as it picked its way

along the trail. Nothing near the kind of horseflesh that
Shuttle still was, he was nonetheless preferable to walking,
and she would sell him to the army once she was done with
him.

"Mama, Mama, how much farther is it?" Martha wanted
to know. Riding behind Thomas, she had to twist slightly to
look back at her mother, but never for a second did she let
go her firm clasp of Thomas's waist.

Sarah shook her head, motioning down at the sleeping
Anna whose chubby cheeks drooped to the jaw as her head
rested on her mother's right arm. If Sarah spoke loudly
enough for Martha to hear her, Anna would surely wake
up.

Still, once again, Martha asked impatiently, "How far,
Mama?"

Sarah pointed to Thomas, wanting Martha to ask him.
He could give her some sort of answer, Sarah thought, even
though he'd never been there before. But Martha persisted,
and every so often she looked back to her mother, whining
some question or other and setting her mother's patience
on edge.

They rode on like this, in what felt to Sarah like an
amiable silence, until past midday, when the springtime sun
was warm on their faces and the horses were thirsty. At the
next creek they would stop, even if Sarah had to wake up
the baby. They would make it to Turkey Creek by dark if
they kept up this pace. Thomas rode without ever looking
back, and Sarah wondered if he was remembering, as she
was.

"A fine place to stop," she called out to the riders in front
of her when at last they approached a tiny creek that ambled through a piece of grassy swamp before them. "The
horses need a bit to drink," she added.

Shuttle slowed to a stop, and the children slid down from
their high perch, but Thomas remained in the saddle. For
the first time in the four hours they'd been riding, Sarah,
pulling up beside him, had a chance to look in his face.

"Are you all right, Thomas?" she asked quickly, startled
by his pallor. "What is it?"

"Must be . . ." He mumbled something she couldn't understand. ". . . feel so weak . . . let's keep goin'."

"I'll get you a drink," she said, reaching to her bag for a cup. "The heat's too much for you." She'd taken three cups with her to the fort, and thank God she'd remembered to bring them along home. In seconds she was down, and carrying Anna at her hip she was off to join Gavin and Martha at the stream where they scooped up water in their hands and tried to douse each other with the excess.

"Now don't be gettin' yourselves soaked," she cautioned them, "or you'll get your uncle Thomas soaked, too. He's not feelin' himself just now. He won't want to be wet, too."

Gavin and Martha stopped their play at the stern sound of her words, and Sarah hurried back to where Thomas sat slumped on the big chestnut gelding. He took the cup and got down one swallow before he handed it back to her.

"Can you ride, Thomas?" she asked, looking up at the ashen face and vacant eyes that had just hours before been Thomas.

"Always," he said, closing his eyes after the brief attempt at humor, and Sarah patted his forearm, then lifted the children to her own horse and led his. Stepping carefully into the gummy riverbed, she held her skirts just clear of the knee-high water with the same hand that held the reins. The other hand she used to help herself balance against the slow but pervasive current.

Halfway across, more confident of her footing as she entered the shallow side of the creek, she hurried ahead, Shuttle stepping evenly along behind her, never so much as straining at the lead. Once at the bank, Sarah at last took a moment to look back to the children. The plodder she'd bought that morning, named Duke, instead of following as she'd thought he would, stood his ground on the other side with the children on his back.

Perhaps she wouldn't have to go all the way across but could call to him from the shallows. As she once again stepped into the water, she called his name and clicked her tongue softly. "Come on, Duke," she called again, once more clicking her tongue.

Duke looked up with enthusiasm that surprised Sarah and headed into the water as Sarah breathed a prayer of thanks that she'd not once again be called into that mucky mess a few feet in front of her. But the prayer was not finished before Duke responded to the coolness of the water and dropped to his knees, tipped to the side, spilling all three children into the water as he threw himself this way and that, a great thrashing heap of legs and hooves and mane.

Sarah, her skirts forgotten, took a running leap for Anna, who bobbed just inches from Duke's hooves. Catching one tiny finger, Sarah pulled Anna toward her as the toddler blinked the water from her eyes. After Anna was safe on land once again, Sarah dragged her sodden skirts through the water to carry Martha and Gavin across. Then she grabbed Duke by the reins and gave a jerk she hoped rattled what teeth he had left before they started on their way again.

When the sun began to sink in the sky they were going to be cold, Sarah knew, but there was no point stopping to try to dry anything by a fire. If Thomas got off from Shuttle, he might not be able to get back on. At least he wasn't wet. They would have to keep moving. And at the next creek she would have to lead Duke and hope he didn't pull her in with him.

She, now, was the plodder. Her pace was slow. Her skirt slogged against her, the hem heavy as if it were filled with rocks. Every few steps she looked back to Thomas for some sign of change or improvement, but now he just lay clutching Shuttle's well-brushed mane, so well used to the horse and it to him that he could ride it in his sleep. Thank you, Lord, for that favor, Sarah prayed. She prayed, too, that Thomas's sickness wasn't what she feared it might be, what so many of the soldiers contracted in the backcountry, and died from—smallpox.

"Dear Lord, dear Lord," she prayed, over and over. "Don't take him now when I've just found him again. And don't let the wee ones get it. Take me, Lord. Aye, take me, but not them."

Behind her she heard the children's voices, saying over
and over a rhyme they wanted Anna to learn. So far the sun
was warm and they did not complain of their wet clothes.
Why, then, was she growing colder with each step she took?
The voice within her told her she was weak, and she con-
fessed her weakness again and again before the Lord as she
walked, praying for forgiveness, until fatigue made the
praying stop.

A blankness came over her in the way dusk was coming
over the rolling hills they travelled between. It would be
well past dark when they reached Turkey Creek, but here
the trail was more familiar. Fever now racked Thomas's
slender body, telling her the sickness was what she feared.
She'd covered his back with the damp cloths from her bag,
for once thankful Duke had wanted a bath. But soon
Thomas shivered convulsively and bothered Shuttle so that
Sarah had to tighten her hold on the reins. In a few moments, it was the fever once more. Then the children fussed
from hunger and tiredness and fear of the dark and the
night noises of birds. And then Sarah, herself ready to drop,
saw ahead not the darkness of their place as she'd expected,
but instead, a light.

Their approach had already been signalled by the whin-
nies of other horses near the house. All day Sarah had been
wondering what she'd find after leaving her house empty
for three months. Woodchucks and skunks didn't take long
to move into uninhabited buildings. She'd prepared herself
for a mess, for having to clean up whatever might have been
dragged in or chewed up or messed on, but she'd never
prepared herself for other people. Sarah drew Thomas's
musket from the sling beside his saddle and loaded it. Then
she took the children down from Duke's broad back and
huddled them behind a brush pile Jamie had made last fall.

"Stay here until Mama comes back for you," she told
them in a hushed voice, "and don't go away."

"Why are you talkin' like that, Mama?" Martha wanted
to know.

"I don't want to wake uncle Thomas," she said, "and I
want to get the house ready for you—there might be a

skunk in it and I don't want you all to smell. Now be quiet. Mama will be back as soon as she can."

Lord, let them sleep, she prayed, and climbed on Duke herself to ride the rest of the way to the house. Before they got there, though, the door swung open and what looked in the darkness to be a rather small man stepped out.

"Lookin' for a place to sleep?" he asked. "You're welcome to the floor."

"I'm Sarah Lowe," she said. "I own this place. And your name?"

"Cobb," the man said. "We—my brother and me—thought the place was abandoned. We—"

"I've been at Fort Ogchachee for three months, as you could've found out if you'd but asked."

Despite the darkness, which kept her from actually seeing the man's face, Sarah was aware of a change in his manner and put her finger to the trigger of the musket.

"We don't do much askin'," the man said in a London backstreet kind of accent. "We're used to tellin'."

Now his brother appeared as a silhouette in the doorway, hiking up his breeches under the shirt he'd obviously been sleeping in. "What does she want, Cobb?" he asked, his voice deeper and older sounding than his brother's.

"Says she owns the place," Cobb said, never taking his eyes away from Sarah's. She watched him just as carefully, counting on it that he hadn't yet been able to discern Thomas's limp form on the other horse.

"Tell 'er come on in," the man in the doorway said, laughing. "The place could use a woman's touch," he snorted.

"Aye, aye, it could at that." Cobb reached out and slid his hand up beneath the damp, mud-caked skirt Sarah still wore, quickly passing thigh and heading for small clothes.

Just as quickly, she brought up the musket and aimed at the man in the doorway. "Leave me alone or I'll shoot!"

The man Cobb stopped his groping and looked behind him to the doorway, then back to Sarah. "I don't believe you can hit 'im from 'ere," he said, his fingers hungrily seeking skin beneath layers of muslin. He'd no more than begun to peel back the damp fabric when Sarah kicked out at him with her left foot, accidently discharging the gun at the same time.

Screaming at the noise, her eyes blinked rapidly. Then she heard another shot. For a moment she lost sight of the men in the darkness, then saw them running for their horses. One of them was limping, holding his leg. She looked to Thomas and felt the nudge of his pistol on her arm.

"Load it," Thomas whispered, trying to sit up.

Sarah took the gun and did as he said, not an easy task in the dark. Thomas touched his fingers at the reins and Shuttle turned about toward the escaping brothers. Thomas fired one last shot, but the intruders were already on their way.

Once again Thomas slumped against Shuttle's neck as Sarah dismounted and ran to the house. The lamplight revealed two dead crows and bird excrement on every surface, wood splinters from the woodchucks she'd expected strewn about on the floor, and shards of glass from her one window scattered like stones at the riverside.

Taking the lamp she turned and left. Roof or no roof, she would not spend a night in such filth. Leading Duke and Shuttle, who still carried Thomas, Sarah started for the lean-to barn, then detoured to get the children, fearing they'd been frightened by the shots. Instead they lay snuggled tight to each other, all asleep. One by one she carried them to the barn, covered them with the damp saddle blanket Duke wore, then headed to make Thomas a bed in the straw. But for her there would be no sleep this night. She loaded the musket. Then the pistol again. And she waited.

20

Thomas woke to a calamity of chickadees. He could hear them chirping their break-of-day song, their tiny brown wings fluttering as they flew in through a makeshift door. Then he saw Sarah, her head on his arm, and he remembered where he was. He pulled her as close as he dared without waking her and closed his eyes again. He felt her move. Heard her get up. Felt her lips touch his cool forehead. She began to tiptoe away.

"Sarah," he whispered, not opening his eyes. She stopped a moment, looking back he knew, then started away again. "Sarah," he said a bit louder. She stopped and looked back.

His eyes opened against the morning light and met Sarah's, holding them. Then they drifted shut once more like window shades drawn silently by some invisible hand.

"Thomas?" She rushed back to him and knelt down, her face close to his.

"At last we spent a night together," he said, a peaceful look upon his face, his eyes unopened, "though it took near death to do it. 'Twas me finest sleep in many a week."

"Don't talk," she said, hushing him. "You're too weak, you don't know what you're sayin'."

At that he opened his eyes. "I feel better," he said softly, "and I know exactly what I'm sayin'. Besides, I think the worst is past."

"Shhh, shhhh." Over and over she whispered it, holding him now and rocking back and forth, side to side as she would one of the children.

"I'll be gettin' up presently," he said, his eyes brightening a bit. "I've had the inoculation. I've not got the smallpox except in mild form. I'll be all right," he said, stirring from her arms and propping himself up on his elbows.

"You didn't!" Sarah said, aghast. "Inoculation is to tamper with the will of God!"

" 'Tis to keep God's children from dyin', Sarah, when they could be saved." So Elizabeth had told him once, for he, too, had had his doubts about the new technique which so many in Charles Town were trying. Elizabeth had a way of letting her love of people and the land take precedence over the notion of a willful, angry God, and he wondered once again why God had worked as He did to mate Elizabeth with a man she did not love.

"But you can't put off your dyin' to suit yourself. Only the Lord knows the day and the hour."

Thomas shook off a slight dizziness as he pushed himself into a sitting position. "At least I'm glad I wasn't too sick to fire me pistol last night, or we might all have had worse than smallpox to die from."

A moment's silence fell between them as they both looked toward the house where the two men had been run off. "You're right, you know," she said finally. "You're always right. No doubt God sent you here to help me. . . ."

Thomas sensed her uncertainty, her questions. "Then let's find those wee ones some food if I'm to be such a help," he said. Trying to stand, he broke into a sweat. He was weaker than he thought. Sarah shot up beside him, steadying him, her body familiar as he leaned upon it.

"Let's have you stay here while I find somethin' for 'em," she said, "for I've no mind to carry you should you take a weakness."

Thomas's face felt cool under the beads of sweat. White as the morning's cream, I am, no doubt, he thought as he leaned back against the log wall of the barn.

Looking about him, at the crude shelter and out to the poor cabin, Thomas was struck by the hardness of life here in the backcountry. Far removed in terms of civilization and progress from Charles Town, it was not unlike the Pennsylvania frontier he'd left for another world, except that here the settlers were more scattered, making any kind of court or law enforcement next to impossible to organize or enforce. It would be hard to know where to begin in creating order. In the meantime, settlers, including lone women like Sarah, were at the mercy of debauchers and thieves. Thomas wondered what to do. He should be getting along back to River Plum to get Gray started on the indigo, for Gray needed prodding on such things. Then again, who was to say if the weather was fit for planting in Williamsburgh?

He watched Sarah laugh with the children as they talked about Duke's swim in the river yesterday. She hugged them and made the day's plans with them over the breakfast of bread she'd brought from the fort, now compressed into a thin, flat, slimy sheet after having been soaked with river water inside Duke's saddlebags. She might have been back with Sheela, joking about a prank at a husking bee or frolic. She had aged, matured. But she was still Sarah.

"You'll not be leavin' today and I hope you know it," she told him as he stood up and stretched.

"I'd planned to," he said. " 'Tis three days' ride from here to River Plum, and by the time—"

"Nay, Thomas. If you could but see yourself you'd know you'd be ridin' nowhere this day. Your face—what I can see of it—has no color at all. And look at you tremble."

"I'm a little weak, nothin' more. Wouldn't harm me from ridin'," he said, as the children ran to inspect the house and look for their cat. "But I might stay a day at that . . . 'tis fine to be seein' you again, Sarah." He looked down at her, afraid to say what was in his heart. "I've never missed a day's thinkin' of you." He tried to smile at this last, to dilute it somehow. To mask it.

"Surely you've had other lasses to think about since you've been gone," Sarah said. Her hair, the color of the Carolina red earth, sparkled where a beam of sunlight touched it. Her bare toes wiggled below her mud-caked skirt. "Have you married, Thomas?" she asked.

"Nay, Sarah, I've not had the luck to marry, though I'd hoped to. Last year. Elizabeth Rawlins was her name. Her father'd made other plans for her, though. Married her to someone of his choosin' . . . I seem to have trouble with fathers," he said, then clicked his tongue and sighed.

"And you love her still?" Sarah's voice was low, hesitant.

"You know that those I love I never quit lovin'." He watched her face for some sign of a response, but got only an "I'm sorry, Thomas," before she ran off toward the house.

Thomas watched her go. She had the same light step she'd had as a lass of eighteen, and her body was still lean and trim, her hair still a bundle of willful auburn twists. He pounded his fist against the pole that held up the front corner of the lean-to, and waited a few minutes before he took his first slow steps after her.

"We were lucky, it seems," Sarah said as he came through the door. "They mustn't have been here long, for the trunk's not emptied. The Lord was with us."

"I'll see to coverin' that window for you, Sarah," he said, seeing her jump when a bird flew in through it. He could pretend as well as she could that what had been said had not been said. "Too bad the bastards had to break it for you."

"Thomas, your words! Remember there's children about."

"I'm sorry to offend you, but callin' 'em by a different name doesn't change what they were—scum, nothin' more."

"They were once children of God who fell to the Devil. We ourselves may do as much."

"So we may," Thomas said, looking at her. The new religion was strong in her and he found it odd but said no more. His own religion had been reduced to little more than church on Sunday in the years he'd been so busy with the building of his business. In Charles Town there were folks of every religion, all busy with the business of getting rich. Here in the backcountry, things were different.

Thomas found scraps of lumber stacked behind the lean-to, and fashioned them into two crude shutters.

"Have you some leather, lass?" he asked, returning to

the house. "I'll hang these shutters for you, and you'll be able to close and open 'em at your will."

Sarah produced some scraps of thick deer hide from inside the trunk, and Thomas continued his work as Sarah busied herself scrubbing down the cabin's log walls. He was aware of a tingle that was more than a response to the cool spring morning.

"I'll be leavin' as soon as we're finished here," he said, not looking up from punching the leather.

"But you might get the fever again. You might fall sick and have no one to help you."

"I'll have no more of fever. I had the Devil's own inoculation, remember?" he teased, still working but looking at her from the corner of his eye. "What I'd like is to see you back to the fort. Jamie'll ne'er forgive me if I let you stay here alone."

"Jamie hasn't forgiven you for stealing me heart and never givin' it back." Sarah stopped her scrubbing and turned to face him. "At first he didn't care, for he'd won me hand and that was all he wanted. But the movin' and the restlessness started soon after, almost as if he'd chase you down . . ."

Sarah moved closer, the space between them filled by no absent Jamie but only by sheer pulsing energy that rushed between them.

"Nay," Thomas said, forcing out a little laugh he didn't feel and laying his work on the table. "Jamie would ne'er do that. Jamie's by birth a restless one. He's a good man in his own way." Thomas was repeating what he'd had to tell himself during the years when he'd ached for the loss of Sarah. The ache sharpened to a stab as his eyes caressed her, and he stood and took her in his arms. "If I've done any stealin', though, I have to tell you I don't regret it," he said, "but I meant no harm, and by God no unhappiness for either of you."

Their lips met, hungry for reunion. Dirty from the trail, tired and edgy from cleanup and illness and intruders, still there was nothing for the two of them but each other.

"We make our own unhappiness," Sarah told him, resting her forehead on his shoulder as she caught her breath. "Or happiness." Her eyes widened, her lips curving into that well-remembered smile.

Bending to kiss her once more, Thomas paused at the sound of hoofbeats, then reached for his musket propped by the door.

"No need, Thomas," Sarah said before he could raise it, " 'tis only a neighbor, John Biggard."

Still on his guard, Thomas followed Sarah outside to meet the visitor, whose horse was lathered and laboring for breath. Biggard wore a flat, wide-brimmed, Quaker-style hat and a beard that fell to midchest. His eyes showed a mixture of tiredness and terror, and before they could greet him he was shouting to them.

"Vagrants! Murderers! Ready your musket, Jamie—" Biggard stopped then, and took another look.

"This is Thomas Gairden . . . my cousin, who's brought me home," Sarah explained, half choking on the lie before she asked, "It is two ruffians you've seen, ridin' together?"

Biggard nodded his heavy-jowled head. "Hit us in the dark of night . . . ruined—" Biggard started, then stopped. "Knocked me cold where I lay in bed. Stole what little money we had." Again he stopped and looked at them. "Were you not harmed by 'em, then?"

"We surprised 'em," Thomas said, extending his hand as he caught the suspicious look in Biggard's haggard eyes. "Drove 'em off and so far they've not returned."

Biggard ignored the hand Thomas held out to him, reining in on his horse to ride out as he'd come. " 'Tis a witch you've brought back to Turkey Creek, Gairden," he said, his jowls shaking indignantly. " 'Tis her ways have brought this wickedness upon us, and no doubt yours with it!" He shouted this time, saliva slushing about his lips as he spoke, and galloped off before Thomas could question, or explain.

He looked to Sarah, and the children who now clung about her skirts. Her head was hung a bit, but a fire of defiance leaped in her eyes and her chest heaved in and out as she fought to control herself. He waited. His eyes asked the question.

" 'Tis nothing new," she managed at last. "I was caught butcherin' a black chicken once, with a broom laid flat across the doorstep, on the same day a child drowned in the creek. A child who knew how to swim. I was given the blame—and the blame for many such takin's place since that—though I know not why."

"And now you're a witch? Fine neighbors you have here, lass."

"They go to me same meeting, and still they think me evil."

Thomas saw a tear begin to form. "The fear of witches runs strong when times are bad. 'Twill pass," he said. And hoped he was right.

It was near noon when Thomas returned from Biggard's. He'd ridden off after the other man despite Sarah's objections, determined to set her reputation straight as well as to help the frightened cracker if he could. Both attempts proved futile, for he found himself unwelcome and unheard. Another neighbor woman had been summoned to help the ravaged Fealty Biggard, and John continued in his wild-eyed daze, harnessing the horse to the plow and driving it mercilessly about half-cleared fields.

Thomas's trip unsuccessful, he nonetheless took a cue from Biggard, and harnessed Duke to Jamie's plow when he returned. It was near sundown when he quit for the day, weaker and more tired than he'd realized as he walked about the small, rolling plots of land in this claim of Jamie Lowe's.

It was quiet when he got back to the house. The children in crisp, white nightgowns were already dozing, uncovered, on the big bed in the corner of the cabin's single room. The new shutters stood open to let in the evening breeze, and on the table he saw a bowl of mush and slab of corn bread set out. He knew it was for him. Soundlessly he ate, already feeling aches in muscles unused since he'd plowed Andrew Roberts's fields in Bartram, and soundlessly he made his way to the lean-to in the blue-black twilight of a warm evening.

He knew she was there when he walked under the roof and through the flimsy door. Then he saw her, in her own crisp, white nightgown. A cloud against the darkness.

"Sarah?" he whispered, though there was no need, no one to hear him but her.

"I needed to talk to you—away from the wee ones," she said. "I'm sorry for my words this mornin'. You were right to try to help John and Fealty . . . I just . . . I . . ."

"You what, lass? You were angry and ashamed for bein' called a witch? Can't say I blame you. I knew the temper'd wear itself out—I've known you awhile—remember?" In one step she was in his arms again, just as she'd been when John Biggard had shattered the day with his shouting and accusations. She was soft, so soft, against him and her hair was loose about her shoulders. His every sense of touch was heightened at her nearness and he felt, rather than saw, the loveliness of her. The satin of her skin as his fingers loosened the bow at her throat. The smooth lines of her shoulders as the gown fell down about them on the curve of her full breasts.

"I remember every moment we ever spent alone together, Thomas Gairden," she said as his lips brushed along her jaw and down her neck. He felt her head drop back to give him room for more and his lips hurried down the arc of it to the supple skin at the gown's edge. "And I want us to remember this," she said, breaking the embrace enough to slide the cotton fabric free of her arms. The gown fell to her feet where she'd spread blankets on a bed of pine needles.

"I want it, too," Thomas said, his arms once more about her, his kiss on her lips. "I want it, too."

In the morning rain that turned this backcountry clay into mud, Thomas saw the world turned seventy shades of green. The wheat he'd planted six days ago was already beginning to sprout, its slender, lime-colored spikes poking fearlessly above the gooey ground. Smells of rich earth and new life filled the moist air, and he drew them deep into his lungs.

A week of pale-sunned spring days had passed before the

ain. A week of precious nights under the stars or in the ean-to had been the culmination of years of longing and he satisfaction of mutual joy, before Sarah slipped quietly back into the house to waken with the children.

He stood behind the lean-to this morning, eyeing the and that rolled gently to the creek—land that had come to ife overnight—and made his plans. It was still too early for he planting of corn here in the backcountry where there vas still the chance for an early frost. And there was indigo o be planted at Williamsburgh—only now there was the natter of Sarah to consider. He couldn't leave her here alone, that much he knew. Just now he wasn't sure he could ever leave her at all.

"Run to the creek and have your bread," Sarah told the children as Thomas took his seat at the table.

He tousled the golden curls of Anna and Martha and garnered his morning kisses from them before they picked up their stick dollies and bread. From Gavin, Thomas got a manly "good day" before the five-year-old trailed his sisters out the door, banging his play musket in pursuit.

"God speaks to us through the children," Sarah said, watching them go. "And these children love you, Thomas. As I do."

Thomas took her hand across the table. Felt her love and resolve. "Ah, Sarah," he said, "how I've loved you, too. Still, you know I must be goin'. I've delayed overlong and Gray'll be wonderin' if he's got a partner still. I think 'tis best I leave this day. The longer I stay, the harder 'twill be to go." He saw her eyes drop. She'd known as well as he that this moment must come.

" 'Twas God's will you know," she said, eyes still focused on the table, on their clasped hands. "He sent you to me for a purpose—to save me life, and to take me away from Jamie." She looked up. "God willed us together, Thomas, and only our own false pride drove us apart—I too proud to wait for you, you too proud to marry 'til you had money. I'm goin' with you this day, where Jamie'll never find us. God's will be done."

Thomas had expected a protest at his leaving, but not

this. To run off together? It was done, but it was rarely
pleasant in the end. If ever caught, Jamie might have Sarah
stoned. He might see Thomas hung.

"I can't say 'twas not God's will, Sarah, nor can I say
'twas the Devil's. What I once wanted so much at last is
almost mine, but I cannot claim it, for Jamie claimed you
first, and Jamie's you are."

"I'm yours, sure as me mother's in her grave," she told
him, bending across the table and kissing him lightly on the
forehead. "And Jamie need never know."

Thomas caught a daft note in her reasoning, heard the
same shrillness in her voice she'd had the morning he'd
followed John Biggard. He took a breath, started to speak,
then stopped, then started again.

"Do you think Jamie couldn't find us if he wanted to,
lass? Biggard could put half the pieces together for him,
and guess at the rest." Thomas felt her hand flinch a bit at
this thought.

"Still I'm goin' with you," she said, drawing back. "I'll not
stay here for Cherokee meat or the back o' Jamie's hand. I
won't!"

"Sarah," he said, "God's will or no, you're still married to
Jamie, and despite the way our bodies have been runnin'
away with us, I can't take you as me wife just because it
pleases me." He stood and looked out through the open
door, his back to her.

"You cannot—or you will not?" she asked, her voice
sharp in question.

" 'Twould be wrong and you know it," Thomas said, turning back to her. She still sat, kneading her folded hands
back and forth in front of her on the table.

" 'Tis a fine time to worry about wrong, Thomas, after
the days we've spent."

"To love each other's not wrong, Sarah. We know now
that our love's a lastin' thing, somethin' we'll have—and not
have—all our lives."

"You'd leave me here with a man who beats me? Who
frightens the children? Why do you think they love you so,
Thomas? Well, I'll tell you why. 'Tis because their father's

ne'er spoken a sober word to 'em in their lives. He's never neld 'em on his lap or sung 'em to sleep as you've done."

"Nay, I didn't know it. But I believe it," Thomas said, seeing desperation in her eyes. "Jamie's had a taste for the jug all his days, though he used to be a happy sot. We all change. Our little flaws grow bigger in life just as they do in the weavin' of a piece of cloth. Aye, Sarah, I know your words for truth, and since a weaver's pledged to weave truth with trust, I must ask you to trust me now. Let me take you and the wee ones with me to River Plum where you'll be safe."

"And what about Jamie then?"

There was still a sharp edge to her voice that bothered Thomas, but he knew it must be her fear. He drew her up and into his arms. "We'll leave word for Jamie that I've taken you there for safety. That way there can be no thought that we've run off together. 'Cousin,'" he said, smiling his all-knowing half smile. "When Jamie comes for you I'll speak with him."

Thomas saw apprehension even yet in her eyes. "I'll not let him hurt you, lass," he told her, holding her close and kissing her forehead, then her lips. "But I'll not spirit you away like a thief, either. I'm done with runnin' from things. We'll leave word with the Biggards where Jamie can find you. You know, I never could refuse you."

"You can't refuse me?" Sarah said. "I seem to remember the past a wee bit different from you. You knew full well I wanted you for me husband, but you wouldn't ask. You know, I thought to have you back then so there'd be a babe and we'd marry, but instead I decided to see how much I could hurt you. *You* refused to stop me from seein' Jamie." Sarah's face was red with tears and anger and remorse.

"I can't refuse you now, tryin' to make up for that time. I'm tryin' me best to make it up to you."

She gave Thomas a long, hard look, and he saw again a wildness in her eyes so unlike the old steady Sarah it was almost like looking at a stranger. She had either forgotten, or else was ignoring, that he had tried to convince her not to marry Jamie, had asked her to marry him instead. She was the one who had refused to change her plans. Thomas watched as the wildness left her eyes and she collected herself, drying her tears.

"So we leave today," she said, and went out to call the children.

Thomas started to follow, then stopped. Cherokees and outlaws he'd always known he might face on the trip home. Alex Gray, too, might want his scalp now that he was late for planting. These things he could imagine. But he could not so quickly digest all that had passed between him and Sarah, or see how it would turn out. Perhaps it was as Sarah had said. Perhaps he had tampered with the will of God.

21

Williamsburgh District
South Carolina
July 1756

When she returned to River Plum after Sunday meeting,
Sarah was still hearing the Reverend Aldworth's words in
her head, even though they were Anglican words. He'd
read from *The Book of Common Prayer* with no more conviction than one might read from a news gazette. But he'd
shouted a scripture commanding the people to cease to do
evil, to cleanse themselves. Judge not the fatherless son, it
had said. The white-wigged Englishman spent the day marrying couples and baptizing their "engagement babies," and
Sarah could tell he counted these people little more than
heathens. Those in the district who were not Presbyterian
waited long months for the visit of a minister and nature
had a way of taking its course without clergy. She, herself,
knew about that.

"Your Presbyterians had themselves a bit o' fun this day,
Alexander Gray," Sarah said at dinner on an afternoon of
stifling, muggy heat. She watched his face but he showed no
emotion other than calm self-satisfaction softened by whiskey. "Brought dogs and stink and ran 'em through the
meeting to bother the Reverend Aldworth," she went on.
"And one of 'em looked familiar . . ."

"A River Plum cur?" Gray wanted to know, chewing on a
tough piece of pork rind as he spoke. "One might've run
away, I couldn't say."

Like his name, Gray's hair was streaked through with
silver, and at thirty-five he was still a good-looking man, if a
bit haggard. But there was an air of danger about him,

possibly because he was never quite sober, Sarah thought. She was not sure how much to say.

"Elvia Willar told me that over near Mill Ferry the reverend was robbed of his nightgown. The thief put it on and climbed in bed with a woman, then spread it about that the parson had bedded the poor—"

Gray's laughter stopped Sarah, his mouth open and the half-chewed pork rind pasty on his tongue. "Aye, 'twas it so? Damned genteel Anglican—no more than he deserves." Gray took another piece of meat, still chuckling.

"The Anglicans are no more loved at Turkey Creek than they are here, but I say any man of God should have respect —even the snifflin' little nickin you call the leader of the Presbyterians hereabouts. He's not got much to say, but he's a minister all the same and would have no stinkin' dogs in his church. He might remind his flock of that." All this Sarah said evenly, careful not to direct it at Gray himself. Across the table, Echoe, as always, remained silent. How much did she understand? Sarah wondered. In four months here, she'd managed to get no more than two or three words at a time from the sad-eyed chattel, yet the young woman had a wise, knowing look to her.

"I'll be leavin' tonight," Gray said, changing the subject. "Back in a day or two. I've left Bruff his orders for the Negroes. You can see they're carried out."

"I . . . I'll not know how. I've not—"

"Bruff knows what to do. You've only to keep an eye on him that he gets out there himself. He'll do the rest."

"But the Negroes—"

"He'll take care of 'em, I said," Gray repeated.

"I see," she said quietly, looking at the table. "I've not been around Negroes much is all."

Again Gray laughed. "Scared of 'em are you? They're no trouble long as we've got the weapons. I paid dear for 'em —they'd damn well better work," he said, still amused. "I'll be seein' Thomas in Charles Town, I wager. Any message for him?"

Gray looked her straight in the eye. She looked back without so much as a blink, hearing his inference.

"I . . . I think not. No doubt he'll be comin' this way himself soon."

"Thomas? Doesn't often . . . of course, with you here it may be different." Gray laughed in a way that made her feel unclean.

"I doubt that. Thomas is a busy man," she said.

"Huh, that he is," Gray said, but his words had a bite to them. "I'll just tell him you can stay at River Plum as long as you like," he said lazily, then pushed back his chair.

Sarah felt color rise to her cheeks but held her tongue. She felt Echoe's eyes on her.

"Echoe!" Gray shouted. "Get me a change of clothes and some food."

Almost before he'd finished speaking, Echoe began to rise from the table, but still Gray shouted, "Now!" Sarah jumped in her chair and rose, too, heading out to the kitchen to tell the slave woman Effie to fix a bag of bread and dry venison for the master.

"I said 'Echoe,' " Gray called out, stopping Sarah. The Cherokee girl hurried past her and out the door.

"She has little enough to do," he said to Sarah's back, softening a bit. "And like a Negro she needs to do what she's told to do."

Sarah turned. "Why do you keep her?" she asked suddenly.

"Pleasure, mainly," Gray said without embarrassment. "And you may've noticed there's no overplus of women hereabouts—unless you're willin'?"

"I'm married, Alexander Gray," Sarah said, setting her jaw. "I'll thank you to remember it."

"Aye, and I shall," Gray said, his eyes sweeping over her. "I most certainly shall, though 'tis my guess Thomas forgets it easy enough."

Sarah turned and continued on her way out to the kitchen, though there was no need. And this time Gray did not try to stop her.

The next day, sunlight lingered long into the evening, heating the already oppressive air. Sarah kept the children indoors as much as possible to spare them from the hungry mosquitoes that swarmed the swampland near the river and even up to the clearing where the buildings sat. Rich planters took their families to the city for the summer, or to summer places on high ground away from the swamps, but Gray remained at River Plum most of the time.

Thomas, of course, had been in Charles Town most summers. Sarah did not know where he was this summer, for there'd been no word from him since he left her at River Plum near the end of April. Perhaps he was in the city, or then again he might be once more off with the militia. Whatever the case, she could wait. She'd waited so many years for him. She would wait some more and one day he would come to her again. She knew it, for what she felt inside her was surely God's will.

Sarah tucked the children in that night, all three in one bed so they could be covered with the fine gauze netting Thomas had left for them. She, though, could not sleep, and sat rocking in the parlor. She heard the buzz of a mosquito, and then the sound of a horse approaching at full gallop. Perhaps Gray had forgotten something?

Rising, she went to the window and looked toward the barn. She saw the horseman talking to Bruff. The tangle of golden red curls and familiar broad shoulders told her, even from the back, that Jamie had come for her. Automatically, an ingrained response sent her to the kitchen where she found a jug and a bit of bread, and brought them back to the house, then sat down to wait for what she knew would come.

Within seconds, Jamie burst through the door as if the house were his own and strode toward the table where Sarah sat. She did not stand to greet him.

"So, here you are, me lovely wife," he said. Sarah saw the red lines that ran about in the whites of his eyes, and the feral way the leaf green irises danced left and right, up and down. He'd been drinking.

"A little kiss," he leered, leaning in close and smashing his lips and stubbled beard upon her face.

She returned his kiss as best she could under the pressure, but tensed as his lips drew away. Crack! came the palm of his broad hand against her cheek and jaw, knocking her from the chair. She felt her shoulder bruise as she hit the floor, then a blow from Jamie's boot pitched her over to her other side. She cried out, covering her middle, but once again the boot came, this time at her thigh. Sarah drew her knees up in pain, cowering behind the overturned chair. In a single movement, Jamie threw the chair aside and lunged for her once more.

A tiny whimper was all that escaped her lips as his brawny body fell down on top of her, startling her from her pain. Looking up she saw Echoe, expressionless, holding one of the large sooty rocks from inside the fireplace.

"Some day I do same to Gray," the Cherokee girl said, her eyes narrowing as she stared at the still body of Jamie Lowe.

The coldness in that look made Sarah, for a moment, forget her own pain.

"God forgive us." Sarah slurred the words, unable to move her jaw. Echoe set the rock on the floor, rolled Jamie off Sarah and onto his back, then helped Sarah up.

"He want to kill you." Echoe's eyes never left the spot where Jamie's body lay sprawled on the floor.

"Nay." Sarah started to shake her head as Echoe helped her into a chair, but stopped when pain stabbed at her jaw. "He'd not kill me, for then he'd have no one to maul about."

"All white men mean," Echoe said. Sarah watched her as her eyes, like rings of obsidian, fixed on Jamie. "Evil," she said, almost to herself, then left for a moment and came back bringing cloths soaked in cold springwater to bind Sarah's jaw.

"Many white men are good," Sarah said.

"Who?" Echoe shot back, indignant, as if Sarah were lying.

"Thomas is," Sarah said. "William Willar—"

"Thomas left you here with child," Echoe said, and spooned some of the whiskey set out for Jamie into Sarah's mouth. "That evil."

The whiskey burned and nearly choked Sarah. Coughing racked her throat and she fought against moving her jaw. At last she managed a swallow.

"Shhhh!" Sarah pointed to Jamie. "How know you that?" she asked in a throaty whisper.

"I watch. I see your body grow thick at middle," Echoe whispered back.

"But—"

"I help you," Echoe offered. "Not care about men."

"Thomas does not know about the child," Sarah said, "and I mayn't tell him."

"I not tell," Echoe assured her, wringing out the cold pack and then holding it to Sarah's cheek again. "And I not speak to Gray. He stole me from my father, not trading as he says he did. He evil. My people come for him one day. . . . Until they do, I not speak." She firmed her hold on the cold pack as she spoke until Sarah winced.

Echoe bent and touched Jamie's neck. "Not dead," she announced without emotion.

"Sometimes I wish he was." Piercing pain radiated throughout Sarah's jaw and into her neck and eyes, making words all but impossible.

Echoe led Sarah to her mattress on the floor in the children's room, tucking her in like one of them.

"There *are* good white men," Sarah said once again. Echoe's face was little more than a silhouette in the light of the room's single betty lamp.

"Women good," Echoe replied with the closest thing Sarah had seen to a smile in all the time she'd known her. Then, like a night shadow, she was gone.

In the morning Sarah found Jamie still lying by the table, bound hand and foot with leather thongs, but Echoe was nowhere to be seen.

It was not until midday that Jamie began to stir. "Sarah?" he groaned. Lifting his aching head, he saw himself bound hand and foot in a strange room. "My God! What's happened to me head?" he shouted, closing his eyes as he cringed in pain. "Sarah?" he called. "Sarah!" He screamed this time, and Sarah, coming in from the kitchen, jumped.

"Jamie. I'm here, Jamie. Calm yourself now, Jamie," she said, stepping nearer, but not too near, and keeping one of Gray's heavily carved walnut chairs between them. "You were out of your head last night, Jamie. Too much whiskey. You fell and knocked yourself out." Sarah quickly asked God's forgiveness for this lie of protection. "We tied you to keep you from hurtin' anyone," she explained. Sarah could not be sure Echoe would come to her rescue this day as she had last night and she held her ground behind the chair.

Jamie turned his head slowly to take in the room's pleasant, imported furnishings. "So, our Thomas's doin' well for himself, eh? This looks to be a place I might want to stay. And Thomas most sure wouldn't turn away an old friend."

Sarah's fingers squeezed the chair's back tightly, thumbs nervously sliding back and forth over the pointed finials of its back. Jamie was still half-drunk.

"I'm sure he wouldn't, Jamie," she said, blankly, "but 'tis Alexander Gray, his partner, who runs River Plum Plantation and this house, and it's to him you'll have to speak about stayin' on." She paused, looking straight at her husband. "Thomas's not here."

"So I've heard," Jamie said, fighting the pain as he pushed himself up on his elbows. "You see, I spent some time o'er a jug with Master Gray yesterday at Truman's Ford Tavern, and we're well acquainted now. In fact, I told him a thing or two about our friend Thomas that was of great interest to him, and I'm welcome here at River Plum as long as I choose."

With this, Jamie smiled once again the self-satisfied smile Sarah had long ago found so pleasant. Years of living with him had taught her such a smile almost always prefaced violence or disaster of some sort. She felt herself stiffen.

"You told him what then?"

"That his partner's a wanted horse thief and robber." Even bound, Jamie had no fear. "Told him Thomas was a murderer, too."

"Jamie! You know better than anyone Thomas's innocent."

"Is he now, lass? Or did he steal me wife, along with her father's horse and money?"

"He stole nothin' that wasn't already his," Sarah said.

"Me wife was his? Aye now, there's a nice one." Jamie began to try to twist himself free of his bindings.

"He's not taken your wife, only brought her to safety. You might thank him for that." Sarah fought to keep down the color she felt rising in her cheeks.

"According to Gray, Thomas has quite an eye for you, though it may be he's still too much the gentleman to do anything about it." Jamie chuckled, but his full lips were turned down at the corners and his brows were knit into deep wrinkles.

Sarah bit her tongue, but kept her eyes on Jamie's twisting hands.

" 'Tis no matter, love," Jamie went on, motioning for her to free him. "And Thomas is in no danger now. He'll just have to part with some of his money is all."

Sarah did not move from behind the heavy chair. "Gray means to threaten him with tellin'?" she asked.

"Seemed to be his thinkin' when he left the tavern."

Sarah's swollen jaw quivered at Jamie's smugness, but still she did not speak.

"Forget it, lass. From what I hear Thomas can well afford whatever Gray asks of him. He's a tight one that Thomas. Always was. You're lucky you didn't marry him."

Sarah let the comment slide.

"And what about Turkey Creek?" she asked. "Are you plannin' to let go to the four winds all that we've worked for?" Jamie had always taken pride in the way he could transform wilderness into farmland, this being the third homestead he'd worked in his young life.

"Turkey Creek? And what's that compared to this? Gray told me how Thomas cheated him out of two loads of deerskins when they first come down to Charles Town, and how Thomas made the money while Gray did the work. Thomas owes Gray. And Gray's willin' to cut me in. By the looks of things hereabouts, we can afford to sit on the Turkey Creek land as long as we like."

"Aye, but what'll you do here? You know nothin' of indigo or rice. You'll go mad just watchin' Bruff and the Negroes do the work and havin' no say in it yourself—"

"Nay, milady. The idea of a few Negroes to do me biddin's quite pleasin'." He stopped and looked at her, his eyes piercing. "And I'll be here to see that you've no ideas about runnin' after Thomas once again," he said, hissing the words.

"I didn't run after Thomas," she said. "Nor him after me. I'd left the fort to see if you were among the militiamen camped outside, for I'd had enough of the fort and those Godless, drunken British officers. I wanted to go home. Thomas offered to take me there, and when he did—sick as he was with a fever—we came upon two rogues like as not to kill us, but Thomas ran 'em off." Sarah watched his eyes for belief or disbelief, but found neither. "And Biggards were hit next—Fealty ravaged, their goods stolen. Thomas wouldn't leave me alone there, and I wouldn't go back to the fort, so he brought me here. Biggards knew all that, for we left word with 'em."

"Biggards knew all right!" Jamie shouted. His rough hands tightened into fists. "They knew Thomas was no cousin of yours . . . You and Thomas spent a week together in me own house—for all I know in me own bed—and then rode off together."

"Biggards are gossips and fools!" Sarah shouted back, finally as angry as her husband.

"Why? Because they think you're a whore? A witch even? I'm not so sure they're fools. Anyone can see deviltry in the way you've been actin'."

"So I'm actin' strange? You may remember that you left me alone at Turkey Creek to go off with your Indian fightin' friends. If the regulars hadn't ridden through and given us transport to the fort, we'd like as not have our hair hangin' on some Cherokee scalp post long since." The isolation of the day he had left flooded over her once more, this time fueling her anger. "And maybe that's just what you wanted,

Jamie Lowe. Maybe you hoped to never see me and the children again. Well, all I can tell you is that you came within a hare's whisker of it, and if it hadn't been for Thomas, those thievin' rogues would've gotten us if the Cherokees hadn't!"

Jamie, for once in his life, was quiet. His head dropped to the side and he lay back flat on the floor.

Sarah took one tentative step and then another from behind the chair, then stooped at Jamie's feet to undo the bindings, all the while waiting for one of them to fly into her face. But Jamie lay still, not moving so much as to offer up his hands to be untied. She waited a moment, then moved to undo the rope at his wrists. Her heart hammered loudly, but still there was no movement, no sound.

Jamie lay with eyes closed, his color now pale except for two reddish spots of sunburn on his cheeks. Sarah rose to leave, half-afraid to turn her back, half praying God's forgiveness for not telling the whole truth. Then she stopped.

"Sarah," she heard from behind her. "Have you ever loved me as you loved Thomas?" he asked quietly.

A long moment of morning sounds—children playing outside and Negroes talking on their way to the fields and horses neighing and cattle bellowing—fell between them before Sarah answered.

"Nay," she said, and kept walking.

22

Charles Town
July 1756

"Madame Borque." Governor William Lyttleton bowed graciously as he kissed her hand and introduced himself.

"She is known as 'Crickie,' your excellency," her husband said, "and I as Michel. We are most pleased you could join us this evening, Governor. It will be a fine opportunity for you to meet the many planters like ourselves who come to the city to escape the fevers."

"Thank you, Michel. Crickie." The governor nodded and looked about the room as he talked. "I've not had much time for socialization since my arrival. Ye Cherokees and ye French who incite them demand the most of my attention . . . you may have heard we plan to mount an autumn campaign to Fort Loudoun." He looked to the Borques for assent and Crickie murmured a yea as the governor continued. "Then there is the matter of ye French neutrals quartered at Sullivan's Island."

"Oui. We've heard there are many of them to be disposed of. Where will you send them?" Borque had to raise his voice to make himself heard over the voices of the other guests.

"That is something I hope to speak about here this evening—if you'll allow it, Crickie."

"Most certainly, Governor," she replied, dropping her eyes politely.

The smile Crickie gave the governor faded quickly as she and Michel stood alone at the door of the second floor parlor to receive other guests. Her Watteau gown of lemon silk was of the newest style with the cap sleeves comfortable for summer, but still she felt warm and uncomfortable. She flipped open the carved ivory fan her mother had sent from England just last week and moved it slowly back and forth. There was, however, little relief.

"Do not look so bored, *ma chère*," Michel said, smiling as he chided her. "We do not wish to drive our guests away early."

"These are your guests, Michel. I am here only as a courtesy to ye new governor. When he leaves, I retire. I am certain Margaret will be only too happy to take my place."

Across the exquisitely appointed room, Margaret talked with a small group of people, but Crickie saw that her eyes came back again and again to Michel.

"You are too gracious, dear wife," Michel said through his teeth, still smiling. "That must be why I married you." Michel nodded to a couple making their way to the refreshment table.

"We both know why you married me, Michel. There is no need for sarcasm." Crickie took a deep breath. The man had lost his power to intimidate her, but he owned her all the same.

"But I do so enjoy our little games of words, Crickie," he said, accenting the last syllable of her name as he always did. "Not as much as some of our other games, of course." At this he twisted the ends of his moustaches, and raised one eyebrow in false allure. Crickie chose to ignore him.

"Mother has asked that Margaret come to her in London, you know," she said, smiling demurely as she gazed around the room. "She wishes Margaret to meet some of the young gentlemen of marriageable possibility there. . . ."

"Margaret is free to do as she pleases, *ma chère*," Michel said, unruffled. "But I doubt she will choose to leave her friends here."

"And if Mother insists?"

"Perhaps your mother will have to come for her then, for I cannot carry her to the ship and tie her there to make her go. Can I?"

Borque's cloying complacency was more oppressive than

he heat just then. "I believe I shall ask the governor to
ddress the guests, Michel," Crickie told him. Before he
ould answer she had snapped her fan shut, and walked
.way.

The guests remained standing, but turned their attention
o where Governor Lyttleton stood before one of the open
balcony doors, catching what breeze he could. He tugged at
his paisley cravat, then began.

"The colony has a need to disperse the Acadians still
sheltered in Charles Town. As most of you know, they claim
o be French neutrals—Catholics from Nova Scotia who
promised to neither aid nor arm the French on the main-
and, yet who refuse to swear allegiance to our King, even
hough the Crown gained control of Acadia in the Treaty of
Utrecht long decades ago—seventeen-thirteen to be exact.
Because of this refusal, the Crown had no recourse but to
see them deported and resettled among the colonies where
hey may have no opportunity to consort with their former
French allies in any way at all. They are to be sold as
indentured servants to pay for the cost of their passage, and
I ask tonight, as loyal subjects of the King, that as many of
you as possible make plans for the purchase of a few of
hem."

There was a hum in the room as people chatted among
themselves about the governor's request.

"We've enough help for the house now, but can use help
in the fields and gardens," Crickie said, the first to offer.
She caught Michel's look of displeasure. He wished her to
manage the plantation, but to do so without any unneces-
sary expenses, that he might spend more freely. Still he
would not dare to object before his guests or the governor.
Crickie smiled her first genuine smile of the evening at the
thought.

"Ah, your commitment to the Crown is admirable, madame. There are many common laborers among the group.
Many tradesmen as well—but they go quickly. Just this day
a man named Gairden bought the indentures of eight weavers . . ."

At the sound of Thomas's name, Crickie ceased to hear

the rest of Lyttleton's statement. Thomas had been gone for over a year, with the militia she'd been told.

". . . they will be ready for discharge Friday next," Lyttleton was saying. "Those not sold will be dispersed to the parishes at first opportunity lest they otherwise band together to further French interests during this time of conflict." Lyttleton's tone of command turned cordial when he spoke again to Crickie. "Send someone for them, madame," he said, "and have your factor inscribe the papers for you."

Crickie opened her fan once again. "I prefer to handle such matters myself," she said, polite but firm. "We may take more if they look fit."

The governor nodded with a lengthy bow of the head. "As you wish, Madame Borque," he said, "though it's little place for a lady."

"I shall see, sir." Crickie fanned herself disinterestedly.

"Pray consider my advice, madame. There are many among these Acadians of unsavory nature, which, of course, is why we are having such difficulty placing them. It was my hope tonight that your husband, with his French ancestry, might take pity on the poor wretches and persuade some of his friends to do likewise."

"And if they do not?"

"Those not bought will be sent to St. Michael's and St. Phillip's parishes to labor in any way we can find for them. Their food alone here in Charles Town is an oppressive drain on the exchequer."

"I'm certain you have helped to place many of them with your words here tonight, excellency."

"Madame, you are most kind," he said, then paused. "Before I take your leave might I inquire into ye origin of your most unusual name?"

"Crickie? It was given me by my father, Lieutenant Colonel Carlyle Rawlins of His Majesty's Royal Guard, and taken from my middle name, Crichton. I was named for my mother's family, ye Crichtons of Crichton Place in London. My mother and sister Deborah are living there once again."

"I know of Crichton Place, certainly," Lyttleton said. "To

hink I travelled so far to meet one of that family. I am
ionored."

"And we are honored by your presence, and by your
efforts for our colony."

Nodding crisply, the governor backed away and into conversation with Andre Moire, then Michel, then from group
o group around the room. A smart man, this Governor
Lyttleton, Crickie thought. His predecessor's concern had
always been to expand the colony's borders. Lyttleton appeared to have more of an interest in local problems. Already he was popular in Charles Town. In six weeks he'd
met the right people, done the right things.

Crickie moved about the room, too, speaking to the
guests. She asked the musicians to begin the music for
dancing. Well over a year ago at a party like this, she had
first danced with Thomas Gairden. . . . Crickie flashed a
smile across the room to Margaret, surprising her, then
turned to take the hand the governor offered. She thanked
him silently for telling her that Thomas was back.

Madame Borque knew the Sign of the Shuttle had been
closed for well over a year. She'd been told by an attaché to
the governor's office that its owner had been among those
who left with the First Charles Town Militia Unit in March
of 1755. His original enlistment was for only one month,
but he had remained at Fort Prince George, the attaché
said, according to the pay list.

Of course the pay list was over six months old by the time
it got to Charles Town, but it was still evidence of where
Thomas had been for part of the year past. He had a duty to
the militia, she knew. And she knew just as well why he
wanted to get as far away from Charles Town as he could
for as long as he could. She had Borque and her father to
thank for that.

Why she felt she would see him this day when she ferried
to Sullivan's Island to buy the Acadian indentures she could
not say, yet the feeling persisted. There could be nothing
between them now, yet she could not forget what had been
between them once. She owed herself the small pleasure of

seeing him, if nothing else, for her pleasures in life were few just now.

The cool breeze of the ferry trip ceased when the passengers debarked at Fort Sullivan. The air was still and the sun broiling as they made their way inside the gates. Crickie wore her old Gipsy hat and carried a fan she kept constantly in motion.

The group lined up inside the thick, palisaded palmetto walls of Fort Sullivan, where Philip Tuthill, recently appointed Commissioner of Indentures for Acadian Affairs, sat with his secretary at a table shaded by a canopy of heavy, cream-colored canvas. Tuthill was a pinched-faced little man with one aberrant eye, and perspiration streamed from beneath his white wig. He was what was known as a "placeman"—sent from London by the Crown, placed in his position over local men better qualified for the position. His secretary, Louis Ducray, a native of Charles Town, was a prime example of the result of such favoritism, and there were many other examples as well, from the Customs House to the Council Chambers.

"May I ask how many of ye Acadians are to be placed," Crickie inquired of the commissioner. A pleasantry. A stall. There was no sign of Thomas anywhere.

"Nearly a thousand, I'm afraid—but we've plans made for them all," he added hastily. "Those not sold will be relocated in the neighboring parishes." He wiped his reddened face dry and tugged at his tight collar.

"So the governor told me," Crickie said. "Will families be kept together?" Another stall.

Tuthill stammered. "I-I-I'm not certain."

Crickie looked once again to the mass of French neutrals before her. The booty of war, they had been taken like property and dumped in a strange place among people who both resented and feared them. Over half of them had died at sea, she'd been told. Sadness and hopelessness cried out from the dark beauty of their eyes. Men like Michel grew rich through gambling. People like these lost everything through living on the wrong side of a treaty line.

"Ye Acadians will find no real home here, I fear," Crickie

old him, "despite our efforts. They long for home. It is in
heir eyes."

"So they do." The voice behind her was Thomas's. She
turned with a whirl of skirts.

"Thomas Gairden! I can't believe it's you!" she cried
with delight as he took her hands in his and stepped back
for a long, head-to-toe look. She felt the roughness of his
palms and saw new lines in the familiar face. A year in the
backcountry had seasoned him, browned his skin. But his
eyes, the mystery and wonder of his eyes, were unchanged.

"Aye, I've been away. With the militia," he explained as
she drank in every detail of him. "But me duty's done for a
bit and I'm back in Charles Town to tend to business—lucky
enough to hire some weavers already trained in Acadia. 'Tis
a day of true good fortune for me."

"For them, as well."

"Aye, for them, too, I hope. They've suffered, these folks
have. Sickness killin' over a hundred of them I heard. Kept
in quarantine. Forced labor. Curfews. I'm a little surprised
you're takin' some to High Garden since they pledge no
allegiance to your King. Does it not bother you?"

Crickie looked down a moment before she answered. "Is
George not your King as well?" she asked.

From Thomas she got only a quizzical smile and lift of
the eyebrows.

"I do not think them traitors, at least, as so many do,"
she went on, "and they are a bargain."

Thomas laughed, then caught a look of disapproval from
Tuthill. Thomas had been here less than five minutes and
already he was impatient with the little bureaucrat.

"Still watchin' the deep pockets, are you?" he asked,
taking Crickie by the arm and leading her out of Tuthill's
earshot.

"I am," she said, smiling. Crickie noted the trim tailoring
of Thomas's coat as he took her arm. A crisp, gray wool
worsted, the coat was trimmed in pale lavender. The vest
beneath it was a deeper lavender brocade. His silk shirt was
thin and cool looking.

"And High Garden's still in your competent care, un-hampered by your sociable husband?"

"Michel wishes me to run ye plantation as I always have," she said, lowering her eyes.

"I'm certain he does," Thomas said.

Crickie caught his double meaning. "I'd have it no other way," she said, emphasizing each word.

Thomas looked away. "I'm certain you wouldn't," he said, and Crickie felt the pain of his words.

He shifted his weight, moving to the right a step or two so as to have his back to the table where Tuthill and Ducray still sold indentures to a small line of takers.

"I want to thank you for getting me to take the inocula-tion," he said, changing the subject. "Smallpox was bad in the backcountry. Lots of men died, but I had only a mild attack . . . met an old friend on me travels . . . when I was sick. Sarah Roberts—Sarah Lowe now."

Crickie saw his eyes search her face for a reaction. They'd talked of this Sarah. She recalled the name. Also the face. She was the Sarah on board the *Endeavor* the first time Crickie had ever seen the unforgettable Thomas Gairden. She had been Thomas's first love. "Was she well?" Crickie asked.

"As well as a woman tryin' to manage three wee ones at a settler's fort can be. Her husband was gone fightin' Cher-okees. She'd had no word from him for months." Thomas shook his head. " 'Tis a waste."

"I'm sorry, Thomas," she said. And she was. She wished no ill to anyone he loved. He had a whole life apart from her now, and she could only wish him well in it. "I don't know whether to say I hope he comes back to her . . . or that he doesn't."

"I can't say either . . . What about Borque, though? Is he treatin' you well, Elizabeth?" Thomas asked. "That's all I'm wantin' to know. I've stayed away more than a year, all the while wonderin' if you'd made the right choice."

Crickie drew in a deep breath. "I had no choice, Thomas. My place is at High Garden," she reminded him.

"But is he treatin' you well, I'm askin'?"

"He . . . He . . . I see very little of him," she admitted.

"And even that's too much?"

Crickie lowered her eyes. She did not have to answer, for he knew Thomas knew her meaning.

"He doesn't deserve you, Elizabeth," Thomas said. He shook his head and clicked his tongue in the same way she remembered. "Even more, your father doesn't deserve you. Your High Garden doesn't deserve you."

"Charles Town thinks High Garden was my father's gracious dowry to Michel. Michel's philanthropy is legend in the city—he's bought the support of those he wants. And if I expose him for what he really is, all I've done in the past year—no, years—would be for nothing, and I would look the fool."

Thomas stood listening, arms folded across his chest. "You're like the British Army regulars, Elizabeth Rawlins—Borque. Must be your father's trainin'. Once you've committed to a plan, you stick to it, no matter what it costs you."

Crickie wasn't sure how to answer. She heard in Thomas's words a hint of the pain he still felt at losing her to Borque, and at the same time a charge of inflexibility. "Ye cost has been dear," she said at last, meeting his eyes straight on. His eyes closed just a moment as he nodded.

"I want at least to know that you're safe," he said.

"I'm that if I'm anything," Crickie replied. She laughed a bitter little laugh. "Michel would not harm ye plantation boss."

She stopped a moment, greeting another acquaintance passing nearby. "You will be always in my thoughts and in my prayers, Thomas, but you must stay out of my sight—Michel is a jealous man."

"Then I should stay nearby, to help you if you need it. I'll be in Charles Town a good amount now. And some at Williamsburgh—we have an indigo crop, thanks in part to you. I've—"

"Stay clear of Michel, Thomas," she said, interrupting

him to emphasize her message. "For your safety and mine Please."

"For yours, I will," Thomas agreed, "though I wouldn' mind a go at your undeserving mate—must be *my* militia trainin'."

Crickie looked nervously about, trying to smile so that anyone noticing her conversation might think it no more than the renewal of an old acquaintance. Michel would relish punishing her for an indiscretion should he find out. She had to leave. She wanted to stay.

"Good to see you again, Thomas," she said, offering her gloved hand for a kiss. "We all do appreciate the help ye militia has given our regulars in fighting ye Cherokees. And now, good fortune to you with your new weavers." All this she said loudly enough to be heard by Tuthill, if he were listening, then took her clutch of papers and went to select an Acadian family for purchase, though she knew not for what. Her real purpose this day was already accomplished.

"It seems to be your lucky night, Monsieur Gray," Michel Borque said that evening as Alexander Gray snapped the ace of hearts over his queen and won the evening's final hand of hearts, along with a handsome pocketful of pounds.

"Aye, the winds o' fortune are blowin' at me back for sure," he said. His boast escaped most of the players, who were already rising from the table, putting on their waistcoats and readying to leave. It was past two in the morning, and the other patrons of Dellap's Inn had long since retired, including proprietor Godfrey Dellap, who left the lamp extinguishing and door locking duties to Borque, his most regular customer.

Michel Borque, though, had a ready ear for any news of fortune. Pouring Gray another glass of whiskey, and refilling his own supply of rum, Borque turned his full attention to the stranger. A quantity of whiskey might be required of this man, he thought, for his face gave away little.

"You have had the good pleasure to learn that the bounty on indigo may be raised, then?" Borque ventured, hoping to draw him out but knowing little of how to start other than that the man was a planter from the Williamsburgh District.

"Always good news when the Crown's willin' to spend a little of its coin on us poor bastards here in the flower of the colonies. Aye, and I'm lookin' for a fine crop, though it's me first. The land about River Plum's a fine spot for it."

"Have another," Borque said, filling Gray's glass once again. "We'll drink to your very good fortune . . . and my own, for at High Garden we, too, anticipate a most bountiful crop."

At this last, Borque noticed the man's eyes raise a bit, though it was still not possible to read their meaning.

"High Garden you say?"

Borque nodded.

"Home of a fine lady named 'Crickie'?"

"It is," Borque said, now more intrigued than before. "Do you know her?" he asked. "She is my wife."

At this, Gray laughed, a deep, shoulder-shaking laugh that made Borque suddenly uncomfortable.

"So you're the one stole me partner's lass away from him," Gray said, chuckling. "Won her in a card game, was it? God in heaven, to think I've been playin' cards with you and bettin' no more than a pound or two. You're a gambler, by God. Pleased to know you!" he said, taking Borque's small, well-manicured hand in his own rough, callused one and pumping it eagerly.

"You, Monsieur Gray, are a partner of Thomas Gairden?" Borque could not believe such news, though he had often wondered at Gairden's source of funds and knew he must do more than run a weaving manufactory. Competition from imported goods and slave labor made the market a narrow one. Most tradesmen stayed in Charles Town only a short time and then went on to planting. Gairden was different. This helped to explain why.

"A bit of a poor relation partner I be," Gray said, less effusive. "But I'm goin' to change all that, for I've learned somethin' of Thomas that'll get him out of Charles Town on the next ship that sails for Philadelphia—leavin' me River Plum and whatever else he has." Gray paused. "Leavin' me a rich man." He raised his eyebrows and gave Borque a look of knowing camaraderie before slamming down his glass and beaming a broad smile to Borque to fill it once again.

"Do you think Monsieur Gairden is a rich man?" Borque asked, lowering his eyes so as not to look too eager for information.

"Not so rich as a Laurens or a Drayton, mind you, but rich enough. And like all Scots, he has the short arms and deep pockets—what he gets, he knows how to keep. . . . Makes it hard bein' his partner."

Borque looked deep into the glass of golden rum before him, all the while keeping his lips formed into a pursed smile beneath his perfectly trimmed moustaches.

"Perhaps with your luck running as highly as it is this evening—or morning—as it may be," said Borque, stretching every *e* sound as his thick French accent became thicker through fatigue and liquor, "perhaps . . . you might like to cut the cards on this good fortune and see if chance should further smile on you." Borque reached in his pocket for a pouch of pipe tobacco and checked for reassurance to see that his special deck of cutting cards was in place. Satisfied, he nodded and asked with the raise of an eyebrow for Gray's opinion on the matter.

At once, Gray shed his vacant look. "I think you're a bit too willin'," he said, rising and at the same time reaching for the waistcoat pocket from which he'd just seen Borque take the tobacco. With one hand he held Borque in his seat while his fingers probed deep into the pocket and seized the deck.

"You scaly French bastard!" Gray sneered, stuffing the deck into his own pocket. "And this is how you got your High Garden, too, I'll wager. . . . Well, once is enough, laddie. For anythin'. 'Tis you I should be exposin' to the fine people of Charles Town, not Thomas." He took his hands off from Borque's chest, but Borque remained shrunken in his seat, clearly afraid of Gray's powerful arms and hands.

"But then, you may be more useful to me free than in the gaol. And if you ever want to see these again," Gray said,

rawing the deck of marked cards beneath Borque's nose
ke a bottle of smelling salts, "you'll give me the help I
eed when I ask for it. Understand?"

Borque nodded. "*Oui*, monsieur."

"I'll be around to your house tomorrow midday," Gray
old him. "Don't be gone."

"I have every expectation to be at home, monsieur," Bor-
ue said, quickly regaining his composure once the threat
f physical danger was less imminent, "have no fears."

"Good," Gray said, backing toward the door. "You're
oin' to be a most valuable asset to me finances, I can see."

Borque watched impassively as Gray went out, then
oured himself another glass of rum. He'd lost count of just
ow many he'd had tonight. Too many. He started to pour it
ack. Then quit, gulped it down, and poured himself an-
ther.

23

"No French speakin' in the manufactory," Thomas said, and the eight men standing before him nodded solemnly. "Not that I mind the sound of it, you understand—just that I've not learned it."

Hearing no objection—hearing nothing, actually—Thomas went on.

"Now . . . Durong, Verstille, LaPierre, and Quessy—you'll have to teach me how to say your names," Thomas said, reading off from their indenture papers, "you men are listed as weavers. You'll be workin' here at the manufactory for the time bein'. I want each of you to weave a yard from the pattern at your loom so I can see your work."

"The looms—how are they threaded?" the young weaver called Durong asked.

"The looms are threaded for coverlids—patterns pinned on the loom castles. I've a new one I'll be bringin' in, too," he said. "I'm callin' it 'Braddock's Defeat'—for the general who died losin' the war for us up in the Ohio. You might like that one," he quipped to no response. The faces were blank. Either they didn't understand or understood too well. Thomas didn't know which. "Just use your own judgment," he said as an afterthought.

For the first time, Thomas saw a spark of interest on the four faces and forged on. "Only three looms, as you can see. One of you'll have to make warp. You can alternate at the looms as you like. I'll be back in later to see how you've done."

"*Oui*, monsieur," Durong said automatically. "That is, yea, Master Gairden."

"'*Oui* monsieur' I understand," Thomas replied with a Scot twist on the French words that made the new men chuckle at last. " 'Tis about all I understand, too. But me name's Thomas, and you're welcome to call me by it."

Thomas's good humor was not altogether easy for him. In their months of internment at Sullivan's Island, hundreds of the Acadians had run away. Perhaps he would return to find these men gone, too. But they were weavers like himself and he owed them his respect as fellow craftsmen.

"I'm placin' me trust in you lads, to work hard and to work well," he said, showing the other four men to the door. "Good luck to you." Then he turned to the others. "Let's go."

"Where?" the man named Rene Fourrait wanted to know. "Are we not to be weavers also?"

"Not yet. Your papers say you men have worked as joiners and carpenters as well as weavers. You'll be helpin' first on the buildin' of a new manufactory over here on Elliot Street. Me friend, Henry Jones, has but a small crew and needs more help. When 'tis finished we'll have a shop and me office in front, dyers and fullers in back, along with some warehouse space, and the looms upstairs—enough looms for all of you."

"Office?" Fourrait asked. He was younger than the rest, alert but sullen.

"Aye," Thomas explained. "I do some tradin' and other business along with me weavin' . . . No slave tradin' if that's a worry to you, though that's most surely the way to riches. Nay, rice . . . indigo . . . skins . . . those are what I know."

He stopped midstride and turned to the unwashed, hungry-looking men with him. There was no spark of interest here as there'd been with the weavers.

"Forgive me if I talk too much for you. You talk a bit."

No one spoke up.

"Do you have family here?"

Fourrait spoke up once again. "Our families were torn apart when we left Grand Pré. They are lost—dead on the ships, or from poor food. Or the heat. Sold like the slaves

. . . This place is hell." Fourrait spat on the ground. The other three men did the same.

"The Crown has a way of makin' life like that, I'll not argue. But here in Charles Town they sometimes look the other way and let us run our own affairs. While you work for me I'll treat you well. Feed you well. And do me best to help you find your loved ones." Thomas saw the doubt in their eyes. "Came on one of those ships myself some years back, and I know your feelin's. But this place's been good to me. Work hard and you'll do well, too."

Ozick Olivier looked from one to another of his countrymen. "Do we work on Sunday?" he asked for all of them.

"Nay, not on Sunday," Thomas said, "though we'll work daylight to dark most other days. Are you Catholics all?"

The men nodded without hesitation.

" 'Tis of no matter to me . . . though you're lucky my last indentured man, Dugald Mackay, is gone now, for he had some other opinions . . ." Thomas laughed to himself as he remembered Mackay and wondered if he'd made his way to the Ohio Valley. The lovely Mary had married another.

"Henry," he called as they reached the building site, "I want you to meet my new men: Fourrait, Olivier, Fougasse and Chop."

"Chop?" Henry Jones asked the question Thomas had already asked.

The Acadian smiled. "The British were not always such enemies," Tobias Chop said, his accent every bit as French as his name was not.

"Well, then," Henry said, "there's hope for peace among us yet," and shook hands with the men, repeating their names with his own Scots' burr, except for Chop, which seemed to sound the same from both tongues.

"Walls are comin' right along, eh, Henry?" Thomas said. A crew of masons worked on scaffolds, laying up courses of orangey red brick that had only a month ago come from London as ship's ballast.

"Aye, we're makin' good progress—and will do even better with eight more hands. Any of you laid bricks before?"

Tobias Chop said he had, and just as quickly Henry took them off and gave them jobs.

"Show 'em the way home tonight, will you, Henry?" he called after them. Jones waved and nodded, busy with the new men.

"Home. Home," Thomas said aloud, clicking his tongue at the thought. The house he'd had Henry build over a year ago, the one he'd hoped to share with Elizabeth Rawlins, would at last be lived in. Not by a family, of course, but instead by a scruffy lot of refugees. Not much different from me, he thought, and walked back to check on the weavers.

The moment Thomas saw Alex Gray's face back at the Sign of the Shuttle, he felt a sharp pang of guilt. It had been almost four months since he'd left Sarah and the children at River Plum, promising Gray to find a place for them as soon as he could. Instead, he'd come back to Charles Town and thrown himself into rebuilding his business, and into denying what had happened between him and Sarah.

"So, Thomas, you've got yourself a wee building project goin' near the wharf, I hear." Alexander Gray drew his head back slightly, raising his stubbled chin and narrowing his eyes.

"So I do," Thomas answered, waiting for Gray to say what he'd really come for. " 'Tis time I got me own fullers and dyers and quit payin' someone else to do it for me. I may not beat the English at their own game, but I can try. How's the indigo?"

"Fine, Thomas, fine," Gray nodded confidently. "I'd say I'll make a thousand pounds on it alone this year," he said.

" 'I'll'?" Thomas asked.

Gray's small smile broadened into a healthy grin. "Benefactor," he said. His smile leveled. "I'm making the thousand pounds because this day you're ceasin' to be owner of River Plum."

"You're payin' me off then? That's—"

"Nay, you're payin' yourself in a manner of speakin'," Gray said.

A two-day growth of gray beard and bloodshot eyes did not obscure the wily look of Gray's face. With a sword at his side he couldn't look any more like a pirate, Thomas thought. "And just how is that?" he asked.

"I've a mind you'll be forgivin' me debts when you hear the news I have for you, partner." Gray's eyes rolled lazily from side to side.

"Sarah?" It had to be about Sarah.

"Nay 'tis not your Sarah, though I must say she's one spirited little lass I wouldn't mind leapin' to me bed," Gray offered. "But 'tis from your past . . ."

At once Thomas knew. And he felt a familiar tic at his right eye.

"A horse thief and a robber I've got for a partner, it seems," Gray said, matter of fact. "Blood on your hands, too."

"Sarah told you that?" At once Thomas tensed.

"Not Sarah, nay." Gray shook his head, pleasure at Thomas's anguish plain on his face. " 'Twas her husband—Jamie, I believe he said his name was."

"Jamie's come for Sarah?" Again Thomas cursed himself.

"That he has, Thomas, and not a happy man, either, at havin' to chase his wife clear across the colony where she's gone with an old suitor . . ."

"But—"

"But that's another matter entirely, Thomas," Gray said, smooth as a glass of Ulster whiskey. "I'm tellin' you that forgivin' me debt on River Plum will keep me lips sealed about your doings to the north—but I'd also be needin' the other parcel of land you just bought, to make me even quieter."

"That's larceny, Gray, and I'd be a fool to give in to you even if I was guilty—which I'm not. No doubt Jamie forgot to tell you that part—how I worked four years for Sarah's father and left not even takin' all of what was mine. About how he helped set up my escape to make me look the more guilty. Go on, believe what Jamie Lowe tells you, but Sarah's already told me the charges were dropped. You've a ne way of thankin' me for helpin' you when you were in eed."

"And what about the deerskins you cheated me out of to tart your business. You'd be gone back north weavin' draw-rs for folks if you'd not had that money to start with."

"I cheated? 'Twas me weavin's we traded those Catawbas or the deerskins. You had no tradin' stock." Thomas heard iis own voice crack, high-pitched in disbelief.

"Aye, but without me, there'd have been no tradin', for ou'd have run from 'em if I'd let you."

"I'd not have cheated 'em, at least. I should've known hen—"

"That you were dealin' with a dangerous man?" Gray aughed. "But you didn't care then, did you, lad? You were n the run from Pennsylvania and happy to find any way ou could to get your start in the Carolinas."

Thomas could not deny there was an element of truth in vhat Gray said. Only it was so twisted. "You know I never planned to keep River Plum from you, Alex. 'Twas business, 1othin' more. Lending's me business—you know I'm no planter."

Gray shrugged. "You're like the rest of these low-country ξents. You want all the land here, and all the land up there, oo. A poor Ulsterman like me can't go against money like ours."

"You could if you'd leave the bottle alone, Alex," Thomas said, quietly, composed again. "I'm goin' back with you to River Plum and talk to Jamie myself."

"Come along, partner. You'll find what I say's true. You're wanted for a horse thief back in Pennsylvania and you'll hang for it if I tell the right people."

" 'Tis the whiskey talkin' in Jamie. He knows no court would see me hanged."

"I'm tellin' you only what the man told me, Thomas . . ." Gray's face was a mask of innocence.

"If you're lyin', Alex . . . if you and Jamie have cooked up this little pot of mush . . . you'll be seein' River Plum for the last time." Thomas felt his breathing quicken. He clipped his words short.

"Hah! I'd not go!" Gray raised his eyes to the ceiling, unconcerned.

"If you're lyin', you'll give it up or I'll have the justice of the peace see that you're driven off." Thomas paused. Looked Gray in the eye. "We'll see who's the dangerous man."

"Aye, we'll see," said Gray, not giving an inch. "We'll see," he repeated and started for the door.

"Not so fast there, Alex. I'm ridin' with you, just to keep matters fair. Like our old days on the Wagon Road," he said, closing the door to his small office behind him. It was a good day's ride to Williamsburgh, which meant he'd be away the better part of three days. A poor thing to do with eight new men to train, but he had no choice. He couldn't trust Gray to keep quiet while he got things in order.

"Durong, you're in charge here until I get back," he said, seeing that the young man had woven more than the older ones. "The job list's on the wall by the door. Keep the men busy. Henry Jones, upstairs, can show you to me house where you'll eat and sleep."

Durong nodded. Thomas hoped he understood. He hoped the new men would still be here when he returned, whenever that might be. And he hoped that Jamie's words were whiskey words.

24

Gray had been gone only two days when Sarah Roberts Lowe knelt, tearless, beside the body of her husband. It had been dumped in the red dust of the path east of the house by two Cherokees she didn't know, and one she did.

"They be back for Gray," called Echoe from the rear of a small, skinny, spotted horse. She rode behind a bare-chested brave to whom she clung tightly, not even loosening her grip when the horse came to a complete stop before Sarah. "This one no good either," she added, looking Sarah square in the eye for one brief moment before the horse raced away.

Jamie lay on his back, and only his blood-streaked clothing identified him. His scalp was gone, half of his face torn away.

"God! Help me, God. Help me!" Sarah screamed, covering her face at the horror. Back and forth and around she threw her head as the cook, a slave woman named Effie, cowered behind her in the doorway, shaking with fright.

"Jamie, Jamie, you didn't deserve this. God forgive me, Jamie, for me wrongs to you. God forgive me," Sarah cried, then ceased speaking and only keened, trancelike, over the faceless corpse. She never heard the slam of the door, or knew that Effie ran to the fields to bring back Oliver Bruff, the overseer.

Bruff sent Effie for whiskey and she brought it out in a small china cup. "Drink this," he said. Sarah snapped her head away, moaning and shaking. Bruff took her by the shoulders and drew her back, away from the body. "Drink," he said. Again she twisted away from him. "Drink, ma'am," he said, more softly this time, but Sarah pushed away the cup, screaming.

" 'Tis what killed Jamie. He'd not have been killed by any man but for drink!" Her eyes gaped, wild with the horror she had seen, and she threw her head down on Jamie's chest, sobbing. Seeing her quiet a bit, Bruff lifted and carried her to the house.

"Stay right with her, Effie," he said, taking a swallow from the jug the servant had left on the table. "Give her something. Anything. Try the whiskey again." Wet and grimy from working alongside the Negroes as they cut indigo, Bruff scanned the yard for any sign of horses, his arms swinging restlessly at his sides.

Effie prevailed where Bruff had not, spooning the homemade fire down through Sarah's parted lips. She was almost still for a moment.

"I want me wee ones!" she screamed then, breaking her short lull. "Where's Gavin? Martha? Anna?" With each name her voice grew higher, harsher.

"They right upstairs in they room, ma'am," Effie said. Not much older than Sarah, she was wide across the cheekbones with a flat nose. She'd become a favorite with the children in their months here, amusing them with games and homemade toys when they came to her kitchen. "I fetch 'em for you."

Sarah started to follow her, her body now springing from the bed like rock from a slingshot, but Bruff's field-ready hands stopped her.

"She'll bring 'em, ma'am," he said. "Let her."

Sarah looked at this man, holding her back from her children. Who was he? She pulled her shoulder away, angry, frightened, then used her sleeve to wipe away the sweat that ran down her brow and into her eyes mixing salt with salt, her eyes burning as she watched and waited. The whiskey warmed her and she tried to rise once again to go to the children, but the world fell away as she lifted her head, split into a restless dream of Jamie and the rogues at Turkey

Creek and her and Thomas fighting Cherokees. Over both dreams, a silent, blank-faced Echoe, presided.

When Sarah opened her eyes the next time, she heard the low voices of two men in the next room. Jamie? she wondered. Then she remembered.

"Gavin! Martha! Anna! Come to your mother!" Reeling as she got out of bed, Sarah felt the gritty white sand of the floor stick to her feet. Before she could take a step, though, she saw a face she knew.

"There, there, lass," Thomas said, " 'tis over, Sarah." He opened his arms and she went to him. Pummeled him with her small fists.

"Cry it out now. Cry all you want," he whispered as she finally collapsed against him, sobbing, a limp sack of cares and desperation that he lifted easily back onto the bed. "I'll take care of you, don't worry."

Sarah fell back into a fitful sleep, with Thomas and Effie taking turns watching over her. Effie had seen Echoe ride in with two other Cherokees, but didn't know what they'd said. Everyone else had been in the fields. Until Sarah came out of her shock, the unanswered questions would remain. Effie hummed mournfully, praying as she rocked by the bedside, while Thomas and Gray talked outside.

" 'Twas a terrible thing for her to see, I'll admit it," Gray said as the two men lounged in the heavy, white oak chairs on the south veranda, watching the stars begin to take their places in the eastern sky. To the west, clouds obscured the doings of the heavens and the moon was ringed with a tinge of white Thomas's father had always told him meant a change in the weather. After weeks of searing heat, rain would be welcome, even if it did slow down the indigo harvest. Gray would want it to nourish the crops. Thomas wanted it to wash away the blood.

"We'll have to take turns on guard," Thomas said.

"They'll not be back, if I know 'em," Gray said. "They've got their Echoe and that's apt to be enough for 'em."

"You're mighty sure of yourself, Alex," Thomas said, not looking at him.

"I know Cherokees," he said. "They want what's theirs, but once they have it they're gone. They're not fighters."

"Have you no remorse that a man was killed here this day, man," Thomas said, sickened at Gray's cavalier attitude, "and that it was your stealin' of the lass Echoe brought it on?"

"Jamie Lowe was an Indian fighter, for god's sake, Thomas. Did you never think they might have trailed him here—that it was him they were after? Is it not a wee bit odd they struck when I was gone and not when I was here? Me life's as good as a piece of eight coin, and I'm about to begin livin' it again—as soon as you sign your papers for me."

Thomas took a long, slow look at the profile of the aging Ulsterman in the twilight. There was no Jamie to confirm Gray's accusation. Sarah was in no condition to be asked about it. And Thomas knew he was as innocent as a man could ever be. Still, inside him, there was no tie to this land. It had brought him profit, but always profit at a price. When a warp string broke on his loom he cut it out and replaced it with a stronger one. He would do the same with Gray.

"I'm willin' to sign back to you your original two hundred acres, Alex," Thomas said without thinking further. "And the slaves you bought yourself. The River Plum that was yours is goin' to be yours once again—but what I've paid for I'll keep. I'll not hinder you. Nor will I ever help you again. Once Jamie's buried and I've seen to a place for Sarah, I'll be gone, and hope never to see you again. I'll give you no more. But I'll tell you this: I'm guilty of nothin'—except a poor choice in partners, it seems."

"Hmmp," Gray said, crossing his legs. "Now who's sure of himself? There's still the matter of the charges. What if I don't like your terms?"

"You don't have to like 'em," Thomas said, springing out of his chair and looking down at Gray, eyes blazing. "You only have to take 'em—and you'd damn well better do it before I change my mind or you won't have anything."

Gray remained slouched in his chair, hands hanging limp over the ends of each arm.

"I'll take 'em . . . since Lowe's gone and your lovely Sarah in there's not like to talk against you. Course I don't really need 'em," Gray said, "as I happened onto some other information during my most profitable trip to Charles Town that will keep me cozy for a long time."

Thomas stood, arms folded, impatient. "That's fine, Alex. Just fine. Play your games. I'm goin' to bed," he said and turned to go in.

"Don't you want to know who 'tis will be takin' your place?"

Thomas stopped. "Nay."

"Aye, but you do, lad," Gray purred, "for 'tis someone you know. Someone you knew, at least."

Thomas opened the door.

"Well, I'm tellin' you, whether you want to know or not. 'Tis your old friend Michel Borque—the one married your lass Elizabeth. . . . He's got some secrets of his own, it seems. And he's willin' to pay to—"

"His way with the ladies is no secret in Charles Town," Thomas said, turning back, "and if he thinks—"

"Nay, lad. Slow down. 'Tis not the women he wants to keep secret—he likes braggin' on women. Nay, 'twas the marked deck of cards I found him tryin' to use that put him in my debt."

" 'Tis no surprise," Thomas scoffed.

"Nay, not for you I'm sure, but 'twould put a damper on his games in the city," Gray said, still unperturbed. "And when you think your lady Elizabeth was robbed of her fortune—and you of her hand—by a man who cheats at cards, 'tis a bit dicey, isn't it now?"

Thomas took a deep breath, thinking. "You're not much of a swindler, Alex, if you go givin' your secrets away like that."

"To you? Why not? I know you, Thomas. You'll do nothin' about it. You'll pine and whine—but you've got no spine when it comes to women, lad. And anyway, the damage's already done there. But your friend Borque wants none of his fun spoiled at the gamin' tables, and he's willin' to pay."

"You deserve each other, Alex," Thomas said, suddenly tired. He left Gray to sit by himself watching the dark clouds roll in from the west and sipping from a jug of his homemade whiskey. Before long, Gray's head would drop to his chest in his nightly stupor.

Thomas threw his blanket on the floor, but heard the whimpers that came from Sarah's bed, soon mingled with snores that came from the veranda.

"If you want Alex, you Cherokees, he's yours for the takin'," Thomas whispered to himself, and closed his eyes.

"But, Mama, the sun's out. Why can't I go to the river?" Gavin asked the day after his father was buried. The curls of his red hair toppled this way and that, and his freckled face was filled with six-year-old defiance. Martha and Anna waited nearby, their eyes wide and wondering.

"Nay! You'll not be goin' outside. 'Tis muddy." Sarah grasped at any excuse to keep the children in, short of telling them the Cherokees would get them. Of course, she knew the Cherokees wouldn't get them. The Cherokees hadn't killed Jamie. She had done it herself.

"We'll be good, Mama," said Martha, wide-eyed, twisting her finger nervously in a yellow wisp of shoulder-length curl while Anna tugged impatiently at her other hand. Like Gavin, both girls wore dark, everyday clothes, and no shoes.

Sarah heard, but didn't listen. It was my telling him I'd never loved him as much as Thomas that did it, she thought. Put him off his guard and let the Cherokees get to him. And it was Echoe, seeing Jamie beat me. It was not a matter of Cherokee versus English, but of woman versus man. That was what killed Jamie.

"Mama?" Gavin asked once more, quietly.

Sarah knew that only God could save her from the fires of hell now. Only prayer and the grace of God.

"Nay!" she shouted. Then calmer, "Nay, you'll get to the parlor with me and read from the Bible. Only by puttin' the Lord before your worldly desires can you get to the grand and glorious kingdom where you'll see your father one day." She shooed the children to the parlor, never hearing the footsteps of Thomas, who entered by the back door and stood outside the parlor, listening, concerned.

"With the Reverend Aldworth gone from the Cruikshanks'," Thomas told her that evening as they walked along the river, "they've room for you and the children for a while if you won't come back to Charles Town with me."

"I can't go with you—and I'll not be stayin' here," Sarah said. She fidgeted at her hair, tucking in unseen strands. "I'll be goin' back to Turkey Creek within a day or two, soon as I feel up to it. 'Tis me home." Patting her head over and over to find lost strands of hair, she kept her eyes on the small paper fan she flickered at her cheek.

"You'll not be goin' there and be the prey of the Cherokees again," Thomas said. "I'll not allow it."

"There's no more to fear from the Cherokees," she said. "They can do no more to us." She spoke without emotion, eyes darting from the fan to the trail they followed through the coarse swamp grass of the upper bank. Back to the fan. Off to the river.

"You don't know that, Sarah. What about the children? Do you think you can protect 'em? And not just from Cherokees but from men like those we chased off—men who run wild in the backcountry because there's no law to stop 'em? You can't. And I can't let you try."

"But me church is there, Thomas. And I need it." Didn't he know anything? Couldn't he tell she had to confess? To be cleansed? His great dark eyes were not on her but far away on the sun that shimmered atop the black water. "Those people know me." She heard her voice become shrill with him. "If naught else, I can go back to the fort," she said.

"To the fort? I thought you wouldn't go back there?" Thomas gave her a sharp glance, puzzled. "Anyway, you couldn't live in the fort forever, and God knows when the Cherokee troubles will end. The treaties are broken as fast as they're written. Who knows how long the Saluda and Savannah will be trouble spots?"

Thomas stopped, picked up a stone and skipped it across the water. A score of little circles noiselessly appeared and disappeared behind it before he spoke again. "You're mine to take care of now, Sarah. Long after you should've been. Long after you wanted to be. Don't run away from me again. You've lost the father of your children and you're—"

" 'Tis not completely true," she interrupted, walking a few steps beyond him. Thomas turned. "The wee bairn I'm carryin's a Gairden," she said, her voice little more than a trembling whisper.

She felt Thomas's eyes search her midsection, seeing nothing. Using the flat of her hands she pulled the gathers of her petticoat to the side, stretching the worn fabric across the mound of belly just now beginning to show, and watched as Thomas's eyes blinked. Blinked again. She stood there waiting, but he made no move to come near, to touch the spot, to wait for the tiny movement she was beginning to feel.

"A Gairden?" Thomas placed one foot on a mound of mossy sod, rested his hands on his hips. Looked at her again. "I—" He stopped, knitting his eyebrows, then took a breath as if to speak.

"A Gairden," Sarah said again. "A son, I'm sure, by the feel of him. Too wee yet to be Jamie's, if that's what you're wonderin'."

He turned his head away from her, rubbed his chin slowly against his shoulder. Sarah looked away, too, up the river. I shouldn't have told him, she thought. She turned her back to him and felt a tear begin to run. Then she dropped her fan.

Thomas had picked it up before she could so much as bend her knees, and returning it, he lay his hands at her waist.

"I've a family once again," he said, looking down into her eyes. Before she could answer, he lifted her off her feet until it was she who looked down at him.

"Put me down, Thomas," she said. She saw his puzzled look, but gently he lowered her back to the ground, smoothed her skirts and straightened her sleeves.

"We're to be married at last then, lass." He slipped his arms around her waist again, though her hands were folded

etween them. "How things change. . . . 'Tis a gift to us,
is new life, to take the place of Jamie's. . . . I know 'tis
o soon," he went on, thinking aloud. "And yet too long. If
'd claimed you that day six years ago, you'd not be in this
lace now. We'd be . . . in Philly, me with a little weavin'
hop and maybe makin' a pound from smugglin' as the
azette says they're all doin' up there. But then we'd never
ave come to Carolina, or seen the miles of sand flats and
lack rivers, never known the beauty of Charles Town—or
ad the pleasure of all these mosquitoes!"

Thomas loosed one arm from about Sarah's waist and
lapped the back of his neck, then swept down Sarah's back
o chase away more of the biting pests. The sun was now no
nore than a tint on the horizon. The Black River beside
hem was dark as its name. Shadows gave way to dusk.
arah was silent, her fidgeting passed into a dull torpor. She
eard Thomas's words, but could force out none of her
wn. She heard his excitement as he planned for them.

" 'Tis soon, but people will understand. No widow's safe
n the colony. Or her children. She must—"

"I can't marry you, Thomas," Sarah said, reviving again.

"You can't . . . ?"

"I can't, Thomas." Sarah felt no emotion, put none into
er words.

"Not tomorrow maybe. Or the next day. But by month's
nd sure. You can't stay at the Cruikshanks' forever. You
an't go back to Turkey Creek. You must come with me
nd—"

"Nay, Thomas," she said, with some force this time. "You
now I love you. But 'twas me love for you killed Jamie. I
old him—"

"You told him about the bairn?"

"Nay, I told him none of that, but when he asked had I
ver loved him as I did you, I couldn't double-tongue. I told
him nay. And in his anger at me, he forgot to guard against
danger and was killed. The blood is on me hands. I can't
wash it off. But I've promised God my life in place of
Jamie's. I'll take no more pleasures in life—and God knows
a life with you would be me greatest pleasure. I'll shun all

worldly things and spend me life in prayer makin' up for
what I've done."

Thomas sucked in a chestful of the cooling evening air
before he answered.

"You think Jamie's death your punishment for lovin' me?
You think Jamie had nothin' himself to be punished for?
Jamie beat you, lass. Jamie left you to suffer the Cherokees
on your own at Turkey Creek. Jamie dragged you halfway
across the colonies with ne'er a thought to buildin' a life for
you or the wee ones—with ne'er a thought for anything but
Jamie Lowe."

Thomas's chest heaved higher with each fault of Jamie's
he enumerated. Sarah stepped back, out of Thomas's arms,
fanning away the mosquitoes that buzzed about her.

"Jamie's not worth givin' up your life for, lass," Thomas
reasoned.

Sarah took another step back, drew her skirt back over
the mound of baby once again, and massaged it slowly.
" 'Tis a child of lust, Thomas, and you know it. I can feel the
mark of the Devil on it." Once again Sarah felt her head
quiver. Reached for loose hairs she couldn't find.

"You feel no such thing, lass." Thomas smiled his half
smile. "You're grievin' and you—"

"I know what I feel, Thomas! Our sins are to be upon the
bairn unless we repent!"

"Before God, I *do* repent!" Thomas cried out. "I repent
the sin of not marryin' you when I should've. I repent the
sin of lovin' you while you were the wife of another. I
repent the sin of adultery. But I will not repent my words on
Jamie, for they were truth. And I will not repent wantin' to
care for you, for wantin' to see my bairn raised up under my
own roof—or for wantin' to make up to you all I should've
given you before."

"But 'tis *my* hands stained with Jamie's blood, sure as if
I'd done the deed myself. And I'm to take me punishment!"
Sarah screamed the words until her chest hurt from the
screaming, from the explaining to one who couldn't know
her sin. Forearms twisted upward and fists clenched, her
bent body pleaded that he hear her and understand, then

straightened. She ran for the house. Away from explana-
ions and away from Thomas.

He was left among the hum of the river evening. The
here-and-there bubble of the water. The buzz of mosquitoes and snap of beetles. The song of frogs. But in his
ears was only the resonance of Sarah's pain.

25

Charles Town
January 6, 1757

"You're certain you won't change your mind," Thomas had
said to Sarah five months earlier, before returning to
Charles Town. He'd seen her safely to the Cruikshanks, and
it was under the shade of a towering oak near the road in
front of their house that Thomas had spoken his last words
to her.

"You know I can't," she'd said.

The vacant look on her face had haunted him in the
months that had passed since that day. What she was holding behind the veil of her eyes he could only guess. Grief.
Guilt. Fear. All of those emotions. But love, too. He knew
that somewhere, too, she loved him. In time, when she'd
adjusted to Jamie's death, she'd be able to love again. But
he'd known he'd have to give her time, and that was difficult.

Summer and autumn passed slowly and the new year
arrived with a stealth. There were stacks of orders to keep
Thomas's new weavers busy, and he had the new manufactory to organize, new warehouse space to fill. He hired a
fuller and was still looking for a reliable dyer. His days were
filled with buying and selling, weaving and details. But his
days were empty days.

He'd been invited to spend this day, "Old Christmas," at
Fenwick Hall with the family of Edward Fenwick, a member of the Assembly who Thomas knew better as a horseman. While Thomas had avoided York Course—and any
other place he might see Elizabeth or Borque—since his
return to Charles Town, he had renewed his friendship with

he planter Fenwick, and advised him on the purchase of a
ine new colt last spring. After dinner today they were cer-
ain to have a look at the string of horses Fenwick raced
from Charles Town to Virginia.

Thomas had worked the early part of the day at the
manufactory along with Durong and the others.

"Durong, tell your men the rest of the day is theirs to
spend as they like. Our cook, Miney, is fixing a feast for you
back at the house. I'll be off to Fenwick's for the day."

"*Oui,* monsieur," Durong said. He was a small lad, no
more than eighteen, fastidious in his dress even though it
was no more than a plain linen shirt and camlet breeches.
He kept his heavy beard closely shaven and the black waves
of his hair neatly combed back. Today he wore a cravat of
red wool at his throat in honor of the old holiday tradition.

Thomas was bid "Happy Noel" from the other Acadians,
whose English was becoming very good now, and whose
smiles were genuine for his gift of the time off. Though they
had no family, no priest to say Mass, and no certain future,
they had fallen into an easy routine here at the new manufactory, and Thomas knew he had been lucky to find men of
such skill just when he'd needed them, especially Durong,
whose work was exceptional.

Riding out of the city, Thomas saw the signs of Old
Christmas around him. A pile of wood scraps and logs and
poles was ready to be set as a bonfire in the evening. Fire-
crackers snap-snapped and the sound of guns could be
heard outside the city wall. The aroma of countless Old
Christmas feasts hung sweet on the cool air. It was not a
holy day with gift giving, like the December 25 Christmas,
but rather a day of celebration with friends, an occasion for
large parties and feasts.

The two-story brick house known as Fenwick Hall had
been built in 1730 by Edward's father, and now Edward had
added two flanks to it—one a coach house, and one a stable
for his thoroughbreds. Inside the house, wide cypress
panels covered the walls, all trimmed with fine moldings
and carvings of cypress and pine. Thomas was welcomed

immediately by Fenwick, greeted by the other guests, most of whom he knew, and then led directly to the horses.

"I'm eager for your opinion, Gairden," the amiable Fenwick said, stopping before the stall of the growing colt. A short, full-bellied man, Edward Fenwick carried himself confidently, and judged horses with a shrewd eye. "Will he make it for a stud or not?"

The stable boy brought the almost one-year-old out of his stall and led him down the lane. The horse was a rich brown with fine legs and bright eyes. Full of energy and ready to run, he whinnied merrily and tossed his head back as far as the bridle would allow.

"Looks like a lively one," Thomas said. He nodded approvingly, eyeing the walk of the young animal, thinking of how much he'd grown since last May when he'd seen him at three months. Fenwick was commenting to him and the other men who'd come along about the colt's spirit and training, but Thomas wasn't listening. The image of the foal growing to maturity touched him. Set off other images. Birth. Growth. Birth.

"—wouldn't you say, Gairden?"

Thomas smiled, apologetic. "I'm sorry, Fenwick, I was thinkin' of the future of a stud such as this one and not listening as I should've been. I'm hopin' you'll remember the man helped you buy him when he has some promisin' offspring of his own."

The men laughed, and moved on to look at other horses, some of them newly imported from Ireland, but Thomas's mind remained far away.

"Fenwick," he said as they walked back to the house, "I'm feelin' a bit poor—like a heavy meal's not what me stomach should take just now. Will you excuse me to your good wife? I think I'd best ride back to the city."

"Why not stay here until you feel better, man? We've rooms upstairs for guests."

"Nay, Edward, but thank you. 'Tis best to be home at such times, and Charles Town's but a short ride. Air may do me well, too."

"As you wish," Fenwick said, patting Thomas on the back. "You will be missed."

"I thank you again." Thomas tried to pull himself up a little slower than usual onto Shuttle's back, to look at least a bit ill though he was not. Fenwick waved him farewell, and he was on his way.

Out of sight of Fenwick Hall, Thomas gave Shuttle his head. They had a much longer ride ahead of them than the one to Charles Town.

"You've a visitor," Esther Cruikshank said. The tiny old woman, her mouth a persistent pucker about a white clay pipe, saw Sarah pause a moment in the thrashing of her head and contorting of her face. Sarah had been laboring since midnight, sometimes screaming to God, sometimes silent. Just now she was restless, irritable. "The man brought you here—Gairden," Esther went on, laying her hand to Sarah's head to check for fever. "He's ridden all night from the look of him."

"Nay!" Sarah snapped, pulling her head away from Esther and keeping it there, her body arching and stiffening, but Thomas was already at the bedside.

Esther left the two alone, whispering, "Quiet her," to Thomas before she turned to leave.

Sarah remained, as she had been, face away from Thomas, body stiffened in a spasm of exquisite pain.

"Sarah," he whispered. "Oh, Sarah, 'tis me doin', this agony of yours." He reached for her clenched fist, and she did not pull away, but did not relax. Gently, his large hands massaged her small one. "Let me help you, Sarah. Please. Let me. Let me." His voice was hoarse, frightened. He'd not expected this.

"No one can help me," she said, pulling her hand from his and pressing hard upon the belly Thomas could see moving, even in the gray light of sunless dawn. "Ahhhhhh," she moaned.

Thomas reached for the door only to find Esther ready to open it from the other side. He looked away as she checked

Sarah once again, her knowing fingertips poking here, there on the belly, then inside.

"He's moved," the old midwife said, never taking the pipe from her mouth. "Got himself in place. 'Twon't be long now." She straightened the bed, trying to make Sarah comfortable, if such a thing was possible.

Thomas noticed the old woman's tired eyes. "How long's she been at it?" he asked.

"Started in the night last night," Esther said. " 'Tis been a long one." Then she motioned for Thomas to follow her out of the bedroom.

"Have you broken your fast?" she wanted to know.

"Nay. A biscuit and ham at Ford's Ferry Inn last eve is all. But I've no hunger now, thank you." Thomas watched as Esther cooked mush over the low fire. Her whole face lay wrinkle upon wrinkle, all radiating out from the circle where her lips sucked the pipe, and she moved in stiff, sticklike motions.

Mr. Cruikshank sat in his chair, half-asleep. Thomas, too, felt fatigue begin to catch up with him, but knew he could not sleep. He stood by the fire while Esther checked on Sarah once more, then returned.

"That your bairn in there tryin' to be birthed?" she asked, with all the force her age and experience commanded.

"Did Sarah tell you that?" Thomas returned, wondering.

"She tells naught, just moans for the Lord to take her. Prays to die. The sound of your voice's the only thing's made her quiet in all of it."

Thomas paused, his long arms extended to the heavy beamed mantel of the fireplace, his eyes absorbed in the flames.

"I came for the child," he said. "Aye, 'tis mine." He waited for the condemnation he expected to appear on Mrs. Cruikshank's face. It did not come.

"Ah," she said, nodding. "So there's guilt *and* grief she's battlin' in there. A bad pair. I've birthed over a thousand bairns in me time, but never seen the like of her carryin' on.

Still once you marry her and see to the wee ones, she'll forget."

"She'll not marry me," Thomas said, looking into the fire once again. "She's made that plain." Thomas heard Sarah cry out and looked to Mrs. Cruikshank, who made no move to go to her.

"Have you beat her?" the old woman wanted to know, a scowl set in her eyes.

"Nay," he replied with an ironic smile. "Nay," he repeated, shaking his head once more, trying to figure it all out for himself. "She had a husband who beat her. And left her. Thought of no one save himself. But she made one mistake—with me—and now she's bound herself to a life of repentin'. She can't—"

"You look to be a man of means, Gairden, whatever your mistakes. We all make 'em, just don't tell folks. She'll marry you, have no doubt of that. I've opened the door to matrimony before, and she's no worse off than some I've done. Whether the bairn's first or the weddin's first is of no concern to the Almighty, as long's there's both. Now get in there and tend the woman to give me a minute's rest."

"But I—"

"If I hear screamin' I'll come runnin'," she said, reassuring him. "Just talk to her—and listen. If she starts pushin', call me quick."

Thomas took a deep breath. It had been a long time since he'd seen anything born. Even the last foal from his mare had been born before he got to the stable. Horses were like that. Fast. All business. People were different.

"Where's Esther?" Sarah asked as he walked in.

"Outside," he said. He saw her shiver under her blankets. Saw the perspiration on her forehead. With two fingertips he tilted her face back toward him. She closed her eyes. "She thinks the father should help with the comin' out as well as the puttin' in, she says. I'll get her in a second if you need her."

"You told her?"

"She guessed," Thomas said, stroking her brow. His fingers combed into place the damp auburn tendrils of hair around her face.

"Ahhh!" she cried, and almost at once Thomas called for Esther who made a quick assessment, then commanded, "Push, lass, push!"

Thomas supported Sarah under the shoulders, lifting her so that she was almost sitting, and half whispered, "Come on, Sarah . . . come on, Sarah," in her ear. His face next to hers, he felt the clenching of her teeth, the tight scrunching of her facial muscles against the pain.

"Good, lass, good," Esther encouraged. "Keep coming, keep coming . . ."

In a gush of fluids and flesh, a black-haired baby girl gasped her way into the world early on the morning of January 7, 1757. As determined as her midwife was to clean her up, the babe was determined to satisfy her hunger, and her tiny squalls were answered by Esther Cruikshank's crooning. Not more than a minute went by before she was snuggled by her mother, her tiny mouth homing in on the nipple of Sarah's breast as her father looked on.

"An angel couldn't beam any more'n that," the old midwife told Mr. Cruikshank when she woke him from his sleep in the chair and sent him off to bed, then went herself. The little family was left to bind together as it would.

"I love you, Sarah," Thomas whispered after Esther had gone. Lying beside Sarah, he was half-afraid to touch her, half-afraid of not doing all he could to seal her and the baby away from any further pain or suffering or aloneness.

"I've longed to hear you say that again, Thomas," Sarah murmured, turning toward him some, the baby warm between them. "Though I shouldn't," she added.

"God gives us miracles, Sarah," he said, his lips meeting hers, gently, then again. "The greatest of 'em is love."

A lock of his black hair brushed her face. "You've labored a bit, too, from the looks of you—cheeks sunk, no color." She closed her eyes as she spoke.

"Nay, the labor was all yours. Still I'd like to call the wee lass 'Ceara'—for me mother—if it pleases you," he said.

"Ummm . . ." Sarah nodded, drifting off to sleep without really answering.

Thomas, though, felt no fatigue. Only joy. He would watch it all—the sleeping, the suckling, the baby movements, the mother movements.

Moving closer to kiss his daughter's tiny head one more time before he got up to take his place in Esther's rocking chair, he touched the firm, hard mound of Sarah's breast where the baby suckled. Afraid of hurting Sarah somehow, he still could not help but brush his lips over the smooth whiteness of the breast as well as the baby's head next to it.

He thought she might have stirred pleasantly at the sensation. Perhaps she was not asleep. He couldn't tell.

Thomas slipped off from the bed, pulled the rocking chair up close and sat down. His fingertips memorized the soft down of the baby's hair and tiny ear, then traced the rise of first one full breast, then the next. As he did, milk began to run from the upper nipple. With one finger he wiped away the wetness. He licked the finger sweet with his own miracle, then leaned back in the chair, and slept.

❈ Part Four ❈

1761

26

Charles Town
February 1761

Thomas paced the length of Shrewsbury's Wharf and fixed his eyes on the morning sky, gray with the mist of late winter. He folded his arms across his chest to warm his hands and pulled his neck down inside the tall collar of his waistcoat. As he walked, his eyes narrowed, his brows wrinkled, his lips tightened. It was quiet at the wharf, early yet. In the damp of almost dawn Thomas walked, alone with his thoughts.

At home, Sarah and the children would be asleep for some time yet. When they did wake, the children would be about their lessons. Sarah would be about her prayers. Just now her world was flayed open by news of further Cherokee uprisings in the backcountry, and her hours of prayer were abbreviated by bursts of shrieking as she remembered Echoe, and Jamie's faceless corpse, and Turkey Creek. Sarah would eventually calm herself, become a loving mother, a cordial wife, before she drifted away once more, folding her hands in prayer, her mind far away. Try as he would, Thomas did not know how to unlock the door to that secret, volatile space inside her. And in the meantime, he saw that the outbursts frightened the children, especially his beloved four-year-old Ceara, too young to understand that her mother's ravings had less to do with Cherokees than with her own demons.

The first year they'd been married, Thomas had held out hope that Sarah's guilt over Jamie would drop away from her like an old cloak. With the second year he'd faced the realization that it was going to take time. In the past two years he'd begun to wonder if even time could heal Sarah's wounds—for certainly he could not, and his failing railed at him in quiet times like these.

Against the morning mist, the masts of the schooner *Prosperity* swayed gently on the bay swells, and Thomas could hear the crew's activity on board as they readied to cast off. It seemed a poor morning to set sail, though there was a bit of a breeze. A poor morning all around, he thought, muttering an "uggggh" through his teeth. The whole city had whispered about Michel Borque running off with Margaret Rawlins for over a month now. And he'd heard that Elizabeth had secluded herself at the home of her neighbors, the Youngs, not just to seal herself away from the scandal, but because Michel had taken from her not only her reputation but also her home. He'd sold High Garden to Alexander Gray for what nefarious reasons the gossips of Charles Town could only guess. The latest rumor had Elizabeth leaving Charles Town to attend her mother in London.

Nothing more than a passing comment from the *Prosperity*'s captain had led Thomas to believe she'd be taking this vessel, but knowing her bent for privacy he took a chance that she'd book passage on a ship such as this, mainly a cargo vessel, and that she'd board just before the ship sailed, hoping to avoid the inevitable stares of those who both pitied her and laughed at her. It had been five years since he'd spoken to her that day at Sullivan's Island, five difficult years for both of them. Today, thoughts of all that had been and all that should have been wrapped him like the mist wrapped Charles Town, and the only way to lift it was to see her one last time.

At the sound of a chaise, Thomas hurried back down the wharf. He recognized the graceful step of the woman who got out the way he might recognize a coverlid he'd woven; both would be ever part of him. He waved. She looked up at him, then over to the schooner. Thomas broke into a run.

"Elizabeth! Wait!" he called out, and once more she looked back. "Wait!" he pleaded once again.

As the Youngs' driver retrieved her one small trunk from

the chaise, Crickie stopped and watched Thomas running toward her, his coat flapping at his thighs. He was not smiling, she could see as he approached, and his dark eyes looked tired and drawn. Yet his face had a well-remembered warmth about it. She felt a quiver in her lower lip and turned her head.

"Never look away from me, lass," he said, taking her by the shoulders and turning her chin back toward him with the gentle pull of one finger.

The driver hurried up the ship's ramp and left the two alone. Crickie closed her eyes and allowed herself a deep breath.

"I thought to never look on you again, Thomas. . . . I can never look at anyone here again. Michel and Margaret have made certain of that."

"Not at all, Elizabeth. There are many who understand you're not at fault, who are angered at your loss of High Garden. In time—"

"They'll forget? Nay, Thomas, they'll never forget. How could they? In the whole history of ye colony there's been no act so base as this. I'm the coward for running from it, I know, but—" She saw Thomas begin to speak but stopped him before he could say what she knew he would say. "Ask me not to stay, Thomas, for it cannot be. You've a wife and family now—"

"A family, aye. A wife—" Thomas paused, looked away himself now. "Ah . . . I don't know . . . Married I am, but Sarah's lost inside herself most of the time. Plagued with memories of things no woman should have had to live through. I don't want the same to happen to you."

Crickie heard the rattle of chaises along Bay Street and saw the city coming to life. She was at once restless and taut. "But it already has," she said. "Don't you see? And I was lost to you the day my father first put himself into ye debt of Michel Borque. My father thought these colonies a game. A whim. I can never forgive him for thinking my life the same."

"Never's a long time, lass. You're apt to see your father again one day and you might find you feel better if you're willin' to forgive. And forget. Don't do as Sarah's doin' and live forever in the past."

Crickie's cheeks reddened with shame and anger, and her breath was quick. "We've had little of luck between us, Thomas." She dropped her head, looking down to the arc of her trim travelling skirt. "And now we're to part forever, for I cannot stay. We—"

"We cannot know what forever is, lass. I once thought I'd be an Ulster weaver 'forever.' I once thought I'd live in Philadelphia 'forever' . . . I once thought we might be man and wife 'forever.' Only one thing's forever, and that's change."

The gray-haired driver shuffled back down the ramp. "Captain almost ready, Madame Borque," he said, not quite looking at her.

"Thank you, Raimund," she said. "You may go then." The black man nodded once again before ascending the chaise and turning it about, back to Bay Street.

"So, I must be going, Thomas," she said, drawing back and still not letting her eyes meet his. She could not let him see the defeat and humiliation she felt.

"I'll be leavin' again myself, soon—militia's to assemble at Monck's Corners for a new assault on the Cherokees holdin' Fort Loudoun. It seems that business will never be done."

Crickie heard him try to make this easier for her. She tried to answer but felt her throat tied in knots at holding back the emotions inside her.

"Look at me, Elizabeth," Thomas said, once again taking her by the shoulders and turning her face to his. "Don't run away. Stay. Face the people. Let them know what really happened."

"What really happened can never be discussed, Thomas. It is dreadful enough that people *think* they know what happened. Nay, once I might have faced it, but not now."

"I'll not ask you to do what feels painful to you—enough others have done that already. I only need you to know that you've a friend here who wants to help, to—"

"You I shall never forget, Thomas," she said. "And

you're right—never is a long time. But for me, all happiness and position are gone from this place. I must count myself fortunate to have my mother's house to return to."

In one quick movement she pressed a kiss firmly against his cheek and was up the ramp and across the deck without ever looking back.

Thomas watched her go, a tiny figure running into the deepening mist, and on his cheek he felt not only the mark of her kiss, but the tears she'd left behind as well. He took one last look at the *Prosperity* and gave a bitter chuckle at the irony of the name before he walked the wharf back to Bay Street and headed for the manufactory.

In the weeks that followed that misty morning at the wharf, the *South Carolina Gazette* kept Thomas and the rest of the city informed of what was taking place not only in the backcountry, but in the rest of the colonies as well. For what was to South Carolina "The Cherokee War," was part of a much broader battle England was fighting to keep its place on the North American continent. Its quarrel was less with the Indian tribes, upon whom they depended for their lucrative fur trade, than with the French. Her treasury badly depleted from numerous wars with the English and Spanish, France saw profit in the fur trade, too, and needed Indian allies to help maintain the colony of New France.

The fighting that in the colonies became known as the "French-Indian War" was one part of what the *Gazette* said was being called in London "The Great War for Empire," for the Crown was also at war in France and Austria, and in the Caribbean. Thomas could tell from the reports that the British Army and Navy were spread thin—and that was one reason they had been inclined to let people on the colonial frontier fight their own battles. In the past four years, however, tribes that had been friendly to the Crown—the Cherokees among them—had grown weary of British vacillation and lack of support. They could not continue to supply hides if their hunting grounds were overrun by settlers. They could not defend themselves against French intervention if the Crown did not supply ammunition in return.

Out of such frustration came the increasing number of attacks on backcountry settlements, and at last, on the British forts themselves. The worst of these was Fort Loudoun, farthest from Charles Town at the junction of the Tellico and Little Tennessee rivers. Under siege since the beginning of the war, it would no doubt have fallen early on but for the help of the Cherokee chief Attakullakulla, a peacemaker known as "the Little Carpenter." He and others from his tribe took supplies to the soldiers on rainy nights, hoping to go unnoticed by their people. But the willingness of some Cherokees to aid the English only served to anger the warriors who wished them gone, and attacks increased.

In August of 1760 the garrison, surviving on nothing more than one pint of corn per day for each soldier, decided it could hold no longer. Its Captain Stuart and his lieutenant, James Adamson, went to the Great Warrior of the Cherokees for terms and were granted permission to retreat with arms and ammunition to Virginia or Fort Prince George. When the soldiers left the fort three days later, twenty-five were killed and one hundred twenty were taken prisoner. The Little Carpenter spirited away Captain Stuart who returned to Charles Town a few months later with his firsthand account of the massacre.

When he got there, plans were already underway to relieve Fort Prince George, now the focus of Cherokee activity. Although a good distance separated the fort from Charles Town, city residents remembered well Indian attacks of forty years earlier, and began to fear another encounter. Some, like Sarah Roberts Lowe Gairden, were plagued by memories much more recent.

"Goin' off to Williamsburgh, are you?" she asked, coming into the bedroom where Thomas was packing together a few things to take with him for the march on the Cherokee territories.

"Why . . . aye," he lied, his eyes on the small leather bag into which he had stuffed a white linen shirt, two pairs of stockings, and a battered old hat he wouldn't need but often wore when he went to Williamsburgh to check on his holdings there. His uniform was at the manufactory, as were the few other supplies he would need to take along. "I didn't want to worry you with the mention of it. . . . I may be gone a good while this time."

"Not mixin' with Alex Gray again, Thomas? Promise me—"

"Nay, lass. Gray's no longer at River Plum, I hear. 'Tis sold to another. Nay, I've land enough for now, but I'm thinking of plantin' up there." He offered the only excuse that seemed plausible. Anything to quiet her. He saw the familiar wringing of the hands and slight widening of the eyes. " 'Tis March now. Time enough to work plots for corn if I can hire some men."

Thomas looked at his wife and tried to smile. How fragile of spirit she was, this Sarah of his, that he could not share with her the simple truth that he was needed to help in the colony's defense. That the mention of the word *backcountry* would send her screaming and raging down the long hall of their home's second story. That he could not share with her his apprehension about the nature of the Cherokee War, about the way it was being fought, about leaving the children, about leaving her. It was not in him to lie maliciously, but lies like the one he'd just told Sarah were the only thing that buffered her against the real world in which he was forced to live without her.

He tried again to smile, raised one corner of his mouth and winked at her. "You'll not notice I'm gone, lass. You'll be busy with your own plantin' here, for the gardens behind the house call out for your hand. The small bushes need prunin', young flowers will need their way cleared from weeds." Thomas went on cheerfully as he changed into the kind of everyday clothes he would wear for riding to Williamsburgh—or in this case the green, where he would meet the other militiamen. From the corner of his eye, he saw that she still wrung her hands as she paced back and forth in front of the closed bedroom door. No more than aye and nay did she say as he kept the conversation going while he pulled on his tall riding boots.

"I've spoken to Miney and Joe, given them their instructions for while I'm away. They'll take good care of you,

Sarah—the wee ones, too. Never was there a better pair than those two. That's how they earned their freedom from the Gordouns." He stopped his line of chatter, rose and went to Sarah, taking her in his arms and looking down into her eyes. "To think I hired two former slaves to care for this house when it was an empty house, when I didn't even know that you lived in this same Carolina. Now they're still here, to help you and take care of you when I have to be away. Fortune smiled on me when they came—but not as much as when you came, Sarah. Always know that."

Thomas bent to kiss her lips. He felt her begin to respond, then stop, the way she had a habit of doing. She was so close, then so very far away from him. He held her there a few moments anyway, and she did not resist. She was warm, but her soft curves were gone and a starved body left behind. Her arms were hardly bigger than Martha's or Gavin's, and her shoulders were sharp corners against his chest.

"When I get back," he said, still holding her, "let's take the children on a holiday—to the beach perhaps. They do so love the water. We could—"

From delicate doll to stinging spider, Sarah sprang out of his arms and flew back against the door, arms outstretched and body arched in defiance. "You'll not be back and you know it!" she screamed. "You're goin' off with another! You've a woman on your mind, Thomas Gairden, and I can tell it. Those the Devil haunts can tell no truths." The green-gold of Sarah's eyes seemed to darken as she spoke, a stark contrast in her pale face, and Thomas watched as her long, thin fingers gripped the door casing.

"Nay, lass," he said. "You know I've no one but you. You're me wife, married at church and in all legal ways. Come now, you're havin' a joke on me, just like when we were young in Bartram. But I know you too well, lass." Thomas forced what he hoped was a pleased-looking smile, not at all sure she was joking.

"I know Elizabeth Borque's husband left her. I know you loved her once. And I know it's to her you're runnin' now!"

At this, Sarah's volume was such Thomas feared even the neighbors might hear.

"Sarah! Shhh! You know nothing of the kind. I've never—"

"You've always wanted her. Always. No matter what you told me. 'Twas always her in the back of your mind. 'Twas always her fine ways and fancy clothes!"

"Nay! I'll not hear this from you, Sarah, for I'd love you now as I've always loved you if you'd but give me a chance. If you'd stop your keenin' and moanin' for Jamie and give a thought to the livin' you'd see you have a husband, and four children—not three—who love you more than they dare say. Don't let yourself lose it, Sarah. Don't throw it away." Thomas felt his chest rise and fall. He caught his breath, watching as Sarah's arms loosened their hold on the door casing and her head drooped to her chest.

"I love you, too, Thomas, God help me," she said. Tears streamed from her eyes and sobs shook the frail body now sagging against the door. Thomas started toward her, reached to take her in his arms once more. "If you'd only not killed Jamie I could forgive you," she sobbed, "but the Lord commands we do no killin', and you've broken that rule. I pray for you, man. I do. But 'tis of no good, for you've a fair Devil's tail of your own now. Poor Thomas. You were once a good lad . . ."

Sarah's voice trailed off in a river of sobs as Thomas stopped inches before her, unsure, at first, of what he'd heard. In the parlor, the clock struck nine. Time he was going if he was to meet his men at half-past. "Sarah? Look at me, Sarah." He lifted her chin with barely the touch of his fingers, but her eyes were blank, faraway. "You know I didn't kill Jamie, or have him killed. You know I'd take no life like that, don't you?" He raised her chin just a bit more, so that her eyes would meet his, but she closed them. Her lips quivered, pinkish waves on the tear-salted white sea of her face.

And this time, Thomas could not take her in his arms. He was not angry. Not threatened, indignant nor hurt. Just empty. Unfathomably empty just then at that closing of her eyes. He stepped aside and touched her arm as he reached for the doorknob, just as she drooped to the floor, flopping her head to her knees in an agony of prayer. Thomas closed the door soundlessly and left, forgetting his bag on the bed behind him.

"Not gone yet?" his cook Miney asked when he went out to the kitchen behind the house for a word with her. The small black woman was cutting open a long, large-scaled fish and her deft fingers quickly cleaned out the cavity before she rinsed it with a ladleful of clear water. Her hair was tied under a white scarf and her sleeves were pushed up high above her elbows. She did not cease her work as she talked.

"Nay, Miney. There's a bit of a problem with Mrs. Gairden. She's in another one of her confusions. This time she thinks 'twas me killed her first husband. . . . I didn't tell her I was off to the Cherokee War, just as we discussed, nor did I tell the children. I know it won't be easy for you and Joe while I'm gone, but I'll be back as soon as I can. Keep telling her I'm at Williamsburgh. She believes you when she believes no one else. And when I stop by the manufactory, I think I'll ask Paul Durong to stay here while I'm away. That should help both you and the wee ones. Sarah, too. Perhaps."

"She'll be all right again in a while, Mr. Thomas," Miney said. "I take her some sassafras tea and put her to bed for a nap. She wake up and forget it all. Don't you worry none, Mr. Thomas."

"Watch her for me, you and Joe. Call Dr. Garden if she should have another bad spell. He can give her something . . . do something." Thomas folded his arms across his chest and sighed, thinking. "I shouldn't go. I should find someone else. I can't—"

"Course you should go. What good are you doin' here that Joe an' me can't do? We watch those wee ones like our own if we had some. We take care of your Sarah. You got your job to do. We got ours."

"Woman's right," came Joe's deep voice from behind Thomas. "Get that uniform on an' go. This is our home,

too. We take good care of it—and Mrs. Sarah—for you."
Joe dropped an armload of firewood into the box inside the kitchen door.

"I know that," Thomas said. "If it weren't for you two, I couldn't think of leaving. I just—"

"Might do her good to be on her own for a while—ever think about that?" Miney asked. "Maybe she need time to miss you a little." Miney raised her eyebrows knowingly as she scaled the fish.

"Might," Thomas said, a bit more hopeful at last. Looking from Miney to Joe, he said his good-byes, then hurried down the street to the stable to mount Shuttle for the long ride to Monck's Corners where the provincials and regulars would meet.

$\clubsuit$

27

The Indian Territories, South Carolina
June 1761

Steep hills rose from the sandy banks of the Little Tennessee River where 2,800 British and provincial troops marched in the early morning sun. At the front of the columns rode forty-seven of the force's Chickasaw and Catawba scouts. To the rear rode the provincial regiment of Colonel Thomas Middleton, escorting the cattle and provision train bound for Fort Loudoun, the colony's western outpost.

Last year's expedition of six hundred regulars and militiamen, led by Colonel Archibald Montgomery, had been turned back by the Cherokees. The defeat had cost the British fourteen cannon, eighty small arms, one thousand pounds of powder and two thousand pounds of ball. This year the enemy, now commanding all of the land west of the mountains known as the "overhills," would be well armed and waiting. Lieutenant Colonel James Grant, a former Indian trader who was commander of this year's expedition, did not intend to make the same mistake. Long columns of uniformed British officers and regulars were followed by provincial enlisted men who assembled for the first time in uniform, albeit uniforms different from those of the regulars. As they marched into the steep-walled valley there was a watchfulness and a wariness that kept everyone on guard.

Lieutenant Thomas Gairden, in a coat of gray worsted with red lapels, rode at the rear of the supply train next to Lieutenant Colonel John Bankson, a prosperous Charles Town factor well connected in the colony and in London as well. Bankson was red of cheek, and purple finger veins marked his nose. With his paunchy middle and spindly legs he cut an oddly contrasting figure to the tall, well-proportioned Gairden.

"Old war-horse?" Bankson wanted to know, eyeing Shuttle's proud head.

"Gettin' there," Thomas replied, patting Shuttle fondly on the neck. "He's been in Cherokee country before. Twelve years on him now, and not as fast as he used to be, but fast enough for this kind of work."

"Yea, the pace is steady, but not speedy," Bankson quipped, then added, "unless the Cherokees come riding over those hills. Then things will change."

"I hear 'twas bloody up here last year with Montgomery," Thomas ventured.

"So I've heard," Bankson replied, glancing back over his shoulder. "But even that was not as bad as at the fort. They say the men were down to nothing more than rotten horsemeat and a pint of corn a day before they sued for terms. Little Carpenter was all that saved them."

"Aye, if only he could convince the rest of the Cherokees to give up the fight, this little journey of ours wouldn't be necessary." Eyes right, eyes left, eyes up, eyes constantly seeking the slightest movement of a thornbush, or bit of dust on the valley wall, Thomas rarely looked at Bankson as they rode.

"We need to settle these boundaries with the Cherokees once and for all," Bankson agreed. "The last two governors spent a king's ransom and still made no lasting treaties. Let us hope Bull can do better. If he doesn't, the backcountry will soon belong to the Cherokees again. 'Twould make business difficult." Bankson's eyes, too, roved the tops of the hills as he spoke.

"Aye, and the Crown's going to have to decide what it wants more—peace and trade with the Indians or more lands for folks to plant. Like Morning Man, that Chickasaw scout told me: 'I always hear white men say "Damn the Cherokees—but they never kill any."' Truth is, most of them mean us no harm. 'Tis a few warriors make the wars."

"I think you're right. Montgomery last year did little more than burn a few abandoned houses and pull up some corn. That's why the Assembly replaced him. Perhaps this trip will be different, eh?"

"I'd gladly get by with no killin'," Thomas said. "Seems a waste. And the way the regulars fight, standin' about like red targets, 'tis no wonder the Cherokees have been able to keep 'em out of the overhills towns."

"You're wearing a British uniform now aren't you?" Bankson asked rhetorically. "As I am?"

"Not like the regulars we're not, and you know it, John. They've given us uniforms and made damned sure we don't look the same as they do. They've given us, the officers, the same pay they've given regimental officers, but not the same respect. Not at all."

The two men rode side by side in silence for a few moments, then Thomas went on. "You notice they've stuck us back here like a bunch of shepherds, don't you? I see no redcoats guarding cattle and supplies."

"You sound like Middleton now," Bankson said, chuckling. "He's already at odds with Grant over being stuck at the rear. I say if we can get these supplies to Fort Loudoun we're doing more for the colony than a regiment that kills a hundred Cherokee warriors. It's all in one's point of view, actually."

"Middleton's a good leader of men," Thomas said, "and we need that, too. We need both supplies and leadership—until now, neither the Crown nor the Assembly's seen fit to give us both at the same time. At least we know our militia can hold its own with these regulars—we're a damn sight better trained than we were when I came to Charles Town ten years ago."

"I agree, Thomas. Let's hope we—"

Bankson hadn't finished his sentence before shots began to ring out from the tops of the river bluffs.

"Dismount! Load!" came the command from the front of the column. Horses skittered, whinnying in fear.

"They're coming right for us!" Bankson screamed. "Form a line west of the wagons!"

"Form up west of the wagons, lads!" Thomas repeated as is men began automatically to take their positions and to repare to fire. From the corner of his eye he saw a hun- red or so of their own regiment ride for the hills on the ight flank to meet the attackers. Another hundred came iding to assist the rear of the supply train. Quickly he tied huttle to the tongue of the nearest wagon as he called out rders to his men.

"Where are the regulars? We need reinforcement!" Thomas called to Bankson, but no answer could be heard. Rifle balls sang their way into and around the frightened attle and horses—and men—trapped in the bottom of the alley. Every panicking animal strained at its lead rope, its oice part of a stampede chorus.

Down the hills the Cherokees rode, darting, shooting, larting away again. Thomas knew the tribe must be vastly utnumbered, and yet they came, whooping and crying out s they raced about the heights of the valley walls.

"Wait for the ones close enough to shoot at or you'll vaste your ammunition," Thomas called to his men. Watch close!"

"Yessir," one of his men answered back to him, ducking s a shot flew over his head.

Eyes on the soldier, Thomas didn't see if it was that ball, or another, that hit a target behind the lines, only heard the reat snort of pain that came bellowing from behind him nd turned about-face knowing the voice. Shuttle was hit, knocked on his side. His sinewy legs pawed wildly, tangling n the wheel of the wagon where he was tied. Blood oozed rom a hole in his chest and a great cut the length of his oreleg exposed layers of muscle that bulged salmon and ed against his chestnut hide. Tender brown eyes now wide vith fright and pain, Shuttle whinnied and gasped as he hrashed.

Taking one last quick shot, Thomas dodged behind the ine and ran to the horse.

"There, lad, there," he said, trying to get to the reins, but he kicking of Shuttle's powerful legs would not cease. Thomas leaped to the other side of the wagon tongue, out

of the way of the hooves, as Shuttle strained against the
ties, pulling the knot tight. Thomas's shaking fingers fumbled again and again before he found enough slack to free
the hurting animal. When at last he did, Shuttle struggled
to his knees, then with a crouplike cough, fell to his side
and thrashed no more.

"Lieutenant! Lieutenant!" Thomas heard Middleton
calling to him. The thunder of cannon now joined the ringing of the rifles. "Leave that horse alone and see to your
men!"

Thomas heard the words but could not move. Tears
rushed to his eyes and he let them run. "You didn't deserve
such pain," he said under his breath, not that anyone could
have heard him had he spoken aloud, for the battle was a
constant volley of bangs and pops, orders, and the baying
and braying of animals still alive. "God damn the Cherokees," he said, picking up his musket and firing at the
nearest rider. The warrior's spotted horse fell beneath him
but Thomas found no sweetness in revenge. He heard a few
men cheer as the horse went down and shots riddled the air
as its rider retreated.

Again and again the horse tried to get up and follow its
master, but one back leg was useless—broken or paralyzed.
Thomas reloaded and shot again. The spotted horse suffered no more.

Fighting continued throughout the morning, shot and
cannon echoing in the valley for nearly three hours. Then,
at midday, as abruptly as it had begun, the shooting
stopped. The last Cherokees withdrew over the top of the
valley walls. The provincials readied for another attack, but
it did not come.

"How many dead?" Thomas asked Bankson late that
evening as they sat inside their tent. Bankson and Middleton were just back from a conference with Colonel Grant,
and the rest of the camp was quiet.

"A dozen or so. Fifty or more wounded. We were lucky."

"And them?"

"Like Morning Man said, we never seem to kill any of

them—not many, at least. Three or four found on the hillside, a couple of horses."

"They got none of me men, but I lost me horse," Thomas
said, swallowing hard.

"Sorry, Gairden," Bankson said, sipping Madeira from a
flask. "At least you didn't have to eat him the way they did
up here last year. To die in battle's a noble end to any life."

"Dyin' in battle's fine when at least you have a prayer of
fightin' back. He had none, thanks to me." Thomas paused
and kept the rest of his thoughts to himself. "Will they be
back?"

"Morning Man thinks no. He thinks the Cherokees low
on ammunition or they'd not have ridden off as they did.
But the other scouts are still out. Our regiment is to camp
tomorrow at an abandoned village called Echoe just ahead
and guard the provisions. The regulars will go on to the
settlements of the middle towns."

"I see," Thomas replied absently, hearing only the word
Echoe. The Cherokees were at once more than faceless
men riding down the hills toward him. They were real people, with daughters named for beautiful hills, with land and
families to protect. He lay down atop his blanket and loosened the collar of his stained linen shirt.

"You look as though you know it," Bankson said.

"I've heard the name," Thomas said, "only 'twas that of a
Cherokee maiden. She had a hand in killin' Jamie Lowe—
me Sarah's first husband."

" 'Tis no wonder then you were eager to make this expedition. A chance to avenge that death?"

Thomas sighed, exhausted from battle and hollow with a
sense of loss that was becoming all too familiar. "I don't
know," he said. "Jamie no doubt gave as good as he got
. . . I don't really know what happened except that since
that day Sarah's never been the same."

"Fear of Cherokees has worked on the minds and hearts
of many in the backcountry and low country, too. Once this
is over, and there's a treaty, there's many will rest easier—
maybe your Sarah among them."

"I hope you're right, Bankson. I hope we're doin' more here than killin' men and horses."

"We are, Gairden. The colonel says we've beaten the worst of them. This could be the end of all battles with the Indians."

In the darkness, Thomas could just make out the silhouette of Bankson, sipping his Madeira in the still, humid, evening heat. "Ahhh," was all he said to the mellow, half-inebriated Bankson. He doubted such a thing, for he doubted the British command as he doubted the Crown's intentions toward the colony itself. As he doubted that even such a mighty thing as permanent, guaranteed peace with the Cherokees could bring Sarah back to him.

"Good night, Bankson," he said, taking one last glance at the vacuous look on his tentmate's face. How can some men find easy answers in battle while others find only more questions? Thomas wondered. He lay there listening as Bankson dropped his flask and began to snuffle in sleep. Why do some thrill at the victory over another while some feel empty? Why does peace come only through war? Suppose it was me killed instead of Shuttle? What then for Sarah and the children? What was achieved this day? he wondered, picturing the smoke-filled valley dotted with bodies. And what will come tomorrow?

28

Charles Town
December 1761

Thomas remembered the neat, well-established Cherokee village long after he'd returned to Charles Town in late July after the fighting was done and Middleton's provincials departed the area leaving Grant and his men behind. Echoe's four rows of thatch-roofed dwelling houses had been white-washed both outside and in with ground oyster shells. Each had had a small garden of corn and vegetables. Most had had small outbuildings as well, for storing corn or keeping fowl. The thick mud walls of the houses kept them cool in summer, and inside, the fur-covered platforms softened with mattresses of long cane splinters had made for comfortable sleeping. It was every bit as much a town as Charles Town, only smaller. And older.

He thought of the Indian women who had lived at the camp. Of how he had expected to see the Echoe he knew, but hadn't. Could she have told him what really happened that day at River Plum with Jamie Lowe? Would it have made any difference if she had?

The Cherokee War was over now, though. Low on ammunition and weary of battle and dissension in the tribe, the Cherokees were ready to settle, but by no means beaten, since they retained possession of the overhills. Just this week, on December 18, the Little Carpenter had signed the treaty agreeing to return all three hundred prisoners, slaves, horses and cattle held during the fighting, along with surrendering Fort Loudoun. He also agreed to allow the English to build other forts, and to execute any tribe member who murdered an Englishman. The French were to be excluded completely, and a settlement line was drawn forty miles west of the Keowee, forty miles east of where the English wanted it. The English would reopen trade once all prisoners were released.

Thomas read the terms of the treaty in the *Gazette* as he waited for Sarah to come down for dinner. The terms were not as rigid as most in the Assembly would have hoped, and there was still discussion as to whether the Indians should be simply contained or completely pushed out of the backcountry. Editorials and letters to the editor in the *Gazette* argued the issue back and forth and Thomas read them with interest, knowing that only one thing could be said with certainty about the Cherokee War: that the provincials could fight. He'd seen them season with each day of march and night of encampment. There was a sense of unity among them, and they often boasted that the regulars would have been massacred without them.

His thoughts strayed back to Echoe as he remembered his troops and their months in the backcountry. Once again he relived the loss of Shuttle. Almost heard the great gasps and thrashing in the horse's battle against death. Heard . . . nay, that was only the children running in the upstairs hall, coming down for dinner. It was already after three. They were late.

"Gavin. Martha. Anna," he greeted them. "And where's your little sister?" Sarah's three children—now his, too— were growing up all right, he thought as he looked at them. Gavin had Sarah's serious nature but the girls were pure Jamie through and through—dimples and curls and laughing eyes. Somehow the features suited them better than they had their father—or is it just that I've come to love them? he wondered.

"She was still putting her shoes on," Gavin reported. "She'll be right down."

"Probably had to get the doll Miney made for her, too," Martha suggested.

"Ah, she would need her dollie I'm sure," Thomas said, going back to his paper. He'd read no more than a line or two, though, when he heard a thud from above him as though something heavy had fallen down. Ceara was so curious . . . such a climber . . . Up the stairs he bounded with the children at his heels, but the nursery was empty. Then, from down the hall, inside Sarah's room, came another thud.

In an instant, Thomas was through the door with the three children right behind him. Before them on the floor, Sarah held Ceara's head between her hands, pounding it again and again against the pine floor. Her bony fingers spread like a web against the raven black of Ceara's hair and her thumbs pushed down on the child's eyes, holding them shut.

"Sarah! Stop! Stop!" Thomas shouted, lunging for her. Pulling her off from Ceara he felt a wave of revulsion as he saw that she'd stuffed a wool stocking into the child's mouth to silence her. Pried loose from the child, Sarah's frail arms pulled free of his grasp and her fingers clawed at his neck as she twisted back and forth, then back again, against his every attempt to contain her.

"She ran down the hall, don't you see?" Sarah screamed. "She's not to do that! I'll not have it! She must be punished. Her sins on earth must be punished as ours all are! God has told me—"

"God's told you nothin' of the kind, Sarah," Thomas said, his teeth clenched to hold back his own anger as he held her wrists while she pulled and twisted and wrenched and clawed.

"Get Joe," Thomas called to wide-eyed Gavin. All three children turned and ran, but little Ceara crawled to the corner and curled up there, hiding her head between her knees on the floor.

"God tells me she must be punished! She must be punished, don't you see? For she is a child of sin. She is wickedness incarnate! She is the child of—"

"Stop it! Stop it now, Sarah," Thomas shouted, losing a grip on the normally quiet woman who was now animallike with strength. Her wrist slipped through his grasp and she reached for his eye just as the slap of flesh on flesh cracked the still air of the chamber.

"Strike me?" Sarah shouted hysterically. "You strike me? You evil monster! You are Satan! Satan!" she shrieked, lurching toward Ceara once again but stopped by Thomas's firm hold on her left arm.

Ceara curled tighter into a ball as she sensed her mother's attack. Seeing her fright, Thomas gave Sarah's arm a quick twist behind her back. Surprise and pain echoed in the piercing, inhuman cry that shot from her and like an empty water bag she collapsed backward onto the down mattress of her stately poster bed.

The servant, Joe, ran in just as Sarah fell and took Thomas's place next to her, ready to subdue her if necessary, while Thomas gathered Ceara in his arms and tried to stop the sobs that shook her. With a quiet word and gentle kiss, he held her close. Still all of what she had seen, and heard, could not be kissed away, Thomas knew, and he rocked her back and forth in his arms as he looked to the spent Sarah, now vacant of memory or reason, who lay limp on the bed guarded by Joe.

"When she gets like this, it takes days for her to get better," Joe said, watching her. "I'll have Miney come put her to bed."

" 'Tis time we put her somewhere besides her bed, Joe. I can't have her hurtin' the children. Get Miney to come see to my darlin' Ceara, here," he said, placing a soft kiss on the child's dark curls, "and we'll take Mrs. Gairden to the hospital before she gets another burst upon her."

"Yes, sir," Joe said quietly as he took one last look at Sarah before he left. Finding her still quiet, showing no sign that she knew what lay before her, he tiptoed from the room.

"Does your head hurt, darlin'?" Thomas whispered to the child in his arms. She shook her head. "Aye, that's good then. Your mama loves you as I do, but she's sick—sicker than I realized—and she'll have to see a doctor." The child nodded against his chest, her body still vibrating with shock. "Your mama wouldn't want to hurt you, ever, and I'll see that no one else does either. I promise."

Ceara kept up her nodding and shaking until Miney

came to comfort her. She did not speak, and she did not cry. But her eyes had a haunted look to them that was odd for a four-year-old. Seeing it gave Thomas the courage to do what he'd been dreading.

One hour later, Sarah was installed in the Charles Town Hospital amid wailing and pain such as he had only previously imagined.

"I know not how to help these people," Sarah said, her wild eyes imploring him to help her. "They've too much pain . . . the doctor must see to them . . ."

"You can help, Sarah," Thomas said, realizing she did not understand that she was a patient like the rest of them. Her physical violence had subsided once Miney administered some of the medicine Dr. Garden had sent by while Thomas was off with the militia, but beneath the sag of her body lay an animation of mind that manifested itself through ceaseless movements of her lips and eyes, and the never ending wringing of her hands, always folded, as if in prayer.

On the ride home from the hospital, Thomas barely heard Joe's attempts at consolation as he struggled with what he'd just had to do. He had lost Sarah completely now, it seemed. He'd lost her first to a ruffian who loved a fight far more than he loved her. Thomas had married Sarah because he'd loved her once, because he'd fathered her child, because he'd hoped they could once again have what they'd had at seventeen. But she'd changed too much— they'd both changed—and no matter how hard he'd tried to make it all like it had been in Pennsylvania, it hadn't worked.

Perhaps he'd not given himself fully to Sarah. . . . Perhaps he'd held back without even knowing it, for if Sarah was distant, the memory of Elizabeth was always very close. Though in all the years since she'd married Borque he'd spoken only those few words to her on the morning she left for London, she had remained real, if not attainable, to him. If Sarah was his youth, Elizabeth was his coming-of-age. His love for Sarah had endured murder and even madness, but Elizabeth had remained a sweet memory he could call up when life with Sarah overwhelmed him. Perhaps he'd relied on that too much. . . . Perhaps Sarah had had more sane moments than he'd realized, for even she had sensed his feelings for Elizabeth. . . . Perhaps if Sarah had seen a doctor sooner. . . . Perhaps . . .

Thomas's mind was far away when Joe pulled the chaise up in front of the tall brick house. He needed to talk to the children and explain about the hospital. He needed to give them all of himself—not some split version that would be little better than Sarah had given them. At a nudge from Joe, Thomas stepped down and entered the wrought-iron-clad door. It was less than a week until Christmas, yet the house wore no signs of festivity, and he was certain there were no gifts for the children. For one brief moment his mind ran back to High Garden and a Christmas past. But in the next moment, as he hung his hat on the rack by the door, he returned once more to the present. He took a deep breath, and vowed never again to look back.

❧ Part Five ❧

1765–1766

29

Charles Town
October 1765

Thomas sat at a loom in his factory on Elliott Street this afternoon, beating shot after shot of woolen weft onto cotton warp. Almost all of his yarns were imported from England now. The few spinners who brought him yarn to be woven would not make a week's wages in a year.

Paul Durant stood at one side of the huge blanket loom across the floor from Thomas, and at the other side stood eight-year-old Ceara, returning Durant's throw of the shuttle with one of her own that did not always make it the whole distance through the shed. Durant was infinitely patient, Thomas thought as he watched them. He liked having his daughter sit next to him on the bench but always became anxious when she wanted to try the weaving herself. Durant, though, gave her as much time and attention as she needed, and she'd come to feel at home here in the manufactory where she now spent the greater part of every day.

"You don't have to do that, you know," Thomas called over to her. "When I was your age I was hired out as a drawboy to the old weaver Kinloch, and I had to work all day. But you don't have to. We need to be sendin' you off to Miss Girardeau's school with Anna and Martha one day soon."

Ceara never missed her catch of the shuttle as she spoke to her father, ignoring his words about school. "Was that before you knew Mama?" she asked.

Thomas paused, and lost the rhythm of his weave. " 'Twas long before I knew her," he said carefully. " 'Twas back in Ulster that I took me trainin' from the old man.

Your mother I didn't meet until . . ." Thomas sighed, remembering it all. "Until I was about fourteen and her folks
moved to New Buildings. I'd lost me father that year. Me
mother the next. Your mama's folks came to be the family
I'd lost."

"Did you like her?" the little girl asked.

"Aye, lass. She was me first true friend." He forced a
smile even though he could hear the question behind the
question. Had her mother always been so frightening? That
was what Ceara really wanted to know. The other three
children had adjusted gradually to their mother's being
gone, but Ceara had never forgotten her mother's constant
faultfinding and punishment, and finally her attack.

Thomas had not forgotten either. Sarah had spent a
week at the hospital after her attack on Ceara, but her
periods of violence became so frequent that the hospital
had no way to manage her treatment short of caging her
like a mad dog, and that Thomas would not allow. Instead,
he had taken her to Williamsburgh and hired the old midwife, Esther Cruikshank, to care for her. She kept Sarah
confined to her room, cared for her like a child, tried to
keep her safe from herself. But one day, after more than
two years, she had brought in breakfast and found Sarah
dead of her own hand, hung from the rafter above her bed.

That had been a year ago, and in the aftermath of Sarah's
death, Ceara was fretful at home, even with Miney and Joe
to care for her as they always had. She followed her father
like a shadow, going with him to the manufactory, to meetings, to the stable, anywhere he would permit. And he
found it hard not to indulge her. The undivided attention
he'd never been allowed to give Sarah he now showered on
Ceara.

And what he couldn't give her, Durant did. The olive-
skinned, slightly built Acadian was the only one left of the
eight Thomas had hired seven years earlier. Two had run
away the first year, trying to find family elsewhere. One had
died in the smallpox epidemic of 1760. The other four had
left by boat the next year to return to Nova Scotia, but when
they were again commanded to take the English loyalty

oath before they could land, they refused and sailed instead
for Santo Domingo, or so the *Gazette* reported.

Only Durant, a man without a family much as Thomas
had been, had remained. He'd come to Charles Town Paul
Durong, but later anglicized his name to help him blend in.
Still he was lonely, and his Catholic faith was alien to most
in Charles Town. Now a free man, having served out his
indenture, he was Thomas's assistant not only in weaving
but also in the management of the business.

Just now their business, like every other one in Charles
Town, was caught in bad times. With the French and Indian
War settled by the Treaty of Paris last February, there were
debts owed to the Assembly for the costs of the militia.
Additionally, there were few remaining contracts with the
British Army for supplies—no more blankets for the frontier. And there was no longer any illicit trade with the
French—a means by which many had grown wealthy during
the seven years of the war. The British, too, had heavy war
debts which they hoped to repay by increasing exports to
the colonies at the same time they decreased imports from
the colonies, and by enforcing trade laws that had long been
ignored.

The new clock on St. Michael's spire chimed the five
o'clock hour, and Ceara mimicked the gonglike sound, to
Durant's amusement.

"Time we were joinin' the rest of the folks at the Customs House, Paul," Thomas said, sliding from his bench
and putting on his jacket. "I'll see Ceara home first and
meet you there."

"I want to go, too," she begged, forgetting the shuttle
and running to her father's side. "Please."

"Nay, lass. 'Twill be lots of talk of laws and tariffs and
things that are of little interest to wee lasses such as yourself. Miney will be waitin' for you with a sweet when you get
home," he added.

"I don't want a sweet. I want to go with *you*," she begged.
"Please . . ."

She had a dark beauty about her—his own black hair,
eyes half hidden by lush rows of long lashes. She had her

mother's small hands and high-boned cheeks sprinkled with a half-dozen pale freckles. She got on well with Martha, Anna and Gavin and thought them her full-siblings, not half-siblings as they really were. Sarah had wanted it that way. Thomas had agreed. Still, every glimpse of her reminded him that she was flesh of his flesh and sometimes it was almost impossible to hold back the truth. No matter how much he tried not to indulge her, he found her pleas irresistible. He wanted to grasp every fleeting second of her childhood, for there were likely to be no more wee Gairdens in his life. Just now he lifted her into his arms, giving her a hug and a quick kiss.

"Aye, then, have it your way, for we're not apt to be there long—just long enough to let 'em know what we think of the Sugar Act and this new Stamp Act they're talkin' of. But after dinner I must come back to the manufactory and you must stay at home with your embroidery and I'll have no begging about it. Agreed?"

"Aye, Papa," she said and let herself down to take his hand. "Come, Paul," she said, holding out her other hand, "let's go."

Durant took her hand with a mannered "*Oui*, mademoiselle," and the three were off to Bay Street.

"Burn it! Burn it!" Thomas heard someone shout as they approached the brick Customs House on the wharf. This afternoon's *Gazette* had carried news of upset in Boston and Philadelphia over the Sugar and Stamp Acts, and a similar rally had been hastily planned by some of the concerned artisans in Charles Town.

" 'Tis a scunner, this tax business," Thomas told Henry Jones as he joined him near the back of the crowd. "When we've been taxed for the war, then lost our contracts after the war was over, for them to tax us more has a smell about it."

"Aye, and Tuthill's the worst of 'em, naught but a puppet for Grenville, who sets these taxes on us," Jones agreed. The housewright still wore his leather apron and carried a basket of tools. "Why, they call this the Sugar Act, and they're taxin' even the importing of silk, which is bound to cost you in your business."

"Aye, 'tis. But more than that, I've a sore spot for these redcoats who fill the streets. If our colony needs defendin', 'tis in the backcountry where ruffians run loose and where the peace of the Cherokees and the settlers is still an uneasy one. But is the army out there to watch the boundaries? Nay, they're here. In Charles Town. They're here, Henry, to see the King's laws are enforced, not to defend us from anything."

Jones nodded in agreement. "Kings see to the linin' of their own pockets first, 'tis true."

Of the fifty or so protesters, a few were strangers, but most were merchants or artisans, like Thomas. Some were women, but most were men. Among them were Ulster Scots, Germans, French, English—first, second and third generation immigrants all mixed together. The real wealth and power of Charles Town, though, its largest factors and planters like Evan Forcher and Henry Laurens—these were not here. They could afford the extra few pence on a bolt of silk or a case of wine. Others could not. Some *would* not.

All eyes, even those of little Ceara, were on the Customs House steps as the crowd chanted "Tuthill, Tuthill, Tuthill," waiting for the newly appointed tax coordinator to face them and defend his London masters.

"Let's go home, Paul," she said to Durant, who held her up so that she could see.

"Not yet, little one. I do not want to miss this opportunity to see Monsieur Tuthill ridiculed, as he was once so happy to do to my people," the Acadian said. "One day you will understand why that should never be done to anyone." The little girl looked at him with admiration. Before she could ask him another question, the crowd quieted long enough to see just what Tuthill did have to say for himself.

"Gentlemen!" he said, raising his arms to quiet them further.

"And gentlewomen," a woman in the crowd called out, raising laughter from the whole group.

"Gentlemen. And ladies," Tuthill started once again.

"Many of you are Englishmen, as I am. You *know* the costs of the empire and that we must share equally in paying for them. We—"

"But we don't share equally, Tuthill, and you know it!" an angry voice cried from the crowd. Thomas identified it as the lawyer, Edmund Stoweman. "Those of us here in Charles Town will pay much more dearly than those in the backcountry. If the tax is to pay the cost of the colony's defense, then let those most in need of defense share in the cost."

"All will share equally. London assures it. And I—"

"London is a long way from Charles Town. Just because the people there don't want to be taxed more doesn't mean we should pay for 'em!" came another voice from the crowd, and a roar of support followed it. The *Gazette* had made it clear that public sentiment in England did not favor further taxation.

"You are not paying for them, but merely for your own defense—"

"We've paid for our defense already—that is what our Assembly has done. We'll not pay again!" came the voice from the woman who had spoken earlier. Again, the crowd erupted into cheers of assent.

"You people need to take your charges to the Assembly. I can do nothing for you. I am a placeman named by the Crown to enforce the laws," Tuthill said, "not to deal with bullswool such as you." Turning to reenter the Customs House, Tuthill went only a step or two before one of the protesters in the front row caught him by the coattail and dragged him around again.

"Our Assembly has naught to do with these taxes," Stoweman said, speaking up once again. "Parliament has voted these, and we've no one there. Taxes from our own Assembly will be paid as levied, but these new taxes—"

"Prime Minister Grenville has announced a one-year decision period for the proposed Stamp Act, may I remind you," Tuthill said, clipping his words like an angry school teacher reprimanding a naughty class. "If the colonies come up with a better method of raising the necessary funds, the Stamp Act will not go into effect. I advise you to go to your homes and come up with a solution rather than acting out such uncivilized scenes in my presence. Any further activity of this nature will force me to call out the regulars. Fines imposed will be severe and painful."

Durant leaned toward Thomas's ear. "Listening to him is severe and painful enough for me," he said with a laugh. "I'm going home."

"Good night, Paul, and thanks," Thomas said. Paul Durant would go home to a boarding house, as Thomas once had, with no one to care where he had been or why he had been there. At least Thomas had the children. Sarah's children, now his. And Ceara. He could never manage the raising of them without Miney and Joe, and even with their help he found himself racing between manufactory and home and school to keep abreast of their needs and activities. His mind drifted away from the angry voices of the crowd for a moment. To Ceara's pretty face so close to his. To Sarah's, now gone. To Elizabeth's, so far away.

"Thomas." Henry Jones elbowed him. "They're askin' who'll sign a letter to the *Gazette* opposin' these new taxes. Are you with 'em?"

Thomas raised his hand, as he saw Jones doing. Looking about, he saw that everyone present seemed to be willing to be identified as opposing the new taxes. Ceara followed her father's lead and thrust her arm defiantly into the air, her face determined and unsmiling.

"See there, Tuthill," Stoweman called out. "See the hands raised in opposition. The city will hear of this day. And as other cities do the same, the Crown will hear of this day."

Tuthill's high-bridged nose wrinkled in a sneer of disgust. His small eyes scanned the crowd, trying to take in every face to record it for future retaliation. "Writs of assistance will be issued for any of you suspected guilty of smuggling, or other crimes against the Crown. You might be careful with your threats."

"A redcoat tryin' to enter my house with a writ to search it had better be ready to face the barrel of a musket," a tall man at the far side of the crowd called out. Hoots and cheers rose in the heat of the late afternoon sky.

"The regulars will carry muskets of their own, good fellow," Tuthill stormed, and this time turned on his heel and went inside the Customs House without hindrance other than the catcalls and torch swinging of the restless throng.

As Stoweman organized a sign-up sheet for the newspaper letter, Henry Jones leaned to Thomas and slapped him on the back. "Should give Tuthill somethin' to think about after he puts his head on the pillow tonight, eh?" Jones chuckled.

"Aye," said Thomas, "and I don't think he's heard the last of it—nor have we." Thomas pulled his mouth up at the corner and clicked his tongue, then tipped his hat to Henry in good-bye.

Lowering Ceara to the street, he took her hand and walked along, matching his long stride to her short one. Something about all this reminded him of leaving Bartram. Something about it was disturbing—something else was exciting. Inside him was a tight feeling he hadn't had for some time. Anticipation? He didn't know if he'd know anticipation anymore. Dread? Nay, he was not the type to dread what he did not already know.

As Thomas walked, he wondered. He felt a small hand squeeze his. And he squeezed back.

The *Gazette* came out three days later with the grievance letter and the names of those who had signed it. Thomas scanned it, found his name listed with the others, and nodded silently. Many names were missing that could have been there, mainly merchants and factors whose livelihood depended on good relations with England. There were those who sided with the King because they were British subjects first, colonists second. Many others, like Thomas, had it the other way around.

While Thomas was still reading, a young errand boy entered through the front door of the Sign of the Shuttle and handed Thomas a message from Evan Forcher.

After he had skimmed the brief contents he tossed it to Durant.

"Hmm," the Acadian said, smiling, as he read Forcher's request for Thomas to meet with him in his offices, "that didn't take long."

"Nay, it didn't," Thomas said, with a knowing raise of an eyebrow. Then he turned to the boy. "Tell your master I'll be there in one hour as he asks."

Thomas exhaled a noisy sigh. "So already it begins—or is it just continuing? The subtle pressure to go along with things even though the times are bad? Somewhat easier for Evan than 'tis for me, as he knows damn well." Thomas sat at his desk, checking accounts past due, as Durant made warp at the warping frame on the wall nearby.

"He'll have his day, too, no doubt," Durant said. "Any man can be pushed too far, no matter how generous the benefactor's been in the past. In matters of love and money, there is always a breaking point. Forcher simply has not reached it yet."

Thomas could just as well have left for Forcher's office along with the errand boy, for he was distracted and got little done in the hour that followed. The idea of speaking with Forcher, who had obviously just read the *Gazette*, bothered Thomas more than he wanted to admit. Taking sides was not easy in a city like Charles Town where everything—business and social—was linked.

When at last the St. Michael's clock struck four, Thomas slipped on his coat and hat and walked the three blocks to Evan Forcher's warehouse.

"Good day, Evan," he said, walking in through the open door, and closing it behind him. There was no need for everyone in the warehouse to hear them air their differences.

"Thomas! Good day. Thank you for coming." Forcher smiled broadly as he rose, gesturing for Thomas to have a seat.

"Stool's fine," Thomas said, avoiding a more comfortable, upholstered chair. "Somethin' on your mind, Evan?"

"As a matter of fact, yea."

Thomas prepared himself for Evan's views on the tax protest as Evan searched his desk for something.

"Ah, here it is . . . I've received this day, aboard the schooner *Fair Winds,* a letter I think you may find interesting. I thought you should see it at once."

Thomas unfolded the letter, written in an unfamiliar hand, and began to read.

Dear Evan,

I regret that it has been some years since I have had occasion to correspond with you, but now a matter of great importance requires that once again I ask your assistance.

A letter from my dearest daughter, Crickie, arrived at my quarters in Antigua some six months past urging that I return to London to sit at the bedside of my wife, Judith. Resigning my station to another, I boarded the first vessel, but arrived in London too late. Judith was taken to God's almighty hand this first day of August 1764, one week before I arrived.

Had I not been called to London, I would have made, instead, a voyage to ye Charles Town, for I had met, in that same week when Crickie's letter arrived, the true wife of her supposed husband, Michel Borque. Travelling with the lieutenant governor to the great sugar island of Barbados, I made the acquaintance of the family Borque, including the woman Marguerite—I am almost pained to report such similarity—his abandoned wife. The family supposed him long ago lost at sea—had no knowledge of his travels to Antigua or Carolina or wherever he may now be—yet the wife had not remarried, occupied as she was with the raising of their six children.

As you can see, such a situation casts a different light on my agreement with Borque, and it is because of this that I beg your assistance. If you are still in possession of the document signed by Borque and myself, it is my wish that you examine it to determine any legality that might restore to me ye High Garden plantation, since the agreement with Borque was, in effect, a fraud.

As you may imagine, I would not ask such a favor were there not some urgency, but my situation is dear, my debts are great, and I must find some means to right myself. You hold the only copy of our agreement, and you are therefore my best hope. I sail for Charles Town in the week next aboard the ship *Courier* and will be most pleased to meet with your good countenance when it lands, hoping you may present me with another opportunity to prove myself in ye Carolinas now that my career in the military is once more behind me.

Carlyle Rawlins

Thomas read the letter, then handed it back to Forcher. "I don't believe a word of it," Thomas said, shaking his head.

"Oh, believe it, Thomas, for Carlyle Rawlins may be a poor gambler, but he's not given to lying. Unfortunately, his loss of the plantation had nothing to do with Michel Borque's amorous activities. Rawlins was in debt to him for gaming, and Borque's liable for no fraud in that, unless, of course, Rawlins could prove he cheated—which, so many years after the event, he certainly cannot. I am, therefore, in the unhappy position of having to inform him that there is no chance of his regaining his plantation through the courts, and no way of regaining his fortune except by starting once again with new land."

"And how would he do that with no money? He would have to borrow . . ." Just then, Thomas thought he caught the drift of Forcher's thinking. "Ah, I see. Rawlins will need money and you do not care to make the loan, knowing his history of heedless squanderin'. But you think I might—"

"Nay," Forcher shook his head and waved his hands for Thomas to stop. "But I'm wondering if I might prevail upon you to speak to Gray. If I know Rawlins, he means by coming back here to regain High Garden. Gray's moved from one thing to the next—perhaps he's now tired of the responsibilities of a plantation—ready to move on elsewhere. I would like to be able to tell Rawlins which way the wind blows."

"Gray was always itchy of foot, but he's put that behind him now. He's quit his gamin' and even his drinking and turned himself into a respectable planter married to a respectable woman. He made a nice profit on the sale of River Plum from what I hear, and wrung favorable terms from Borque before his hasty departure, plus he's had four very fine crop years to regain his investment. I'd say Gray is on his way to becoming a wealthy man and not likely to sell out."

"But you could talk to him?"

"I could, but I'd rather not. Gray was once me partner, but we've travelled many a different road since then. He's made a pastime of tryin' to beat me—sold River Plum so he could buy High Garden, knowing what Borque had planned with Margaret Rawlins but never tellin' anyone. He knew full well I'd have bought it for Elizabeth, so he kept his dealings secret. We've not spoken since. His life may look respectable to those who don't know him, but I know better. Save your time, Evan. Let Rawlins talk to Gray if he wants to."

Speaking of those days past brought back memories Thomas had kept well hidden over the past few years. Elizabeth left without a home. The scurvy Gray living at High Garden in her place. Borque and Margaret running away together.

"Then you'll do naught to help the woman you once loved regain her position here?"

"Elizabeth? I would do anything to help Elizabeth. But we're not speakin' of her, are we? The letter says nothing of Elizabeth. Rawlins speaks only of himself. For all we know, Elizabeth has remarried. She never planned to come back here."

"She'll be with him, I'm certain."

Thomas tilted his head a bit, as if he hadn't quite heard Forcher. "When she left she said she'd never be back, and I believe she meant it."

"Lisette has visited her in London, Thomas," Evan said quietly. "She's most unhappy there, confined to the family house in Crichton Place with little to do other than make polite conversation. While her mother was living, of course, she was occupied with her care, but now there is nothing for her except her father."

"Her father! Her father *is* nothing! Her father has caused her naught but despair."

"Her father was once the object of all her affections, and I doubt he's completely lost that place in her heart, despite his follies. You and I may find his actions most thoughtless and unwise, but she is still his daughter. Deborah is married now. Only Crickie and her father are alone."

"Will you make a loan for Rawlins's new start then, Evan?" Thomas looked Evan Forcher in the eye, factor to factor. Business.

"I'm not in the business of charity, Thomas. I've too many other planters overborrowing their limits just now to take on another. I'm prepared to offer Rawlins a position here in my offices where he can be watched over, and still maintain his dignity and social position. But I'm not willing to fund another plantation venture for him just now."

"Another time perhaps, when things are better?"

Forcher was thoughtful. "Perhaps," he said, "though things are not so bad now that I'd sign my name to a letter in the *Gazette* the way you did."

"Ah," Thomas said through a half smile, "so you did have another reason for askin' me here."

"Nay, Thomas, not at all. I'm merely saying that protesting at the Customs House will do nothing to change taxes. Only Parliament can do that for us."

"Aye, and who in Parliament is going to do that for us, Evan? We've no one there to speak for us."

"But we do owe our share in payment for the war, Thomas. Surely you agree to that?"

"We *fought* the war, Evan. Are we payin' ourselves then? A tax was already levied by the Assembly for expenses, and that sent to London. Are we to be taxed twice for the same thing?"

"The new tax is to be spent here in the colony, for our continued defense," Evan said.

"*Pppllllffff,*" Thomas responded, blowing air through his

lips. "Have any redcoats been sent to the Ninety Six o[r] anywhere else on the frontier? Nay, they're quartered here in Charles Town. They're not defendin' us, Evan—they're *guarding* us. Guarding us, and the King's tax money. Ope[n] your eyes, man!"

Forcher paused for a moment, considering the argument then brushed it off. "No one likes taxes, Thomas. Neither you nor I. I simply choose to make my protest to the gover nor."

Thomas smiled at the concession. "You're closer to the governor's ear than I've ever been," Thomas conceded. "and may do more good for folks with him than all of us against Tuthill. But one way or another the Crown's got to leave us alone. We can take care of ourselves."

"You're so right, Thomas, and I believe they'll see it that way in time. But the Crown is heavy with debt, just as Rawlins is, and like him is grasping at straws to make it up."

"Perhaps you could loan to the Crown then, Evan, and let me take the Rawlinses under me wing." Thomas raised his eyebrows. The statement was part joke, part query.

"They're both bottomless pits, Thomas," Forcher cautioned.

"But then we all have our causes, don't we, Evan? I'll be needin' your help if money's needed by Elizabeth, for she'll never take it from me—it'll have to go through you."

"Agreed. I would be most happy to serve as your agent—even your partner—in such a 'cause.' "

"Well, then, Evan," Thomas said, shaking the other man's hand and smiling, "we'll see what we can do to help these needy Londoners when they return to the colony."

Thomas left Forcher's office, scampered down the stairs and whistled a jig tune as he walked down the street. He'd be watching for that schooner, and when it landed, he knew what he would do.

When the *Courier* arrived one bright October morning three weeks later, Evan Forcher and Thomas Gairden were on Motte's Wharf to meet her. This day was a far different one from the day he'd seen Elizabeth off four years earlier, a day of mist and fog and parting words. This day's sun warmed the face and shoulders of the two men watching the schooner bob lazily along on the bay swells. Their eyes strained to see familiar faces on deck.

When the ship was no more than two lengths away, Forcher made out the form of an aged Carlyle Rawlins, and when it docked he could see up close the changes almost fifteen years' time had wrought in the face of the other man. His skin was still bronzed from his months in the Indies, and his belly was rounded from food and drink. His travelling clothes were well pressed and of the latest fashion. Carlyle Rawlins knew how to keep up appearances, at the very least. But his eyes were tired under loose skin that sagged over them, and his hair was a silver gray.

"Allow me to introduce Thomas Gairden," Forcher said once his own greetings were done.

"Ah, Gairden," the older man said, appraising him. "I recall a letter from you once before this unfortunate Borque business. Pity. Ah, but that's passed now and your life's gone on. Evan says you've done quite well for yourself."

"Well enough," Thomas said. He felt twenty again under the older man's scrutiny.

Rawlins still reeled a bit, adjusting his sea legs to land legs once again, and tipped against Forcher.

"Forgive me, Evan, I'm a bit wobbly yet. Is your chaise about? I feel the need to be seated."

Evan snapped his fingers for his driver to bring up the chaise and Rawlins immediately headed in its direction. "Are we not to wait for Crickie?" Forcher asked.

"Crickie would not make ye voyage," Rawlins said without looking back. "I've come alone."

The engagement brooch Thomas had purchased hung heavy in his breast pocket. "Alone?" he said, hurrying after the swaying Rawlins. "Evan said—"

"She would not come back to Charles Town." Rawlins stopped as he came to the side of the chaise. "I'm sure you can understand why."

Beneath the man's brusque manner, Thomas detected a note of defeat.

"But you've come—"

"I had no choice. I was no longer well favored at Crichton Place. So you see, she would not come . . . and I could not stay." He looked to Evan as he slid onto the seat of the chaise. "I pray you have good news of the situation at High Garden." In the space of the fifty yards he'd walked from the ship's ramp to the chaise, Rawlins had gone from confident traveller to weary sojourner. The change, and the bitter disappointment inside him, left Thomas speechless.

"We'll talk about that later, Carlyle," Evan said, taking his place across from the slumping Rawlins. "There may be a way . . ."

Forcher searched for something to say, but Rawlins saw his meaning instantly and finished for him. ". . . to save face? Perhaps. For now, I need no more than a place to rest and some unspoiled food to eat."

"My house and my pantry await you, Carlyle. Thomas, you'll join us, of course."

"Nay, Evan, thank you, but I'm certain Mr. Rawlins wants to rest."

"And since Crickie's not here there's very little in an old soldier to interest you, eh, Gairden? I understand. After a life in the army one becomes a good judge of men, and I can see the disappointment in your face right now. It was not me you came to greet but my daughter. If it makes you feel any better, I know she remembers you. Lisette Forcher —it's Lisette Langlois now, isn't it, Evan?—Lisette told her of your wife's death. I had hoped that the opportunity for this voyage would improve Crickie's spirits once again, but instead it only made things worse. She is a determined woman and it is her wish never to return to Carolina again. If you wish to see her, young man, you shall have to go to London."

With that, Rawlins nodded sharply and Forcher motioned for the driver to go.

Thomas watched the chaise roll away, then spat on the wide planking of the wharf. Young man, indeed. Thomas began the walk back to the manufactory with measured steps. The past three weeks had been a lovely dream, in

hich he and Elizabeth were reunited, even united in mar-
age, and living on happily with the children in the big
ouse on Meeting Street. There was no past in this dream.
lo Borque. No Sarah. No wars or smallpox. No death. No
ieutenant Colonel Carlyle Rawlins, Esq.

Thomas kicked at a wood chip lying near a stack of fire-
ood on the wharf. Reality was something altogether dif-
erent. Reality was that Elizabeth was who she was—and
ie was not coming back to the whispers of Charles Town.
Jnless he went to London to fetch her—and that he could
ot do. All at once he was not sure that she would come
ack even if he sailed to London after her. Thomas kicked
t another wood chip, then hurried on down the street. He
ad children to raise. A business to run. And by God he'd
ever get it done with dreaming.

Ie'd spoken to no one of Elizabeth's coming, and he'd told
o one of his disappointment when she'd not arrived, but it
vas not difficult to tell that something was bothering
Thomas Gairden.

"May I sit with you today, Paul?" Ceara asked, coming
nto the manufactory one morning a few days later. "Papa
loesn't want me by him anymore."

"Of course your papa wants you," Durant told her, lifting
ier up onto the smooth bench beside him, "but he has
nuch on his mind."

"What?" she wanted to know. Her small hands threw the
abby shuttle while Durant's larger ones threw the indigo
pattern thread of the coverlid he was weaving.

"That I don't know, but I see it, too. Your father's been
very quiet. He may be worried about the new taxes. Or
ibout a shipment late in arriving. He rode to Williamsburgh
oday—perhaps it's something there that's bothering him.
Anyway, one day when he is ready for us to know he will tell
is. Until then we must pay attention to our work and hope
he problem goes away soon."

Ceara felt Durant's warm smile and leaned against the
comfort of his soft shirt, but still she wondered. Was Papa
getting like Mama had been? Mama had been quiet like

this—and then gotten loud and— It was her turn to throw the shuttle again, and she kept her rhythm just as Paul kept his, but all the while she thought of her father and did some worrying of her own.

30

Was it worse, Crickie wondered, for people to think that her husband had run away with her sister, or for people to think she'd been so foolish as to marry a man already married to someone else? Was she Elizabeth Crichton Rawlins Borque? Or just Elizabeth Crichton Rawlins? Was it worse to be without money or without respect?

These questions Crickie had pondered again and again during the weeks of her fifth crossing of the Atlantic. Once, during a particularly bad storm, she'd thought the ship might be lost altogether and save her the quest for an answer, but the captain had prevailed and the ship was saved, herself along with it.

One thing, however, had never been in question. She still loved Thomas Gairden. She had never quit loving him. When Lisette Langlois had told her Thomas's wife had died, Crickie had wanted to return to Carolina immediately. But then she remembered how long it had been since he left. Perhaps there was someone in his life already. After all, he had four children to care for. Lisette had been travelling in Europe for almost a year, so she had no knowledge of Thomas's comings and goings. Many women would wish for a man such as Thomas. She could not expect him to be waiting for her. He did not even know she was now curiously unmarried. There was no correspondence between them. Probably nothing between them any longer.

And as for making the voyage with her father, that had been out of the question. She'd not been able to let go of the anger built up at her father since the loss of High Garden and her marriage to Borque. His arriving too late to see her mother alive was the last straw. He cared for no one but himself, and she finally recognized it.

Crickie looked out across a calm and sparkling Atlanti The *Somerset* cut boldly through the water, sails filled with crisp November breeze. At this rate, the Carolinas lay n more than one week ahead. She had in her reticule a ver small sum of money left after having paid off her father debtors with the funds from the sale of the family home— once her grandmother Crichton's home—in London. A least her mother had not lived to see that final loss. Eve her father had left before the sale was completed. Onc again he had left her to carry the burden of his prodiga ways. This time, though, he'd left before he ran throug more than the house was worth, though he came close. Sh had enough left to pay her passage and to carry her for while as she started her life anew.

A letter from her old neighbor Mrs. Young had indicate advancing age made it difficult for her husband to manag their plantation, and it was here that Crickie pinned he hopes. Her High Garden neighbors had been the onl friends to stand by her after Michel left. They knew he capabilities. As the *Somerset* glided up the Ashley River she intended to disembark at their wharf—she'd taken th precaution of giving the captain a false name—to slip i unnoticed and make her offer to take over for them at modest salary, and to gain enough, within two or thre years, to purchase land of her own. She knew indigo. Sh knew rice. She knew little else.

"Crickie?" white-haired Edward Young asked as sh stepped from the ship. "Can it be? Your father said—"

Crickie took the wrinkled hands he held out to her an kissed him lightly on both cheeks. "Father does not kno I'm here—and won't, if you'll help me."

"You know we will help you in any way we can . . . but don't understand . . ." Edward had failed considerably i the four years Crickie had been away, and the surprise o her arrival had him in a state of complete confusion.

"I think it best that Papa and I keep our distance, but th distance between Carolina and London was far too great There was nothing for me there with Mother gone . . . n purpose . . . and, as you may as well know, no money. I've come to ask if there might be a way that I can assist you, and once more stay with you for a time—until I might purchase land of my own."

In Charles Town she would have to wear a stiff facade, but with this old friend she could be honest, and was. Tears rolled from her eyes and she dropped her chin to hide them.

"You never should have left us, dear Crickie," the old man said. "How you could have helped us these past years —but of course your mother needed you, too. We are old, we are tired. We need your youth and spirit here, for the new owner of High Garden is not nearly so generous as you once were. We welcome you, and it is not we who will help you, but you who will help us. Come. Let us walk to the house and toast your return. This is cause for a celebration!" he said, then whispered, "even if it is to be a 'secret' celebration!"

Crickie smiled and blinked away her tears. The deed was done. The worst was past. She smelled the heavy scent of white pines that dotted the slope between the river and the house. The late season air was a caress, nothing like the chill of London. Warblers and swamp frogs echoed their evening calls. Soft shadows of live oak and magnolia lay quiet on the dry grass of early winter. Smoke from a dozen cooking fires drifted from beyond the big house. The shrill whinny of two horses near the fence sliced the silence of this great, gentle world. But only for a moment. She was home.

It was a warm day in April of 1766 when the bell jingled on the door of the Sign of the Shuttle. Thomas, Durant and Ceara all looked up.

"Paul, take Ceara on back to Madame Girardeau's, will you please? 'Tis time for the afternoon session."

Durant took his cue and helped the little girl into her bonnet, then hurried her out the door.

"Good day, Thomas," Alexander Gray said evenly. "Ashamed to introduce your old partner, are you?"

"Nay. Not at all," Thomas said, sizing up the other man.

" 'Tis just that when you appear out of nowhere, there's always a reason—usually one I don't like. Ceara's still recoverin' from the loss of her mother. I try to be careful of what she hears."

"Aye," Gray said, nodding. He wore a fashionable powdered wig, and Thomas was struck by the change in his countenance just by the mere covering of that gunmetal gray hair of his. But the eyes were the same, and his face never lost its "I know something you don't know" look.

"You're lookin' well, Alex," Thomas managed.

"Living well's what does it," Gray replied. "High Garden's been good to me."

"Hmm," was all Thomas could say. All he had to say. Gray understood.

"No need for hard feelin's, Thomas. You know I bought and paid for it—building it up every season—but that's not what I've come for, though 'tis on the same subject."

Thomas raised his eyebrows, waiting.

"She's here," Gray said simply. "At Young's plantation. Runnin' the place, if I know anything about it. Saw her out with an indigo crew yesterday as I was hunting."

"Sorry, Alex. Couldn't be. She's in London. Won't ever return to Charles Town. Even her father said so."

"Fathers can be wrong. They can be dead, too. I did a bit of checkin' up on you, Thomas, and found Andrew Roberts died six years back. But the charge of horse thief against you stands—in case you're wonderin'. I'll not be botherin' about it, though—no longer any need. At last I'm richer than you are, Thomas." Gray winked and chuckled. "But anyway, I tell you I wouldn't forget a woman like Elizabeth Rawlins. If you're so certain she's in London, 'tis your business and none o' mine. Good day, Thomas."

Gray turned leisurely about with a swing of one arm, and Thomas shook his head at the transformation of his old partner from Indian trader to planter. What did Gray want of him this time, conjuring up such a tale? Whatever it was, he'd not give Gray the satisfaction of asking, that much he knew. He was done with the likes of Gray.

Back to the loom he went, for just now he was busy with

orders. During the deliberations on the Stamp Act, the colony had decided not to import fabrics from England, and weavers found themselves with more work than they could handle. That offset the decline in his role as a wholesaler of British goods and also helped keep him busy during these months he'd spent debating the ayes and nays of a trip to London. The two letters he'd sent Elizabeth had gone unanswered. Perhaps her father finally was right about something: If Thomas wanted her, he'd have to go get her.

As Thomas wove the fine texture of a mock damask, Gray's words came back again and again. He knew what he'd seen. He was sure of it. But if he was so sure of it, why wasn't he telling her father? And why did no one else in Charles Town know of it? Why only Gray? It was just too convenient to be believed.

Thomas shrugged it off, then came back to it again and again as he beat the fine threads into shed after changing shed. Durant returned with a brief report on Ceara at school, then resumed his work without further conversation. Thomas wove by rote, without so much as a thought to the dance of his feet on the treadles. His narrow fingertips checked each selvage loop by touch and what few adjustments were needed caused no more than a moment's pause in the work. He could finish the yardage for Mrs. Gibbes this afternoon if he had no more interruptions. . . .

"See the children home from school, will you, Paul?" he asked of his assistant. "I'm goin' out for a bit."

Durant nodded, kept on weaving. But knew the unscheduled departure had something to do with the man who'd been there earlier and could only hope it was not bad news.

Thomas rode first to the City Tavern, thinking to find Gray and give him the satisfaction of being questioned further, but Gray was not there. He then rode back to Forcher's warehouse thinking to question Evan, or even Carlyle Rawlins whom he'd managed to avoid the better part of the past six months. He then thought better of it and instead turned right on Bay Street.

"Hear the news?" someone called to him from the direction of the wharf. *"Two Brothers* just brought the word down from New York—Stamp Act's been repealed! Celebratin' tonight!" he shouted. "Spread the word!"

Thomas tipped his hat and rode on smiling, suddenly in more of a hurry than he'd realized. The repeal would be bad for weaving, but good for trading where there was more money to be made. Best of all, it meant the colonies had stood up to the Crown and won! Thomas whooped and kneed his horse into a gallop. In a few short minutes, he was at the Ashley River Ferry, ready to cross.

Once across, he gazed at land that had changed a great deal since that day in 'fifty-four when he'd first ridden to High Garden. More and more rice fields were visible through the branches of sweet bay and honeysuckle just beginning to leaf out. The road was well travelled, now, too. Trees had been cut and the road widened to allow wagon traffic.

Thomas rode on past the turnoff to High Garden. The little sign had given way to a larger and more important-looking one that boasted ALEXANDER GRAY, OWNER. Alex was not a man to hide his good fortune, Thomas thought, chuckling in spite of himself. And there was a nugget of good somewhere in Gray, Thomas had to admit, remembering that it was Gray who'd helped him get his start in Charles Town.

Whatever was going on, if it involved Elizabeth in any way he wanted to know about it. He knew Edward Young only from his two or three meetings with the man at High Garden before Elizabeth was married, but had found him gracious and approachable then. And his family had been close to Elizabeth. Perhaps . . .

Thomas shrugged off the thought. It was not possible that Elizabeth could have returned without his knowing it, without answering his letters. But perhaps her sister Deborah . . . there was some resemblance there, perhaps even greater one now that Deborah was full grown. He'd not seen her in several years.

As he got closer to the plantation, Thomas felt a sense of desperation grow inside him. Would Young even remember him? And what would he think of Gray's tale? Should Thomas even tell him? Perhaps he should say his horse was lame or he was unwell . . .

The bright green of the just planted rice fields and the forests returning to life from their winter's rest surrounded him with their lush beauty. Field hands to the west of the road waved and called out to him as he rode by. He nodded and waved back, not hearing what was said. He had a great sense of not belonging here on this unfamiliar territory, of eyes following him as the horse broke into a gallop. But as the mare made her last graceful strides toward the sprawling brick house, Thomas did not care. He'd come on a mission, and he didn't intend to leave until it was complete.

Seeing no one about to tie his horse for him, Thomas let the mare stand at the bottom of one of the twin stairways that led to the veranda on the house's river side. Still slim and agile, Thomas took the curving steps two at a time and gave a knock at the door. It was answered by a small black man wearing a black vest and white shirt.

"May I see the master, please," Thomas asked as he was shown into the house's central hall.

"Please sit," the man said, backing away and then ascending the broad stairway to the second floor.

As Thomas waited, he took stock of the furnishings about him. Double doors opened into the library which looked to contain hundreds of volumes. Heavy chairs and a large, mahogany desk sat angled in one corner, and near the windows to the river sat an expensive-looking settee upholstered in deep green silk and wool damask. The room had a look of elegance, of permanence and good taste. A book stand with a large volume open on it looked inviting, and Thomas was about to go to it when the servant returned.

"Master Young is not in. May I ask who is calling?"

Thomas wondered if he caught a note of uneasiness in

the man's voice. Servants usually knew the whereabouts of their masters without having to go ask. He took a chance.

"Monsieur Paul Durant," Thomas said, hoping no one but the servant heard the total absence of any French accent in his speech.

"Thank you, sir," the servant said. "Please wait."

Once again Thomas nodded, his heart racing. He walked to the book stand, his back to the door. Paul Durant? How absurd. But if something odd was taking place here, better to—

"Monsieur Durant?" the servant said, returning. "Please follow me."

Thomas followed the servant's quiet steps up the staircase to the second floor parlor. Stepping into the doorway as the servant introduced him he heard nothing the man said. The sight of Elizabeth before him, dressed in her usual working garb of muslin petticoat and dark skirt with a matching bodice, stopped him where he stood.

"Thomas?" she said. "Thomas?" She made no move to come closer, but motioned for the servant to leave, then turned her back and rested her arm on the back of a richly carved chair.

"Aye. Not Paul Durant—I don't know why I said that exactly—except . . . would you have seen me if I'd said 'Thomas Gairden'?" He walked in and stood just behind her, looking down over her shoulder. "Would you now, Elizabeth?"

"I . . . I don't know, Thomas. I don't know if I'm ready to see anyone. I don't know if I ever will be. I . . ."

She turned toward him, and the urge to wrap her in his arms flooded over him though he could tell it wasn't time. He moved a step back, gave her room. She took a step back, too.

"When did you come?" he asked, seeing she was not ready to talk about feelings, or the future.

"November last." She said this with a bit of pride, he could tell. She'd been here six months and no one had even known it.

"I should have guessed," Thomas said. "I should have known when you didn't answer me letters—"

"I have your letters," she told him quietly. "Deborah sent them on to me just two weeks' past. I didn't know how to answer them."

"A simple yea would do," he said, his eyes studying hers. There was silence in the room broken only by one lace curtain brushing a nearby tabletop in the afternoon breeze. "I want to marry you, Elizabeth, before anything or anyone else can come between us again. There's no need for your father's consent this time. There's no need for anything but the two of us to do what we've wanted to for so long."

"But who would you be marrying, Thomas? Elizabeth Rawlins? or Elizabeth Borque, the throwback of a bigamist?" Crickie's words were quiet, but sharp.

"That Borque was a bigamist's no fault of yours, Elizabeth. He could be put to death for such a crime under the laws of the colony. I understand his wife thought him lost at sea. Ha! He planned that the same way he planned to cheat your father at cards and you at marriage. You cannot ruin your life because of it."

"Borque has ruined all our lives, don't you see? He's robbed us not only of our money but also of our reputation, our self-respect. I hope to make my way somewhere in the colony—perhaps on one of the sea islands near Beaufort—away from the whispers, away from the past. I cannot know when Borque may return or what kinds of claims he may place on me. I cannot let anyone else be drawn into such a life."

Thomas was silent a moment. "And I say you cannot stop me. I say that if Borque ever has the poor judgment to come back here he'll be hung before he says so much as a 'good day.' I've no fear of him. Or of people's whisperin'. Folks have whispered about me some, too, with Sarah actin' as she did. And, of course, we never told it about the city that she died by her own hand, but folks seemed to know anyway. They treat me different—like in some way I'd caused it. Even when they're trying to be friendly, I can tell there's something different."

"Still her own hand did the deed, not yours. But when people whisper of Elizabeth Borque, I wear the guilt of one who lived with deceit—I lived as his wife knowing both he and my own sister deceived me. I lived a lie I cannot forget." Crickie's words welled up from somewhere deep and primitive within her, pained and ashamed.

"I suffer me own guilts for Sarah," Thomas said quietly. "We were lovers while she was still married to Jamie—you may as well know it. I'd lost you to Borque . . . I found her once again. . . . And I've no regrets, except that she was lost to Jamie in a way I could never overcome. It wasn't just that she blamed herself for Jamie's murder—she blamed herself for not lovin' him. And I had a part in that."

"We were lovers once, too," Crickie said, lowering her eyes, "but you must never feel guilt in that, for it was I—"

"I had only joy in that, Elizabeth," Thomas said before she could finish. He caught her look of surprise. "But I was guilty of playin' by the rules—askin' your father, honoring your betrothal, watchin' you married, when I should have stolen you as Borque did Margaret and taken us to Savannah or Boston or anywhere out of his sight. He'd have made do with Margaret if you'd not been here." Thomas paused, looked down. "I was weak, Elizabeth. God knows I was weak and it cost you dearly. Since then I've learned something about playin' by the rules—the rules are always changing here in the colonies, and if a man is to survive he has to be bold enough to make some of the changes himself. I learned it too late for us the first time, but I'll not make the same mistake again. The whispers of Charles Town—of the whole colony and London, too—be damned!"

He reached into his pocket where the small crimson box still rested near his heart. "I brought this to the wharf the day the *Courier* landed, hoping to ask for your hand and have the captain marry us there on deck before your feet could touch the streets of Charles Town. Since then I've wondered if I'd ever have the chance to see you again."

He handed her the box and she opened it. The wing-shaped brooch was lined with rows of sapphires and diamonds joined by a single pearl.

" 'Twas made for you, Elizabeth. A row of diamonds for when we met and fell in love. A row of sapphires for our parting. The long row of diamonds at the bottom for our life together now. We can't relive the past, we can't change it, and we shouldn't forget it—not the good parts, at least."

Crickie's fingers touched the finely set stones, took the brooch from its box and held it in the palm of her left hand.

"When I left London," she said, looking at the diamonds sparkling in the late afternoon sunlight, "I told myself I'd come to Carolina but not see you. I told myself it was ye land I was coming back to . . . only ye land, for land would judge me not. I've come through a bitter time, Thomas. And I'm not certain it's over."

"Let me help you make it be over. Marry me, Elizabeth," he pleaded. "I know what you're thinkin'—that you want to wait until everything is perfect again, but I'm tellin' you nothin's ever perfect. I thought I could make it that way once, and now I've learned better. But you and I can weave our lives together the way I do threads in a coverlid. And we can make our own pattern as we go, not live by someone else's design."

"You loved her, didn't you?" Crickie asked out of nowhere. "You didn't just marry her to be a father to her children."

"The youngest one—Ceara—is my own child, Elizabeth, though she doesn't know it. The Sarah I loved at nineteen changed and lived a life of torment—but, aye, I loved her. And I love you. The heart has many rooms, Elizabeth, if we'll just open the doors."

"Will you be wantin' tea brought up, Miss Elizabeth?" the servant Sally asked softly from the hall, breaking the spell Thomas cast with his eyes and words. Before Crickie could answer, Thomas crossed the room, gave the slave a pleasant "No, thank you," and closed the door. Hands behind him on the knob, he leaned back against the door for a moment, his eyes never leaving hers. He saw her bewilderment, her surprise, and crossed back to her, taking her in his arms and kissing her with a gentleness that matured to a deep, shared intensity.

"Ah, Elizabeth," he said, rocking her in his arms, "let me be all to you that Borque was not. I want you for my wife—for my partner. I can help us begin again, but you must do your part, too. We make our own lives, lass. That much I know." Once again he kissed her, slowly, the course of his lips a testimony of the conviction of his spirit.

Drawing back, she lay her head against his shoulder. She was quiet, pensive for a time. At last she looked up at him. The curve of her breast still touched against his shirt and he felt her warmth, sensed a renewal within her.

"If I answer yea, it can be no simple yea, for we both know well there's naught that's simple in this life." Her forehead was lightly lined from years of worry, and in her eyes apprehension lingered like a fawn behind its mother.

"Life's not been simple . . . for either of us. But 'tis far from over, lass," he said, his dark eyes never leaving hers. "We're strong enough to quiet the whispers and make a new life if we do it together, Elizabeth. Life's a race, lass, but we cannot win if we don't run." He raised his eyebrows as he watched for a sign. An answer. But none came. The black eyes that had been so bright, so full of energy, so filled with love for him now were filled with doubt.

Thomas paused. Waited. He and Elizabeth had been apart . . . how long? Five years? And in that time he'd come to know only too well the strange contortions of the human mind—reason to Sarah had been madness to everyone else. Thomas felt the cool of the April breeze that billowed in through the open window as it met the moist skin at the back of his neck. His own perspiration both heated and chilled him.

"Do you remember, lass, that day at the Sign of the Shuttle when I told you there were different ways to win a race?"

Crickie answered only with a tilt of her head and a look of question in her eyes, but Thomas knew she recalled it and went on. "You've won many a race but don't know it, for you thought the purse was money or position. You think yourself second to your papa. You think yourself second to Borque."

Thomas watched her eyes as he spoke, saw the doubt return, and he hurried to explain. "But you've won, lass, for you've done what needed to be done—just as I did when I let Borque race my mare so I could get a better price for her. You saved face for your father when he needed it. You made High Garden all that it is . . . and you managed to free yourself of the buzzardly little Borque."

Thomas raised her chin, and smiled down at her, his eyes carefully appraising her response. "Never think yourself beaten, Elizabeth. Few could do what you've done," he said, holding her tight the way he sometimes did Ceara when she had a night terror about her mother. "Warp and woof, you and I are. We're locked together by our ups and downs, ins and outs—made stronger by 'em."

For a long moment, neither spoke. Elizabeth drew out of his embrace and walked to the window. The heavy lace of the draperies brushed at her wrist as she rested her fingertips in a row on the sill. Thomas stood as he was, arms emptier than he could ever remember. He saw her look out across the newly greening lawn, the pink blooms of the honeysuckle hedge, the deepening blue of the evening sky. But he wondered where she was, where inside her head she was.

"Thomas?" she said softly, still gazing out the window.

He took a step. Stopped.

"Was it all the way you've said? Was it all a race? Was I a prize—no more than a piece of silver?"

"There's no prize to equal what you are, Elizabeth. And even if Borque thought you something he'd won, I'd remind him what the Bible says about the race bein' not always to the swift nor the battle to the strong . . . that time and chance happeneth to us all. Not that he would recognize the words."

Crickie turned toward him once again, tears running freely, glistening against her dark lashes. "I want that to be true," she said, lips and chin quivering as she spoke. "I want it, but I'm afraid to believe it. I've been wrong so many times."

Thomas went to her, wrapping her once again in his arms. "Nay, lass. You've not been wrong. Wronged, but not wrong. This time is different—a different way of winnin' the race—for we'll run it together."

There was no answer for a time, but he felt the sobbing subside as he held her. Still she was silent and the quiet frightened him. "You might be able to win it without me, lass," he said, almost to himself, his lips brushing the top of her head, "but I know I cannot win it without you. Please . . ."

At this last she looked up, eyes reddened, moist but not flowing. "How I love you, Thomas Gairden," she said, closing her eyes at the power of the words. She brought the diamond brooch to her lips and touched it there. "For luck," she said.

He kissed it, too. "For love," he whispered, then kissed her lips. " 'Tis the only prize worth havin'."

DON'T MISS *THE GUARDIANS*—BOOK 2 IN COLEEN JOHNSTON'S SAGA OF THE GAIRDEN FAMILY! AN EXCERPT FOLLOWS:

"Papa!" Lily Gairden cried. "You're home! We've been so worried." She gathered the folds of her black-and-white checked skirt in front of her and swung her legs over the bench of one of the many looms at her father's manufactory in Charles Town, where she was working late, and all alone. Running to him, she felt almost like a child again as he caught her in his arms.

"I had to get home for your birthday, lass. A mite colder than the January you were born. Let me see . . . 1757 . . . 1776. That makes you nineteen—I look at you and I don't know where those years have gone." Once again he hugged her close, kissed the top of her head where her black hair was pinned into a knot. Her arms held him close, too. He was tall, and much bigger to hug than her sister Martha's children. Still, she held him as close as she could, thankful he was home safe. The news of the Snow Campaign here in South Carolina and the fighting around Boston had sounded worse with every issue of the *Gazette*. From the look on Papa's face, the reports hadn't been exaggerated.

"We heard Richardson's men marched through two feet of snow. Did you? And do you still have all of your toes?"

"All ten, but I doubt they'll ever be warm again. Richardson's men had it worse, rooting out pockets of Loyalists from the Congarees to Charles Town. For us, the worst threat was starvation—or thirst. We ended up digging a well forty feet deep—had no water in our fence-rail fort. Still we lost but one man. Loyalists lost none.

We called a truce, and that was it. But Richardson and his men took prisoners. Hundreds of them. Most of 'em now in the Charles Town gaol."

"Such good news, Papa," Lily said. It meant that soon Paul would be back, too. After Lily had come home from school in England last summer, she had grown to think of Paul Durant, her father's partner, as more than just a friend. None of the young men in Charles Town could match his dark good looks or the knowing way he talked to her, looked at her. Paul Durant had never married, and Lily's brother, Gavin, even teased her that Paul was waiting for her to grow up. Since she was a little girl she had dreamed that he would do just that. At last the dream might be coming true. She tried not to seem too eager when she asked the question foremost in her mind. "And what of Paul? When will he be back? Nothing is the same here at the manufactory without him."

"I don't know when he'll be back," Papa said, clearing his throat, "but it looks as though you've done a fine job without us."

Lily sensed his hesitation. "But surely you saw him?"

"There were hundreds of men there, lass."

"You didn't see him then? But where is he?"

The wrinkles in Thomas Gairden's face were even deeper than they'd been when he left, Lily noticed. And he was thin. Life with the militia had been harder than he wanted to admit. She waited for her father's answer a moment, then had a frightening thought. "He wasn't the one?" she gasped.

Thomas looked at her, his eyes glassy, tired. " 'Twould be easier to tell you he was, lass."

"Why? I don't understand . . ."

"I don't know when he'll be back. Or if he'll be back." Papa drew in a heavy breath that whistled in his nose; he'd caught cold sleeping on the ground these past weeks. "I should have told you before I left . . . Paul . . . Paul and I had words. Our first time ever to have an argument. We did not call a truce as the militia did."

"But why, Papa? About what?"

Her father paused. His lips pushed out, drew in. His brows pulled together alongside two deep, v-shaped lines. "About you," he said, softly.

"Me? What about me?" Lily asked.

"He asked for your hand, Lily. I said no."

Lily felt her heart hammer, felt her skin too small to hold all that was inside her. "Without ever telling me? Without even asking me?"

"Aye," her father said softly. "It could not be, lass. He's twice your age, and a Roman Catholic—"

"Too old? You speak of 'too old' but you found no wrong in fathering a child to a woman already married to another?"

"Lily! You'll not speak to me of that—of what you cannot know!"

"I may not know it all, but I know enough to know that what you and Mama did was adultery—and yet now you refuse me Paul because of his faith? I know Mama was a hypocrite—I didn't know you were one as well!"

"I am your father," Papa said, "and I do what is best for you because I love you. You cannot know what being married to a Catholic would mean for you in Charles Town. You would find yourself an outsider just as Paul has always been."

"Then at least I would have someone to be outside with. In all my life, no one has wanted me—Mama didn't, she tried to kill me; you didn't—you wouldn't even tell me I was yours; your new wife didn't—that's why she talked you into sending me off to London. No one, no one but Paul has ever wanted me—and you sent him away."

"I love you, lass, but I'll not see you married to a Catholic. No Scots-Irishman wants that. You were baptized a Presbyterian, and that's what you'll stay."

"This is not Ireland, Papa. And I'm not a little girl anymore. I'm a woman. Don't you see? I have feelings. I have opinions. I'm old enough to be married." She stopped a minute, her breaths quick and shallow, her lips pursed tight against the words on her tongue. Then at last she set them free. "And if Paul doesn't come back for me, I'll never forgive you!" Darting past her father and down the stairs, she ran out the back of the warehouse onto the wharf.

It was freezing cold, unbearably cold for Charles Town even in January, but Lily walked to the far end of the deserted pier, not even feeling it. The steady lap, lap, lap of the water against the pier echoed the throbbing of her head as she thought of never seeing Paul Durant again. She pressed her hands tight over her eyes to hold back the tears. Paul *had* loved her, just as she had loved him. But he had taken the gentlemanly course. He had asked Papa first.

"You should have asked *me*, Paul. Me!!!!" Lily's cry sped off on the gusting wind.

Lily looked at the bottomless darkness of the harbor. Where hundreds of ships normally loaded and unloaded, now only coasting schooners and other small vessels lay at anchor. The piers were quiet, except for the music of a flute from somewhere she couldn't see. The water lapped up almost to the tops of the pilings. Fell back again. Up. Back. Lily closed her eyes and still saw it. The blackness. The depth. The total encasement of all that dropped beneath it. She could step off. Never be heard. Never come back. She would find Paul in that world beyond death.

But no. That was what Mama had done. And this much Lily knew: she did not want to be like her mother, at least not like the part of her she remembered. And she would not ever let herself be like her father, either. And so she only watched the water. Heard it slap the pier. Lost herself in its power. And finally, went home.

A week later, smoke brought an early darkness to the evening air of that same pier. One block over, fire had destroyed all the buildings between Tradd Street and Stoll's Alley hours before, and they smoldered even now at dusk. Rumors that Loyalists were the cause of it all— that they'd set the blaze in retaliation for members of their faction held in the Charles Town gaol—began almost as soon as the first flames licked the afternoon sky.

The warehouse at the Sign of the Shutte was quiet, but the smell of smoke had found its way inside and for once the acrid odor of the indigo vats would have been welcome instead. Lily had avoided the manufactory all week, had moved her things back to Martha's again, after Papa had told her about Paul. She came now only to see for herself what damage there might have been. Papa and three of his weavers were leaving just as she arrived, their faces smudged and their clothes streaked with black from helping to fight the fire. Lily had almost felt sorry for Papa when she saw him, but said nothing. There was no longer anything to say to Papa. "Lock up when you leave" was all he had said to her.

She stood there a good long while, looking at Paul's unfinished spinning jenny and the evidence of him that was everywhere in the big, dark space. A noise at the wharfside door broke off her thoughts. One of the men must have come back for something.

"Who's there?" she called before she slipped the bolt.

"Lily?"

"Yea, this is Lily. Who goes there?"

"Cade McCleod," came the husky whisper. "Let me in. Please."

Lily opened the door a crack to find the unkempt young man cramped inside the door frame so as to hide himself from view of the street. He took a quick look both ways, then stepped inside and leaned back against the wide, heavy door. Breathing hard, he closed his eyes a moment and caught his breath before he spoke.

"So you do remember me after all?" he said between breaths. " 'Twas a chance I took. There was nowhere else to go. The militia's out to find anyone who looks like he might have touched the match in the night, and I've no desire to go back to the Charles Town gaol."

"You've been in the gaol?" Lily felt herself stiffen, but tried to conceal it. "On what charge?"

He waited a moment before he answered, judging

whether he should tell the truth or not, she could tell. Her eyes never left his.

"I went to Dutch Fork was the reason, joined some friends takin' a stand against the Associators."

"Still a Loyalist are you? I thought you might have changed sides by now."

"Never. Anyway, most of it came to nothing, but when the rebel Associators surprised us in our camp, a few of us were dragged off to make an example for the rest. I happened to be sleepin' next to Patrick Cunningham at the wrong moment. He gave the order for us to save ourselves, and he rode off—bare naked, but still he got away—but I didn't make it. Over a hundred of us they brought to the gaol, but finally let us go, on promise of no more armsmanship against the Province." McCleod coughed violently, turning away from her as he clapped himself on the chest trying to loosen the tightness there. "Gaol's a poor place, lass, where I've no wish to return. I'm unwell, with no money, no horse. No one to turn to. I remembered you. A Whig at that, but I—"

"I'll help you," Lily interrupted, "but you must help me, too."

McCleod coughed again and looked at her, surprised. Suspicious, too, she knew.

"I want you to take me with you."

"Take you with me? But where?"

"Anywhere. Just as long as 'tis away from my father."

"I don't know . . . I . . . I'd thought to join Cunningham and the others in St. Augustine and—"

"St. Augustine," she said, nodding. "Anywhere. Just away."

"But Lily, a Whig in St. Augustine would be mightily lonely. 'Tis there the Loyalists are banded together, in hopes of helping the Crown."

"All the more reason to go there with you." Lily spoke with measured determination, taking little pleasure in the words.

"You want to go against your papa? Is that it? And I'm to help? Nay, Lily. That will not be. Your papa's an important man. Your bein' with me would only give him cause to rile the rebels against me anew."

"So you're afraid of the rebels then?" she asked.

"Nay. But there are few of us just now. We need time. We need to pick our battles, not have 'em thrust on us."

"Papa need not know where I've gone. Only that I've gone and won't be back. . . . And I may even be able to be of help to you." Lily raised her chin and lifted her eyebrows, almost smiling.

"But a lass? Traveling with me. I don't know . . ."

"Wait then. Right there, behind those crates, in case someone should come in. I'll be back in a moment."

By the light of a single oil lamp, Lily made her way up to the weaving room and opened the chest that she knew contained some old things of Paul's. She'd looked in it in the weeks he'd been gone, wondering if he would ever be back for it, wondering if she would ever see him again. Tonight, with the smell of smoke choking the air, she knew she would not. Yet he would help her as he always had. She slipped out of her gown and petticoat and into a pair of his worsted breeches and a cotton shirt. She found a coat that didn't match and put it on. Where they were going, no one was apt to worry about dress. An old pair of his boots stood in the corner. Too big. She put on an extra pair of hose and stuffed yarn thrums into the toe. Picking up her own indigo cape, she started back for the stairs—realized she would need a hat. She ran down and checked the back of the door to Papa's office. His tricorn was there. He so often forgot to put it on, always in a hurry. She took it, and stopped to leave a note on the tall writing desk that stood by the door.

"Papa," she wrote. "I've left with Cade McCleod. Ask Elizabeth who he is. Lily."

She read her words once more. They should give Papa something to think about. He'd soon find he would rather have had her married to a Catholic than a Loyalist, no doubt. Putting down the pen, she scampered up the steps to the weaving room once more, picked up her clothing and wrapped it in a coverlid strip just cut from the loom. Half of a Liberty pattern. Well, she thought, that gave things a nice symmetry. This, at last, was her liberty. Let Papa be damned.

Lily and Cade made no more than a few miles each day. She kept her hat on when they met people along the trails that hugged the coast as they made their way south. Some days they rode along hard-packed sand beaches and saw only shorebirds or an occasional weasel. Other days they passed through small settlements where people were glad for company and invited the two "brothers" to stay the night.

"We're headed for land in East Florida," Cade would tell them, doing most of the talking while Lily played the part of his younger brother. "Our folks, they died—the smallpox did it. We buried 'em and left for new lands we've heard of to the south."

And wherever they stopped, Cade would bring the conversation around to the war with England, ever watchful for an unspoken reaction if there was no spoken one. Were they Loyalists? Might they be of help? He was calculating, she knew, what support they might have, especially in the area around Savannah, which Cunningham had told him would be a point of siege. If the British couldn't work Charles Town harbor, they could work Savannah, where there was no organized opposition. From there they could sail up the Savannah River, disembark troops on the southwest side of South Carolina, then break the Charles Town harbor blockade and come from the east as well, locking the Continental troops between them. A neat plan, he thought, should it come to that. The Continentals had no real navy, certainly nothing like the British navy. The harbor was theirs for the taking—and they would have taken it before this but the Crown was set on keeping the battles to the north where it could make use of its landed troops the way it had in Massachusetts. The southern colonies, the Loyalists thought, might be offered a separate peace to join with the Crown against the northern colonies.

"How can the Crown think of making such an offer when there are so many in Charles Town alone who oppose it?" Lily asked as they walked their horses along a grassy river bank on the Georgia coast after they had been traveling several weeks. "Are they not taking much for granted?"

"That is our task, Lily. To turn the tide for the Crown. To get for it the support it needs. Look at the numbers of people we've talked to along our journey who had no feelings one way or the other but just wanted to be left to work their land and make a living. To bring peace and insure that they will be left alone, would they not be in favor of a separate peace if it was offered them? Of course they would. They'd be fools not to."

"But in Charles Town—"

"Charles Town is one place, Lily. The people there think it is the only place, and that everyone should do as they do, think as they think. But other people in other places have other ideas. We're givin' them a chance to be heard. That's all."

"You know, of course, that those are the same words the rebels use when talking about the Crown. They're giving folks the chance to be heard—to let King George know about other ideas—that's all."

"Aye, well, I suppose it is two sides of the same coin, but this is my side."

"Still, you can see the other side, too, can you not?"

"I can't be lookin' to the other side anymore, Lily. That would make me a traitor."

"There'll be traitors on both sides."

"Aye, but we'll be on the winnin' side." He grinned, then narrowed his eyes. "You're not turnin' back on me now, are you, Lily? Goin' soft on your father?"

"Nay. Just thinking how much the same the talk is on both sides. But I've made my choice. I'll stick with it."

Cade gave her horse an affectionate pat on the rump, then galloped on ahead, leaving Lily to her own thoughts.

The spring rains began just as they made their wide

loop around Savannah. Red dust turned to slick mud. Indigo's white stockings turned pink with stepping in it, and the gelding Cade rode, a lovely roan named Comet, looked old and mottled in the downpour.

Lily and Cade had no more than strips of old sail they'd scavenged along the beach to shield themselves from the torrents that poured from the dark skies, and Lily thought even the cold of the night they left had been better than this. Their sailcloth tent was crude at best. Constant wetness plagued them. There was still nothing to warm them at night but the strip of coverlid and the skirt of her gown. Never before had she known one could live so simply and still survive. At first, meals had been slim, mostly rice, but after they'd worked two weeks for the man just below Beaufort, and earned in trade an old musket of his, with powder and balls, Cade shot squirrels and pigeons for their supper. During his months with the Loyalist troops, he had become quite good at cooking meat and foraging for greens.

Rain fell through the night in what was now the first week in May. In the morning, it was still falling. They had quartered for the night on high ground, but even so they awoke wet and aching with damp. Cade found a few sticks less wet than the rest of what was about them and started a small fire, which was mostly smoke, just outside the end of their makeshift shelter. Lily crept as close to the fire as she could and still keep the sail cloth over her head, and Cade did the same, holding his hands out, palms down, to catch what heat he could from it.

"Can we cook rice over it?" Lily asked, seeing no more than a few orange embers beneath the sticks.

"Not good rice, but some kind of gummy rice, I suppose," he said.

Lily laughed, tired from a restless night of listening to the rain and knowing she was wet and getting wetter and hearing Cade turn first right, then left, then right again, trying to make his body forget how unpleasant it was. This stretch of country was little settled and they'd had no idea of how far they might have to ride to find shelter for the night. Better to hold up where they had, they decided.

But it wasn't only the rain that had kept her awake, Lily knew, and she wondered if it was only the rain that kept Cade tossing about as well. They had been on the trail over three months now, ambling along the Atlantic coast, two brothers looking for new land, except for times like this, when Lily's hair fell loose clear to the small of her back and her hat was off and she neither looked nor felt like a brother. What would Papa think if he could see her now? Sodden, unwashed, traveling with a young man—a Loyalist? She almost wished he could see her. And Paul? What if he, too, had gone to the other side to spite Papa? What if he had gone off to New Orleans where it was said there were many Acadians? Or to the north? She would never know, thanks to Papa.

"You're quiet," Cade said, watching her. "Rain's sorrowful, isn't it?"

Lily's eyes remained fixed on the embers' glow. " 'Tis. That 'tis."

"Lily?" Cade's voice seemed to call to her from far away as she lost herself in her thoughts. "Lily," he said again. "You have smells of weeks on the trail."

She felt his eyes on her, felt him lean close enough that his shoulder touched hers. She turned to him, then looked down at her mud-stained breeches and hose. She shook her head lazily and pulled her fingers up through the long locks of her black hair, then continued to stretch her arms upward, her fists touching the wet sail cloth overhead. "And you don't, brother?" she asked, pretending a yawn as she felt unbrotherly feelings stir inside her the way they had a way of doing at quiet times like these.

"The rain is ceasing, and the sky is brightening in the east. The river's bound to be warm, for the rain's not a cold rain. We could clean ourselves a bit before we go on this day."

His words were ordinary. Matter-of-fact. Except that Lily saw the face that went with them: the teal-tinged eyes that at every other time challenged her, but that at this time did not look into hers; the voice that did not call her 'brother' this time; the shoulder that touched hers just a little closer now. She felt the spark, like flint on tinder, begin to flame. Man to man? She was the one who'd wanted it that way, but he'd been the one to keep it that way, careful to sleep away from her no matter how cold the night, careful not to help her from her horse anymore nor to touch her in any way at all, careful to bathe fully clothed, as she did.

"Perhaps we should . . ." she said, not moving her shoulder away from his. "But let's wait a bit . . . for the sun to warm us." She looked to him for a response and saw him breathe deeply, felt him shift away, then lean toward her. He touched his lips to hers, eyes open as hers were. Did she want this as he did? Lily closed her eyes and felt the gentleness of his rough hands in her hair, then under it on her neck, then caressing the curve of her back. She arched closer, and he pulled her onto his lap, never taking his lips from hers. The dampness of her clothes, the wet sail cloth above them and the little smoking fire faded from her mind. Secure in his arms, Lily was warm, and thoughts of war were very far away. . . .

***THE GUARDIANS* BY COLEEN L. JOHNSTON —BOOK 2 OF THE GAIRDEN LEGACY. COMING IN EARLY 1994 FROM ST. MARTIN'S PAPERBACKS!**

She was a pawn in one man's quest for power.
A man who stole her legacy and ignited
a passion deep within her...

BLOOD RED ROSES

KATHERINE DEAUXVILLE

"A DAZZLING DEBUT...
A love story to make a medieval
romance reader's heart beat faster!"
—ROMANTIC TIMES

Heading for a new life in California across
the untracked mountains of the West,
beautiful Anna Jensen is kidnapped by a
brazen and savagely handsome Indian who
calls himself "Bear." The half-breed son of a
wealthy rancher, he is a dangerous man with
a dangerous mission. Though he and Anna
are born enemies, they find that together
they will awaken a reckless desire that can
never be denied...

SECRETS OF A
MIDNIGHT MOON
Jane Bonander

IN THE BESTSELLING TRADITION OF
BRENDA JOYCE